LA CINDERELLA
BY
AMANDA BERRY

MILLS & BOON

Dear Reader,

My interest in writing an ex-rock-star hero came about through watching a couple of TV documentaries, including "Heavy—the History of Metal." I expected grunts and expletives; what I heard were articulate, clever and often well-educated men looking back over extraordinary achievements in music.

Alice Cooper, Johnny Rotten…great guys.

A lot of them had been through the mill with drugs, alcohol and relationships, but those who'd come out the other side were bad boys made good. Still with that self-deprecating humour and world-weary twinkle that make rogues so irresistible to romance readers.

Another profession that often gets stereotyped is the librarian. What fun, I thought, to put these two together. Drop by my website, www.karinabliss.com, and tell me if you thought so, too.

Happy reading,

Karina Bliss

WHAT THE LIBRARIAN DID

BY
KARINA BLISS

First published in Great Britain 2011
by Mills & Boon, an imprint of Harlequin (UK) Limited,
Eton House, 18-24 Paradise Road, Richmond, Surrey TW9 1SR

© Karina Bliss 2010

ISBN: 978 0 263 88897 3

23-0711

Harlequin (UK) policy is to use papers that are natural, renewable and
recyclable products and made from wood grown in sustainable forests. The
logging and manufacturing processes conform to the legal environmental
regulations of the country of origin.

Printed and bound in Spain
by Blackprint CPI, Barcelona

New Zealander **Karina Bliss** was the first Australasian to win one of the Romance Writers of America's coveted Golden Heart Awards for unpublished writers. It took this former journalist five years to get her first book contract—a process, she says, that helped put childbirth into perspective. She lives with her husband and son north of Auckland. Visit her on the web at www.karinabliss.com.

To my sisters—
Carolyn, Janine, Deryn and Natalie.
All women supremely capable of bringing a
strong man to his knees.

Acknowledgements
Thanks to Cheryl Castings, who suggested the
name Matthew Bennett in a "Name a character"
contest I ran through my website.

PROLOGUE

Seventeen and a half years earlier
Suburban New Zealand

EVERYONE SAID ONLY a weirdo would turn down a date with Mary O'Connell's older brother, home from university for the holidays. And Rachel was sick of being a weirdo.

Tentatively, she followed Steve's lead in the kiss and wiggled her tongue. He responded with a flattering groan. Sweet sixteen and *finally* been kissed. She shivered, more from the loveliness of the thought than his gentle stroking of her bare arm. Then he touched her breast and she shied away. "Don't do that."

"I can't help it." Breathing heavily, Steve stared into her eyes. "You're so beautiful."

"Am I?" She stripped the wistful note out of her voice. "Don't be crazy." She was passable, that was all. When she wasn't in her school uniform she wore clothes that were Mom's idea of what a young lady should wear. Rachel pulled at the button-up collar of her pink blouse. She hated pink. And plaid skirts. When she left home she'd always wear bright colors.

"You *are* beautiful." Steve's voice vibrated with intensity. "And smart. And funny." He loomed closer again and her nervousness must have showed because he stopped with such an understanding smile that Rachel felt like a silly little girl.

Sure, they were a bit isolated, sitting here in his Toyota Celica, but across Hamilton Lake, suburban lights twinkled like stars.

And obviously they couldn't have a conventional date in case someone reported back to her parents. She shivered again, knowing how her father would react if he found out. But some risks were worth taking and Rachel yearned to live.

They'd drunk beer, which she'd only pretended to sip, watching Steve anxiously. But he'd stopped after one can. And he'd asked her about all sorts of subjects and listened—really listened—to the answers. As if her opinions mattered. Not even Chloe, her best and only friend, did that. Normally it was Rachel's job to listen.

His sincerity reminded her of Holden Caulfield, the hero in her favorite book, *Catcher in the Rye,* except that Steve was good-looking. Not that looks mattered; Rachel would hate to be shallow. And Steve said it was his favorite book, too. It must be a sign. Before she lost her courage, she leaned forward and initiated another kiss.

This time when he touched her breast Rachel let it linger a few seconds before she removed his hand. "I should really be getting back," she said. "I've got an exam tomorrow." She took her education very seriously. It was her way out.

Steve didn't get annoyed; he simply nodded and started the engine, and Rachel's last doubt dissipated. When he dropped her off at the end of the street he lifted her hand and kissed it, a French gesture that thrilled her all the way to the bone.

"Say we can do this again," he begged, and she nodded because her heart was too full to speak. *I'm in love.*

Same time
Long Beach, Los Angeles, U.S.A.

"GOT YOUR FAKE ID?"

Devin shouldered his bass guitar, checked his jeans pocket and nodded, but his attention wasn't really on Zander. With a sixteen-year-old's fascination, he was watching a stripper across the bar.

His brother's volatile temper had left him a bass player short an hour before a gig, and Devin was the last-minute replacement. Now he was discovering heaven had many layers. The stripper winked at him and he blushed and dropped his head.

Then caught Zander exchanging grins with the drummer, and scowled.

His brother nudged him. "And don't tell Mom I brought you here."

"You think I'm stupid?"

"Yeah."

It *was* seedy, the kind of place where people carried knives. Dimly lit, pungent with marijuana and sticky underfoot. But Devin didn't care. As they set up their secondhand equipment on the tiny platform that constituted the stage, his heart pounded harder and harder until he thought he'd pass out.

This was his chance to become a permanent member of Rage instead of the awestruck kid brother sitting in the corner of the garage. When the band let him. On the rare occasions, Devin would go up to his room afterward and create riffs on his bass or Zander's discarded electric guitar, which Devin played upside down because he was left-handed.

Zander had heard one, liked it and used it in one of his songs. After that, Devin had got more garage time. He knew every chord by heart—which was why he was here. So they didn't lose out on three hundred dollars. Devin wondered whether he could ask for a cut.

"Don't screw this up," muttered Zander as he made his way to the microphone. Devin decided not to push his luck.

Instead he wiped his damp palms on his Guns 'N' Roses T-shirt and waited for his brother's hand signal, too scared to look around in case he caught someone's eye and got knifed, or worse, kicked out for being a kid. He couldn't lose this big chance.

Chris, the lead guitarist, gave his shoulder a friendly punch. "Breathe," he encouraged. Devin gulped as Zander grabbed the microphone and faced the band. His eyes and grin were wild and a charge crackled through the air and surged through Devin. He grinned back.

His brother raised one arm, revealing a flash of white abdomen between T-shirt and low-slung jeans. He must be the only person in L.A. without a tan, Devin thought irrelevantly, then Zander mouthed the count—*three, two, one*— and swept his arm down.

With Chris, Devin struck the first note of "Satan's Little Helper," and forgot his nerves, his hopes, forgot everything except coaxing emotion from his guitar. Lost himself in the music.

Much later, drenched with sweat, dazed from adrenaline overload, he sat at one of the scratched wooden tables in the bar. In the round of drinks, he mistakenly got a beer and drank it because he was so thirsty.

Zander noticed his empty glass. "Only one," he warned, but he was too busy lapping up female attention to stop Devin accepting another.

After two beers he sat with a silly grin on his face, not feeling shy, not feeling anxious, not feeling anything but cocky. "Am I in, bro?" he called. Zander shrugged.

"Until we find someone better."

And Devin thought, *No one will be better than me. I'll make sure of it.*

He sneaked a glance at the stripper again and she wasn't looking at him as though he was a stupid kid anymore, because being in a band somehow changed that.

I'm in love.

CHAPTER ONE

"Isn't this the second marriage proposal you've turned down?" asked Trixie. "Face it, Rach, you're a heartbreaker."

"With that imagination you should be writing fiction, not shelving academia." Kneeling on the floor, Rachel Robinson snipped through the tape on the carton of books addressed to Auckland University library, then glanced at her assistant.

"I'm a thirty-four-year-old librarian, not Scarlett O'Hara, and Paul is probably breathing a sigh of relief right about now." At least she hoped he was. He'd been upset last night—and she still was. Both of them had expected her to say yes.

"That's another thing," said Trixie with the bluntness of youth. "Rejecting proposals is poor policy for a woman who wants a family. You may look twenty-nine but your ovaries are knocking thirty-five."

Normally her protégée's homespun lectures were entertaining, coming as they did from a twenty-year-old Goth-wannabe with dyed black hair and a nose stud. Today they struck a nerve. "Maybe I'm meant to devote my life to my work."

"Now that's just crazy talk."

At the other end of the counter, a student approached

the help desk and pressed the buzzer. "Yours," said Rachel thankfully. The first day of the university year didn't start until tomorrow, but the smart ones were getting in early.

Trixie bent and gave Rachel a fierce, parting hug. "I hate it when you're unhappy. Go tell Paul you've changed your mind."

So much for putting on a brave face. Hauling the books out of the carton and stacking them under the counter, Rachel wished it was as simple as that. Lately her left brain didn't know what her right brain was doing. Tentatively prodding her feelings, she found no regret or remorse, only a guilty seam of rock-solid relief.

Standing, she closed her eyes, breathing in the heady smell of institutional tranquility, and tried to internalize it. *Help me,* she prayed silently. *Why do I run every time I'm close to marriage?*

Someone cleared his throat and Rachel opened her eyes. A man waited, impatiently frowning at her.

He was dressed in faded jeans with slashed knees and a too-tight olive-green T-shirt stretched over muscled biceps. Ruggedly tanned, he had sun-streaked russet-brown hair curling past his collar.

It wasn't that he had a five o'clock shadow at nine-thirty in the morning that screamed "bad boy." To Rachel's eyes, that simply made him scruffy. And most certainly his menace wasn't in his boots, butter-soft leather and, good Lord, purple?

No, it was the arrogant way he stood—feet planted wide, arms folded across his impressive chest. It was the dragon tattoo curling the length of one muscled arm. But mostly it was the sleepy sensuality in the hooded hazel eyes casually scanning Rachel as if she were part of a female buffet. She got the impression he was already very full but might possibly squeeze in dessert—if it was handed to him on a plate.

The woman in her bristled, but the librarian mustered a professional smile. "Can I help you?"

The man didn't smile back. "I heard there was a library tour for those new to the college." His voice was deep, his accent American.

Rachel reached for her timetable. "You're a day early, but if you give me your name I'll book you in for tomorrow."

There was a brief hesitation. "Devin Freedman."

"Devin. Spelled *o-n* or *i-n?*"

His mouth relaxed its tight line. *"I-n."*

"I can give you an informal look around now if you like."

For some reason his guard went up again. "I don't want any special treatment."

"You must be a student," she said drily. "If you were a lecturer you wouldn't say that."

Narrow-eyed, he assessed her, and Rachel nearly told him to lighten up. Then a thought struck her. "Oh, Lord, you *are* a new lecturer."

A smile broke through the guy's suspicion. It did strange things to Rachel's stomach. Or it could be she'd been too upset about Paul to eat breakfast.

"No," he said, "not a lecturer. And I would appreciate a tour. It's going to be hard enough tomorrow being the oldest student here."

"Don't worry, we have quite a few adult students. I assume you're part-time?"

"Full-time."

Rachel hid her surprise. Except for the boots, he didn't look as if he could afford to pay the fees without working.

On the other hand, with that body, he probably made good money working nights in a male revue. She said briskly, "What degree?"

"Bachelor of commerce."

"Okay, Devin…my name's Rachel Robinson and you're in luck. I'm the subject librarian for business and finance. Follow me." She spent the next fifteen minutes walking him through the library, while he listened intently, saying little. "You're American," she commented at one point.

"No."

Okay, we don't do small talk. "We have a few library tutorials of interest to you. Let me get you some brochures." She led him back to the counter and started rummaging through a filing cabinet.

"I'm *sure* I saw him come in here." The voice was female, very young and slightly breathless.

Another responded with a giggle, "Do you think he'd sign my bra?"

Startled, Rachel looked up. Devin had vanished and three teenagers milled around the entry, two girls and a boy.

"You promised you'd be cool about this if I brought you," the youth complained. Then he caught Rachel's eye and lowered his voice. "Shush, let's just go in and look."

"Can I help you?" Rachel asked in her best librarian's voice.

The boy dropped his gaze. "Uh, no, we're just looking for someone."

"Famous," added one of the girls, smoothing down her skirt and scanning the rows of books.

Rachel stepped into her line of sight. "So you're not here to use the facilities of the library?"

"No," the girl replied, "but—"

"Then it's better if you wait outside for whoever—"

"Devin Freedman." There was worship in the boy's tone.

"—you're waiting for," Rachel continued. "If you're sure he's here?"

That sowed enough doubt for them to start arguing among themselves as they left.

When they'd gone, she looked for Devin and found him leaning against a bookshelf in aisle three. He straightened at her approach, his expression wary. "As I was saying," she continued, "we have a few one-hour tutorials of interest to you. A library and resources overview, an introduction to our online library catalog…" She stopped because he wasn't listening, then added softly, "And I can show you the staff exit when you're ready to leave."

His attention snapped back to her. "Thanks."

"I'm sorry, I still have no idea who you are," she admitted.

"That makes two of us." He saw her bafflement and shrugged wide shoulders. "I was a guitarist in a band that did well."

And now you're going back to school? But he probably had enough of people prying into his private life. "That's why I don't know your name then. I don't keep up with contemporary pop."

He winced. "Rock."

"Excuse me?"

"We were rock."

Something in his pained tone made her smile. "Was that like comparing Gilbert and Sullivan to Puccini?"

An answering glint lit his eyes. "Sorry, I'm not an opera buff. It's always struck me as a bunch of overemoting prima donnas going mad or dying."

"Whereas rock and roll…?"

Devin laughed. "You're right," he conceded, "no difference." He thrust out a hand. "Anyway, thanks for your help." She took the warm tapered fingers, careful to avoid the dragon's tongue flicking at the tip of one knuckle. "I'll hang around a bit longer till the coast clears," he added. "Read the brochures."

"If it's any consolation, they run a tight ship here," she said. "I doubt you'll get harassed past the first day."

"That's one of the reasons I chose this campus. I wanted fossilized conservatives dressed in…" His gaze slid over her gray pin-striped trousers and pale blue satin blouse with short puffed sleeves. "Thanks again."

Rachel felt a spike of irritation before her sense of humor kicked in. What did she care what a guy wearing purple boots thought about her vintage fetish? Still, she gave the boots a pointed look before she said kindly, "You're *very* welcome."

The edges of his irises were bright green, with copper-brown starbursts around the pupils. When he smiled with his eyes the effect was unnerving. "Ma'am," he drawled, flicked an imaginary hat brim, then strolled toward a reading nook.

Smart aleck. People rarely challenged Rachel and never teased her; the world of academia was a civilized one. She sighed.

"Hell bod," said Trixie, coming up beside her. Then she started. "Hey, isn't that—"

"Devin Freedman," said Rachel knowledgeably, and went back to unpacking books and brooding on why someone who was desperate for kids couldn't cross the first threshold.

As though she'd conjured him, Paul reeled through the library's double doors. Rachel gasped. The side part that normally flipped his gray-streaked black hair rakishly over one eye zigzagged across his skull as crookedly as he now staggered across the navy carpet.

His corduroy jacket—the same soft brown as his eyes—had pizza stains on it and the blue chambray shirt that normally buttoned neatly under his chin flapped open halfway down a pale hairy chest. And the designer jeans...

Rachel rushed over and jerked up his fly. "You're drunk!"

"Are you surprised?" His voice rang loudly.

"Shush...."

She tried to drag him into the staff office, but he clutched at the countertop, swaying slightly. "You led me on!"

Heads began poking out from the aisles of books as readers took an interest. "Paul, please," she begged. Regardless of whether she deserved this humiliation, he was jeopardizing his job by showing up inebriated. She had to get him out of here. Rachel grabbed his arm again, called over her shoulder, "Trix, help me."

He flung them both off with a dramatic gesture, ruined by a loud belch. "When I've had my say."

Until last night she and Paul hadn't seen each other in six months because he'd been on sabbatical, studying some obscure Germanic dialect in Munich. Their reunion had come to an abrupt end on the way back to his apartment from the airport, when he'd proposed to her.

And Rachel had said no.

Their eighteen-month relationship had come to an even more abrupt end on his front doorstep as she'd desperately tried to explain a decision she couldn't justify except by describing her feelings. Unfortunately, terms like "panic" and "claustrophobia" didn't help him take the news any better.

Paul swallowed. "You broke my heart."

"It's not like you were crazy in love with me," she reminded him gently. In fact, they'd never been as fond of each other as when they'd been apart and their unremarkable sex life had been supplanted by romantic telephone calls and e-mails.

He refocused on her with bleary-eyed outrage. "I proposed to you, didn't I?"

"Well, yes," Rachel admitted. "Kind of."

"Guess we should think about getting married," had been his exact words. But their relationship had always been fueled by pragmatism, not passion. Paul wanted an independent, low-maintenance wife to support his brilliant career. And she wanted to start a family with a nice guy. Because Trixie was right, Rachel was running out of time. And her dating pool had always been the size of a goldfish pond. She was too self-sufficient for most guys…and too smart to pretend to be someone she wasn't.

Paul seemed to realize she wasn't reacting as she should. His face crumpled and he started to sob with a drunk's easy tears. "You really don't care, do you?"

Rachel blanched. Had his affections run deeper than she'd thought? "Of course I care." But much as she hated hurting him, she couldn't marry him. Even if only her right brain knew why. Seeing their audience growing, she tugged desperately on his arm. "Please, Paul, let me take you into the office, make you some coffee. You're doing yourself no good here."

"No!" He wiped his face with his sleeve and nearly fell over. "I don't want to."

"Oh, for God's sake." Devin Freedman appeared from out of nowhere and tipped Paul over one of his shoulders. "Where do you want him?" he asked Rachel.

CHAPTER TWO

THE SMART-ASS LIBRARIAN looked at him with none of the self-possession she had earlier. In fact her big gray eyes were haunted. "In here," she said, ushering Devin into the office. "Trixie, take over." With trembling fingers, she pulled the venetian blinds closed, then shut the door and leaned against it.

Devin dumped the drunk on the couch and ran a professional eye over him. He'd quit bawling and was rolling his head from side to side and moaning faintly. "Some kind of container might be useful," he suggested. "He'll hurl at some point." Rachel looked at him blankly and he tried again. "Barf." Still nothing. Where was a translator when he needed one? "Throw up…vomit."

"Oh…oh!" She scanned the room, then found an empty cardboard box and bent over to pick it up. It wasn't the first time he'd noticed she had a nice ass. Rachel placed the box by the couch and backed away, her expression guilt-stricken. He suspected he knew what was worrying her. "Alcohol makes some people maudlin," he offered. Particularly those who took themselves way too seriously. "Don't worry about it."

"You don't understand," she murmured. "He proposed yesterday and I turned him down."

"That's no surprise. There must be a fifteen-year age difference."

"Seven years. I'm thirty-four." Devin's age. She didn't look it. The librarian shook her head. "Not that age matters. The important thing now is that—"

"He's acting like a wimp?"

"No!" She took a protective step toward the drunk. Anyone could see she had a conscience. That must be painful for her. "Paul had every right to expect me to say yes. I meant to say yes, only…" Her voice trailed off.

Paul sat up and grabbed the box. Rachel retreated and they both turned their backs, but couldn't escape the awful retching sounds. "Only you realized you'd be making a terrible mistake," Devin finished. Maybe the vintage clothes were an attempt to look older?

"I drove him to this." The librarian's slender throat convulsed. "And he's not the first man I've let down. I…I'm a heartbreaker."

As one who'd been given the description by the world's press, as one who'd dated and even married the female heartbreaker equivalent, Devin was hard put not to laugh. Only the sincerity in her pale face stopped him from so much as a grin. She really believed it, which was kind of cute—if a little sad. And he thought *he* was self-delusional at times.

Not that she wouldn't be pretty with a hell of a lot more makeup and a hell of a lot less clothes. The fastidious restraint of all those satin-covered buttons and dainty pearl earrings made Devin itch to pull Rachel's sleek dark hair out of its practical ponytail. Mess it up a little. Understated elegance was exceedingly bland to a man whose career had depended on showmanship.

He'd deliberately dressed down to fit in today, and thought

he'd done a pretty good job until the librarian's gaze had fallen on his boots. No jewelry except one signet ring and one modest earring…hell, he was practically invisible.

The sound of retching stopped and they turned around. The drunk—Paul—had pushed up to a sitting position and was wiping his mouth on some copier paper. White-faced and sweating, he glared at Devin. "Who do you think you are, manhandling me like that?"

Devin shrugged. "Someone had to stop you making an ass of yourself."

But Paul had already turned on Rachel. "I hope you're happy reducing me to this state."

"She didn't force alcohol down your throat," Devin said quietly.

The librarian swallowed. "Paul, I'm sorry. I had no idea you cared about me this much."

"You think everyone's as lukewarm as you are?" Paul balled the paper. "I did *all* the caring in that relationship. All the work in bed. You—"

"Have really, *really* bad taste in men," Devin said, because Rachel was hugging herself and obviously taking this Paul's rant way too seriously.

The librarian seemed to remember he was there. She straightened her shoulders. "Thank you, but I can handle it from here."

"You sure?" She was obviously out of her depth. "He's likely to get more abusive. I can toss him in a cab for you."

"Thanks," she said awkwardly, opening the door, "but I'll be okay." Devin got the impression she wasn't used to accepting help. Any more than he was used to offering it. For a moment he had an odd sense of his world shifting. But it had shifted so often lately he ignored it.

Something incongruous about her appearance had been bothering him, and as she bit her lip Devin finally figured out what it was. Her mouth—lush and full—was more suited to the L.A. strippers he'd shared stages with in the band's early performing days than a prim librarian. He grinned just as Romeo grabbed the box and started hurling again.

Rachel stiffened. "I'm glad one of us finds this funny."

"Your mouth doesn't fit your profession," he explained. "It's like seeing something X-rated on the cartoon network."

He didn't think to censor himself because he'd been a rock star for seventeen years and never had to. And got a sharp reminder he was no longer in that world when she shut the door in his face.

"Lucky the librarian fantasy never made my top ten," he told the door.

DEVIN WANTED TO BE treated as normal, and yet once his amusement wore off, Rachel's reaction gave him a profound sense of dislocation.

She'd looked at him without his fame in the way and hadn't liked what she'd seen. It was a scary thought, because whoever she saw was someone he was going to have to live with for the next forty plus years.

He strode across the road from the library into Albert Park, then stopped in a stand of tall palms that reminded him of L.A.—his home before his life depended on leaving it. For a full five minutes he looked up through the fronds to the blue, blue sky, homesick. Then he started walking again, around the quaint Victorian fountain, past oaks and a lot of trees he didn't recognize.

This must be how refugees felt in a new land…displaced, wary. And yet he'd been born here, was still a citizen, though he'd left for his father's country when he was two. He breathed in the smell of fresh-mown grass, only to regret it wasn't L.A.'s smog.

"Your pancreas is shot to hell. Any alcohol and you're dead." The doctor had been blunt, and left him sitting in a private hospital room full of flowers from fans. The band had imploded at the same time as his health…. What the hell he was going to do with the rest of his life?

His car keys fell out of his hand; someone bent to pick them up. Another teenager—shit, this place made him feel like a dinosaur.

"Are you okay?" Gray eyes, intense in a pale face. Lank blond hair.

"Of course I am." The kid stepped back and Devin took a deep breath. "I'm fine…thanks." He couldn't rush the ascent, but had to stop and acclimatize, then kick up a bit more. He reminded himself that the surface was there— even when he couldn't see it.

"You're Devin Freedman, aren't you?" Nervously, the kid hitched up his baggy jeans. "I heard you'd be studying here this year."

Living on a remote part of Waiheke Island since his arrival in New Zealand two months earlier, Devin had got used to being left in peace. *Something else to give up.* "Yeah," he said grudgingly, "I'm him."

In his drive to take control of his life, Devin had started taking online accounting courses to decipher his financial statements. A tutor had suggested university. When Devin stopped laughing he'd thought, why not?

And already his growing fiscal knowledge had paid off. He'd appointed a new financial advisor who'd found disturbing anomalies in some of Devin's statements. It looked like someone had been ripping him off; unfortunately Devin suspected his brother. But he needed to be very sure before he acted.

"I'm a huge fan. *Darkness Fell* was a work of genius."

"Not *The Fallen* or *Crack the Whip?*" Rage's final albums.

The kid looked at his feet and shuffled. "I really liked the early stuff. I know the others sold well… I mean, not that's there's anything wrong with commercial albums…."

Devin put him out of his misery. "You're right, they were crap." By that point the band had barely been speaking.

"But you still had some phenomenal guitar riffs and—"

"You play?" Devin asked, cutting short the hero-worship. He gestured to the expensive guitar case slung over the kid's shoulder.

"Bass mainly, but also some electric and acoustic—like you." The next words came in a rush. "Would you sign my guitar for me?" At Devin's nod, he unpacked a Gibson and scrambled in his bag for a Sharpie.

"What's your name?"

"Mark White."

Devin hesitated with his pen over the guitar.

"Your autograph will be fine," insisted Mark. "I hate phoniness, too."

Grinning, Devin signed, then handed back the bass. "See you around."

MARK MANAGED A CASUAL NOD but sank onto a bench as soon as Devin disappeared. Mark's knees were shaking. He clutched the neck of his instrument, looked at the manicured gardens of Albert Park and thought, *I imagined that. No one meets a legend, a god among bass players walking through freakin' rose beds.*

He glanced down at his guitar and for a moment panicked because sunlight was bouncing off the lacquer and he couldn't see it. But then he adjusted the angle and there it was scrawled across the maple. "To Mark, stay honest. Devin Freedman."

And Mark grinned because one part of him wanted to run back to his apartment, jump on his computer and flog it on eBay, and the other wanted to sleep with it under his pillow. *You are one screwed-up dude, Mark.*

So what was new?

Still, he let himself be happy, because it wasn't every day a guy got to meet his all-time hero. Then he looked toward the campus and his smile faded under the familiar gut-wrenching nausea, anger and terror. She was here… somewhere.

Mark had seen the University of Auckland envelope at the adoption agency when he'd asked the woman to check his file, claiming he was in an open adoption. Funny how people didn't care about hiding envelopes. The woman had been very kind, considering he'd been lying to her. "Do your parents know you're here?"

He'd lied again. "Sure."

Abruptly, Mark stood and began walking. Why had his birth mother started out wanting an open adoption, then changed her mind and severed contact? The question had been eating away at him every since he'd discovered he had a different blood type to both his parents.

He'd searched through his parents' private papers and found correspondence from an adoption agency. Mom and Dad still didn't know he knew…and Mark tried not to blame them because it was clear *she'd* made secrecy a condition of adoption.

But his anger…his alienation had spilled over into his misbehavior. It had been a tough twelve months on everybody. He'd only talked his parents into letting him enroll at a university four hundred kilometers away because "honest, Mom and Dad, I see my future now and it's all about getting an education and being normal like you want me to be."

Like I used to be. When I knew who I was. But Mark had another agenda. He would confront his birth mother. She would sob an apology and beg his forgiveness. He would say, "You had your chance," and walk away. Just like she had.

He'd worked out that she'd been seventeen when she had him. That made her thirty-four now.

It shouldn't be too hard to find her.

THE FADED BLUE SEASIDE cottage was one of Waiheke Island's first vacation homes, and unlike its newer neighbors, it was tiny and unpretentious. Not for the first time, Devin thought how well it suited his mother. He jumped the seaman's rope fence and strode down the white shell path, giving a cursory pat to the concrete seal balancing a birdbath on its nose. Then he caught sight of the front door and frowned.

It was wide open and a gardening trowel lay abandoned on the doorstep. His pulse quickened, and though he told himself not to panic, he shouted, "Mom!"

Three heart-stopping seconds of silence and then a faint reply. "I'm out back."

Devin walked through the dim interior to the rear garden, a sprawl of crunchy grass, lichen-covered fruit trees and roaming nasturtium. "How many times do I have to tell you to shut your damn door? Anyone could walk in."

Holding a red bucket, his diminutive mother looked

down from the top of a stepladder leaning against the peach tree. "And how many times do I have to tell you this isn't L.A.?" She dropped a handful of small white peaches into the half-full bucket, then ran a hand through her short gray bob. "Any leaves in my hair?"

Devin put his hands on his hips. "Should you be doing stuff like this?"

"I'm not going to have another heart attack, honey." Katherine held out the bucket. When he took it, she climbed sedately down the ladder. "Not now they've replaced the faulty stent."

He reached out and helped her down the last couple of steps, and her hand seemed so frail in his. Briefly, her grip tightened, reassuring him with its strength.

Still, Devin said gruffly, "Is it any wonder I'm paranoid after two emergency flights in two months? If you'd listened to my advice earlier and got a second opinion—"

"Yes, dear."

Reluctantly, he laughed. "Stay with me another week." He owned the adjacent headland, sixteen acres of protected native bush shielding a clifftop residence.

"I've only just moved home. Besides, you cramp my style."

"Stop you doing what you're not supposed to, you mean," he retorted.

"Dev, you're turning into the old woman I refuse to become. I'm sure I wasn't as bossy as this when you were in recovery."

"No," he said drily, "you were worse."

She ignored that, instructing him to pick some lemon balm for herbal tea on their meander back to the house. "How was your first day at school?"

"The other kids talk funny." Ignoring the kettle, he turned on the espresso machine he'd installed.

"Make any friends?"

He gave her the Devin Freedman glower, the one that *Holy Roller* magazine had described as the definitive bad rocker look. Being his mother she simply waited. "No, but then I don't expect to."

"You know I'm on the mend now, darling, so if you want to go back to L.A.—"

"I don't," he lied. "Got anything to eat?"

"There's a batch of scones cooling on the counter."

He burned his fingers snatching a couple, but feeding him distracted his mother from the subject of his future.

Five years earlier, when he'd quit rehab for the second time, she had told him she wouldn't spend her life watching him self-destruct, and had moved back to her native New Zealand. It had been a last-ditch effort to snap him into reality. Devin had felt nothing but relief, then added insult to injury by minimizing contact. It hadn't stopped Katherine from being the first person at his hospital bed.

Now she needed him to take care of her. Whatever she said.

His older brother, still living stateside, couldn't be relied on. A keen sense of the ridiculous had kept Devin's ego in check over the last crazy seventeen years, but the planet wasn't big enough for Zander's, who still blamed Devin for the breakup of the band.

The truth was Devin had held Rage together for a lot more years than its flamboyant lead singer deserved.

So if it turned out Zander had been screwing him over… well, Devin didn't think he could put even his mother's peace of mind before his need for justice.

CHAPTER THREE

"HE LOOKS LIKE HE NEEDS a friend," Rachel said to Trixie two days later. She'd noticed the teenager yesterday during library orientation. Now, as then, he walked around with his shoulders slightly hunched, blond fringe falling over his eyes and a scowl on his young face that did nothing to hide his apprehension. She remembered what it was to be young, alone and terrified. "Maybe I should go talk to him."

"Oh, hell, you're not starting a new collection of waifs and strays already, are you?" Trixie complained as she sorted a pile of books for reshelving. "We're not even a week into the first term."

Rachel stood up from her computer. "You were a waif and stray once, remember?" Trixie had been a scholarship kid who'd practically lived at the library in winter because she couldn't afford to heat her flat. Rachel had given her a part-time job, which turned full-time when she'd graduated last year.

"Which is why I'm protecting you now," Trixie reasoned. "You're useless at setting boundaries."

"Tell me about it. I keep getting bossed around by my junior."

The boy reached for a book on one of the shelves and

the backpack slipped off his scrawny shoulder, spilling books and pens. A red apple rolled across the carpet. Rachel started forward.

Trixie caught her by the arm. "Leave some time for yourself this year. Especially now that you're single again."

Rachel freed herself, but the teenager had already fastened his backpack and was slouching out the door. She turned to Trixie. "Don't do that again," she said quietly.

Under her pale makeup, Trixie reddened. "I was only trying to look out for you."

"Thanks, but I don't need a babysitter." She needed that reminder occasionally.

Ducking her head, her assistant nodded. Was there anything more pathetic than a sheepish Goth?

"You're a good friend," she added, "but, kid, I'm bruised not broken." Trixie had no idea what Rachel could survive. "Anyway, Paul rang and apologized this morning."

Trixie's head jerked up and her kohl-lined eyes narrowed. "I hope you told him where to stick it."

"Mmm." She'd been tempted, but being in the wrong was punishment enough for Paul. Rachel knew how that felt.

"And you reckon you don't need looking after?" Disgusted, Trixie picked up a stack of books and headed for aisle three. "At least date guys who can handle their drink." She pointed one black-painted nail. "Someone like him."

Beyond Trixie's finger, Rachel saw Devin Freedman scanning titles in the business section. Instinctively, she sucked in her lips to minimize their natural pout at the very moment he chose to glance over. Amusement warmed his eyes and she froze.

Instead of politely looking away, he folded his arms and grinned, waiting to see what she'd do. Mortified, she turned her back on him and blew out a puff of irritation. Dreadful man.

When she'd recovered her composure, she turned back to find him standing right in front of the counter. "Hi, Heartbreaker," he said casually. "How'd it go with Romeo the other day?"

Rachel frowned. "It's not a subject I want to discuss with you. And please don't call me that."

"You're still pissed about the comment I made about your mouth," he guessed. "I did mean it as a compliment."

She snorted. "That I have a mouth like a hooker? Still, it's better than a sewer, I suppose."

"Actually, I was thinking stripper," he replied lazily. "But I love the outraged dignity. Put me in my place again."

"I'm a librarian, not a proctologist," she said sweetly, and he chuckled.

This guy had a thicker hide than an armadillo, and momentarily, Rachel envied him. She might have accepted Paul's apology, but it would take a long time to forget being called cold and unfeeling. She had too many feelings; that's why she protected herself. Maybe she should be grateful for any compliment, however insulting. At least Devin meant no harm.

"Look." She adopted a conciliatory tone because one of them had to be a grown-up. "I *was* annoyed the other day by your comment, but I shouldn't have shut the door on you. That must have been hurtful and I'm sorry."

"You think you hurt…" This time he laughed out loud. "You're really quite sweet under that Miss Marple exterior, aren't you?"

She realized he was referring to today's vintage outfit— a high-waisted black skirt paired with a white ruffle-front blouse, herring net tights and pewter ribbon-tie patent shoes. The man had just delivered another backhanded compliment.

Almost, almost she was amused. But Rachel's ego was still too battered. She eyed his designer stubble and rumpled roan hair. Today the boots were black and the faded jeans set off by a black leather belt, complete with a big, ornate silver buckle, that sat low on his narrow hips. "At least I don't look like a cowboy after a week on the trail. Even Trigger made more effort."

His eyes narrowed appreciatively. But before he could answer, a shocked male voice said, "Rachel!" Looking left, she saw several of the university's top staff. The vice chancellor flanked by her two deputies…one of whom was Rachel's boss. "Why are you insulting Mr. Freedman?"

In that split second she comprehended that if the vice chancellor was in attendance, Devin was donating money—lots of it. "He's…" she began, then stopped. *Arrogant and cheeky, that's why,* didn't seem like a good enough reason.

Devin decided to help her out. "Oh, Rach and I are old friends." He could read every emotion that crossed her expressive face. The smart retort she had to bite back, the irritation at being beholden to him, a begrudging gratitude. "That's why I suggested meeting in the library." He twinkled at her. "She creates such a congenial atmosphere."

She twinkled back. "So exactly how much cash are you giving us, *mate?*" Oh, she was sharp, this one. Still, Devin's appreciation was tinged with annoyance. He liked to keep his philanthropy private.

The vice chancellor looked surprised. "I thought we were all keeping this a dark secret?"

Devin's gaze pinned Rachel. "We are."

Her chin rose. "Now that's not a tone to take with an old friend."

He'd never been great with authority and it amused him that she wasn't, either—unless it was hers. On an impulse Devin leaned over and planted a light kiss on her compressed lips. "Well, see you later…old *friend*."

He could almost feel the daggers thudding into his back as he steered the vice chancellor and his deputies toward the cluster of red leather armchairs out of view.

He'd discovered this space two days ago before Paul had disturbed the peace. Each corner of the library was glassed-in with floor-to-ceiling windows. Outside, towering silver birches swayed in Auckland's constant wind, their leaves dappling light and shade across the utilitarian carpet. Sparrows peppered the branches and their noisy chirruping gave Devin an illusion of companionship.

He wanted solitude, yet when he got it, his thoughts became bleak. Too often lately he'd found himself in his mother's cottage, which only made her worry about him. And that was intolerable.

The vice chancellor introduced himself as Professor Joseph Stannaway. Like his companions, he wore a suit, his short gray hair neatly marshaled to one side, and his strong face unlined…probably because he wore an expression of permanent solemnity. "As I said to your representative," he began as they took seats, "we wanted to thank you personally for your generous donation."

"Really, there's no need—"

"And to try again," the chancellor interrupted with a smile, "to persuade you into an official ceremony. It would garner a lot of media attention, which could only be good for the university's profile. Perhaps the bank could produce one of those large checks…what do you say?"

Playfulness didn't sit well on the man—he seemed too educated for it. It must be hard, Devin thought dispassionately, to devote your career to higher learning and then have to be grateful to someone who'd made a fortune writing lyrics like "Take me, baby, before I scream, you're the booty in my American dream."

"I'm sorry." Devin deliberately shunned all publicity. Sticking his head up over the trenches for the paparazzi to take another shot at? Never again.

The delegation spent the next twenty minutes trying to change Devin's mind with flattery, which only irritated him, chiefly because in the past it might have worked. Maybe that's why he got so much enjoyment from Rachel's barbed observations—they were novel. Of course, the kiss would really stir her up; a sensible man would regret it.

He grinned as Stannaway droned on. Not, unfortunately, one of Devin's attributes.

RACHEL WAS REHEARSING her rebuke to Devin the next day when the boy she'd noticed came up to her station.

"What can I do for you?" Her smile must have had an edge because he eyed her warily as he shoved back his hair.

"I was wondering if you had any lists of all the university staff…you know, like everybody, not just the lecturers. And their ages."

"Not here. You might be able to access some information through the registrar, but there's possibly some privacy issues around their release."

His face fell. "Oh."

"What's the name? Maybe I know the person and can save you the trouble."

"Um, she's an old friend of my parents. I was just hoping I'd…recognize something when I saw the list."

Poor kid, he really was desperate for a friend if he was hunting down such tenuous connections. "Where are you from?" Rachel asked kindly. She was supposed to be leaving on her morning break but this was more important.

"A farm outside Cambridge."

"Really? I grew up in Hamilton." They were only twenty minutes apart. "Small world. First time living away from home?"

He swallowed. "Yeah."

"It's hard initially, but you'll find your feet soon. A lot of the first years are in the same boat, all scared—"

The teen glowered. "I'm not scared."

Damn, wrong word. If Devin hadn't rattled her, she wouldn't have chosen it.

"I see you've got a book there…would you like me to check it out for you? It will save you joining the queue at the front desk."

It was a peace offering for hurting his pride, and he took it. "Yeah, thanks." He handed over the book along with his library card.

Which didn't work. "They do this sometimes at the beginning of term," she said. "Let me just check that all your details are filled in…." The screen came up. "Mark…nice name. Okay, one of the library's ID codes is missing."

Glancing at his address, she noticed he wasn't living in residence, which was a shame; he'd make more friends that way. She nodded at the guitar case by his feet. "You know, the university has a lot of music clubs you might be interested in."

"I'm not really a club-joining kind of guy."

About to reply, Rachel caught sight of his birth date and her breath hitched. *June 29, 1992.*

"Something wrong?"

"No." Her fingers were suddenly clumsy on the keyboard as she reminded herself of the facts. On average, there were sixty-four thousand births a year in New Zealand. Which meant around one hundred and seventy-seven people—eighty-eight boys—shared her son's birthday. But she had to ask. "So what do your parents do?"

Mark frowned. "You need that for the form?"

"No, it's processing."

"Mom's a teacher." Rachel's pulse kicked up a notch. "And Dad's a farmer."

Not a policeman. As always, the disappointment was crushing enough to make Rachel feel sick. Her fingers were damp on the keyboard; she wiped them on her skirt, chiding herself for an overactive imagination. She gave the teenager his card.

"Here you go. All sorted now."

Mark shoved it back in his jeans. "He used to be a cop," he added, and the smile froze on her face.

Someone who knew how to keep her baby safe, she'd thought when short-listing the applicants with her social worker.

"Are you okay?" Mark asked.

"Fine." Her heart was beating so hard he must be able to hear it. Rachel loosened the top button of her shirt, suddenly finding it difficult to breathe. There was only one way to know.

"You have something in your hair," she said abruptly, reaching out a trembling hand.

"Yeah?" He started flicking his fingers through the blond strands, "What is it?"

"A…an insect…let me."

Obediently, he leaned forward, and she brushed the hair away from his right ear. "Turn your head a little."

Just at the hairline behind his ear, she saw it. A birthmark the size of her thumbnail. Rachel gasped and he broke away, raking both hands through his hair. "What! Did you get it?"

She stared at him, unable to speak. Tall like his father, with his fairer hair. His eyes—shock jolted through her—were the same color as hers, but the shape was Steve's. "It's okay," she croaked, pretending to flick something away. "It was a moth."

"A moth." Shaking his head, Mark picked up his guitar case. "Jeez, the way you were going on I thought it had to be a paper wasp at least."

No, don't leave. "You've heard of bookworms, haven't you? Lethal to libraries." Rachel memorized his features. "The term also applies to certain moth larvae. From the family *oecophoridae.*" Outwardly she smiled and talked; inwardly she splintered into tiny little pieces. "Of the order…now what was it?" *My son, my baby. You grew up.* "Starts with *L.*"

Mark shifted from one foot to the other.

"Lepidoptera," she said brightly. "Of the order Lepidoptera." The tiny bundle treasured in her memory, gone forever. But her son—her grown son—was here, and the reality of him shredded her with love and pain and need.

"Wow," he said politely, stepping back from the counter. "That's really interesting."

"Wait!"

"Yeah?" He was impatient to get away from the crazy woman, and how could she blame him? With all her heart she wanted to say, *I'm your mother.*

But she couldn't.

Two years earlier, she'd written a letter to the adoptive parents through the agency. *If he ever wants to meet his birth mother, please give him my details.*

Their reply was devastating. *In keeping with your wishes at the time, we've never told our son he was adopted. We're very sorry at the pain this must cause you, but you must understand to do so now would be detrimental to our own relationship with him.*

"Have a good day," she rasped.

THE WOMAN WAS A WEIRDO. No doubt about it. Mark stopped outside and shifted his guitar to his other shoulder so he could tuck the book into his backpack.

He didn't have a class for another hour and he stood uncertain, glancing across the narrow, tree-lined street bisecting the university. Buildings in this part of campus were angular and geometric, to Mark's eyes, hard and unfriendly shapes for the university's social heart, holding the student union, the theater and the student commons. It was lunchtime and he was hungry, but the overflowing cafeteria was too raucous. Too…intimidating. He'd wait until later, when it cleared out somewhat before grabbing something to eat.

Coming from a small community where everyone knew everybody, he'd thought finding his birth mother would be relatively easy.

But the university employed hundreds, and trying to

access lists only led to awkward questions. He certainly couldn't tell the truth.

And he missed home. He missed his parents, which he kinda despised himself for because he hadn't been all that nice to them before he'd left.

He still couldn't believe they weren't really his. That all the things he'd built his identity on—inheriting Dad's musical ability and Mom's aptitude for math—were a lie.

He wasn't from the clan of Whites whose roots in the area went back four generations. His multitude of cousins weren't his cousins and his grandparents weren't his grandparents.

A group of students swept down the footpath, laughing and horsing around, nudging him aside like he was invisible. His classes were made up of eighty to a hundred strangers in huge auditoriums.... In a week he'd never sat next to the same person twice.

And so many of them seemed to know each other. How had they made friends so quickly? What was wrong with him that he couldn't?

He'd thought staying with his air hostess cousin in her city apartment would be cool, but Suz was away two weeks out of four. And when she was home, her boyfriend was nearly always over, so Mark tended to hang out in his room. The guy was a stockbroker and a real phony.

Another bunch of kids brushed past, knocking the guitar case off his shoulder. Devin Freedman caught it before it hit the ground.

"You need to get out of the line of fire." Still carrying the case, he stepped back into the library's portico before handing it over. "It's Mark, isn't it?"

He remembers my name. Suddenly Mark's day got a whole lot better.

DEVIN REMEMBERED THE KID because he had a good guitar. "What are you studying…music?"

"Business… I'm in some of your classes."

"Really?" Devin hadn't noticed him, but then the teenager wasn't big on eye contact.

Mark obviously misinterpreted his surprise because he blushed and added in a rush, "But I'm not some wanker carrying his guitar case around all the time to be cool. I busk in town during lunch breaks. That's why I've got my acoustic today." He shrugged in a belated attempt to appear unconcerned. "The money keeps me in beer."

Devin kept a straight face. "Not something parents allow for in their budget, I guess." He looked toward the cafeteria and braced himself for stares. Having cut short the meeting, he had to hang around for his next class, and damned if he was going to go hungry because a bunch of kids would gawk at him. Delaying the moment, he asked, "Made any friends yet?"

"No. I mean I'm sure I will…."

Devin realized he'd hit a nerve. "Me, neither," he said easily. "First day everyone wanted to sit with me. The dean gave a stern lecture about harassment and now nobody does. Who'll let me copy their homework?"

The kid laughed; it sounded like he really needed to. What the hell. "Had lunch yet?" Devin had been going to ask the librarian as a peace offering, but she'd gone home sick, which was odd because she'd looked fine half an hour ago.

Color rose under Mark's pale skin. "If you're asking because you feel sorry for me—"

Devin raised his hands to the sky. "Fine, we'll sit by ourselves like a couple of geeks." He started walking across the road, heard Mark scramble to catch up, and hid a grin.

"Since I'm doing you such a favor," Devin growled, "you're buying."

The kid shot him a glance. "Hey, you're the rock star," he protested.

"Which makes you the groupie," Devin drawled. "I'll have a coffee and a doughnut and it better have sprinkles."

CHAPTER FOUR

RACHEL CAME BACK TO WORK two days later, all cried out. The aftereffects—sore eyes and red nose—led credence to her flu story, which only made her feel more guilty. A childhood of enforced deception had given her an antipathy to lying.

She was in an intolerable situation, aching to see her son but with no excuse to do so. Instead she had to depend on the occasions he chanced into the library during her shift, and not surprisingly, after her babble on Tuesday he tended to give her a wide berth.

Friday afternoon she'd just begun an informal workshop on finding and searching business resources when Mark and Devin came in together and joined the seven students already standing in a circle around her. Ignoring Devin, she smiled a welcome at Mark and summarized her intro. "Okay, everyone, let's move on to search strategies." *Act cool,* she told herself, *he needs to think of you as normal.*

As she distributed the handouts, Devin murmured provocatively, "Your hair's much nicer down." Rachel turned her back on him. She hadn't seen him since the kiss three days earlier, and he wasn't a bit repentant. But a slap on the wrist would have to wait for privacy.

She got the opportunity twenty minutes later, when she dismissed the group. To her surprise, Devin had asked some intelligent questions, made notes, acted like a regular student right down to calling her Ms. Robinson. "Can you stay behind a moment?" she asked him.

"Sure. Mark…go ahead, buddy, I'll catch up to you."

Rachel forgot her prepared lecture on respecting people's boundaries. "How do you know that boy?"

"Who, Mark? He's one of my classmates…nice kid. But no need to be jealous. You're still my number one sparring partner." He eyed her folded arms. "I expect you want an apology for that kiss."

"That would be nice."

"I know I *should* be sorry. Will that do?"

A smile trembled on her lips. If Mark hadn't been involved she might have enjoyed this outrageous man. "About that teenager," she said. "Wouldn't you rather hang out with people your own age?"

Devin raised a hand to his impressive chest in mock horror. "Why, *Mrs.* Robinson, are you coming on to a student?"

"Are you *ever* serious?"

He considered her question. "Oddly enough, all the time I'm not teasing you. You know, maybe we should go on a date, explore this little attraction we've got going."

"So little I'm completely unaware of it," she retorted.

"Really? I thought you were a clever woman." He leaned closer. The man had charisma; she gave him that. The innate confidence that came from a lifetime of being desired. Lucky him.

Surprise came into his extraordinary eyes. Rachel thought it was because she'd held her ground. Until he sniffed. "Your perfume," he said, "it's sexy as hell."

He smelled good, too. She banished the thought. "What were you expecting, lavender water?"

Devin blinked.

"But you're right," she added coolly. "I am clever. Too clever for you."

He grinned, sending his charisma wattage through the roof, then to Rachel's relief straightened up. "Maybe you'd enjoy slumming," he offered.

"I won't lower my standards."

"The professor being such a class act."

Rachel's cheeks heated, but she held his gaze. "Speaking of classes, don't you have one?"

He glanced at his watch. "Damn, it's still hard working to a timetable. One more thing…don't mention the donation to the university to anyone."

It occurred to her that he'd bought himself a place here. Lovely.

He misread her disgust. "Please."

Before she could answer, Mark came back into the library. With a cursory nod to Rachel, he said, "Hey, Dev, we're late."

"You were supposed to go on ahead…never mind." Devin turned back to Rachel with a rueful smile. "I'd better run. I'm teaching that boy too many bad habits." With a casual wave he left.

She watched them leave with a disquiet that turned into real alarm when, on her break, she took the opportunity to research Devin on the Internet. Though his musical achievements proved substantial, Devin Freedman was a man who comfortably juggled the seven deadly sins and still found time to break a couple of commandments.

The hair rose on the back of her neck when she read he'd admitted to using recreational drugs. He was also an unrepentant drunk. When, two years earlier, a writer for *Rolling Stone* magazine had asked if he had a problem with alcohol, Devin had replied, "No, we're very happy together."

He'd collapsed on stage eighteen months ago amid frenzied rumors of a drug overdose, then effectively vanished from the media…resurfacing in New Zealand before Christmas, pulling a Marlene Dietrich "I vant to be alone."

There were a couple of pictures of him, Stetson pulled low, mirrored sunglasses hiding his eyes, palm outstretched to the camera. Otherwise nothing but speculation about the guy nicknamed the Prince of Excess.

Rachel shut down the Internet connection and stared unseeing at her screensaver, a model of the mountain bike she wanted to upgrade to. Her own experience of him did nothing to reassure her.

Beneath the banter he was self-indulgent and arrogant, a man who did what he wanted when he wanted, with no thought for other people.

And her son was under his influence.

"So, MARK…HI!" Even to Rachel's ears, her tone was too tinny; too bright. She'd been waiting five days for this opportunity to talk.

The teenager glanced at her, startled. "Hi." He returned to scanning the library shelves.

"Need some help?"

"No, I'm okay, thanks." He'd been taught nice manners; she'd already noticed that. It warmed her…and it blistered like acid.

"Are you sure? After all, that's what I'm here for!"

Rachel laughed and it was a silly, high sound. She felt like a thirteen-year-old trying to impress a crush.

"Here it is." Mark took a textbook off the shelf. "Well, see you."

She fell into step beside him. "So, how are your classes going?"

"Um, fine."

"Do you spend much time with Devin Freedman?" She hadn't intended asking so baldly, but he'd picked up speed.

He slowed at that, his gray eyes suspicious. "A bit…why?"

"What about out of school?"

He stopped at the bank of high-backed chairs that made up a study corner. "Look, if you want his autograph I think you should ask him for it yourself."

"His auto—" This time Rachel didn't have to force the laugh. "Oh, no, I'm not a fan."

"She's a friend, aren't you, Heartbreaker?"

Rachel jumped. One of the chairs swung around to reveal Devin.

"I wish you'd stop calling me that."

"What…friend or heartbreaker?"

"Both."

He chuckled and the light flashed off the heavy silver link chain around his neck. Today he'd accessorized his faded jeans, olive T-shirt and scuffed brown cowboy boots with way too much jewelry—silver hoop earrings and three rings including a skull with diamond eyes. Mark looked from one to the other, then plunked himself into a chair. "Oh, you guys know each other. That's cool, then."

About to tell Devin to take his boots off the coffee table, Rachel paused. "Sure, we're friends," she said. Advising Mark to be careful around the rocker would sound less hysterical if he thought it came from personal experience. "So, Devin—" she paused, trying to think of something "rock n' roll" to say "—how's it hanging?"

The twinkle in his eyes became more pronounced. "It's *hanging* fine, thanks for asking…. What are you up to?"

The blush she'd managed to hold back through his innuendo heated her cheeks. "The usual. Actually, I'm due in an acquisitions meeting so I'd better go." She looked at her son. "Bye, Mark."

His nod was friendly. "See ya."

She waggled her fingers at Devin, who waggled back. "Definitely up to something," he said.

Fortunately, he was gone when she came out of her meeting forty minutes later, but Mark was still there, poring over books. Hungrily, Rachel studied him, noting the way he chewed his lower lip when he concentrated.

The hand cupping his chin was big; his body still had some catching up to do. And he was boyishly thin, his bony shoulder blades sticking through the striped T-shirt as he bent over the table and took notes. Surely he was too young to be fending for himself….

With the discipline of years of practice, Rachel stopped torturing herself. She had to trust the people she'd chosen for him. Had to accept he wasn't her son—but theirs.

As though sensing her scrutiny, Mark glanced up and grinned. Something had made him happy. Encouraged by his first smile, she approached him. "Devin gone?"

"Yeah, but we're meeting later." Obviously bursting with news, he added, "I finally talked him into showing me his guitar collection."

"In town?"

"No, at his place on Waiheke. You been there?"

Rachel sat down. "No." His adoptive parents weren't here to protect him and she was. "Listen, Mark, Devin might not be the best person to hang around with. He has a history of drug and alcohol abuse…." Her voice trailed off under his look of contempt.

"Aren't you supposed to be his friend?"

"Devin knows when I disapprove of his behavior." That at least was true. "I just want to make the point that you're only seventeen years old and living away from home for the first time. That makes you vulnerable—"

"Stop right there," Mark interrupted. "Let me get this straight. I hardly know you and you're giving me a lecture?" Shaking his head, he stood up, sweeping his books into his bag. "Who the hell do you think you are— my mother?"

"SHE'S RIGHT," said Devin when Mark repeated the conversation. "I'm not the kind of person you should be spending time with."

They stood on the deck of the Waiheke ferry watching the whitecaps as the boat surged against a brisk northerly toward the island that lay forty minutes off the mainland.

Their fellow passengers were a mix of commuters holding briefcases, tourists and the alternative lifestylers who'd once had the place to themselves. Now the island's slopes were dotted with homes of the wealthy. Yet there was still a lull, a lazy charm about the place. Nearby a businessman loosened his tie, while two kids raced across the deck to the bow to point out the island to their mother.

Cool for the first time that day, Devin breathed in the salty air and felt the tension he always carried ease a little.

"You don't sound that bothered about it," Mark replied.

Glancing sideways, Devin saw the kid's hurt expression. *Oh, great.* He still didn't quite know how Mark had talked him into inviting him over; it had something to do with Devin feeling he owed him.

A week and a half into university life his brain felt close to exploding under the weight of new information, and Mark had helped him out more than once, explaining concepts. The kid was bright, no doubt about it.

And so puppy dog enthusiastic about music. Devin remembered that kind of devotion; he still mourned its loss. Maybe that was really what this was about. He was warming himself at the fire of the kid's idealism. "Listen, Mark. Don't expect too much of me. You'll only be disappointed."

"I don't… I mean, it's not like… Look, I don't have to come if you don't want me to."

Devin laughed. "What are you going to do, jump in and swim back?"

MARK WAS DISAPPOINTED at his first sight of Devin's house. From watching reality TV shows on rock stars he expected some sort of mansion with white pillars, wrought-iron gates with a security keypad, a six-car garage and an entourage…definitely an entourage.

Especially since they rode from the ferry terminal to Devin's property on a customized Harley-Davidson.

But albeit secluded—and white plaster—the place was pretty simple, a long, low-lying building with no distinctive features that Mark could see. Inside was better. Mostly white with red feature walls and white leather furniture. Art covered every wall, from big canvasses of bold swirls of color to old movie posters and some hot nudes. He recognized an Andy Warhol and wondered if it was an original.

The house perched on a cliff with dramatic glass walls toward the sea. Mark stood at the window and gazed out across the expanse of water and beyond to the far horizon. Below, several seagulls hovered in the updraft. "Wow."

Musical instruments were scattered around the enormous open plan lounge—an antique snare drum, various types of guitars. A microphone in the corner and he spotted speakers so small they had to be state of the art. Memorabilia, but no Grammys or awards. Mark was disappointed.

Then his eyes fell on a bass guitar. "Is that the Fender Precision?"

"Yeah."

"Can I touch it?"

Devin smiled. "You can play it."

"No shit!" Reverently, Mark picked up the instrument, running his hands over the strings. One of rock's most distinctive riffs had been created on this very bass. He became aware of Devin watching, and froze, embarrassed to show himself up as a meager talent.

"You want a drink?" asked Devin. "Coke, Sprite, juice?"

"A Sprite would be good."

When Devin had disappeared down the hall, Mark turned on the amplifier and played the Rage anthem right through, thrilled to the bone. When he'd finished, Devin still hadn't returned, so he picked up an electric guitar and started playing his own riffs. As an only child, growing up on a farm from the age of twelve, he'd often relied on his own company. That's when he'd begun to play guitar.

He played one of his songs right through, forgetting his shyness, trailing off when he noticed Devin standing at the door holding two glasses.

"You're good."

Mark blushed. "Thanks," he said diffidently.

Devin put the drinks on the table, picked up his bass guitar and said, "Play that last one again."

Mark did, and Devin accompanied him, adding tonal qualities Mark would never have dreamed of. "I like that song," said Devin. "Whose is it?"

"Mine."

Devin looked up. For a long minute he didn't say anything. "Let's try that again," he suggested.

Mark spent the next two hours in musical heaven. He didn't ever want the day to end. But eventually Devin stopped and glanced at the clock. "I'm hungry. How about you?"

"Starving."

Mark followed him into the kitchen and sat on a stool while the rocker opened his fridge and inspected the contents. "I've got a better idea. How about we go eat with my mom."

CHAPTER FIVE

DEVIN WAS WALKING THROUGH Albert Park en route to class the next morning when he glimpsed the librarian sitting by the circular fountain.

Her gaze immediately dropped to the open book in her lap, but he'd been around enough stalkers—and better ones than this—to know he was her target.

Her skills needed work, but her choice of location was sound. All the park's paths converged on the historic fountain, with its bronze cherubs and their water-trickling orifices.

He hid a grin. This should be interesting. Of course, she had no idea he knew she'd warned Mark to shun him. He braced himself for verbal sparks.

As he approached, she looked up in feigned surprise and Devin was conscious of another spark. One that with any other woman he would have called sexual…if she wasn't wearing a fifties-style calf-length dress in a red-and-white diamond check with a matching fabric belt. Did this woman own *any* clothes from this decade? Red suited her, though. He particularly liked the matching lipstick.

He stopped in front of her. "Of all the fountains in all the world, somehow we meet at this one."

"Isn't that a coincidence!" She looked past him—checking for Mark—then back with such undisguised relief that Devin was provoked to tease her.

"You don't happen to have any Tylenol, do you?" He put on his shades to hide his amusement. "I'm too old to keep partying this hard."

She frowned slightly and he read her thoughts. *Had Mark been with him?* But the only way to get information… She opened her bag. "Sure."

Devin sat down next to her and lifted his face to the sun. It was only eight-thirty but already humid. The scent of the park's roses was heavy in the air.

The breeze changed direction. Fountain mist drifted toward Rachel, forcing her to move closer. She wasn't wearing perfume today but she still smelled seductive. How did she do that? Maybe he shouldn't torment her by making things up. He and Mark had eaten at Katherine's, then been cleaned out in a friendly poker game with her elderly neighbor before the kid caught the 9:00 p.m. ferry.

Rachel said way too casually, "I didn't think you knew many people here." Fishing.

He took the pills she offered, shiny in their silver foil. "Heartbreaker, when you're a rock star you can always find people to party with." There was no bitterness in the observation. He'd long ago accepted that his real friends were people he knew before he'd become famous.

Except they were still treating him as fragile. Another reason to stay away from L.A. He was too close to broken to shrug off someone else's doubt. How ironic that the only person who looked at him without deference or sympathy was this woman.

"Well, the last ferry from Waiheke leaves at midnight," Rachel ventured. "So I don't suppose things got too out of hand."

She'd checked the ferry timetable? Her concern for Mark seemed a little excessive. "Oh, I have plenty of room for sleepovers and no one minds three to a bed." Her lovely mouth tightened. "But it was all pretty tame…some bourbon, coke…" Devin winked to make sure she'd make the connection to the drug, not the beverage. "A hot tub filled with twenty of my closest friends, and rock blasting over the sound system…"

He noticed as he ran out of rock star clichés that she'd slid almost to the other end of the fountain edge, and he had to bite the inside of his cheek. "It was a spontaneous thing or I would have invited you. We could have done with some classier chicks."

Devin had a sudden image of her in a hot tub, incongruous and unexpectedly appealing. It had been too long since he'd had sex, but the months of therapy and rehab had left him feeling like a peeled onion, exposed and vulnerable.

"Was Mark with you?" she asked bluntly.

"The kid? Hmm, let me just think…. We started the evening together. So hard to recognize people when they're naked and wet." He stopped when he saw the stricken look in her eyes. "I'm kidding."

"Please leave him alone."

He frowned, puzzled. "Who is that boy to you?"

For a split second Rachel looked guilty. "No one. I…I just don't like seeing minors being led astray."

Devin's sympathy evaporated. Ignoring the fact that he'd just given her reasons to be concerned, he got pissed. She was being officious, no doubt basing her assumptions on what she read in the press. Well, if she expected depravity… "If you don't want me corrupting minors, then give me someone my own age to play with." Lazily, his gaze traveled down her body, deliberately provocative.

Angry color flooded Rachel's cheeks. She stood. "Grow up!"

"Where's the fun in that?" Devin stood, too, stretched and yawned. "You know, I like a feisty woman, and this heartbreaker reputation of yours has me intrigued. Any time you want to take a ride with me—"

"I wouldn't take a walk with you, cowboy," she interrupted heatedly, "let alone a drive."

"Darlin,'" he drawled, "who said anything about a car?"

BY WEDNESDAY OF THE following week, Rachel had confronted an unpalatable truth. Mark was deliberately avoiding her. She knew he'd been into the library because his online history showed he'd been taking out books. But he was obviously timing his visits around her shifts.

She'd blown it, warning him against Devin. In hindsight, it had been a stupid thing to do. But she seemed unable to do anything except react to her emotions where her son was concerned.

The yearning to see him was terrible, as bad as giving him up had been.

Fortunately, he'd struck an acquaintance with Trixie—it seemed only Rachel couldn't make friends with him—so she was able to gather crumbs of information. It was through Trixie that she knew Mark still spent time with Devin. Apparently the rocker had become some sort of musical mentor, which Trixie thought was the coolest thing to happen to Mark, and which Rachel thought was the absolute worst.

But what could she do about it?

As she walked to the downtown parking lot after her shift, a thread of music in the city cacophony distracted her from her gloomy musings. Glancing up, she saw Mark strumming guitar with another teenager outside The Body Shop, their voices straining over the blare and honk of rush hour traffic. A meager collection of coins lay scattered in an open guitar case. Rachel stepped into a nearby doorway where she could watch unobserved.

Mark's reluctance was evident as he joined in the choruses; he obviously knew he had an indifferent singing voice. She was to blame for that. The other boy's voice was stronger and well served by a song that was both melodic and haunting.

She wasn't an expert, but Rachel could see nothing in his performance to excite a music legend into mentorship. Her fingers tightened on her bag. Was that relationship more payback from Devin?

He'd breezed into the library several times this week, always calling across the room, "Keep me posted about that ride, won't you, Heartbreaker." Rachel had fielded a lot of interested questions from fellow staff members who were agog at the thought of one of their own attracting a rocker.

As if.

She knew damn well that Devin was baiting her as punishment for sticking her nose in something that didn't concern her. What she couldn't judge was how much of that depravity was feigned to annoy her.

In her worst moments, she even considered telling Devin the truth. But Rachel had kept this secret too long to trust it to an undisciplined rocker who probably had looser lips than Jagger.

The song finished; the buskers took a break. Flipping his hair out of his eyes, Mark caught sight of Rachel and scowled. She responded with a tentative smile and stepped forward. "Can I talk to you privately for a minute?"

"I don't need another lecture."

"I want to apologize."

He searched her face, then shrugged. "Back in a sec, Ray." They walked down the side street a few feet. It was quieter here. She steeled herself.

"I know my concern seemed intrusive—"

"It was the disloyalty that got me."

She swallowed. "Disloyalty?"

"To Devin," Mark said impatiently. "I mean, the guy's your friend."

"Oh."

"He's the one you should be apologizing to."

Rachel murmured noncommittally and Mark's expression grew even sterner.

"Especially when he agreed with you that he was a bad influence."

That surprised her. "He did?"

"At least until you read him the riot act. Then he said I could hang out with him as much as I like." Mark grinned. "Maybe I should accept your apology."

Rachel bit her lip. So she'd provoked Devin into doing the very thing she'd set out to prevent. Mark really was better off without her. Except…this was the only chance she'd ever have to know him. "So are we okay again?" *Will you stop avoiding me?*

"I guess." He was already looking beyond her as he waved to his mate. "Yeah, coming! So is that all you wanted?" He was taller than her by a few inches. *Amazing.*

Through force of will she matched his casualness. "Yes, that's all." As he walked away, Rachel knew she'd never be anything to him other than as the loopy librarian. Unless… "Mark?"

He turned back impatiently. "Yeah?"

"I will think about apologizing to Devin."

He nodded in approval; she basked in it all the way to the parking lot.

She'd always had one imperative for her son. To keep him safe. And that hadn't changed.

If the only way to Mark was through Devin Freedman, then so be it.

In the driver's seat of her Honda hatchback, she passed a hand over her face, suddenly exhausted. She felt as if she was on a teeter-totter, up one minute, down the next. For years she'd worked hard to achieve serenity. Her childhood had held no security…even the long periods of relative peace were the only uneasy calm before an impending storm.

As an adult she'd organized her life into neat compartments. Now the drawer was a jumble again.

She needed to start thinking smarter. Apologizing wasn't a fix; somehow she had to scrutinize that damn man. Then she could judge him herself.

An idea occurred to her and she grew thoughtful. If she befriended the rocker, then Mark's attitude would soften toward her, providing an opportunity to get to know her son.

Not quite the threesome Devin had had in mind when he'd tried to shock her. Rachel chuckled. She'd thought of a way to get what she wanted *and* extract a little revenge on Mr. Rock Star.

The next day when Devin called across the library,

"When are you going to put me out of my misery, Heart-breaker?" Rachel smiled.

"Right now."

THINKING HE'D MISHEARD, Devin moved closer. "Excuse me?"

Rachel beamed at him. "I'm saying yes to a date. Well, really, it's a way of apologizing for hurting your feelings last week."

Hurting his… Okay, now he *knew* she was joking. "I realize I was out of line," she continued earnestly, "and this is my way of making it up to you."

Devin folded his arms, leaned on the counter and waited for the punch line. And waited.

"How does tonight sound?"

Good God, she was serious. He was so flummoxed he couldn't think of an excuse. "Umm…"

"Seven o'clock suit you?" Without waiting for a response, she wrote it in her diary in neat script.

"Look, this really isn't necessary. No hard feelings."

"No, I insist. And my goodness, you need a reward for all that persistence. Which is sweet of you, incidentally."

Devin winced. "The word *sweet* should only be applied to situations involving whipped cream and a supermodel," he said, and sparked a frown from her. His confusion gave way to suspicion. *Wait a minute.* The librarian didn't want to date him any more than he wanted to date her. This was counterterrorism. Intrigued, he decided to beat her at her own game.

"Give me your address," he drawled. "I'll pick you up."

"Maybe it's better if we meet at the restaurant."

"Except I'm still deciding where to take you."

Reluctantly, Rachel found a piece of paper and wrote down her address.

"You know, I'm kinda nervous about this," he said as he accepted it. "Given your reputation as a heartbreaker and all."

Her eyes narrowed. "Yes, I had decided not to date until I'd got that situation under control. Are you sure you want to take the risk?"

"Hmm, good point." He rubbed his chin. "Maybe I should reconsider...."

Something oddly like panic clouded her expression. It was as if she really cared about this. Then she leaned forward and said softly, "Chicken?"

Devin chuckled. There were so many lessons he could teach this woman. Specifically, never take on a hell-raiser. Even reformed ones were dangerous. "Go ahead," he dared, "break my heart."

CHAPTER SIX

THE LIBRARIAN'S neighborhood was made up of immaculately restored colonial cottages, each with pocket-handkerchief front yards full of lavender and standard roses. *Figured,* Devin thought.

Few had garages, so everyone parked on the street, which meant he had to leave his car a mile down the road and walk. Having been raised in L.A., he bitterly resented it.

He also seriously resented being nervous. It wasn't that he was hot for the librarian, simply that this was his first date ever without the social lubricant of alcohol.

Devin found number eight. The house was the same as every other except instead of being painted cream or white like its neighbors, it was honeysuckle-yellow and the garden was a subtropical jungle of banana palms, black flaxes, and orange and red canna lilies. He was picking up way too much plant lore from his mother. A well-used mountain bike was chained to the old-fashioned porch railing.

Sucker. She gave you the wrong address. Why hadn't he seen that coming? He was about to turn away when the door was flung open. "You're forty minutes late," said Rachel. "I'd just about given you up."

Devin checked his Hauer. She was right. "Timekeeping's never been my strong point." He saw she expected an apology, and shrugged. "Sorry…. So your roommate owns this place?"

"I live alone. You know, I tried ringing the number you gave me—" her gaze traveled from his Black Sabbath T-shirt down to his slashed stone-washed jeans "—but there was no answer."

"The number goes to a message service. Only close friends get my direct line." She actually had to think about why. *Hello, I'm famous.* He caught himself. Channeling his egotistical brother. *Ouch.* "Ready to go?" he asked politely.

"I was beginning to think you'd stood me up," Rachel confessed. "It felt like the high school ball all over again."

So the librarian had insecurities. "Yeah? What happened?"

Her expression shut faster than a poked clam. "I'll just get my cardigan."

Cardigan? He might not be a hell-raiser anymore but Devin valued his reputation. "Haven't you got anything sexy?"

"Yes," said Rachel. "My mind."

Fortunately, the cardigan was a clingy black number and it did have the advantage of covering another hideous buttony blouse. It was a shame Rachel didn't do cleavage because she had great breasts. Turning from locking the front door, she caught the direction of his gaze and stiffened. Oh, great, now she probably thought he wanted her.

"Let's take my car," she said, pointing her remote.

Devin looked at the little silver hatchback emitting a high-pitched beep, and pulled out the keys of the Aston Martin he kept in town. "Let's not."

"So yours is parked close?" she inquired too damn innocently. For a moment they locked gazes.

"Fine," he conceded. "But I'm driving." He held his hand out for her keys, but her fingers tightened around them.

"I'll drive…. I don't drink."

"Neither do I." When she looked skeptical, he added, "Anymore."

An indefinable tension went out of her. She gave him the keys. "You don't know how glad I am to hear that."

"It figures you'd be an advocate of prohibition," he commented as he opened the passenger door.

"I've noticed before that you typecast librarians," she said kindly. "But as your experience of learning institutions is obviously quite new I'll make allowances."

Devin started to enjoy himself. "Now who's stereotyping? Besides, if you don't want to be seen as old-fashioned, you shouldn't dress like that."

He shut the door on her protest and crossed to the driver's side. "I'll have you know this is vintage," she said as soon as he opened his door.

Devin folded himself into the ridiculously small interior. "I know what it is, I just don't like it."

"Is this how you usually talk to your dates?" she demanded.

"Actually," he said, deadpan, "we don't usually talk."

Her lips tightened; she reached for her seat belt and Devin gave up on any expectation of fun. He turned the ignition and the engine spluttered into life. It sounded like a lawnmower on steroids. "I thought we'd drive into the city," he said, "and wander around the Viaduct until a menu grabs us."

"It's Thursday night. We won't get a table unless you've made a reservation. And if you'll excuse my saying so, you won't get in wearing torn jeans."

Expertly maneuvering the toy car out of its tight parking space, Devin snorted. "Watch me."

"IT'S BECAUSE YOU'RE famous, I suppose."

Rachel's luscious mouth was set in a disapproving line. "You make that sound like a bad thing," he joked. Mentally, he confirmed his game plan. Dine and dump.

They sat in a private alcove in one of Auckland's most exclusive restaurants. Through the open bifold windows, city lights reflected in the harbor and the incoming tide lapped gently against the moored yachts.

Rachel unfolded the starched napkin and laid it on her lap. "I wouldn't like to think anyone else missed out on their booking because of us, that's all."

Loosen up, will you? "Bread?" He passed the basket over. She took a whole wheat roll and declined the butter. "Why are you really here, Rachel?" She obviously wasn't enjoying this any more than he was.

She looked guilty and he was struck with a sudden suspicion. "Did the chancellor want you to hit me up for another donation?"

"Of course not." Her shock appeared genuine and he envied it. It must be nice not to suspect people's motives in being with you.

"So you're just punishing me then…for giving you a hard time?"

Her lashes fell, screening her eyes. "Sure."

Maybe he should have chosen his words better. "I didn't mean to imply spending time with you was a punishment," he clarified. "Just that you're not my type." Oh, yeah, that made it better. "I mean—"

"Devin." She lifted her gaze. "I'm not offended. You're not my type, either."

Perversely, he was piqued. "Not a nerd, you mean?"

Her eyes narrowed. "Not housebroken."

He chuckled. "Okay, I deserved that. Let's try and be nice to each other."

There was an awkward silence, then Rachel cleared her throat. "I understand your band produced a fusion of post punk and metal—" she paused, obviously trying to remember research "—which evolved into the grunge and later indie genres."

"And here I thought it was about playing guitar and scoring chicks." Devin dipped sourdough into herb-flavored oil. "Rachel, how the hell did you miss out on rock music?"

"I had…ill health in my teens, which forced me to drop out of school." With tapered fingers she pulled the roll into smaller and smaller pieces. "Then spent all my twenties working days and studying nights to get my library degree."

Devin was attuned to picking up wrong notes; her story was full of them. He shrugged. "Don't tell me then."

She glanced up. "What do you mean?"

"You don't have to lie, just tell me to mind my own damn business."

"You know, Devin, civility has a social purpose. It stops people from killing each other."

He grinned. "I like to live dangerously."

"That's fine," she said seriously, "as long as you don't hurt bystanders."

All alcoholics left casualties in their wake. Devin had to work to keep his tone flippant as he replied, "You say *don't* a lot, you know that? You'll make a great mother."

She said nothing. Glancing over, he saw a bleakness in

her expression that shocked him. He knew that level of despair intimately. Instinctively, he laid a hand over hers. "What did I say?"

"Nothing." Sliding her hand free, Rachel gave him a small smile. "I'd have thought it would be easier studying business at an American university, considering most of your tax is paid there."

He picked up his glass and took a sip of water before answering. "My royalties come in from a dozen countries and I've got more money in tax havens than I have in the States."

"Don't tell me then," she said.

He laughed. "Touché. You're right, I don't want to talk about it."

When she dropped her guard—for about one millisecond—her smile was breathtaking. "Were you aware you have over four million Internet pages devoted to you?"

Devin leaned back in his chair. "If you've done your research there's no point trying to impress you."

"You could tell me your bio was grossly exaggerated," she said lightly.

He could have played that card. It surprised him that momentarily he wanted to. "It's not."

If there were excuses, he wouldn't make them. At sixteen he'd jumped on a roller coaster that had given him one hell of a ride for seventeen years. And if the gatekeeper had said, "Son, you'll be famous, songs you help write will be an anthem for your generation, but it will cost you. You'll all but destroy your body and soul, you'll lose your identity, and when it's over you'll lie awake at night wondering if you'll ever get it back," Devin would still have bought a ticket.

They finished their bread in silence.

RACHEL DIDN'T KNOW WHAT to think. The idea of Mark hanging around someone who could so coolly acknowledge such an appalling past made the hairs on the back of her neck rise.

But she wanted to be impartial—or at least as impartial as she could be with her son's welfare at stake. Heck, who was she kidding? She was a wreck over this. Fine, then. She'd factor in her emotional bias when weighing the evidence. Because it was important to her to be fair. God knows she'd had enough people judging her as a teenager not to jump to conclusions about someone else.

And while Devin was arrogant beyond belief, brutally honest to the point of rudeness and far too confident in his own sex appeal—flashing a charmer's grin to the waitress delivering their meals—he also had an appealing self-awareness.

He took another sip from his water glass and Rachel wondered if she was being lenient simply because he'd given up alcohol. Having been raised by a drinker, she found it was a very, very big deal to her. Surely that meant some sort of rehabilitation had taken place?

But did it extend to drugs…groupies? She didn't want Mark to be exposed to those, either, or any of the character traits she associated with rock stars—excess, selfishness, immaturity. She needed more information.

As she picked up her knife and fork, she asked casually, "Why study here…New Zealand, I mean?"

"When you're running away, the end of the earth is a good place to go." He glanced up from his steak. "I'm sure you read about my meltdown and the band's collapse on the Internet."

"Yes," she admitted. But in his business, "taken to

hospital suffering from extreme exhaustion" was all too often a euphemism for drug overdose or alcohol poisoning. As she ate her fish, her gaze dropped to his fingers, long, lean and powerful—musician's hands. "Do you miss any of it?"

"I don't need the temptations of the music industry right now."

That sounded promising, but his clipped tone told her that she should change the subject. Reluctantly, Rachel backed off. "So, is your brother still in L.A.?"

"Yeah, Zander's re-formed the band, with a new lineup."

Devin's curt tone hadn't changed, but she was too surprised to notice. "Can he do that?"

He shrugged, putting down his fork. "He owns the name, and as the lead singer, he's got the highest profile. For a lot of fans that will be enough."

As Devin spoke he folded his arms so the dragon tattoo on his hand curved protectively over one muscled biceps. It struck her that he was suffering.

"But not all of them," she said gently.

Devin looked at her sharply. "Did that sound maudlin? It wasn't meant to. It was my fault as much as anyone's that the band fell apart." His mouth twisted. "Collapsing on stage disqualifies me from lectures on professional dignity. If Zander wants to try and wring a few more dollars out of the Rage brand, let him…. Shit, I *am* still bitter, aren't I?"

There it was again, the self-awareness that made him likable.

"Speaking of bitter," he added, "how's Paulie?"

It was her turn to squirm. "Back in Germany."

"You let him lay a guilt trip on you, didn't you?" Devin picked up his fork again and stabbed a potato croquette. "I just bet he made the most of it." His gaze trailed lazily over her face. "You're too nice, Rachel. If you ever want tips on how to behave badly, come to the master."

She frowned. "What exactly do you teach your disciples?"

His gaze settled on her mouth. "That depends," he said, "on how bad they want to get." Green eyes lifted to meet hers and a jolt of sexual awareness arced between them, catching Rachel completely by surprise.

WHAT THE HELL WAS *that* about?

Devin washed his hands in the restaurant's washroom, taking his time. He'd made the comment to wind her up, and yet when she'd looked at him he'd been tempted to lean forward to taste that kiss-me mouth. Yeah, and get lacerated by that sharp tongue of hers. And he couldn't even attribute his crazy response to the demon drink. Devin smiled. Still, it had been mutual—the attraction and the immediate recoil.

"I'm glad *someone* is enjoying their evening," said a weather-beaten old man at the next basin.

"It's taken an interesting turn." Reaching for a hand towel, he glanced at the old guy in the mirror. He looked like Santa Claus in a polyester suit—big-bellied, grizzled white eyebrows. Only the beard and smile were missing. "Your date not going well?"

Santa grunted. "I booked our dinner weeks ago and we've got a makeshift table by the bloody kitchen." The old man lathered up his hands, big knuckled and speckled with age spots. "Figure they stuffed up the booking but the snooty-nosed beggars won't admit it."

Devin experienced a pang that could have been conscience; he hadn't had one long enough to tell. Tossing the used hand towel into the hamper, he said casually, "Big occasion?"

"Fortieth wedding anniversary. Drove up from Matamata for the weekend." With arthritic slowness, the old man finished rinsing, turned off the tap and dried his hands. "We're dairy farmers, so this time of the year's a bit of a stretch for us, but the old sparrow wanted a fuss. Might as well have stayed home if we were going to eat in the bloody kitchen." He grimaced. "Sorry, mate, not your problem. Have a good night, eh?"

Devin resisted until the old man reached the door. "Wait!" *Damn Rachel.* "Let's swap tables. It's not a big night for us."

"No, couldn't put you out."

Devin said grimly, "Happy to do it."

"Why should you have to put up with clanging pots and swinging doors?" The old man's face brightened. "Tell you what, we'll join you."

"JUST CALLING TO SEE how the date's going with the rock star?"

Shifting her cell phone to the other ear, Rachel glanced in the direction of the men's room. "I told you, Trix, it's not a date. It's—" *an interrogation that's taken a disturbing turn* "—just dinner."

"Rach, the guy's been in seclusion for months. It's a real coup…ohmygod!" Rachel held the phone away as her assistant's voice rose to a non-Goth squeal. "You should be selling your story to the tabloids! I'll be your agent."

Rachel speared a green bean. "Here's your headline— I Had the Fish, He Had the Steak."

"Obviously you'll need to have sex with him to make

any real money." The bean went down the wrong way and Rachel burst into a fit of coughing. Trixie read that as encouragement. "You can't deny there are plenty of women who've got famous through sleeping with a celebrity," she argued. "You could even get a place on a reality TV show…you know, celebs surviving in the Outback."

Rachel dabbed her streaming eyes with a napkin. "Tempting as the prospect is," she croaked, "I think I'll pass."

"You'll never get famous as a librarian," Trixie warned her.

"Oh, I don't know. Melvil Dewey invented the Dewey Decimal System over one hundred and thirty years ago and everybody knows his name."

At least Trixie's nonsense was steadying Rachel's nerves. So she'd been momentarily sideswiped by the guy's sex appeal. She was female and he was prime grade male.

"For God's sake, *don't* tell him one of your hobbies is finding wacky facts on Wiki." Trixie sounded genuinely horrified. "You'll lose whatever credibility we have."

Rachel laughed. "Goodbye."

"Who was that?" Devin asked from behind her, and she jumped, her nervousness returning. Not for a minute did she believe he was seriously attracted to her, but she had an uneasy feeling he'd try anything—or anyone—once.

"Trixie, my assistant. She—" *told me to sleep with you* "—had a work query."

Devin took his seat and signaled for their waitress. "There'll be another two people joining us." He filled Rachel in. "And this is all *your* fault."

But she was impressed by his gesture—finally, signs of a conscience. And secretly relieved they wouldn't be alone.

She was starting to have doubts about her ability to manage him.

The Kincaids—Kev and Beryl—arrived. Only halfway through the introductions did Rachel realize the downside of Devin's generosity. She'd lost her opportunity to grill him further about his ethics.

"So, Devin, you're a Yank," said Beryl as they'd settled at the table. Plump and pretty, she was like a late harvest apple, softly wrinkled and very sweet.

Rachel tried to remember if Yank was an acceptable term to Americans.

"Actually, Beryl," Devin said politely, "I was born here, but moved to the States when I was two. My dad was an American, my mother's a Kiwi."

Beryl looked from Devin to Rachel. "And now you're repeating history. How romantic."

"We're not—" Rachel began.

"She's my little ray of Kiwi sunshine," Devin interrupted.

Rachel said dryly, "And he's the rain on my Fourth of July parade."

Devin chuckled. Beryl murmured, "Lovely."

Her husband eyed Devin from under beetled brows. "What do you do for a crust?"

He looked to Rachel for a translation. "Job," she said.

"Student," said Devin, after a moment's hesitation.

"You're a bit old, aren't you?" New Zealand country folk were only polite when they didn't like you. Rachel hoped Devin understood that, but the way his jaw tightened suggested otherwise.

"Changing careers," he answered shortly.

"From?" Kev prompted.

"Musician."

"How lovely," Beryl enthused. Rachel suspected she often took a peacekeeper's role. "Would we know any of your songs?"

Devin's smile was dangerous as he turned to the older woman. "Ho in Heels?" He started to sing in a husky baritone. "Take me, baby, deep…"

"Oh, Kev," Beryl clapped her hands in delight. "Don't you remember? Billy—that's the agricultural student who worked for us over Christmas—played it in the milking shed."

"Cows bloody loved it," said Kev. "Let down the milk quicker."

Rachel looked at Devin's stunned expression and had to bite her cheek. "Was it a ballad by any chance?" Her voice was unsteady.

"Slow? Yeah, not that the other bloody rubbish… sorry, mate."

Devin began to laugh.

"Did you know," Rachel said, fighting the urge to join him—one of them had to keep it together, "there was a study done at Leicester University that found farmers could increase their milk yield by playing cows soothing music."

"Is that bloody right?" marveled Kev.

Devin laughed harder.

Kev and Beryl looked to Rachel for an explanation and she dug her nails into Devin's thigh to stop him. It didn't. "Conversely," she said, hoping the effort not to laugh was the cause of her breathlessness, and not the warm unyielding muscle under her fingers, "Friesians provided *less* milk when they listen to rock music."

"Well, I never." Beryl smiled indulgently at Devin, who was wiping his eyes with a napkin. "You Yanks have a different sense of humor from us, have you noticed?"

Devin bought the restaurant's best bottle of vintage Bollinger for Beryl and Kev, who insisted that Rachel accepted half a glass for the toast.

Devin explained to the old farmer that even a sip of alcohol would kill him, then gave Beryl a ghoulish description of how his pancreas had almost exploded.

Rachel thought he was laying it on a bit thick, and told him so while Beryl and Kev debated the menu. He looked at her with a gleam in his eye. "You see right through me, don't you, Heartbreaker?"

"Heartbreaker yourself," she said tartly, but somehow it came out as a compliment.

"Frenzied Friesians," he murmured, and Rachel gave in to a fit of the giggles.

CHAPTER SEVEN

DEVIN SAT BACK and admired her. Laughter lightened Rachel's seriousness, made her accessible. He was pretty cheerful himself. For the first time in New Zealand he didn't feel like an outsider.

However weird his life had been as a rock star, it had nothing on Beryl and Kev and the obscure facts that popped out of Rachel's luscious mouth. There was something appealing in the librarian's quirky nerdiness. She didn't give a damn about his fame or his opinion and Devin wanted her.

In a corner of the restaurant, a guitarist propped himself on a bar stool and started strumming on a Lucida. The playing was average but his voice was true enough for the flamenco ballads.

Kev thought Sinatra would be nice and requested "Blue Moon," then sang along in a surprisingly good tenor. "Played the captain in the local production of Gilbert and Sullivan's *H.M.S. Pinafore* last year," he confided to Devin. "Bloody great night this, mate. All it needs is dancing."

On the quiet, Devin handed over some bills to the management and a few now-empty tables were cleared away. Delighted, Kev and Beryl did an anniversary waltz, moving lightly around the floor. One number led to another.

Touched by the elderly couple's obvious nostalgia, other diners joined them.

The effects of champagne still sparkled in Rachel's eyes. Devin held out a hand. "Shall we?"

"I haven't danced for years…you okay with a shuffle?"

She did better than that. As long as Devin distracted her with conversation, her body moved with his in perfect rhythm. She only stumbled when she concentrated on the steps. Which was unfortunate, because Devin didn't want to talk—he wanted to savor the softness of Ms. Rachel Robinson.

So he encouraged her to expand on her theory of why musicians were so often good at math. "They're both about playing with nonverbal patterns so there's a lot of commonality there."

As she warmed to her subject Devin found he could get away with an "Mmm" and a "Really?" Gradually he drew her closer, until her body was right where he wanted it.

"Mmm."

THERE WAS SOMETHING in that last "Mmm" that jolted Rachel into awareness that she was dirty dancing with Devin Freedman.

One of his muscular thighs cleaved snugly between hers, his chest was a wall of hot muscle against her breasts and his "Mmm" still vibrated on the top of her head, where he'd been resting his chin.

And the hand supposed to be around her waist was caressing the upper curve of her bottom. About to protest, she became conscious that both her hands were in exactly the same position on *his* anatomy. She jerked back. "Excuse me a minute."

In the bathroom she splashed her face with cold water

and sprinkled a few drops down her neckline, appalled and ashamed. Obviously, three sips of five-hundred-dollar champagne was an aphrodisiac. Why hadn't there been a warning on the bottle?

"Remember you're here to assess his character," she admonished her guilty reflection.

Rachel put her hair up in the tight ponytail Devin hated. She'd outgrown her partiality for bad boys after the last one got her pregnant.

Back in the main restaurant, the music had stopped and a small group—which included Kev and Beryl, diners and kitchen staff—milled around Devin, who stood with his arms folded, scowling. The dragon on his forearm was a guardian across his chest.

Kev caught sight of Rachel. "Talk him into it, love…all we want is that song the cows like."

One glance at Devin, and Rachel knew not to try. "We don't have that kind of relationship," she said quietly, hoping to remind people of their own tenuous connection to him.

"We weren't trying to be pushy or anything, mate," Kev assured Devin, who raised a skeptical eyebrow.

"Of course you weren't, Kev," Rachel answered. She took Devin's arm, unconsciously patting the dragon. His hand closed firmly over hers. "I imagine if Devin picks up a guitar in public the media will start hounding him."

"I'm not going to give up my privacy." Under her hand, the muscle relaxed. "But I could have explained it better." His thumb began a gentle circuit of her knuckles. "I'm sorry for being so defensive."

Everyone apologized then, with back slaps and hand-shakes all around. Devin signed autographs, a camera was produced and he stood patiently while everyone had their photo taken with him. Rachel shook her head when he held out a hand for her to join them. She needed to reestablish some distance.

He closed it and her pulse sped up at the heat in his eyes. "Shall we go?"

"No," she said firmly, practicing the word. "I promised Kev a dance." Satisfied that Devin had got the message, Rachel dragged the bemused farmer to the dance floor.

SHE WANTED HIM.

That was all Devin needed to know to be patient. While Beryl went off to get a recipe from the chef, he sat at their table and ordered coffee, watching Rachel on the dance floor. In one date, he'd gone from indifference to fascination. He wasn't used to challenge in his relationships with women. He decided he liked it.

He cast his mind back to his two marriages, the first in his late teens, to an indie rock chick in an all-female band. He'd wanted a port in the storm, but Jax had proved to be as angry offstage as she was on it.

Ten years later he'd hooked up with a Swedish actress during one of his frequent blackouts. It had been a trophy marriage on both sides, the mirror over the bed reflecting two clichés going through the motions of intimacy. They'd separated after three months.

There was no point regretting a past he couldn't change; still, Devin couldn't help wincing.

He heard a muffled ringing and tracked it to a cell phone in Rachel's bag. It wasn't a model he was familiar with and a text message flashed up when he tried to answer the phone.

Dnt blow chnce 2 screw a rck str. Trix

He stared at the message, then replied, Nt tht kd of grl?

A few minutes passed. R now, rmber our tlk!

Grimly, Devin returned the cell to Rachel's bag. He was a trophy date, and the librarian was only acting hard to get. Increase her chances of banging a celebrity, he guessed. The fact that it had nearly worked infuriated him.

When Rachel arrived back at the table five minutes later, he regarded her coldly. "I've settled the bill."

"Are you sure you don't want me to contribute?"

"Let's not spoil a great evening."

"What's wrong?"

"Nothing." He pulled himself together—never let them know you care—and steered her toward Beryl and Kev. They left with a promise to visit if they ever got to Matamata. Wherever the hell that was.

"Close to Hamilton, where I grew up," said Rachel. She filled the silence on the way home with Wikipedia trivia. If Devin hadn't known better he'd have said she was nervous.

But he did know better. His anger grew hotter, barely contained. Outside her house, he handed over the car keys, shoved his hands in the pockets of his jeans and turned away. "Good night."

"I said I'd lend you that book on music and math. Wait, I'll run and get it."

Another ploy. Damn, this woman needed a lesson. "Sure," he drawled.

He undressed her with his eyes as she led the way to the house. Rachel opened the door and started groping for the light switch. "It won't take me long to find it."

Devin cut the game short. "I'll bet." He stepped inside and spun her around to face him.

"Wha—"

In the darkness, he found her mouth. She wrenched away from him. "What on—"

"Don't tell me you haven't thought about doing this?"

She hesitated too long.

He kissed her again, pulling her close, cupping the nape of her neck with one hand. With a moan, she settled into him and he forgot everything but exploring that incredible mouth—moist, full, bitable.

Following her lead, he kept it tender, reveling in the contrast between her tentative tongue and the unconscious pressing of those lush breasts against his chest.

They came up for air.

"Do you always kiss like that?" she gasped, and he struggled to remember she was using him. And then felt disgusted all over again.

"Why, are you taking notes?" Backing her up against the wall, he nudged her thighs apart and ground his erection against her. "If you want to screw a rock star, this is how we do it, babe—standing up, right here, right— Owww!" He reeled backward from a knee to the groin.

"You narcissistic bastard!"

"Okay, I get it." Devin groped for the wall behind him. "You changed your mind."

"Changed my—" The light snapped on and Rachel advanced on him. "I was never going to sleep with you!"

"Take a look at the text messages on your mobile and let's cut the crap."

"What?" Frowning, she pulled the phone out of her handbag and checked it, then looked up, exasperated. "So one of Trixie's stupid jokes allows you to treat me like a groupie, is that it?"

Devin eyed her closely. "Was it a joke? Or something to boast about?" He'd been caught before.

She drew herself straighter. "I've never met anyone with such a high opinion of himself. What gave you the idea I was even interested?"

"Oh, I don't know…. Maybe it was when your hands were on my butt." When she blushed, he folded his arms. "Quit acting coy. I even asked you if you'd thought about it."

Her mouth tightened. "Kissing you. That's *all*."

"Kissing?" Devin stared at her incredulously. "When a grown woman tells a guy she's thinking about it, Heart-breaker, he's not imagining kissing."

"I didn't give you permission to imagine anything, mate. And if you've ever dated a grown woman I'd be very much surprised." Color high in her cheeks, she opened the front door. "Now, please leave!"

"Happy to," Devin said grimly. Didn't she know how many women wanted to sleep with him? "Frankly, I'm amazed I hit on a cardigan-wearing, pass-on-the-butter, book nerd anyway."

As he walked out, he caught his shin on the serrated pedal of the mountain bike. "Sh—"

The rest of the expletive was cut off as Rachel slammed the door behind him.

Dammit, that gave her the last word.

MARK WAITED ALL MORNING for Devin to notice he had hurt feelings. By lunchtime he gave up.

Walking to the cafeteria between classes with Devin, he stopped abruptly. "I waited for you an hour at the ferry terminal last night." It was two hours but he didn't want to seem that much of a loser.

Devin looked at him blankly and Mark's sense of grievance grew.

"You invited me for a jam session, remember?"

"Did I? Sorry, buddy, I forgot." Devin continued walking, as distracted as he'd been all morning.

Mark's hurt smoldered into active resentment. "You know what?" he said to Devin's back. "Since you obviously don't even notice I'm around, I'm gonna skip lunch and catch up on some homework in the library."

Turning impatiently, Devin scowled at the last word, and Mark immediately regretted his temper. "I'm sorry, okay?" he said. The last thing he needed to do was piss off one of his few friends here. "It was just...well...never mind." He'd had a frustrating few days piecing together a staff list from old yearbooks and faculty newsletters, but it wasn't comprehensive or age-specific. He'd have to visually scan every female staffer on campus and confront anyone who seemed the right age.

"What? I'm not mad at you." Devin walked back to him and Mark avoided his eyes. Sometimes the musician saw too much. "Why don't we get food to go and I'll give you that guitar session I promised you now?" They were blocking the path through the quadrangle and Devin steered him to one side. "I've got an apartment in town and our next class isn't for a couple of hours."

"You have another place?" Mark was impressed.

"Yeah, I bought it to stay in the city during week, but found I prefer going back to Waiheke. Mom uses it more than I do." Devin hesitated. "Do me a favor? A textbook I need has come into the library. Go pick it up while I get the food?" He handed over his library card.

"Is it because you don't want to see her?"

Devin said evenly, "What makes you say that?"

Immediately, Mark knew he'd said the wrong thing. "Um, because she told me you were a bad influence? Except that…I mean…she said she was going to apologize."

"She did. Everything's sweet."

It didn't *sound* sweet. And the guy's scowl had come back. "So you don't think she's—"

"I don't think of her at all," Devin interrupted. "Let's meet back here in ten minutes, okay?"

"Okay."

He started walking to the library, then hurried back, scrambling in his pocket for change. "Dev…let me give you some money." He didn't want the rocker to think he was a leech.

For the first time that day Devin's expression softened. "My treat."

Rachel was behind the counter when Mark walked into the library, and her face lit up when she saw him. She always looked so pleased to see him that it made him feel slightly awkward. But he guessed being cool wasn't in a librarian's DNA.

Then he caught sight of Trixie in a black leather dress and kick-ass boots and revised his opinion. She'd told him she'd toned down her look for the library job…only one pair of earrings and her most conservative nose stud.

He kind of had a crush on her even though she was three years older and scary. She was dealing with someone but called out, "Have you been to that vegetarian café I recommended?"

He nodded. In the farming community he came from, everyone ate meat. But you didn't argue with a militant vegetarian, you meekly ate your lentil stew and tried not to be on a bus when the gas hit.

"So you like vegetarian food?" said Rachel. She always sounded like she was filing away information for the FBI.

"Love it," he lied, and handed over Devin's card to collect the reserved book. Rachel looked at the name and her smile faded.

"Devin said it was okay for me to collect it," Mark stated. Maybe they had a policy or something.

"That's fine."

She found the book. "He told me what you did," Mark added, and she froze with the book over the scanner. Gray eyes lifted to his.

"Apologized," he prompted. "Good on you. Friends shouldn't fall out." It occurred to him that he'd helped smooth the way. It was nice to do something for Devin for a change.

"Have…have you seen Devin today?"

"Yeah, we're heading over to his apar—" He stopped, wondering if Devin wanted him telling his business. "We're going to hang out for a couple of hours." He really shouldn't be so proud of it, but Mark couldn't help himself. It was such a buzz to be an icon's friend. Well, not really a friend. But then Devin was encouraging his songwriting and…

Rachel was turning Devin's library card over and over in her hand. "Did he mention we had dinner last night?"

"No." Some of his smugness at being the peacemaker dissipated, then Mark laughed. "He stood me up for you, you know that?"

HER SON'S FACE transformed when he laughed. It was like glimpsing land after spending six months in a leaky boat. Rachel swallowed hard. She'd seen him shy, angry, solemn, even a little melancholy, but she knew instantly. *This is who you are.*

She started to laugh with him, then registered the implications of what he'd said. He thought she and Devin had kissed and made up.

She'd gone to bed in a rage, tossed and turned until 2:00 a.m., thinking about the cutting things she could have said to Devin, and wishing she'd kneed him harder.

Then she got up and cleaned the grout in the shower with an old toothbrush. Labor-intensive cleaning was Rachel's cure for insomnia; generally she'd be back in bed within fifteen minutes because she hated cleaning.

This morning the shower was sparkling. So was the range hood.

Mark looked at his watch. "I'm gonna be late meeting Devin."

He took the light with him. There was no question whose side Mark would be on when Devin told him about their disastrous date.

Even mistrusting Devin, Rachel had been temporarily disarmed by the Freedman charm. She still couldn't believe she'd fallen for it. Now she would become public enemy number one.

Rachel recalled Mark's laugh, their shared moment, and tears pricked her eyes. She hurried into the staff bathroom.

Five minutes later, Trixie barged in and found her, sitting on the floor and dabbing at her face with toilet tissue.

"Rach…ohmygod, what's wrong?"

Her red-rimmed eyes made a denial stupid, so Rachel said what she needed to believe. "Nothing I can't handle." She managed a smile. "Don't worry about it."

Trixie's boots squeaked as she crouched in front of her and took her hands. "Says the woman who never cries? I don't think so."

"Don't give me sympathy, please. I'll get worse." Standing, she went to the sink and splashed her face briskly with cold water. Defeat wasn't an option. She'd just have to think of another way to watch out for Mark. "Anyone on the counter?"

Trixie ignored her. "Didn't the date go well?"

Better for Trixie to think that. Rachel met her assistant's gaze in the mirror. "Devin saw your text message."

"About screwing a rock star?" Trixie's eyes widened. "Didn't you tell him it was a joke?"

"Egotists rarely laugh at themselves."

"What a butt-head."

Rachel remembered the feel of Devin's butt. "The misunderstanding wasn't one-sided," she admitted. "I should never have kissed him back." In the cold light of day she couldn't understand why she had.

"You kissed!"

Damn. "Let's get back to work, hey?" She turned the handle but Trixie leaned against the door.

"Just tell me what the kiss was like."

Fantastic. "Like kissing a wet dog. Look, the whole date was a bad idea, but no harm done."

"Then why were you crying?"

"Because…" Unable to tell the truth, Rachel floundered.

CHAPTER EIGHT

"BECAUSE YOU ACTED LIKE an asshole, Rachel's really upset."

Devin looked down at the baby Goth barring his way into the lecture hall. "You're the text sender…Trixie, isn't it? And this is another one of your oh-so-funny jokes. Because Heartbreaker doesn't get upset, she gets mad."

The young woman frowned. "No, this time I'm serious. I don't know what went down, other than the fact that you kiss like a wet dog, but—"

Devin laughed. "You see? Mad."

"You made her cry."

"I doubt that." He tried to step past her; she blocked him.

"I found her in tears this morning. She tried to make light of it, but Rachel never cries. I mean never. Even when her dad died a couple of years back."

He didn't need this. It had been enough placating Mark. Devin figured he wasn't due to make another apology for at least a year. "You're making too big a deal of this."

"You mean it isn't a big deal to *you*," said Trixie. "But it must be a big deal to Rachel or she wouldn't be so upset. She's not like us. She's led a sheltered life and hasn't learned to protect herself."

Devin recalled Rachel's well-placed knee. "Trust me, she can take care of herself."

"I mean emotionally," Trixie said impatiently. "She doesn't protect herself against being hurt."

He wasn't used to being taken to task over bad behavior. The band had been on the road so much it was easy to sidestep consequences, and if they hadn't been touring... well, there was the house in Barbados to escape to if he needed to get out of L.A. for a while.

"I'll think about apologizing."

"Really?"

"Sure." But it was a tactic to get rid of her. Devin didn't "do" hurt feelings and he wasn't about to start.

So he couldn't explain how he ended up knocking on Rachel's front door at 6:00 p.m. Friday evening.

When she was feisty he could ignore her, stay pissed. But Rachel hurt niggled at his peace of mind. And that peace was too hard won to surrender lightly.

Her shadow appeared through the stained glass door panel, hesitating as Rachel recognized him. Then she opened the door. They eyed each other warily.

Devin saw immediately that Trixie had been telling the truth. Rachel looked washed out. Suddenly an apology wasn't hard. Whatever his faults, he wasn't such an asshole that he couldn't admit when he was wrong.

"I jumped to conclusions, last night." When she didn't say anything, he forced himself to give more. "I'm still learning to give people the benefit of the doubt instead of suspecting their motives in being with me."

She glanced away. "It doesn't matter. It's not like we expected anything from the date."

"No," he admitted. "We had too many prejudices for that."

"*I* was trying to keep an open mind." Stepping back, she started to close the door.

And Devin realized his arrogance was about to lose him a friendship with the first woman to interest him in years.

"Before I go, let me give you a few more tips on bad behavior," he said brusquely. "Develop an alcohol addiction and get married a couple of times—at least once in a ceremony you can't remember because it was during one of your alcoholic blackouts.

"Try and keep the marriages short and make sure you write a song about eternal love to play at each wedding, which will have you cringing for the rest of your life. Become an arrogant, opinionated prick because no one ever said no to you." Devin stopped, disorientated. Overhead, the sound of a distant rumble drew his gaze. A 747 glinted in the blue sky. Wishing to God he was on it, he sighed. "I'm sorry, Rachel. I guess I'm still getting the hang of normal." He started to leave.

"Normal's overrated," she said behind him, and he turned. She was staring after the jet's vapor trail. "You know how certain songs take you back to key times in your life? Times when you were happy or sad, confused or needing courage?" She looked back at him. "Writing the soundtrack to people's lives is no small thing," she said softly.

Devin cleared his throat. "What was your special song?"

"'Letting You Go.' Sam…Samantha Henwood. I was sixteen."

"I don't know it."

She started to hum, then to sing, and it was painful to hear because the librarian was tone deaf.

Devin put his hands over his ears. "You're killing me."

Rachel smiled and sang louder.

Stepping forward, he clapped a hand over her mouth. Above his fingers, her eyes were still smiling. Devin had never thought of gray as a warm color before, but now he dropped his hand before he got burned. "Will you accept my apology?"

"As long as you admit that the world doesn't always revolve around you."

"As long as you realize it has for the last decade."

"And for the record," she told him tartly, "I didn't eat butter because before Beryl and Kev joined us I intended having dessert. I wear cardigans because I like vintage. Not sleeping with a guy on the first date doesn't make me a prude, and if you *ever* call me a book nerd again I'll ram my mountain bike down your throat."

Damn, but he liked this woman. "I get it. Librarians are people, too." And because he couldn't resist teasing her he added, "Next you'll be telling me you have a vice."

"I do." She hesitated, long enough for his imagination to jump to the bait. "I don't make my bed."

Devin laughed. "Let's try another date."

Her eyes widened. "Why?"

"Admittedly, most of the time we engage in interplanetary warfare and yet…" Devin tucked a strand of loose hair behind her hair. "And yet, Heartbreaker…"

Rachel knew what he meant. There was something between them, an odd, unexpected connection. And that kiss… But it was wrong to use him as a means to Mark, and she couldn't kid herself that that wasn't the primary temptation. She shook her head. "I just broke up with someone I thought I'd marry. You'd only be a rebound."

He grinned. "See, that's what I like about you, you keep

giving me firsts. I've never been the rebound guy before. What's the drill?"

He was incorrigible…and far too appealing. Rachel wavered. He was also offering her another chance to find out more about him. Wasn't that her goal? And a repentant Devin was more likely to reveal himself…. She was skirting dangerously close to her ethical boundaries. Was it fair to use him like this?

"Any sensible person would run a mile," she hedged.

"I've had a million words written about me," he said. "I don't think *sensible* was ever one of them."

Rachel remembered the other things written about him, things he hadn't denied. This wasn't about her. Or Devin. It was about protecting her son. "Maybe we could go out to formalize our peace treaty," she suggested, "but no date. Strictly platonic." Attraction only made things tougher. Her motives murkier. This way no one got hurt.

"Sure." His lopsided, sexy-as-hell grin belied his easy acquiescence. "*The Flying Dutchman* opera is coming to town, isn't it? I've been seeing billboards."

"Next weekend, but the tickets are expensive." Which was why she hadn't booked. Most of her income went toward her mortgage. Rachel remembered who she was talking to when he laughed.

"Consider it part of the apology."

She trusted his meekness even less than she trusted that sexy grin. "As long as we're quite clear," she stressed, "that I'm only using you to get to Wagner."

"I think I can hold my own against a dead guy." Devin's expression grew serious. "So you're not upset anymore?"

How did he know that she'd been… "Wait a minute! Did Trixie make you apologize?" *I'll kill her.*

Devin frowned. "No one *makes* me do anything."

But the apology hadn't been his idea. Rachel stopped feeling guilty about her mixed motives.

"Hi, Mom, it's Rachel."

"Rachel, are you in trouble again?"

Eighteen years later, it was still the first question her elderly mother asked.

"No, everything's fine. I always call Sunday morning to see how you are."

"Well, you know, bearing up." Maureen sighed. "Still missing your father terribly, of course."

"Did you get that book on heritage roses I sent you?" Rachel swapped the phone to her other hand and wiped her suddenly damp palm on her dress.

Maureen's voice brightened. "Yes, it's wonderful, particularly the section on English hybrids." She rattled on about cuttings and placement, and Rachel stared out the window at her wild garden. "And Peggy and I are our club reps in the regional district's floral arranging competition."

"Sounds like you've got plenty going on." Since her father's death, her seventy-nine-year-old mother had taken up a multitude of new interests. Blossomed, in fact.

"Oh, and the most exciting thing? The council is recognizing your father's years of service by naming one of the new benches in the park for him."

Rachel caught her breath. "Well, it's great to hear you're doing so well."

"Honey, did you hear what I said? Your father—"

"You know I don't want to talk about him, Mom, and you know why." She took a few deep breaths because otherwise she'd scream, *He's dead and you can stop pretend-*

ing! But it would do no good. "Please, let's just concentrate on what you and I are doing, okay?"

Her mother sighed. "Okay. I'm sorry about your attitude, though."

A familiar sense of betrayal tightened Rachel's throat. "Listen, this has to be a short call today. I've got a roast in the oven that needs basting." She always made sure she had a good reason for a short call. Because sometimes they were all she could cope with.

"Have you started your charity lunches again?"

"It's not charity, Mom," she reminded her patiently. "Just a handful of first year students desperate for a home-cooked meal." She'd been inviting strays to her first semester Sunday lunches for five years. The event had become such a fixture around campus that staff and counselors would often send lonely scholars to see her in the library. Overseas students and out-of-towners for the most part.

"Well, I'm glad to see you've retained *some* of the values we taught you."

"Take care, Mom."

Hanging up, Rachel wiped her hands on her skirt again. Her jaw ached; she unclenched it. The weekly calls she'd initiated after her father's death, following seventeen and a half years of estrangement, had been a mistake. Foolish to think that after an adult life spent in denial, her mother would break character and admit anything had ever been wrong—with anyone except Rachel, that is.

She gripped her apron in her fist and stared at it in confusion, then with an exclamation ran into the kitchen and opened the oven to a billow of smoke and heat.

Grabbing an oven mitt she hauled out the roasting pan and inspected the sizzling leg of lamb. There was a layer of scorched fat around the base, but nothing that couldn't be saved. If only everything in life was so easily salvaged.

ON WEDNESDAY AFTERNOON Mark stood outside classroom 121 of the human sciences block waiting for the tutorial to finish. A classmate had mentioned this sociology tutor had handed out cake to celebrate her thirty-fifth birthday.

Through the door Mark could hear her voice…at least the tone of it, light yet authoritative. It gave him a strange feeling in the pit of his stomach. The talking stopped, and a shuffle of chairs signaled the end of the tutorial. He moistened his lips and straightened, trying to get some oxygen in his lungs.

The door opened and students streamed out, the industrious ones first, looking at watches and picking up their pace to get to their next class, then the easygoing chatterers.

Heart kicking against his ribs, he nervously looked over every woman coming through the doorway. Too young… too young…too old.

"Excuse me." Mark forced himself to approach the most likely candidate. "Are you Rosemary Adams?"

The blonde shifted her heavy satchel to her hip. "No, the tutor's still inside."

"Thank you," he said through bloodless lips. In the classroom, a dark-haired woman stood with her back to him, vigorously clearing the whiteboard of equations. Mark tried to remember what he'd been planning to say to her but his impassioned yet aloof denunciation had fragmented into a terrified jumble in his mind.

He cleared his throat and she turned around. "Did you forget something?"

She was Maori.

Unable to speak for the crushing disappointment, Mark shook his head and backed out of the room. In the corridor he picked up his pace until he was running, heedless, through clusters of students.

A car horn honked in warning as he jumped off the curb and ran along the gutter because people weren't moving fast enough. Only when Mark reached the park did he stop, doubling over to catch his breath. His disappointment was matched by his enormous relief.

"HALLELUJAH, you're finally going out." Holding a bag of peaches, Katherine Freedman stood on Devin's doorstep and sniffed him appreciatively. "Look hot and smell gorgeous…it must be a woman."

Resigned, Devin opened the door wider and gestured her in, leading the way to the open-plan kitchen. "Okay, who told you?" Five-thirty on a Saturday evening was not the time to be delivering peaches.

"Bob Harvey at the ferry office happened to mention you'd booked in a 7:00 p.m. vehicle crossing. As luck would have it I'm also heading over, for dinner and a meeting with the Coronary Club. How about a lift from the ferry building into town?"

In the kitchen, Devin accepted the bag of peaches and tipped them into the fruit bowl with all the others, unsettling the fruit flies. "You're not meeting her, Mom, and I'm taking the bike."

"You think I can't straddle a Harley?"

"You still look good in leather," he conceded, "and I guess a helmet hides the wrinkles."

She picked up a peach and threw it at him, but Devin was expecting it and made a neat catch.

"Fortunately for you," she continued, "I'm going across with Susan, so you won't have to think up an excuse not to take me." She tut-tutted, eyeing the fruit bowl. "You should probably stew those."

"Yeah, because I'm a 'bottling preserves' kind of guy." Devin poured her a cold drink, then turned to find her rifling through the kitchen drawers. When she pulled out a chopping board and a paring knife, he took them away from her. "And I don't need to think up excuses. I'm perfectly comfortable telling you to mind your own business. Shouldn't you be going home to get ready?"

"Unlike you, I can be ready in five minutes." Katherine took the utensils back. "Now find me a pot." Perching on a bar stool at the marble-topped island, she started peeling and chopping peaches straight out of the fruit bowl. His mom never sprayed her trees and there were spots of brown rot on some. Devin shook his head as she carefully pared away the good flesh before discarding the rest.

Only a couple of months earlier he'd thought he would lose her. "You've got a big birthday coming up." He found the pot she wanted and placed it at her elbow. "How would you like to celebrate?"

"Quietly." Katherine tipped the peaches she'd already sliced into the pot. "I intend staying sixty-nine for at least another four years."

Devin got the compost bucket she had insisted he buy, and cleared away the discarded peelings. "So dinner at the island's best restaurant with your son sound okay?"

Katherine didn't answer. Glancing over, he caught her pensive look. "No big deal if you've already made plans with girlfriends."

"Let me get back to you on that. So tell me all about

your date." Katherine dropped the knife and gripped her thumb. Blood welled above her nail. "Bother!"

Grabbing a paper towel, Devin wrapped it around her thumb, then guided her to the sink, where he rinsed the cut and inspected it. "Nothing a bandage won't fix." He found the first aid kit, dug around for the right size and handed it to her.

"Your date?" she prompted.

"Technically it's not a date." No woman had ever insisted on platonic before.

"Really?" Katherine finished applying the bandage and looked up. "What is it then?"

Devin started to laugh. "Deluded."

You'd have thought a smart woman like Rachel would know better. Nothing could have stoked his interest more than her No Trespass sign. If the librarian had been genuinely indifferent, Devin could have accepted it, but she wasn't. The kiss had proved that. And the challenge inherent in her nonnegotiable decree…what kind of wuss would he be if he let the gauntlet lie?

Katherine rinsed her other hand, still sticky with peach juice. "Don't tell me you've finally met a nice girl," she said hopefully.

"I'm not telling you anything," he reminded her.

"Spoilsport. In that case I might as well go."

"What about the peaches?" he teased.

She poked her tongue out at him. "I know you'll throw them out as soon as my back's turned so give them to me. I'll finish stewing them at home." Drying her hands on a tea towel, she added, "Have you heard from Zander lately?"

Devin stopped smiling. "No." When he'd raised the subject

of financial anomalies, his big brother had cut the phone call short. Since then Zander hadn't returned any messages.

"Careful with those peaches, Dev," Katherine protested. "You'll bruise them."

He slowed the tumble of peaches from the fruit bowl into the bag, and glanced at her. "So, how is he?" While Zander rarely initiated contact, Katherine kept the relationship going by phone.

"I can't seem to get hold of him lately." She busied herself searching in her bag for her car keys, which Devin could plainly see near the top. "But he must be terribly busy arranging the new tour."

Running scared more like, if he was avoiding even Katherine's phone calls.

"I'm sure he'll phone soon," he told her.

"Oh, I'm not worried."

Which meant she was. Unfortunately, the mounting evidence suggested his brother had been siphoning off more than his share of royalties on the early songs they'd cowritten. But surely Zander trusted Devin not to involve Katherine? Damn it, this situation was getting more and more complicated. On impulse Devin kissed his mother goodbye, something he rarely did. "Have a great night."

For a moment Katherine looked startled, then she patted his cheek. "You, too…and I expect to hear all about it." On those ominous words she left.

All going well, he reflected as he closed the front door behind her, the evening's activities wouldn't be fit for maternal ears. Checking his watch, Devin calculated time zones, then rang Zander's cell and left another message: "Call your mother!"

Then he finished getting ready for his date, turning his

mind to more pleasurable thoughts. Like teaching the librarian to forgo restraint, caution and common sense in favor of spontaneity, recklessness and instant gratification. And that was even before they reached her unmade bed. Her so-called vice perfectly complemented the only one he had left.

Sex.

CHAPTER NINE

RACHEL DIDN'T WANT to be nervous.

It made the evening ahead feel too much like a date.

Which it wasn't.

Peering past the mottled green patches in the antique oval mirror on her dresser, she applied a shocking pink lipstick and decided she was satisfied with her appearance. She wore a tight-fitting fifties cocktail dress of pink crepe overlaid with black lace, which had a scalloped edge at the strapless bodice and a mermaid ruffle hem. After straightening the black velvet bow at the Empire waist, she hunted for the lacy tights that went with the outfit. Holding them up, she frowned. They had a run, and the ladder was long enough for a fire brigade.

Reluctantly, she settled for patterned knee-high stockings—figuring the three-quarter-length skirt would cover them. She finished the outfit with a pair of dainty black ankle boots with a high heel, and clipped on velvet bows to match the one at her waist.

Opera presented a rare chance to dress up, but she was also trying to prove a point. Of course vintage could be sexy—look at Dita Von Teese, the famous striptease artist once married to shock rocker Marilyn Manson. Rachel hesitated, then picked up a tissue and scrubbed off the slutty lipstick, replacing it with a less provocative nude shade.

She glanced at the diamanté watch strapped to her wrist. Her car was being serviced so they'd go in his. She hoped Devin was allowing enough time for them to walk to wherever he'd parked.

The full-throttle throb of a powerful engine brought her to the door. Nervously wrapping herself in her fringed silk shawl, she stared at the leather-clad figure on the Harley-Davidson.

Devin lifted the black visor on his helmet. "No pre-car street layout defeats a red-blooded American," he said with satisfaction, then scanned her shawl-swathed figure. "I brought a jumpsuit in case you wore a dress." Reaching into a side satchel, he pulled out what looked like a pair of orange mechanic's overalls, then unclipped another helmet from the pillion.

Rachel finally found her voice. "I'm not going to the opera on a motorbike!"

"Why not? It'll be fun." His gaze dropped to her feet. "Those boots should be okay on the bike."

She tugged the shawl tighter around her shoulders. "What about my hair?" It was piled on her head, with loose tendrils softening the diamanté sparkles at her earlobes and throat.

Devin looked at it critically. "Very pretty."

She had a sudden feeling he was doing this on purpose. "We're catching a taxi."

"Okay." To her surprise, he got off the motorcycle without a murmur. "How long do they take on a Saturday night? Not that I mind missing the first half…"

Rachel held out her hand for the jumpsuit and helmet. "Wait here." Inside, she put on the offending items, knowing better than to check her appearance in the mirror.

When she came out, Devin sat astride the bike, engine idling and his face hidden behind the visor again. "If you're grinning behind that…"

He raised a gloved hand holding two tickets. "Front row mezzanine, overlooking the stage."

Gingerly, Rachel approached the bike. "How do I get on this thing?"

"Put your left foot on the foot peg, then swing your right leg over the seat. Watch out for the exhaust."

She followed his instructions, trying not to touch him, and he checked the position of her feet. "You can hold on to the grab rail or me. If you haven't ridden before you'll probably feel more secure with your arms around my waist."

Rachel reached behind her for the grab rail. "This is fine." She couldn't see his face, but it sounded as if he was trying not to laugh.

"Let's go then."

He accelerated slowly, but her knees tightened instinctively around his hips. The Harley picked up speed and Rachel dropped the grab rail and clamped her arms around his waist, hanging on for dear life. A rumble of laughter vibrated through his torso, matching the rumble of the bike's engine.

She'd never been on a motorbike before, never comprehended the delicious assault on the senses. Speed cooled the air and pushed the scents of the city under her visor. Exhaust fumes, a sizzle of food from passing restaurants, the whiff of trash from a downtown Dumpster, and from the waterfront the salty tang of the sea.

Devin knew the streets well, bypassing traffic lights to detour down narrow alleys. If she wanted to, Rachel could lean out and touch the parked cars, talk to passing pedestrians. There was no barrier between her and the pulse of the neon city, the pulse of the powerful bike vibrating beneath her.

Under the thin jumpsuit the skirt of her dress had hiked up, and Devin's legs warmed her where she gripped him, from knees to inner thighs. Her spirits soared with a heady sense of freedom. Naughtiness was addictive. She could have been a teenager again, but a teenager without responsibility, without the burden of having to make adult choices.

Rachel felt an almost overpowering urge to stand on the foot pegs with her hands on Devin's broad shoulders and yell, "Forget the opera! Let's just ride until we run out of gas." Except she had a disquieting feeling he would agree.

"Hey!"

Twisting, she saw a stranger waving and gesturing from the sidewalk. Rachel waved back. Twice more, she returned salutes—from two openmouthed kids staring out the back window of a passing car, and from an old lady waving her walking stick. Amazing who turned out to be Harley fans.

Too soon they were at an underground parking lot on Queen Street where Devin cruised into a parking bay. In the enclosed space the rumble of the Harley was deafening.

Rachel touched his shoulder and pointed to a sign, Owners Only.

He turned off the engine. "I've got an apartment here," he said over his shoulder. "We'll dump the gear first, then walk across the road to the opera house."

Standing on the foot pegs, Rachel swung her right leg up and over the seat.

That was when she noticed the rubber heel of her dainty boot was on fire.

Taking off his helmet, Devin turned at the sound of Rachel's gurgle of laughter, then caught sight of her smoldering boot. "Hell!" Hunkering down, he grabbed her foot with his gloved hands, wrenched down the zip and hauled off the boot, dropping it on the concrete.

"All those people—" peals of laughter escaped under the visor "—waving and yelling—" she hauled off her helmet, gasping for air "—and I—" another paroxysm of laughter shook her "—I thought they were just being *friendly*." Leaning on the bike for support, Rachel dabbed at her eyes.

Devin inspected her ankle. The stocking wasn't touched. Dropping her foot, he stood up. "What the hell part of 'keep your feet on the foot peg at all times' didn't you understand?"

Without waiting for a response, Devin launched into a blistering reprimand. Rachel bit her lip and tried to stop laughing. It felt almost like an out-of-body experience, looking down at himself—the never-loses-his-cool Prince of Excess—ranting at his passenger on the importance of following the damn rules. Finally he ran out of steam and stopped for breath.

Holding her helmet, Rachel bowed her head. "I'm sorry. I promise to be more careful on the way home." She didn't sound contrite, she sounded as though she was still laughing. And when she raised her head, her eyes confirmed it. "But you have to admit it's quite funny."

Tomorrow it might be funny. Right now he wasn't ready to let her off the hook for giving him such a scare. Scowling, Devin picked up her boot, looked at the indentation where the rubber had melted, then waved it under her nose. "On your leg this would be third-degree burns."

Rachel's face fell. "And they were so expensive," she

said, remorseful for the wrong reason. "One hundred dollars on sale." The boots he wore were worth three grand, U.S. "Will it last through the opera?"

In answer, Devin snapped off the fragile heel. "We'll knock the other one off upstairs. That will get you through the performance at least." Leading her to the elevator, he used his key to access his floor.

The elevator opened into a private lobby. Rachel stepped out and, like all his guests, immediately gravitated to the panoramic view through the hall's archway. "My God, I thought you said you had an apartment…this is a penthouse." As her gaze swung around the living room, with its rough-hewn stone columns and steel spiral staircase, Devin willed himself not to stiffen. Seeing his wealth changed some people. He didn't want the librarian to view him any differently than she did now.

"I like the casual comfort," she commented, stroking the saddle-brown leather couch, "but I would never have picked you as a flower man." She gestured toward the orange poppies on the sideboard, ignoring the expensive cast-bronze sculpture beside it. "Those are a homey touch."

His mother did the flowers. Devin relaxed. Nothing had changed.

"Right," Rachel said briskly, dumping the helmet. "Let's take off this gear, fix my shoe and get Cinderella to the ball."

He peeled off his leathers, but when he turned around she was still in her jumpsuit, staring at him. "I should have told you to dress up," she said in dismay.

Devin looked down at his black jeans and bloodred, V-neck silk T-shirt. The pin-striped jacket had been personally tailored for him by top American designer Tom Ford. A dragon motif, the exact match of his tattoo, was embroidered in red silk down the length of one sleeve and across his shoulder. The whole ensemble, including the red snake-skin boots, cost more than her pip-squeak car. Manfully, he resisted the impulse to tell her that.

She misread his inner struggle as hurt.

"It's my fault," she said. "I should have mentioned that men wear tuxedos to the gala opening night."

He grinned. "It wouldn't have mattered."

"You'll get stared at."

The woman was a delight. "Okay," he challenged, "show me what normal people wear."

Self-consciously, Rachel wriggled out of the overalls and smoothed the skirt of her satin-and-lace dress. Devin shook his head. "As I thought, still channeling the fifties. Although—" he assessed the outfit again "—lose the bow, drop the lace to get some cleavage and Dita Von Teese would probably wear it to the Grammy's."

For some reason Rachel started to laugh. "You've got helmet hair," he said. "Let me fix that." Removing the pins, he ran his hand through the silky, shoulder-length mass to loosen it. She used a peach blossom shampoo and for a moment Devin was back in his mother's orchard, in that fleeting new state he'd come to recognize as peace.

Without conscious thought he lowered his head. His lips brushed Rachel's. They were as soft as petals, and parted in surprise, but he didn't deepen the kiss.

Something in the moment stopped him…a freshness, an innocence. A promise? Shocked, he lifted his head.

Rachel cleared her throat. "We're not doing that, remember?"

"Why?" He needed to know.

She had to think about it, which was good, because he

didn't want to be the only one shaken by this. "I don't know you well enough."

"What do your instincts tell you?"

For a moment she stared at him, then shrugged helplessly, unable—or unwilling—to answer. Devin didn't push it, simply touched his lips lightly to hers and stepped back. He could seduce her; he'd had the power too long to doubt himself. But suddenly this…thing wasn't about what he wanted.

In silence, he levered the heel off her remaining boot with a screwdriver. In silence they walked to the elevator.

RACHEL FOUND her legs were trembling, and it had nothing to do with her reconstituted boots. Something odd had just happened and she felt light-headed and breathless. While they waited for the elevator she stole a look at Devin.

He was watching her in a way that made her want to kiss him. It wasn't desire, it was awareness. He attracted her. He just did.

Before she could rationalize her action, she lifted a hand to the nape of his neck, slowly drawing him down until their lips were inches apart. And stopped. They were both deadly serious. Then he closed the gap and the heat of his tongue set off a rush of sensation. They kissed, broke apart, then kissed again. Her hands roamed restlessly under his jacket and over the silky fabric delineating every taut muscle in his back.

The ping of the elevator sent them springing apart.

The lift doors opened. They looked at each other. Long seconds passed and neither moved. The doors closed. Rachel moved into his arms like a woman used to indulging in spontaneous passion with unsuitable men.

She didn't think, didn't question. She didn't do anything

Rachel Robinson normally did. It didn't seem to be that important. She couldn't stop. Not even when his mouth settled on hers with a possessiveness Devin wasn't entitled to, and his hands slipped under the flounces of her dress and pulled her closer to the erection under his jeans.

Tugging out his shirt, she slid her hands beneath it and across his broad chest to the tight male nipples. His body was extraordinary, every ridge and indentation a moving, living landscape for her exploring fingers. Someone was panting, and Rachel became conscious that it was her and tried to shut up. But he kept doing things that made her gasp as he steered them toward the bedroom.

When they came up for air, she saw a white bed on a black granite floor in a starkly beautiful room that overlooked a thousand twinkling city lights. Devin kicked off his boots, shrugged out of his jacket and pulled off his shirt. The dragon on his right arm glared at her. Under his right pectoral, another tattoo began—an abstract of curves and spirals in the Maori style, tracing over his ribs and disappearing into his jeans.

"You okay?" Devin asked, and Rachel realized she'd stalled.

"Yes." Trying not to feel self-conscious, she unzipped her dress and stepped out of it, remembering too late she was wearing those awful knee-high stockings.

Devin's gaze roamed hungrily over her lingerie and stopped below her knees. "What the hell are those?"

"Sex toys…you never know when you'll need ties."

"Great, let's use 'em."

"Have you no inhibitions at all?"

"None." He took her into his arms once more. When he

bent to kiss her again she couldn't remember which way to turn her head, and they bumped noses.

"Sorry." Her arms were suddenly wooden around his waist. "Devin, I don't—"

"My fault," he said. "I'm overthinking this. To tell the truth, I never had sex completely sober. And I haven't had sex at all for over a year."

Rachel lost her self-consciousness. Of their own volition, her arms lifted to wrap around his neck. "I'll try and be gentle," she whispered, and Devin chuckled. This time when they kissed there was no mistiming, no awkwardness. They'd recaptured the lazy, electric ease that narrowed their world down to this room.

His fingertips were light on her face as he traced her features, watching her through half-closed lashes, a smile tugging at his mouth. By touch, she learned the slight bump in the strong bridge of his nose, the scar under his right eyebrow. Above the raspy jaw, his cheeks were baby-soft.

Her nipples tightened as his thumb dipped between her breasts in the black strapless bra and began a gentle circling under the lace. She pulled his head down for a kiss, warm, liquid, and they fell on the bed, where they bounced on the springs and broke apart, laughing.

Lifting his knuckle, Rachel kissed the dragon's head, then followed its sinuous length up Devin's arm. Under her lips, his skin broke out in goose bumps.

His fingers tangled in her hair. "Before we go too far, let me get some condoms from the bathroom."

Rachel didn't hesitate. "Yes."

He rolled over her to go get them and somehow her bra ended up at her waist and his mouth at her breast, his hands teasing circles on her inner thighs. She pushed him off. "Go!"

Sitting up, Devin cupped her face and smiled. Somehow it was a gesture more intimate than anything they'd been doing on the bed, and her throat tightened. "How did we end up here, again?" he asked.

"Wrong turn I guess," she said lightly. She'd learned a hard lesson eighteen years ago. Never confuse sex with love.

"No," he said. "Sooner or later I would have got you here."

Something in his male arrogance took her straight back to another charmer, and Rachel instantly stiffened. "You... sound like you planned this," she said, watching him closely.

She caught the telltale flicker of guilt before he smiled at her. "*This* I didn't plan." He disappeared into the bathroom.

So good, she thought, stunned, *at faking sincerity.* And oh, my God, she'd nearly fallen for it. Humiliated, Rachel hauled up her bra and covered her breasts.

Except she wasn't sixteen anymore and no man got away with making a fool of her. Reaching for her dress, she paused. She had an idea. Did she dare?

When Devin came back, she was lounging seductively against the pillows in her underwear. Rachel held up the stockings. "Let's use these."

He blinked, then chuckled as he rejoined her in bed, jeans tightening over muscle. "You nearly had me."

"And I want to have you." She dropped her tone to husky. "Tied up."

Half smiling, he scanned her face, and Rachel hid it against his chest, right over the place where his heart should be. His hand caressed her nape and she resisted the urge to turn her head and bite it. "I've always wanted to try it," she murmured instead, "and you're the perfect guy to do it with." Under her cheek Devin's ribs rose and fell in what felt like a sigh. But when she glanced up he gave a lazy shrug.

"Sure, babe, whatever you want."

"Lie down." All business, she looped one of the nylons around his wrist, then tied it to the bedpost.

"You put your bra back on."

Rachel grabbed his other hand. "I'm shy."

"You know," Devin said thoughtfully, "I never thought I'd say this, but I was kinda looking forward to old-fashioned sex for our first time...ouch. Maybe you could loosen the tension on that one."

She yanked his trapped wrist against the post and double knotted the second stocking. "So you're suggesting they'll be other times, then?"

His eyes narrowed. "Okay, what's really going on?"

Rachel clambered off the bed and glared at him. "This wasn't something that just happened. You had every intention of seducing me tonight, didn't you?"

"Yeah, but you changed my mind and then..."

"And then?"

"Hell, I don't know...you changed it back."

With his arms tied to the bedposts above his head he looked like every Amazon's idea of a human sacrifice, pagan, muscular and deliciously vulnerable. Furious at the direction of her thoughts, she bent and scrambled for her dress. "You're pathetic."

"Rachel, you know we're about more than sex."

Hand frozen on her dress, she barely registered his comment. There was a pair of red stilettos under the bed. Lying on their sides at right angles, as if they'd been kicked off in a hurry.

I haven't had sex at all for over a year.

The son of a... Enraged, she picked them up and tossed them onto his washboard abs above the hip-hugging jeans, hoping the heels left a mark. "Next you'll be telling me you're a cross-dresser."

She waited for signs of guilt. For shame. Devin looked at the shoes and started to chuckle. The chuckle grew into a laugh that shook the bed. He laughed until his head was rolling helplessly on his shoulders.

Tears prickled the back of her eyes. It was 1992 all over again.

Rachel picked up her dress and stepped into it, reaching behind her for the zip and jerking it up. It stuck halfway and she pulled harder. Nothing. She spun the dress around to the front.

Devin's laughter subsided. With difficulty, he wiped his streaming eyes on his bare shoulder. "They're my mother's," he said.

"Spawn of Satan don't have mothers." Rachel struggled with the tab. "And funny, isn't it, that you've never mentioned her?"

"Why? I've never heard about your family…. Untie me and I'll help you with that zipper."

"Fool me once, shame on you. Fool me twice, shame on me." The zip still wouldn't budge. Her anger grew.

"Look," Devin said reasonably, "I did my growing up in public. Every stupid thing I've ever done is documented. In rehab I decided the rest of my life is private. Mom's why I'm in this godforsaken country. She's been in hospital lately with a heart condition."

"Old ladies with heart conditions don't fling their shoes under the bed in a 'I'm about to have wild sex' kind of hurl."

He started to laugh again. "Do you use that imagination in bed?" Infuriated, Rachel stopped wrestling with the zip on her dress and dragged down the one on his jeans. "I'm hoping that's a yes," he added.

"You think this is funny?" Her dress slipped and she made a grab for it.

"Rub some soap on the zipper," Devin suggested. "C'mon, Heartbreaker, get my wallet out of my pants—there's a picture of my mom."

"I don't care if there's a picture of your family dog." She yanked off his jeans and dumped them on the carpet, but lost her nerve at the boxers. "I'm leaving you here for room service to find in the morning. Maybe that will make you think twice before lying to seduce women."

Devin started to struggle against his bonds. "Okay, this has gone far enough. Untie me right now."

His panic was the sweetest revenge. "Maybe I'll even ring the media. They love bondage stories involving celebrities."

"I'm serious. Right now!"

"Go to hell." Head held high, clutching her dress under her armpits, Rachel disappeared into the bathroom.

"If you leave me here, I'll sue you!"

"I'll settle the legal bill with what the tabloids pay me!" she yelled back. He heard the sound of cabinets and drawers being opened. "Where's the bloody soap?"

Devin renewed his struggle. "As if I'm telling you!"

She slammed the bathroom door. He tried to reach the knots on his left wrist with his teeth but the librarian had strung him so tight he couldn't get close. Just as well—he'd probably kill her if he got free right now.

"Devin." A faint, familiar voice from the doorway wrenched him from his revenge fantasies.

"Mom," he rasped. "What the hell are you doing here?"

"I host the Coronary Club here Fridays." As her fascinated gaze trailed over his bonds, he heard the sound of approaching voices, then several elderly women appeared behind her.

"Oh, my Lord, Katherine," whispered one of them. "Is this one of your boys?" Everyone behind jostled for a look-see and within seconds half a dozen matrons stood at the end of the bed, checking him out with unabashed interest. And Devin discovered he did have inhibitions left.

He wiggled to try and lift the waistband of his boxers, which had gone dangerously low when Rachel had hauled off his pants, but all that did was draw the ladies' attention lower.

"Anyone getting palpitations, leave the room," said Katherine in a pained voice he recognized from his childhood. The one that usually preceded a grounding.

Devin cleared his throat to bring everybody's attention back to his face. "It's not what you think."

The bathroom door opened and Rachel came out, rubbing a bar of soap on the zip of the dress, which was lowered to her waist. "The cabinet's full of women's toiletries. You've got quite a little harem going—" She looked up and gasped so hard, her lovely breasts threatened to pop out of her lacy strapless bra. Devin didn't much like Rachel's clothes, but her underwear was fantastic.

The expression on her face made her look like a Picasso: it was all over the place. He grinned suddenly. Okay, this was worth it. "Aren't you going to introduce yourself?" he suggested kindly.

Her grip convulsed on the soap, which popped free and flew across the room. The ladies followed its trajectory, then turned back to stare at Rachel, who was zipping her dress up as fast as she could. "I'm not a groupie," she faltered. "I'm his librarian."

"And this is a new approach to chasing overdue books?" suggested Katherine helpfully.

Devin waited for the moment Rachel's eyes widened as she registered their resemblance.

Because, as any bass player knew, timing was everything.

Then he settled back on his pillows. "Meet my mother."

His date squared her shoulders and held out her hand. "How do you do." Then Ms. Grace-under-pressure crumbled. "You see, I thought he had another woman," she explained, clinging to Katherine's hand. "It was your shoes under the bed. They were kicked off as though…" Rachel finally realized she held his mother's hand in a death grip and dropped it. "Well, my mistake."

Color flooded Katherine's cheeks as if she was having a hot flash. Except she'd been through menopause. A horrible suspicion dawned on Devin, becoming certainty when his mother flicked him a guilty look. His mouth tightened.

"*Now* who's got some explaining to do?"

CHAPTER TEN

SOMEONE UNTIED HIM. Devin got dressed, then he and Rachel made cups of tea for the Coronary Club. Because making nice, he told her when she fluttered, panicking, toward the exit, was the way you persuaded people to keep your secrets. It worked with the media…sometimes.

Rachel approached every individual and earnestly explained all the circumstances. Devin followed with a plate of low-fat oatmeal cookies and some high-octane flirting.

Devin and the ladies had a good time. Rachel and his mom skittered away whenever there was the remotest possibility of Devin being alone with them. But he didn't own a cowboy hat just because it looked good.

He corralled his first filly when his mom left the safety of the herd to say farewell to one of her cronies. The elevator doors had barely closed on her full-figured friend when he said behind her, "You had sex with someone in *my* bed?"

Katherine turned on him defensively. "I changed the sheets."

He'd hoped for a denial. "This isn't the fifties, Mom. There are STDs to worry about now, AIDS."

She tried to step past him. "I'm not having this conversation with you, Dev."

He blocked her escape. "And what about your heart

condition? I mean, should you be raising your heart rate like that?"

"Orgasms are very good—"

"Oh, God!" Devin clapped his hands over his ears. His father must be turning in his grave.

Katherine pulled his hands away. "For relieving stress, which in turn reduces blood pressure." Exasperated, she surveyed him. "I did warn you not to start this conversation."

"Well, who is it?" he demanded. "I'm assuming there's only one."

She considered him. "That's none of your business, any more than what you do with Rachel is mine." Her voice softened. "She's adorable, by the way."

Rachel came into the foyer at that moment, shawl clutched around her and staring over her shoulder as though fearful of being followed. Devin waited until she was close. "Looking for me?" he asked, and she started guiltily.

"I've explained our misunderstanding and accepted total responsibility." She avoided his gaze by smoothing the fringe on her shawl. "I don't think you've got anything to worry about." Awkwardly, she held a hand out to his mother. "Nice to have met you, Katherine."

His mom clasped it in both of hers. "And you."

Devin cut short the pleasantries. "How are you intending to get home?"

"I ordered a taxi."

"I'll wait with you. Mom—" his gaze pinned Katherine's "—we'll talk when I come back."

"Devin…we won't." Her tone was equally adamant. "At least not about that. Goodbye, Rachel." She smiled. "I do hope I'll see you again."

"Oh, I'm nowhere near through with her yet," he promised his mother.

Rachel got twitchy as soon as the elevator door closed. "I'm sorry about earlier." Despite her calm tone, she kept jabbing at the elevator button to try to make it move faster. "I jumped to—"

Devin backed her into a corner and kissed her.

She broke free, surprised. "Aren't you mad at—"

He kissed her again. Harder. This time when she came up for air, she was disheveled and breathless.

"It's probably for the best. You and I aren't—"

And again. The woman would not shut up. He could feel the moment she stopped thinking "shoulds" and "shouldn'ts" and started thinking "why nots" and "maybe."

Started seeing him as he'd grown to see her—a fascinating world unexplored. This time when he lifted his head that intriguing glow was back in her gray eyes.

Devin let the warmth permeate through to his bones before he stepped back. "We're even," he said.

"INSERT THE SIXTH NOTE after the fifth to give your bass pattern a lighter, more upbeat quality…yeah, that's it."

Mark tried but he couldn't sustain concentration past a few bars. "I'm sorry." Disheartened, he stopped playing. "I guess I'm not feeling it today."

He watched apprehensively as Devin took off his acoustic guitar and walked out of the living room of his apartment. Miserably, Mark stared down at the view, his bass still hanging from his shoulder strap.

At 11:00 a.m. on a clear summer morning, all Auckland's landmarks were on display—the Sky Tower, the bridge and Rangitoto, the dormant cone-shaped volcano in the harbor. How many chances would his mentor give him, he wondered, before he wrote him off?

Devin reappeared with a couple of energy drinks and tossed one can to him, before sprawling on the couch. "What's up? And don't say keep saying nothing. You know I haven't got the patience for it."

Mark hesitated, but he needed a confidant badly. He rolled the cold can against his forehead. "If I tell you, you have to keep it a secret."

"Scout's honor."

He was momentarily diverted. "You were in the Scouts?"

"No, just pledging their honor."

Mark put down the can and started toying with one of the frets on the guitar. "I thought I'd tracked down my mother yesterday—my real one. Only she wasn't."

Devin whistled. "You're adopted?"

"I only found out a year ago…by accident."

"That's rough." Devin swung himself to a sitting position. "Why didn't your folks ever tell you?"

Bitterness flooded Mark, as sour as old grapes. "Because my Hamilton *birth* mother made it a condition of the adoption." The letter from social welfare had been clinical. 'Our client has changed her mind about open adoption and is only willing to proceed if you agree to secrecy….'"

"Careful of your guitar, buddy."

Confused, Mark looked down; he was torturing one of the strings. Handing the bass to Devin, he plunked himself on the throw rug and hugged his knees. "You're probably thinking, well, why am I looking for her then? But she shouldn't be able to do that without giving some kind of explanation. I mean, how am I supposed to feel?"

Devin started plucking at the strings of the bass, casual notes that somehow reached in and squeezed Mark's heart. "You tell me."

He swallowed. "I just need to know why…. I mean, I'm not expecting anything."

"Are you looking because you want to heal something in you," asked Devin quietly, "or because you want to hurt her?"

Mark didn't answer. Another cascade of bittersweet chords; the vise around Mark's chest tightened.

"Do your parents know you're doing this?"

"They don't even know I've found out I'm adopted." He expected Devin to lecture him, but his dark head remained bent over Mark's guitar. The notes softened, the melody became gently reflective. Mark stirred restlessly. He didn't want to be soothed. "You don't think I should do it, do you? Find my birth mother."

"Would my opinion make a difference?"

"No."

"Then why," said Devin mildly, "are we having this conversation?" The tune evolved into an electric version of "Amazing Grace," languid and hauntingly beautiful.

Mark suffered through the song. He had a sudden intense longing for home, for his parents, for the tranquility of his life before this terrible knowledge had changed everything.

Tears filled his eyes. He blinked hard, but one escaped to trickle slowly down his cheek. Mark froze, reluctant to wipe it away in case he drew Devin's attention. The salty trail stung his shaving rash—he was still getting the hang of a new razor. At last the tear touched the corner of his mouth. Surreptitiously, he caught it with his tongue.

Devin's eyes were closed, his fingers sliding over the strings. "It's okay to have second thoughts, Mark."

"I'm not."

His mentor opened his eyes. "Maybe you should take another year or two before you do this."

"I can't," he said impatiently. "The only thing I know about her is that she works at the university. If I wait and she leaves, then I'll never find her." He stood and started to pace. "And my parents won't help me. I already know that without asking. They always do the right thing and keep their word and stuff…and, well—" he hesitated, not wanting to appear soft "—if they learn I'm looking for her, they might get hurt. Which is also why I haven't told them I found out I'm adopted. Because I have to see her."

Devin struggled for the right words. He had no skill base to handle emotional pain; he'd barely mastered his own. What the boy needed was a student counselor, but Mark would bristle at the suggestion and he didn't want to alienate him.

"Devin?"

Someone who could empathize…someone with common sense and compassion. An insider who could influence Mark toward counseling. It was Sunday. Devin glanced at his watch. Lunchtime. Rachel had turned down his lunch invitation, citing her prior commitment with students.

He put down his guitar and stood. "Let's gate-crash a party."

RACHEL WAS HUNTING through her kitchen drawer for a carving knife when the doorbell rang. "Someone get that," she called into the adjacent lounge, where conversation hummed over the muted strains of *La Bohème*.

"I'll go," answered Huang.

Hunched over the stove, Trixie stirred a pot of

steaming gravy, her brow knotted in concentration. With her kohl-darkened eyes, swirling black skirt and Alien Sex Fiend T-shirt, all she lacked was a witch's hat. Rachel grinned.

"If you do the 'double, double toil and trouble' joke again, I'm letting it burn," Trixie warned. "How you can be so happy slaving in a hot kitchen all morning is beyond me."

"Because bringing people together and feeding them makes me happy." This was Rachel's favorite day of the week, the ritual an affirmation of her dreams—family, community, tradition. If one day she could get Mark here… "I only hope we have enough meat." She found the carving knife and surveyed the joint, steaming gently on the countertop, mentally toting numbers. Jacob, Sarah, Huang, Marama, Juan, Silei, Ming, Dale, Chris…herself, Trixie and—

Devin appeared in the kitchen doorway holding a huge bunch of red gerberas, and her heart gave a queer little lurch that she wanted to be dismay but wasn't. He eyed the knife. "I can see flowers aren't enough."

"What are you doing?" she said stupidly. This morning she'd convinced herself that the man was a scenic detour down a blind alley. She needed to get back on the freeway with its speed limits and clear signs.

"I was hoping you'd have room for extras." Over the flowers he nodded hello to Trixie. "How's the intimidation racket?"

From the stove, Trixie said, "One hundred percent success rate."

"She's promised never to interfere again," Rachel said grimly.

"I might have a job for you, Trixie," Devin continued. "My brother."

Rachel glared at her assistant. "On pain of *death*," she reiterated.

Undeterred, Trixie waved the gravy spoon toward Devin. "Have your people talk to my people."

"Mark, that's you," he said over his shoulder, and Rachel dropped the knife. It hit the floor with a clatter.

Devin strolled forward to pick it up and Mark came into view behind him, blushing as he looked at Trixie.

Delighted as she was to see him, Rachel experienced a pang of regret. Why did her son have to be so irresistibly drawn to the dark side? Then Devin straightened, holding the knife in one hand, the flowers in the other—dark, gorgeous and devastatingly sexy. *Because it runs in the family.*

"You look harassed." Handing her the gerberas, Devin tucked a loose strand of hair behind her ear in an intimate gesture that made Trixie and Mark exchange glances. Too many things were happening at once and Rachel seemed to have control over none of them. "Want us to go away again?"

She gathered her wits. "No, stay! Mark, it's lovely to see you here." Her throat tightened on a rush of emotion and she busied herself finding a vase for the flowers. "Trixie, why don't you take him through to the lounge and introduce him to everybody? I'll handle the gravy. And, Devin, since you've got the knife, would you mind slicing the meat?" She gestured in the direction of the leg of roast lamb.

"Sure, if you don't mind me butchering it."

Her pulse steadied with Mark gone. "Not as long as I get twenty-six slices out of it."

"Heartbreaker, you crack me up." Devin dropped a brief kiss on her mouth and her pulse sped up again. The dragon twisted on his forearm as he began slicing meat with a showman's flair.

Rachel concentrated on stirring the gravy but couldn't resist another glance. The noon sun streamed through the window, glinted off the flashing knife and picked up the red in Devin's stubble. He dwarfed the tiny kitchen, completely out of place against the teal-and-cream cupboards of her country-style décor, with its ceramic roosters, appliquéd tea towels and battered dresser.

This crazy attraction must be affecting her ability to be impartial, because she no longer saw him as a threat—at least not to Mark. So, what…one kiss and the frog had turned into a prince? No, she'd been softened by the fact that he was looking out for his mother. Katherine had sung his praises last night.

What do your instincts tell you?

To jump him.

Frowning, Rachel turned off the heat and put a lid on the gravy. *Keep it simple, stupid.* Now was the time to tell him she'd had second thoughts.

Except then he might leave—and take Mark. She put the vegetables and greens into serving dishes, then returned them to the warming drawer. She'd raise the subject after lunch.

Devin brought over a platter of meat, beautifully sliced. "Thirty-two. Damn, I'm good. You want me to carry this to the dining room?"

Rachel pointed to the two-person oak table in the corner of the kitchen. "You mean that?"

"Don't tell me. It also makes up into a bed at night."

If only he didn't make her laugh. "Put the meat in the oven with the vegetables, then come and be introduced."

"In a minute." Off-loading the meat, he took her into his arms and smiled at her. And Rachel knew it wasn't fair to let this go on any further.

"About last—"

Devin kissed her with the same arrogant confidence he had the night before, bypassing her reservations and tapping straight into the uncomfortable heat she felt for him. "I'd rather talk about tonight."

Such an innocuous statement. Such a wealth of sinful promise.

Flustered, Rachel pulled free, fixed her gaze on his belt buckle and launched into her analogy about the difference between three-lane highways and one-way streets, and knowing what kind of driver you were. Devin balanced on the edge of the table, swinging one booted foot, and listened in polite silence.

She ran out of gas and spluttered to a stop. What had started out as a good idea had ended up a six-car pileup.

"Let me see if I've got this straight." His voice was thoughtful. "I haven't even made a layover yet and already I'm a blind alley?"

She looked up to see the slow-burn grin that always took the chill off.

"You know this road map of yours isn't even accurate," he pointed out. "Paul, the expressway, turned out to be a dead end."

Rachel bit her cheek to stop from smiling.

Hooking one arm around her waist, Devin pulled her closer. "What you need on that map is a rest stop. Somewhere to take a break from the serious business of staying on the straight and narrow, scanning side mirrors, checking GPS, watching for safety signs…"

She couldn't hold back the laugh. "You're incorrigible."

"I love it when you use librarian words." He nuzzled her neck. It felt wonderful. Maybe she was overthinking this. No one needed to get hurt. He was a rock star, for God's sake, and she hadn't lost her head over a guy since her teens. Briefly, her arms tightened around him. To hell with impartiality. By bringing her son here, Devin was top of her hit parade right now.

"Let me introduce you to everybody, and then we'll have lunch." As she pushed Devin toward the living room, Rachel said softly, "Thanks for bringing Mark…to meet other students."

"Actually, I'm hoping for advice," he replied. "I'll tell you about his cock-eyed plan when everyone's gone."

DEVIN SUDDENLY FOUND himself standing alone, amid a dozen students of various nationalities jammed together on the sofa or seated on large cushions on the floor. Conversation dried up as they recognized him. Turning around, he saw Rachel had stopped in the doorway with an anxious expression. "Something wrong?"

She smiled and moved forward. "For a moment I thought I'd left the oven on…but I didn't." She began making introductions.

As he did the rounds, Devin noticed everyone was wearing stickers starting with "Ask me about…" Trust the librarian to have an icebreaker. Shaking hands with a guy called Huang, he looked closer. *Ask me about…*

Growing up in Taiwan.

What it's like to have to study in my second language.

Rodeo.

"You rodeo?"

Huang nodded. "When I first come here to learn English I live in Warkworth with rodeo family."

Devin had friends in the business, and the two of them discussed barrel racing and bull riding for several minutes.

"And where is your sticker, Dev-an?" Huang inquired politely, and those within earshot laughed. The young man's face reddened.

Talking to Mark nearby, Rachel glanced at Huang, then pulled a sticker pad and pen out of her apron, a white cotton bibbed thing covered with cherries. "I'm so sorry, Devin, I forgot."

God, she was sweet. "No problem," he said.

"Ask me about…" She tapped the pen against her teeth while she considered. Devin smothered a smile. Sex, drugs and rock and roll? Rehab? With her hair pulled back in a loose ponytail she looked only a few years older than these kids.

"Being famous," suggested Trixie, and suddenly everyone was chiming in.

"How much money you've made."

"Dating supermodels."

"What it is like," said Huang, "to live most people's dream?"

"That's a silly question," said Trixie, "because there's only one answer. Bloody fantastic."

Everyone laughed.

"Okay, let's go with that one," said Devin. "You're nineteen years old, Trixie, and a rock star—famous, rich, dating studs. Now what?"

She raised one pierced eyebrow. "What do you mean?"

"You've got another fifty to sixty years to fill and you've got nothing left to wish for. What happens when the novelty wears off?"

Baby Goth shook her head. "Never going to happen."

"Eat your favorite food for a week," he said drily, "then tell me you don't crave a change. Eventually it happens."

There was silence as people digested that.

"But you've still got your music," Huang ventured.

Devin turned to him. "And in the first rush of fame you've overcommitted to album contracts. So, yeah, you're busy. Except your record company wants more of the kind of songs that made you famous. And you want to stay famous. Making music becomes a high-pressure business instead of a creative endeavor."

"Then I'd forget about fame," Mark said confidently, "and just write original music for my hard-core fan base. They'd keep buying."

"But not in enough numbers to keep the money flowing in that you've been spending like water."

"Then I'll enjoy what I've already bought," said Trixie. "The mansion and the boy toys." She licked her lips lasciviously and the others laughed.

"Sorry, Baby Goth." Devin shook his head. "The boy toys won't hang around if you're not famous. And how much money you've got left to play with depends on your manager and your business savvy—which has probably been addled by the drugs or alcohol you used to medicate the terror you feel at living the dream and not being happy."

He became aware of the silence, the heaviness of the atmosphere. And he used to be the party guy. Then Rachel's hand curled around his fist, encouraging him, and he intertwined his fingers with hers.

"Listen, I was too young when I got famous," he said. "I didn't know the Holy Grail doesn't exist. But you guys are smarter." They liked that; smiles dawned. He made his final point. "Just remember when you hit the big time in your chosen careers not to tie your identity to it. And leave something left to strive for."

"Life's meaning lies in the journey, not the destination," said Huang.

"Confucius?" Devin asked.

"Cereal box," said Huang.

CHAPTER ELEVEN

"SO YOU WON'T EVEN EAT gravy?" Mark was asking Trixie as Rachel approached shyly with her own plate.

"Nope," said Trixie, "Rach prepares it out of the drippings of little baby animals." As she spoke she moved over to make room for her hostess on the couch. "Sit in the middle, Mark," she added with a shudder. "I can't look at carcasses."

Used to Trixie's theatrics, Rachel sat next to her son, who cast a longing glance at her roast lamb before scraping the gravy off his vegetables. But she knew not to interfere in affairs of the heart.

"There's pavlova and ice cream for dessert," she consoled him, and he visibly brightened.

Across the lounge, Devin perched on a stool, still swamped by students, and she was grateful. It was hard enough acting natural around Mark without Devin's keen powers of observation making her nervous. Trixie noticed the direction of her gaze. "You do realize you're going to be inundated with first-years once it gets out he's been here?"

Rachel shrugged and turned to smile at her son. "I hope you'll come again, too, Mark."

"Sure," he said, looking at Trixie.

Trixie opened her mouth, no doubt to tell him she was

only here because her washing machine had broken down and she needed somewhere to do free laundry. Rachel cut her off. "So how are your studies going, Mark?" Maybe his cock-eyed plan was to give up school?

"Great. Got my first A on an assignment last week." He finished his last roast potato and reluctantly speared a carrot.

"Do you know what you want to do with your degree yet?"

"Well, it's kind of a backup if a career in music doesn't go anywhere. It was a deal I made with my parents." He pulled a face, but it might have been due to the carrot.

"How cool that you've got Devin as a mentor," said Trixie.

"Yeah, but I'm trying not to take advantage of that, y'know? I think he's had enough people using him in his life."

Rachel felt a prickle of unease but dismissed it. Her relationship with Devin had moved beyond Mark. *Yeah, and into a gray area.* So she'd be more scrupulous about keeping a distinction.

"Have you and Devin done the wild thing yet?" said Trixie.

"That question's really not appropriate." Rachel concentrated on cutting her lamb.

"Why, because of Mark? I'm sure he knows the facts of life. He grew up on a farm."

Cheeks burning, Rachel tried desperately to change the subject. "What kind of farm was that, Mark?"

It was his turn to look panicky. Puzzled, Rachel watched color creep up his cheeks, then the penny dropped and she came to the rescue. "Did I tell you about this study on dairy cows they did at Leicester University?"

Within thirty seconds, Trixie's eyes glazed over and she stood up. "Run for cover," she advised Mark. "It's one of her Wikipedia anecdotes."

When she was out of earshot, Rachel looked at Mark. "It's a beef farm, isn't it?"

"Yeah." He ducked his head. "But if Trixie finds out she'll stop speaking to me…or beat me up."

"It could be worse. Imagine what she'd be like with iron in her diet." She met her son's eyes and they burst out laughing.

DEVIN WAS GETTING recommendations on Pacific hip-hop artists from a Samoan student named Selei when the sound of Rachel's laughter made him look across the room. He liked watching her laugh, liked the way it animated her face and made her eyes glow. She and Mark sat side by side sharing a joke, heads together like conspirators.

He was glad he'd had the idea of seeking her advice about… A preposterous idea entered his mind as he stared at them. Laughing, they had a striking similarity in the tilt of their chin and the way their eyes crinkled.

No. He had to be imagining things.

"I've got a compilation CD in my car, Devin," said Selei. "I'll lend it to you." He left the room in the wake of the other students, who were making a rush to the kitchen for dessert.

Casually, Devin wandered over to Rachel and Mark. "What's pavlova, that it causes a stampede?" he asked.

Beryl and Kev's hometown was Matamata. "Near Hamilton," Rachel had said, "where I grew up." Mark's birth mother had been from Hamilton.

"A cake-size meringue smothered in cream and strawberries," said Rachel.

And she was thirty-four. Around the right age.

"New Zealand and Australia still squabble over who

invented it," Mark added. "It was made in honor of some ballerina who toured Down Under a couple of centuries ago."

"Actually, it was only eighty odd years ago," Rachel corrected. "Anna Pavlova, in 1926... Devin, why are you looking at us strangely?"

"I was thinking how odd it was to fight over ownership of a dessert." He reached for Rachel's empty plate, telling himself this was all coincidence. "The food was great, thanks."

"Here, I'll take that." Mark stood and stacked the plate on top of his own, still half-full with carrots and broccoli. "You want me to get you some pav? Rachel?"

"I'll come with you. Devin, stay and enjoy the peace for a few minutes. You've earned it."

He sat on the couch, trying to think. The math worked, but Rachel wasn't the type to have had a teen pregnancy. Why was he so emphatic about that? Devin smiled. Because he couldn't imagine anyone taking advantage of her.

But he was thinking of the grown woman. What would she have been like at sixteen, seventeen? The corners of his mouth lifted again. A Goody Two-shoes without a doubt. Earnest and probably naive. But still uniquely Rachel.

Devin couldn't categorize her. Yes, she was conservative, at least compared to him, but she surrounded herself with people who were outsiders, or rebels like baby Goth. Yes, Rachel was sensible and pragmatic, but last night she'd surrendered—briefly—to passion and spontaneity.

Searching his mind for facts, not feelings, Devin came up with very few. Busy protecting his own privacy, he'd never appreciated that she was doing the same. What did he know about Rachel, really? Only what she'd wanted him to.

No wonder he couldn't get her out of his head.

He remembered how opposed she'd been to his friendship with Mark a few weeks back; in hindsight, her concern had an almost hysterical quality. But then, she looked out for new students. Hell, she had a houseful right now.

Through the open doorway, Devin watched her cluck over her brood like a mother hen. This woman wouldn't have given up a child. He was wrong. Things could stay simple. Simple was how he needed them.

Two HOURS LATER Rachel was on the doorstep saying goodbye to students when Trixie came out with Mark.

"I'm taking him to the new health food store in Grey Lynn and stocking him up on whole foods." Rachel noticed he was carrying Trixie's bag of clean laundry. Mark caught her eye and grinned self-consciously.

Whatever his cockeyed scheme was, it wasn't serious. From their conversation, she'd learned that Mark wasn't planning to leave school. He probably wanted to date Trixie, and hoped Devin would get some pointers from Rachel. Unfortunately, he was doomed to disappointment. Trixie might consider dating a younger man but she stuck to her own kind. Hopefully, the crush didn't run too deep.

"Drive carefully," she said to Trixie.

"Yes, Mom. C'mon, Mark, let's leave the lovebirds to it."

Rachel blushed. Why did Trixie keep doing this to her? "Our relationship hardly warrants that description," she began, and was pulled back into a hard male body.

"Yet," said Devin. His breath on her nape sent a shiver down her spine. "Thanks, guys, we'd appreciate it."

Rachel finished waving them down the street before she turned on him. "You're taking far too much for granted, mister."

"You just don't like someone else taking charge," he said mildly. "But what's that got you in the past? Guys like Paulie you can't respect."

"I respected Paul," she said defensively.

"Notice how you put that in the past tense?" Devin rubbed his thumb between her eyebrows, making her aware that she was frowning. "Besides, if I let you dictate the pace you'll end up thinking about it for another month, laying down rules and parameters and basically taking all the fun out of it." Devin slid his thumb down her jawline, then brushed it across her mouth. "Do you really want me to let you do that?"

His broad chest was very close. In answer she stepped forward and laid her cheek against it, then felt his arms close around her. The trouble was, around this guy she couldn't think. He smelled so good—rugged, clean, masculine. "You have pheromones in your aftershave, don't you?"

A chuckle rumbled under her cheek. "I haven't shaved for a couple of days."

She checked; he was right. Funny how she'd stopped noticing him as scruffy and disheveled. Lifting a hand, she ran her fingers through the stubble. It highlighted his mouth, wide, firm and tempting.

And his hair was soft, too. Somehow all those vibrant red highlights made her expect it to be springy, but it was baby-fine. "It's getting long again," she commented. She could lose her hand in all that rich, wild color.

"You think I should get another haircut?"

She hesitated. "No."

Something started to hum between them, like the charge in the air before an electrical storm. He freed her hair from the ponytail. "You smell good, too. Like roast lamb and gardenias." He kissed her, and she closed her eyes, suddenly weak with desire. "And you taste of strawberries," he said when he came up for air.

"I might have eaten a couple in the preparation," she admitted, smiling.

"Is that why you served yourself so little, or did you go short so the fledglings could have second helpings?" He looked at her with a frank affection he didn't bother to hide. He had no business looking at her that way, as though they had the possibility of a real relationship, a future. It took her dangerously close to needing him, and Rachel had spent her life making sure she didn't need anyone.

"You have the most expressive face of anyone I've ever met," he said. "And you've just gone AWOL on me. Why?"

Rachel swallowed. "That's silly," she said, and kissed him.

The kiss was different, distant. Devin let her go. He'd had enough casual sex to last him a lifetime, and it wasn't what he wanted from her. The realization was a shock; now he was the one who needed some time to think.

"I didn't get to eat much, either," he admitted. "How about we grab a cold lamb sandwich?"

"Good idea, there's still plenty of meat on the bone." She didn't seem the least disappointed by his withdrawal, dammit, leading the way to the kitchen, hauling out the leftovers, the bread, the chutney. The librarian never reacted how he expected. It was one of the most infuriating and charming things about her.

"Put the kettle on," she said. "We'll have tea."

"I'll make iced. It's too hot for the Kiwi version."

"Trixie left some wine in the…sorry, I forgot. Yes, iced tea would be lovely." She started building the sandwich—meat, mustard, tomato. "Do you miss alcohol?"

Devin preferred to have the subject out in the open. "For years I thought alcoholism was a problem I could be cured of, so I could go back to drinking." He found ice in the freezer, a lemon in the fruit bowl. "But when it finally came down to life or death…well, it clarified my priorities. No, I don't miss it."

"And you'll always have your music."

He concentrated on stirring in the sugar. "I haven't had an idea in months. I'm beginning to think I can't write songs sober."

"Performance anxiety," said Rachel. "You'll get over it."

"Oh, will I?" Devin was torn between amusement and irritation. "As the first woman I intend to sleep with— sober—you'd better be more encouraging in bed."

She giggled.

Devin stared at her for maybe two seconds, then strode over and threw her over his shoulder. In the hall he couldn't find the bedroom, which only made Rachel giggle more. At last he chose the right door. Pushing it wide, he paused on the threshold. It was French provincial, the whitewashed furniture all spindly carved legs and ornate handles.

The bed was narrow, piled high with pillows and bolsters, the curved headboard stenciled with fat pink roses. Fortunately, the shabby gilt mirrors on the delicate dresser injected a much-needed sinfulness to the fairy-tale theme.

Dumping the librarian on the bed, he lay on top of her until her giggles subsided and she lay boneless and quiescent under his weight. He became aware of every soft curve and valley of her body. Her eyes darkened with a similar appreciation of their differences.

She wore some kind of vintage dress of pale green cotton with a simple bodice and a full skirt. Devin hadn't liked it until now, when he realized he could flip up the skirt and position his lower body between her bare, lightly tanned legs.

"Your boots are on the bed," she protested feebly. He laughed deep in his throat, then moved to nestle against the silky fabric of her underwear, applying just enough pressure to show Rachel how denim over an aroused male could work for a woman.

They were going to do this slowly, but her surprised gasp stirred a need that tipped his lust into possessiveness.

There was fierce ownership in the way his teeth grazed her nipples through the cotton, then his mouth suckled until she moved restlessly under him. "But my dress… no…don't stop."

His mouth captured her moan as he slid his fingers up her silky thigh and between their bodies. She was wet, hot and ready for him, and they'd barely started.

He'd come if he didn't slow this down. Devin started pulling away his hand and it got tangled with hers as she struggled with the clasp of his belt, then the zipper, shoving his jeans down just low enough to… Her hand closed around him.

"Rachel, wait—"

It was her turn to cut off his protest with a kiss as hot and wild as what they were doing with their hands. Breathing heavily, he grabbed her wrist.

She was beautiful, her soft hair tangled, her eyes unguarded. Devin forgot what he was going to say and kissed her back. Their bodies came together and he remembered. "We need a condom."

"Yes."

She fumbled in the drawer beside her and he noticed her

hands were shaking. So were his. Between them they managed to cover him, haul off her panties. They didn't bother with his jeans. Or his boots. She whimpered as he thrust inside her, and he heard himself answer with a similar helplessness.

Then everything was Rachel, the feel of her around him, the unfocused expression on her face. Their gazes tangled, fierce and soft at the same time. The antique bed was too narrow and their clothes bunched, stalling their rhythm, but it didn't matter. Devin felt a wonder, a wonder that built and carried him to uncharted territory.

She cried out, and the sound took him over the edge. In that timeless moment of release he loved her.

He remembered that as they lay together afterward, catching their breath and staring at the ceiling, Rachel obviously as shocked as he was by the intensity of the experience.

He was faintly embarrassed, unwilling to believe it was possible that someone who'd never considered sex as anything other than fun had been temporarily caught in the emotions of a lovesick teenager.

Rachel rolled toward him with a serious expression and he panicked. If she talked about feelings…

"I think," she said carefully, "you might have one vice left."

In his relief, Devin laughed.

SHE SHOULDN'T HAVE SLEPT with him.

Pretending to be hungry, Rachel took another bite of her roast lamb sandwich, then forced it down with a swig of iced tea. Devin sat beside her on the garden bench in the tiny paved courtyard of her backyard, devouring his second sandwich.

His long legs were sprawled out in front of him; one arm

was slung casually around her shoulders, and in the early summer evening his black T-shirt was a sun trap she wanted to snuggle into. Instead she sat on her side of the bench, nursing her grievance.

The man had grossly misrepresented himself as a player when he was…well, Rachel didn't know what he was. But far from feeling light-hearted and rejuvenated, she was disorientated and vulnerable.

It had taken everything she had to come up with a flippant comment after they'd had sex, when inside she'd felt like a nervy sixteen-year-old wanting reassurance that this meant something to him. She hadn't expected to care, but he'd made her care and he had no right to.

His lazy charm and her own prejudices had lulled her into seeing him as emotionally harmless, and then he'd gone and nuked her when she wasn't looking. *Bastard*. Giving up on her sandwich, Rachel ripped off pieces and tossed them to the sparrows.

"You're not throwing hand grenades, Heartbreaker."

She picked up the jug of iced tea. "Another?"

"Thanks." He held out his glass. "I never did get around to asking your advice about Mark."

The mention of her son was a welcome diversion. "Break it to him gently," she said, refilling the glass, "but between you and me, he has as much chance of dating Trixie as you do of attending Sunday service."

"Maybe God's already answered my prayers." There was a meditative quality in Devin's voice that made her skin prickle. She fumbled and tea and ice cubes skidded across the flagstones.

"Careful." Taking the jug from her, Devin put it back on the ground. "Getting his heart broken by an older woman might be good for Mark's songwriting. Look at what Rod Stewart achieved after meeting Maggie May."

"Mark's too young to start having sex," said Rachel sharply. "If I thought for one minute Trixie was interested—" She stopped, because she was overreacting and Devin's eyebrows were raised. "Of course, it's none of my business." Though she didn't want it, she picked up her iced tea and took a sip, grimacing at how sweet it was.

"You care about teenagers," he said. "That's why I want your advice. Anyway, Trixie isn't the concern."

"So if it's not Trixie…" And Rachel knew from talking to Mark that it wasn't school. She clutched Devin's arm. "Oh, God, he's sick, isn't he?"

He laughed. "Did you see how much Anna Pavlova he ate? No, he's not sick. He recently found out he's adopted, and he wants to find his birth mother."

For a moment Rachel couldn't breathe, then happiness swept over her, a joy so great she couldn't speak. She tightened her grip.

"I want you to talk him out of it," said Devin.

"Why?" The word erupted from her. She flung his arm off and stood up. "Don't you understand how wonderful that is?"

"He hates her," said Devin, and her iridescent rainbow-colored bubble burst.

Rachel walked to a rosebush, where she started pulling at dead flowers. "He hates her," she repeated slowly.

"For giving him up," said Devin. "He's looking for a confrontation, not reconciliation, and that's not good for him. Shouldn't you be wearing gloves to do that?"

She gazed down at the shriveled rose petals in her hand, the color of dried blood, and the tiny pinlike thorns embedded in the pads of her fingers. "Probably."

"Let me see." Mechanically, she went to him, holding out her hand like a child. "For God's sake, Rachel, it's full of thorns." He started pulling them out with long, skillful fingers.

She swallowed hard. "What if she had a good reason for giving him up?"

"We don't know that—we don't even know if she's willing to see him." Pinpricks of blood welled where he'd removed the tiny thorns, shiny beads of bright red. "He's doing it behind his adoptive parents' backs, following his own crazy trail like some vigilante, seeing his mother in every woman's face. He's even got me jumpy."

Pulling the last prickles out of her thumb, he shifted his attention to the few still in her palm. "You want to hear something funny? For a few minutes today I even thought you might be a candidate."

Her insides lurched. "That is funny," she managed to say.

Devin lifted her hand higher and examined it closely. "I think that's all of them."

A teardrop splashed onto her open palm, then another. Rachel couldn't hold them back. For long seconds, they watched the tears trickle along the heart line, then Devin lifted his head, his expression one of shock.

"Or not funny," she said.

CHAPTER TWELVE

"MY PARENTS WANTED ME to keep the baby."

Devin watched as Rachel's hands fluttered like wounded birds before she linked them in a viselike grip. Holding herself together.

"Everyone said how wonderful Mom and Dad were through the whole pregnancy, that it was so like them to turn the other cheek." Her voice was slightly winded, as though she needed more oxygen than her lungs could produce. "I became a pariah when I insisted on adoption."

"Rachel," he said helplessly. She was in agony and he didn't know how to help her. And after her first crying jag, when she'd let him hold her, she'd pulled away. He'd already made such a mess of this he didn't want to force the issue.

It had grown dark in the intervening hour. They'd moved inside and he'd made her hot tea, piling in the sugar. Now they were in the family room, Devin on the couch and Rachel standing in front of the mantel. Her tea sat untouched.

"What about the father…did the boy deny paternity?"

"Oh, no." She gave him a tight little smile. "He and his parents offered to pay for the abortion. And made it clear that keeping the baby made it solely my responsibility."

Devin said softly, "But your parents were supportive?"

"We ended up parting ways over it."

At *seventeen?* And he'd assumed her upbringing was sheltered. "Did you have anybody on your side?"

"A good social worker." Restlessly, Rachel moved things around on the mantel—two gilded candlesticks, an antique clock, a small bowl of potpourri. "So, don't you want to ask me why I gave up my baby?"

There was a brittle quality in her voice.

"No." Devin waited until she looked at him. "I already know your reason was a good one."

Her shoulders sagged. "Thank you," she whispered.

From the couch, Devin held out a hand. "Come here."

She shook her head, returned to straightening the mantel ornaments. "I'm okay."

"I'm sure when Mark finds out—"

Her head jerked up. "Promise me you won't say anything."

"Rachel, you have to tell him," Devin said gently.

"I will, only…" She swallowed. "And this will sound silly, but I want him to like me first."

Not silly, heartrending. For a moment Devin couldn't speak. "Of course he likes you."

"As your friend or Trixie's." She stirred the potpourri with her index finger, round and round, completely unaware of what she was doing. Faintly, Devin smelled orange peel and cloves. "If I spend a little more time with him, build a rapport, he'll be more inclined to listen to my reasons for giving him up."

"You're scared," Devin said. "That's understandable. But waiting isn't going to make it easier."

She pounced on him. "So you *do* expect fallout."

"I don't know how Mark will react," he said honestly. "But I do think he's more likely to read some conspiracy into a delay."

Stubbornly, Rachel shook her head. "It's *my* decision to make, Devin."

"Not if you're asking me to be monkey in the middle. I have a friendship to protect here, too, remember?"

"Obviously not ours."

His own temper flared. "It's because I care about you that I'm trying to get you to see sense, you obstinate woman!"

Rachel snapped on a lamp. Light flooded the room and illuminated the angry color in her cheeks, but her voice was level. "I don't need you to care about me. I need you to butt out of what's none of your damn business."

Incredulous, he stared at her. "We just slept together. I'm a mentor to your son. Of course it's my damn business."

"Exactly. We *just* slept together." She waved a finger at him, an intensely annoying gesture. "Now you're trying to muscle in on my life. I should sue you for misrepresentation."

"Oh, I get it." Devin stood up. "I'm okay to fool around with, but God forbid we achieve any real connection."

Rachel snorted. "Says the guy with two ex-wives."

"At least I got that far." He pointed his own finger to see how she liked it. "You balk before you get to the altar. And you think you don't need advice on relationships?"

They glared at each other. "I know you've destroyed a lot of brain cells," said Rachel, "so I'll say this slowly and clearly. If you tell Mark, I'll never speak to you again."

"Here's a better idea." Devin flicked his gaze over her, as cutting as rawhide. "*Never* speak to me again and I won't tell Mark."

She didn't even hesitate. "Deal!"

"Deal." This time he was the one who slammed the door.

Devin took the 8:00 p.m. car ferry back to Waiheke in a blistering rage.

As he found a seat inside the lounge he decided he was glad Rachel had clarified where they stood before he made a fool of himself. To think that this afternoon he'd understood the allure of a relationship with a normal woman. He snorted. Rachel normal? "Ha!"

The old guy sitting opposite glanced cautiously over his newspaper, then got up and found another booth. Devin barely noticed. The librarian had more baggage than Paris Hilton.

When the boat moored he was first off, opening the throttle on the Harley as soon as he hit the island's backroads. He still couldn't get his head around the fact that she was Mark's mother. What had driven her to give him up? It had to be something bad.

Devin shook off the thought as irritably as a dog with fleas. It wasn't his problem. The librarian had spelled that out loud and clear. Like he'd welcome this kind of complication in his life, anyway, when he'd just got things back on an even keel.

In his vast empty house, Devin turned on all the lights, then stripped to his boxers and pummeled the punching bag in the gym until his arms ached. Mixed with his sweat was Rachel's perfume.

He took a shower and scrubbed himself with vicious thoroughness. It didn't help. Hauling on clean clothes, he settled down to a class assignment, but shoved it aside within minutes and opened the final report from his forensic accountant. Devin read it and his mood grew even blacker.

Checking his watch, he saw it was four in the morning in L.A. Too bad. Devin dialed Zander's cell and was again routed straight through to Message.

"Hey, brother," he said pleasantly. "Just reminding you it's Mom's birthday next weekend and it would be nice if you called her. Oh, and I've had the results back on an independent audit of the band. Seems you owe me about five million bucks in royalties on four of our early hits."

He opened the sliding door and walked out onto the deck, bracing himself against the buffeting wind. "My lawyers suggest I sue, but I figure there's a rational explanation." Far below the glass balustrade, white water boiled and broke over the jagged rocks. Gripping the rail with his free hand, Devin looked down until he'd conquered his vertigo. "I mean, only a lowlife would screw over his baby brother, right, Zand?"

Devin dropped the amiability from his tone. "You've got five days to make contact before I release the hounds."

RACHEL WATCHED DEVIN walk down the path toward the fountain, his head down, brow furrowed. Nervously she stood up, smoothing her skirt against the gusty wind. From the swirling, slate-gray clouds overhead, it looked as if they were in for rain.

She'd barely slept with worrying. This was too important to hope for the best. And Devin had mentioned he had an early tutorial this morning.

Steeling herself, she waited for him to notice her. He walked right past.

Rachel blinked and called after him. "Devin!"

He glanced back, recognized her, and his frown deepened. Now *that* she had been expecting. "Can we talk? Please?"

"No." He kept walking.

Rachel forgot her diplomatic approach. Chasing after him, she caught him by the arm. "Look, I've got everything to lose in this. So quit sulking because I decided against following your advice."

He glared down at her. "Is that what you think our fight was about?"

"Wasn't it?"

He thought about it. God, she liked him for that. Even angry he was willing to question his motives. It made Rachel examine her own more closely. This wasn't just about making Devin keep his word; she needed his understanding.

Scattered drops hit the concrete path, and one splashed cool on her face.

"Maybe my ego's involved," he admitted.

The shower became a deluge within seconds. He took her arm and they ran for cover to the vestibule of the gothic clock tower, built in the 1920s, that was the university's most striking building. Rachel always expected to see Quasimodo swinging from one of the tall spires. At this time of the morning, seven-thirty, there were few students about and their footsteps echoed on the marble floor. Devin positioned himself near one of the massive oak doors and stared out at the pounding rain. Wanting to escape as soon as possible, she thought.

"About yesterday—" she began.

"What really shocked me," he interrupted, still watching the rain sheeting onto the steps, "was how quickly I went from lover to enemy."

"I'm sorry," she said simply. Yesterday, she'd dropped her guard for the first time in years, and his dissent had felt like an attack. The thought of telling a hostile Mark the truth terrified her. She could never make him like her enough to overcome the fear of rejection. But admitting that would reveal her vulnerability. "When you questioned my decision to postpone telling Mark, it took me by surprise. I know you were only trying to help."

All she needed was a little time to rehearse, to win Mark's trust. Was that so much to ask? She was framing her argument when Devin turned his head.

"I've been trying to piece all this together… When did you find out who Mark was?"

"A couple of days into term, but I couldn't say anything to him. As far as I knew, his parents had never told him he was adopted."

"He found out on his own. They still don't realize."

That explained why they'd never contacted her. If it wasn't for Devin Rachel might never have found out Mark knew he was adopted, let alone looking for her. Thank God for him. She felt a rush of gratitude, affection.

"So the first date…it wasn't payback for teasing you. You were trying to assess whether I was a bad influence?"

Rachel swallowed. She guessed where this was leading. "Yes."

Devin said slowly, "And you agreed to a second date—?"

"It wasn't a date. Remember? I was very clear about that." The facts and nothing but the facts. "I hadn't made up my mind about you, and platonic kept things simple."

His forehead creased in a frown. "So you slept with me because…?"

It was her turn to look out into the rain, lessening now to desultory drizzle. "I'd… revised my poor opinion of you, obviously."

"Obviously?" Devin turned her to face him. "You knew I spend a lot of time with him. Dating me meant you would, too."

That stung, but Rachel wasn't here to fight with Devin again. Far from it. "You really *don't* trust people's motives in being with you, do you?"

His gaze didn't waver from her face.

"Okay," she conceded. "The unvarnished truth. I won't say your 'usefulness' didn't bother me, which is why I held off getting romantically involved."

"Maybe you could have tried harder."

Her heart started to pound. "When I accused you of trying to seduce me the other night, you said you'd changed your mind—until I changed it back." She coaxed him with a rueful smile. "Can't I succumb to the same temptation?"

Devin wanted to smile in return, he really did. But he'd been screwed over so many times.

Rachel's tentative smile faded. She dropped her eyes, but not before he'd seen the hurt in them. Instinctively, he reached out a hand.

Head still down, she said, "I'm not asking you to lie to Mark, but…"

Devin returned his hands to the pockets of his denim jacket. "Stay out of it?"

Sun broke through the clouds, glinted off the wet trees.

"It's a lot to ask," she admitted.

"No," he said. "Staying out of it is *exactly* what I want to do."

There was a moment's silence. That was the thing about intelligent women. They didn't need things spelled out when a guy moved on. But he didn't want to hurt her. "The thing is, Rachel, I've had a complicated couple of years." Understatement.

"And you want a simple life."

He wouldn't sugarcoat this. "Yes."

"I completely understand," she said briskly. "This is my mess and I'm sorry for dragging you into it." She gestured to the open doors and they stepped from the gloom into the brighter world outside. Smiling, she held out her hand. "No hard feelings?" The woman had guts.

Devin returned the handshake. "No hard feelings."

FOR THE NEXT THREE DAYS Devin watched Rachel campaign for Mark's friendship with a desperate cheerfulness that made him grit his teeth and turn away. He wasn't getting involved.

But dear God, didn't the woman know how to play it cool? Stupid question.

Around Mark she acted like one of those annoyingly cute little terriers, all wagging tail and eager friendliness as it frisked around your ankles, getting underfoot and gazing up at you with bright eyes begging, *Pat me. Pat me. Pat me!*

Okay, that was an exaggeration—the librarian was a little taller than that and her tail was always worth watching. But it *felt* that bad to Devin. Maybe because he knew how much was at stake. Normally Rachel understood teenagers, but in her need for Mark's approval, she was doing it all wrong. And this was too important for a misstep.

On Wednesday Devin gave up and frog-marched a protesting Rachel into her office.

"What are you doing? I have inventory to clear."

Devin kicked the door shut behind him. "I'm staging an intervention before you completely screw this up with Mark."

Immediately she was defensive. "I'm not."

"Whenever he comes into the library you drop everything to fawn all over him, and giggle at his lame jokes. Hell, he just told me you even let him borrow reference books that are supposed to stay in the library."

"I'm authorized to exercise my discretion." She took refuge behind her desk, behind an attitude of polite condescension. "Was that all?"

"No." Eyeing her with exasperation, Devin sat down and rested his boots on her desk. "So you really don't think your approach with Mark is over the top?"

Frowning, Rachel shoved his boots off. "I fuss over lots of students."

"You don't offer to lend them your car."

"It was raining yesterday and he didn't have a coat, plus his bag was particularly heavy…."

"Uh-huh." Devin put his boots on her desk again. "He's worried you're looking for a boy toy."

She'd been about to shove his feet off again, instead her fingers tightened around his boots in a viselike grip. "That's ridiculous," she said faintly.

"That's what I said." Devin could feel her nails digging through the soft leather. Scratching his eight hundred dollar boots. Gently, he wiggled them free and returned them to the floor. "Fortunately, Trixie had already pooh-poohed the idea."

"Thank God."

"Trixie—" Devin paused, waiting until Rachel looked at him "—told Mark that you've only gone a little crazy since I dumped you. Apparently you miss me."

Her gaze slid away from his, then returned blazing. "Wait a minute. *Who* said you dumped me?"

He had the answer to his unspoken question. "Hey, don't blame me. All *I* said was that we had philosophical differences. It's not my fault if Trixie and Mark read that as 'Rachel wouldn't put out so Devin dumped her.'"

"I wouldn't put… Mark thought…oh, this is horrible." Her defiance spluttered and went out. "Okay, I'll try and pull back my approach." She started playing with a paper clip on her desk.

"Tell him the truth, Heartbreaker."

"His parents are coming up next Friday…. He's bound to show them around campus." Painstakingly, she pulled at the thin metal, stretching it out. "I was going to take a short leave, but we have our annual budget meeting and when it comes to lobbying for your section's textbooks, it's dog eat dog."

"It's pronounced *dawg*."

She smiled but her fingers twisted the paper clip into a tortured Z. "I know I have to tell Mark before then. It's just, well, we haven't got the friendship I'd hoped for."

Devin leaned forward and rescued the paper clip. "How about I invite you both to Waiheke for the weekend? Mark would jump at the offer and it would give you the chance to spend time together in a more natural way."

"Why would you do that?"

He'd missed her, and it seemed she'd missed him, but one of them knew how to play it cool. So he told her half the truth. "We're still friends, aren't we?"

She gave him a crooked smile. "Friends."

CHAPTER THIRTEEN

IT SEEMED APT, thought Rachel, as the ferry docked at Matiatia Wharf on Waiheke early Saturday morning, that Devin lived on an island. She wondered if he realized the significance. With Mark beside her, she disembarked, searching for Devin's tall figure in the crowd.

"There's Katherine." Mark waved to the slight figure at the end of the pier. "Devin's mother." In white capris and a turquoise T-shirt with matching jewelry, Katherine waved back.

Rachel hadn't seen her since being discovered in a compromising position with the woman's son, and she prayed Katherine wouldn't bring it up in front of Mark. But though her eyes twinkled as he made the introductions, Katherine said nothing about meeting her before.

"Dev asked me to pick you up," she said. "He's embroiled in some business calls from the States. I'm to take you to my place and he'll meet us there in an hour."

"He should have rung me," said Rachel. "We could easily have caught a later ferry rather than put you to this trouble."

"Are you crazy? I wouldn't miss this for the world." Really, her eyes were as wicked as her son's. Walking between them, Katherine tucked her arms in theirs. "And I wanted to see Mark again. We had a fun dinner together last time you were here."

As she steered them toward a small cherry-red Fiat parked by the ferry terminal, Rachel tried to work out how these two knew each other. It must have been the night of the "orgy" Devin had teased her about. She'd been such an idiot.

Demonstrating exquisite awareness of a teenage male, Katherine asked Mark to drive "us girls." She sat in the back next to Rachel, pointing out the passing sights. The town's trendy eateries; a view through the pohutakawas down to the harbor; workers harvesting the rows of laden vines across the hills. "That's one of the island's top wineries."

Rachel tore her gaze from the back of Mark's head—how cute, he had a cowlick—and made an appropriate response. They'd had such a lovely time on the ferry. She'd taken Devin's advice and played it low-key, and Mark had filled the silences she'd left for him.

An anecdote on childhood seasickness. A request for advice on an assignment. And, disturbingly, a brief rant about phonies, after he'd read a newspaper article rating the trustworthiness of various professions. Librarians rated highly. Rock stars weren't even on the list.

"We're just coming down into my bay now." Katherine pointed out the window, and obediently Rachel looked at the curve of shingle beach and the colorful iron roofs on the settlers' cottages scattered against the lush green backdrop.

"It's beautiful." She wouldn't think about the frightening confession that lay ahead. This weekend was only about her and Mark having fun together. There would be a happy ending with her son. And in situations where happy endings were impossible—her thoughts turned to Devin—silver linings like friendship. Unconsciously, Rachel sighed.

"We're here," said Katherine.

The Fiat pulled up beside a tiny faded blue cottage so cute

Rachel had to resist the urge to hug it when she got out of the car. She patted the sun-warmed concrete seal balancing a birdbath on its nose. "Devin always does that, too," commented Katherine. "Come in. Mark, you know the way."

Inside, mullioned windowpanes gleamed, and the golden kauri floor sloped downward toward the kitchen, which had an old Aga cooker and lace curtains, and smelled of baking and lemon. Mismatched armchairs with fringed cushions lent a charm to the sunlit dining room, and somewhere Rachel could hear an old grandfather clock ponderously marking time. "I love it," she said.

"Devin keeps trying to buy me a bigger place, but telling him I need grandchildren to fill it usually shuts him up. Earl Grey?"

"Thanks."

Mark asked for water. "I think he'd be a good dad," he said, accepting a piece of homemade shortbread.

"Really?" Rachel thought of Devin with Mark and the other students at her luncheon. "Well, he can be patient when he wants to," she conceded. "And the kids would always have someone to play with."

Katherine fixed her with a meaningful stare. "What he's never had is the right woman."

Rachel bit into the buttery shortbread, still warm from the oven, and diplomatically changed the subject. "Does your other son have children?"

"Zander? No. But that's probably a good thing," Katherine handed Mark another cookie. "He's far too selfish to put anyone's interests before his own."

She caught Rachel's blink of surprise and laughed. "I love Zander, but it would have been a lot better for his personal growth if he'd become a minister instead of a rock star. That was his original choice of career, you know. He was in the choir when he was a boy…though in hindsight I think it was less of a spiritual calling than imagining himself center stage in the pulpit."

The wistfulness in Katherine's voice struck a chord. "Do you see him very often?"

"No." Katherine picked up the teapot and filled two delicate china cups. The perfumed scent of Earl Grey hung in the air. Rachel had always found it slightly melancholic, like pressed flowers in an old love letter. "But I used to say that about Devin, and now he's living down the road. So I don't give up hope." She handed Rachel her tea.

Mark stood at the window, looking out to the garden. "The last of the peaches should be ripe by now. Want me to pick them while I'm here?"

"That's so thoughtful, thank you. There's a bucket on the back step." Through the window, both women watched Mark cross the grass. "Sweet boy," Katherine commented, sipping her tea. "He and Devin picked for me last time they were here, because my son gets so huffy when he finds me up the tree.

"I had a little heart trouble earlier this year," she explained, "and he still treats me like an invalid…. So, Rachel, now that we're alone, tell me how you two are getting on."

Rachel watched Mark swing up into the tree. "Much better now that I've stopped trying so hard," she said, then realized Katherine was talking about Devin.

"Yes, I think women expect rock stars to want kinky sex," said Katherine thoughtfully. "Bondage, threesomes and such, but Devin says he's always been a one-woman man. One at a time, I mean."

Fascination overcame Rachel's embarrassment. "You two talk about stuff like that?"

"Lord, no!" She laughed. "He's such a prude with his mother. And he's terribly Victorian about Matthew—my lover. Since you outed us, I've been trying to get them to meet, but Dev keeps coming up with lame excuses. Actually, I'm hoping you'll help me. It's my birthday and Devin's taking us all to a local restaurant. But he's balking at Matthew joining us."

"I'll certainly see what I can do, but I have to warn you my influence is limited," said Rachel. "We've decided that we're better off as friends rather than…anything else." She gave a self-deprecating laugh. "I mean, a rock star and a librarian takes the 'opposites attract' theory a little too far don't you think?"

"It can work. I was a Kiwi honor student, in the States to research a thesis on symmetric matrices, and the boys' father was a Texas-born biker. I met Ray when I was working part-time at Marie Callender's restaurant. He was managing a Harley dealership down the road in West L.A. and was the smartest man I ever knew." Tenderness lit Katherine's eyes. "Smart enough to follow me back to New Zealand, anyway." She paused then smiled sadly. "He died of cancer when Devin was twelve." She smiled sadly. "I think part of Dev's problem with Matthew is that he doesn't like to see another man in Ray's place."

"That's why Devin likes Harleys," said Rachel slowly, "and cowboy hats."

Katherine nodded. "Are your parents alive, Rachel?"

"My father passed away some years ago. My mother lives in Hamilton." She recited the facts the way she always did, without emotion.

"No siblings?"

"No. They'd pretty much given up on having a family when they had me. Mom was forty-five when I was born, my father forty-nine."

"And you were their miracle."

For a moment Rachel said nothing, looking down at her hands. Heavy expectations, heavy disappointments. "Some people aren't meant to be parents." She'd never voiced the thought before. But she needed to practice surrendering secrets.

"And some are," said Devin, behind her, resting his hands, big, warm and reassuring, on her shoulders. "Mom, how many times do I have to tell you to close the front door? Anyone can walk in. Where's Mark?"

"Picking peaches for me," said Katherine. They all looked out the window and burst out laughing. Mark was balanced precariously on a forked branch near the top of the tree, using his cell phone.

DAMN, HE'D MISSED the call.

Red bucket propped against his feet in the fork of the tree, Mark listened to the dial tone. With his left hand, he absently picked a small white peach.

He checked his messages, saw the last one was from Trixie, and got nervous. He'd told her about his birth mother and she'd immediately offered to check staff records for women aged thirty-two to thirty-seven, teenagers when he'd been born. That would really help, because it was nearly impossible to tell females' ages from looking at them.

Maybe Trixie had found something. Taking a deep breath, he listened to her message. "Just to tell you, I've printed off the list of names, and while you're enjoying yourself in the rock star's mansion, I'll be cross-referencing all afternoon. But don't feel bad about it."

Grinning, Mark replaced the phone in his pocket. She was still pissed that she hadn't been invited, but when he'd hinted as much to Devin, he'd replied, "Tough. Restful women only."

"Are you sure you wouldn't rather be alone with Rachel?" he'd asked.

"Yeah, I would, but she insisted on a chaperone." When Mark looked doubtful, Devin had laughed. "I'm joking. It's just a hang-out weekend, buddy. Good food, a little swimming, a couple of jam sessions and my mother's birthday dinner. Think you can cope?"

Mark had relaxed. "Yeah, your mom's cool."

And he was kind of relieved Trixie hadn't been invited. Although she was a goddess among women, and being in her orbit was still better than floating alone in the universe, a guy liked to be in charge occasionally. Mark had decided he preferred his love unrequited.

As he returned to picking peaches he felt a frisson of excitement along with the old familiar dread. Today could be the day he found out the name of his birth mother.

DEVIN DIDN'T KNOW WHY he was nervous showing Rachel his house. Maybe because this was his retreat, the one place he was truly himself. Maybe it was because he'd decided on the decorating, and having seen Rachel's neighborhood, he figured she'd hate modernism.

But as always, the librarian surprised him. "Vibrant, colorful, brash and in your face—it's you." She held her hands out to the cardinal-red feature wall as though it radiated heat. "I love it." She wandered through the spacious rooms, admiring his art collection, pausing at the nudes. "Ex-wives?"

"Very funny." *The odd girlfriend maybe.*

Rachel walked to the glass wall overhanging the cliff. "I feel like I'm in an eagle's nest."

"That was the effect I wanted…. Let me show you where you're sleeping."

He'd deliberately put her in the bedroom close to his—with Mark shipped to the L-shaped wing at the other end of the house. Rachel frowned as she took in the setup, but Mark was with them so she didn't comment.

But later, as they lay on sun loungers by the pool, digesting one of Devin's Tex-Mex specials, while Mark pitted himself against the swim jets, she said, "I'm onto you, Freedman."

He'd been watching her, lazily thinking her figure was wasted in that polka-dotted one-piece, and wondering if she'd let him buy her a bikini.

He and Mark had spent the past couple of hours messing around with the teenager's songs in the music room, while Rachel made endless cups of hot tea and sat, knees curled under her, on the white leather couch reading a book and seemingly oblivious.

Except she'd tapped her pink-painted toes to the rhythm and her eyes kept raising to Mark. Devin had realized he was showboating, not his skills but the boy's. It was a present he could give her, an insight into her son's talent.

In the end she'd stopped pretending to read and simply listened as Devin fine-tuned Mark's ideas, while the teenager basked in all the attention. *One day,* Devin thought, *I want her to look at me like that.*

He hadn't had a good morning. Today was the deadline

for Zander to respond to his ultimatum, and Devin hadn't heard anything.

Happy birthday, Mom. First thing Monday, I'm initiating legal proceedings against your eldest son.

Devin had even considered canceling the weekend, but Rachel needed this time with Mark. And now a few hours later here he was, strangely content.

"How are you onto me, Heartbreaker?" Her pale skin was reddening in the sun. He unscrewed the lid on a tube of sunscreen and dotted some on her nose. What was it about this woman that made him feel so protective?

"I can do that." She took the tube from him. Oh, yeah, her fierce independence. "And I'm onto you because underneath the rock star bluster you're a kind man—with your mom, with me, with Mark."

Devin hadn't expected that and wasn't sure how to respond. "Keep thinking of me as a selfish prick, then I won't disappoint you," he said at last.

She finished applying sunscreen to her face and slathered some onto her shoulders, skirting the apple-green halter neck of her retro bathing suit. "For an egomaniac," she said thoughtfully, "you have a lot of trouble accepting a real compliment."

He watched Mark splash around the pool. The ego was for music. In his personal life, Devin had never been sure of his identity. People saw whatever image they projected on the famous, and as much as that irked Devin, it also protected him. No one knew who he was. Then he'd stopped drinking and discovered he didn't, either. Now he was trying to find out, and Rachel's remark set the benchmark high. He wasn't used to living up to people's expectations, wasn't sure if he always could.

But she made him want to grow. Could he?

Could he reveal himself to be as vulnerable to rejection as other men? Yet he'd never lacked courage. "You asked me on Wednesday why I'm doing this. It's more than friendship, Rachel. I think I'm in love with you."

Rubbing sunscreen over her legs, she paused, then her movements became brisk. "Of course you are. I'm the first ordinary woman you've spent time with. Understandably, you're dazzled." She started screwing the lid back on the tube.

"You don't like the idea," he said flatly.

"I don't exactly fit the Devin Freedman template, do I? For a start, I'm only a B cup."

Her flippant replies were irritating the hell out of him. Then he noticed Rachel was having trouble screwing the cap on. Taking it from her, he finished the job. "I've never met anyone who avoids risk the way you do. You chicken out if you have to. But if I want to love you, I'll bloody love you, got that?"

"Well, you can't," she retorted. "That was never our deal."

Understanding dawned on him and with it, incredulity. "You're pissed because I'm suggesting more than a fling? If I didn't have a rock star-size ego I'd be insulted by that."

"That's silly." But a telltale blush spread across her cheeks.

"Okay, you know what?" Abruptly Devin stood. "I *am* insulted."

He dived into the pool to join Mark, making damn sure she got wet.

CHAPTER FOURTEEN

RACHEL NEARLY DIVED in after him to apologize, but something stopped her. Probably the cowardice he'd accused her of. But she was still shocked by his casual declaration.

Even her two would-be fiancés had never said the L word—and neither had she. *I love you* had always seemed too extreme somehow for the calm, steady tenor of her previous relationships. Instead they'd talked about fondness, shared interests and goals. Certainly she'd never heard the word from her parents.

The only person who'd ever said he loved her had run back to college, terrified when she'd told him she was pregnant, and left his zealous parents to clean up the mess. Not love, sex. Teenage hormones.

Picking up a striped beach towel, she dried her arms and legs and watched Devin power into a fast crawl, water rolling off his muscular tanned shoulders as his arms sliced through it. And God knows, hormones played their part here. Now Devin wanted to change the rules? Well, what if she didn't want to?

The infinity pool gave the illusion of being open-ended, and for a moment it looked as though Devin was going to swim straight over the cliff. Rachel fought the urge to stand and shout a warning. She didn't want to lose him.

That made her even more afraid.

He surfaced, water dripping from his sleek, dark head, and glanced across the diamond-blue pool. "Come play with us, Heartbreaker." Quick to anger, quicker to forgiveness. *Oh, God, I'm in trouble.*

"Yeah, come on in, Rach," Mark called. "I think I saw a beach ball in the pool shed." He climbed out and, grabbing a towel, disappeared into the small building. She hesitated on the side of the pool.

"Sooner or later, you're going to have to get your hair wet."

"Not necessarily." Rachel slid in up to her waist, felt the prickle of cool water on her sun-warmed skin. Gingerly she fanned her arms through the water. "Maybe I'll stay in the shallow end."

"The hell you will."

Devin ducked under, and the next second a muscular arm wrapped around her waist. As the water closed over her head, Rachel started to protest, then laugh. He released her and she surfaced, coughing and spluttering.

Unrepentant Devin pinned her against the side of the pool with his body, long and wet. "No wimps allowed." His gaze caressed her with the softness of a butterfly's wing. A strange helplessness came over her, as much from fear as exhilaration.

"What's wrong?" he asked.

Because she hadn't considered a future possible with him, she hadn't put any emotional safeguards in place. "I don't know if I can do this."

"Yes, you can." He cupped her chin and lowered his head, his lips cool against hers, persuasive. So very persuasive. She surrendered to the kiss, wrapping her arms around his neck.

"Man, I only left you guys for a few minutes," Mark said in disgust.

Mortified, Rachel ducked under Devin's arm and swam to the side.

"I was drowning," Devin protested, laughing. "She was bringing me back to life."

"Yeah, right."

Rachel climbed out of the pool, avoiding her son's eyes. "I'll make us some lemonade."

"*Lots* of ice," Devin suggested wickedly.

She knotted her sarong around her waist.

"Is that a yes?" he said, and she knew he wasn't talking about lemonade.

"I'll think about it."

Except she didn't want to think, she simply wanted to savor this wonderful lightness, this trembling delight. Thinking would lead to questions like *What the* hell *do you think you're doing?* In the kitchen, Rachel hummed as she cut and squeezed lemons, stirred in sugar and added ice. Lots of ice.

The doorbell rang as she returned to the pool, and she remembered Katherine's request to ask Devin if his mother could bring a date tonight. Better get on that.

Balancing the tray in one hand, Rachel had the other on the door handle when she caught sight of her reflection in the hall mirror. Dumping the tray on a nearby table, she wiped sunscreen off her nose with one corner of her sarong. The doorbell chimed again—and whoever was there held it down.

"Okay, okay, I'm coming." Finger-combing her wet hair, she hauled open the oversize door and blinked.

A fleet of shiny black Mercedes were parked in the

driveway and a dozen beautiful people spilled across the grass between the cars and the house. A burly guy moved forward, scanning first her and then the interior, before stepping aside.

Behind him, a man in his late thirties ranted on a cell phone decorated in diamonds, so dazzling in the sun that Rachel lifted her hand to shade her eyes. His teeth were almost as white, bared in a snarl. "I don't give a shit how you do it, just do it."

A handsome man, he was dressed in white jeans and a white leather waistcoat that oozed like oil over his muscled bronze torso with every irritable gesture he made. A silver chain-link necklace with a padlock hung around his broad neck.

His shaggy blond hair looked to have enough product in it to punch its own hole in the ozone layer, and below his designer sunglasses, his strong, full mouth was currently issuing a stream of obscenities into the phone.

Two gorgeous women in their early twenties, with pneumatic breasts and lips, assessed Rachel as though they were judges in the Miss World pageant and she couldn't even qualify for Miss Congeniality.

One of them stepped forward. "About time. Is Devin Freedman home?"

Before Rachel could answer, the man rang off, his gaze sweeping over her in the same quick dismissal. It stopped at the sweetheart bodice of her bathing suit. "Holy crap, I feel like I'm on Gilligan's Island."

Even if Rachel *had* been the help, these people needed a lesson in manners. She lifted her chin. "Is Mr. Freedman expecting you?"

The man raised one blond eyebrow and took off his

shades to reveal laser-blue, bloodshot eyes. "Don't you know who—"

"Let me check if he's available." Closing the door in his face, she locked it, picked up the drink tray and strolled back to the pool. Devin and Mark were lobbing the ball back and forth with graceful athleticism.

Tempting as it was to dismiss the caller as an encyclopedia salesman, Rachel figured she'd probably caused enough mischief. "There are five Mercedes and approximately fourteen people at the door and on your lawn," she said to Devin. "I think one of them is your brother."

"Cool," Mark said.

"Damn." Devin absently rotated the ball in his hands, then added cryptically, "So, the SOB is guilty." With a frown, he climbed out of the pool, wrapped a towel around his waist and padded through the house, not bothering to dry off. Rachel thought it politic to stay where she was.

"What do you think *that's* all about?" asked Mark as she put the tray beside the sun loungers.

"I don't know." She glanced at her son, torn between removing him from Zander's orbit and staying to support Devin. By the grimness in his expression, he needed it. "Maybe we should catch the ferry back to Auckland and leave them to it?"

"Are you crazy?" Mark punched the ball to the other end of the pool. "Zander Freedman…wow! He might even have some of the band with him. But you can go if you want," he added generously.

Rachel sat down, committing to the role of watchdog. "Maybe," she said, "Zander's here to surprise his mother on her birthday?"

But from the little she'd seen of him, she doubted it.

"I'M HERE TO SURPRISE Mom for her birthday," Zander said. He met Devin's eyes with that same "you question my word, I'll knock the shit out of you," expression he always had when he was in the wrong.

"Not to confess, then," Devin replied, and saw a flicker of culpability before Zander put his shades back on.

"I thought we could clear up that little misunderstanding at the same time." Stepping into the hall, he glanced around and raised his eyebrows. "You downsizing, baby brother?"

"Yep, only five bedrooms, five bathrooms." Devin looked beyond Zander to where the others stood. "You can stay, but your entourage will need to find accommodation in Oneroa. Expect to rough it—I don't have live-in staff."

"Don't panic, I've rented my own place. But there's only one comfort I really need." Without looking around, Zander held out his arm and a blonde stepped into it. "Stormy, this is my brother. Devin, my girlfriend."

Stormy—probably christened Samantha—gave him the rock chick pout. "Hi, I've heard so much about you." He, on the other hand, knew nothing about her. Not that it mattered; she wouldn't be around long. Zander was thirty-seven, but the age of his girlfriends never rose above twenty-five. It was starting to get sad.

"Nice to meet you," he said politely.

Another blonde thrust out a hand, staring at his bare wet chest like a long-lashed limpet. "I'm Zander's P.A., Dimity." Unconsciously licking her lips, she dragged her eyes to his face. "Let me introduce you to everybody."

Resigned, Devin shook hands and exchanged pleasantries with all the people who supported his brother's ego—the stylist, the personal trainer, the publicist, the bodyguard, the dietician, the chef and a couple of buddies and their girlfriends.

He didn't recognize any of them, but Zander was notoriously hard to work for. Devin did pick up some useful information, though. No lawyer in the bunch, which, considering the legal trouble Zander was facing, was either very cocky or very clever.

"We chartered helicopters from the airport." Dimity flicked back her hair. "And we're en route to the estate we're renting." She named one of the newer mansions, built as a vacation home by an Auckland banker, and disparaged by locals as "Miami Vice." "Zander, I'll go ahead and check that everything's satisfactory. I'll leave Security and one of the cars here."

Exasperated, Devin looked at his brother. "I'll give you a lift on the Harley when you want one, and you don't need a bodyguard here."

Head cocked, Zander was studying one of the nude paintings. "Really? You've left some pretty interesting messages lately." But he nodded.

Dimity clapped her hands and hollered, "Let's go, people!"

"Stormy, darlin', you go with them." Zander encouraged his girlfriend toward the door with a spank on her shapely rear. "I need to spend a little one-on-one with my baby brother."

"Actually, that's going to have to wait," Devin said. "I have houseguests."

"The uptight broad who opened the door?" Zander laughed. "Hell, you really are downsizing."

Devin grabbed his brother's waistcoat as Zander sauntered past. "If you're going to be an asshole we'll talk through lawyers."

"C'mon, where's your sense of humor?" Breaking

Devin's grip, Zander draped an arm around his bare shoulders and gave him a none-too-gentle shake. "You're the poster boy for sobriety now. Make it look fun."

Shrugging off Zander's arm, Devin led him through the house to the pool, where Rachel and Mark sat on longues, reading. The teenager leaped to his feet as soon as they came into sight, awe on his face. Rachel glanced warily over the top of her book. Seemed she already had his brother's measure.

Zander walked toward her with hand outstretched and his most charming smile. "So which wife are we up to now? Four?"

Rachel put down the book. "If that's your math, you might want to consider an assistant," she suggested kindly. About to run interference, Devin grinned. His librarian could take care of herself. "And you know very well your brother and I aren't married," she added.

Zander's eyes glittered. "I'm not that great with current affairs, either," he responded, "but tell me your name anyway, babe, and I'll try and remember it."

Her smile lost none of its sweetness. "*You* can call me Ms. Robinson."

Mark gasped, but Zander only chuckled as he turned back to Devin. "I take it back, little brother. You upgraded. But holy shit, she must be hard work. I'll stick with the airheads…."

Astonished, Rachel looked at Devin. "Think of him as a three-year-old in a man's body," he advised, "and you'll know how to deal with him."

"With a spanking, I hope," said Zander. "Dev, remember that time we—"

"And this is Mark," Devin interrupted, "one of my classmates and another musician. Lot of potential as a songwriter."

"It's an honor to—to meet you," Mark stuttered, and Devin was reminded of the first time he'd met the boy. Zander looked bored and he sent him a warning frown.

"Yeah, well." Zander shook Mark's hand. "Good to meet you, too. Always a privilege to meet the fans." It was lip service, but Mark glowed.

From inside they heard a rush of footsteps, then Katherine appeared at the open sliding doors. Spying Zander, she caught the frame for support. "My God, it is true. Alexander Freedman, why didn't you come straight to your mother's?"

"Because I wanted it to be a surprise." He held open his arms. "Happy birthday, Mom."

With a choked little laugh, Katherine flew into his embrace. "This is so wonderful."

She grabbed her oldest son's face between her hands. "Let me look at you…" Deep grooves bracketed his mouth, and under the Californian tan his brother had the slightly bloated look of someone whose excesses were starting to catch up with him. But he still had a steelworker's arms and shoulders; he spent a lot of time lifting weights.

Devin saw worry flicker in Katherine's eyes as she measured the changes, then she smiled. "Still gorgeous. How long has it been? Two years. Oh, Alex, I'm so happy I could cry."

His brother's face softened. "You are crying, Mom. Now c'mon, you'll ruin the leather." Devin tossed him a towel and gently Zander wiped their mother's eyes. "So, you okay…the heart and everything?"

"Yes, yes… Lord, don't you start. I get enough of that from your brother." Katherine caught his hands. "So how long are you here?"

"Only a couple days."

"Oh, Alex, no, why so short?"

Casually, Zander released her grip. "We're doing some early promo on the band's Australasian tour. I've got meetings in Sydney on Monday."

Of course his brother would kill as many birds with one stone as possible. Talking Devin out of a lawsuit, self-promotion and Mom. Probably in that order.

Cloaking her disappointment, their mother said cheerfully, "Well, I'll just have to make the most of you now, then."

"On that note," said Rachel, "let Mark and I give you guys some time alone." The two of them got to their feet.

"You don't have to," Katherine protested.

"That would be nice," said Zander.

"Ignore him," ordered Devin, but Rachel shook her head. Stepping closer, she murmured, "We want to buy your mom a present, anyway. The village is within walking distance, isn't it?" He nodded. "C'mon, Mark."

As soon as they'd disappeared through the sliding doors, Zander turned back to Katherine. "How did you know I was here?"

She laughed. "Jungle drums. I know you've rented every Mercedes on the island, used helicopters to get here and have commandeered the island's best chef for a private party tonight."

"Ah, but do you know the party's for you?"

Their mother melted. "Oh, darling, you shouldn't have gone to all that trouble."

"You're worth it." He dropped a kiss on her head. "Invite whoever you like."

Devin stifled a snort. Yep, lifting his little finger must have been hard. If the prodigal son had come back repentant, fine, but his brother was serving his own agenda, not

Mom's. And that was saving his ass from being sued.
Besides, knowing Zander, the party would be full of music
execs, a local TV news crew, a couple women's mags and
a whole lot of eye candy.

With his arm around their mother, Zander looked up and
obviously read Devin's thoughts, because he smiled. "Isn't
this nice, the whole family together again? Come join the
hug, little brother."

Disgusted, Devin shook his head. Zander was using
their mom to try to guilt him into backing off.

"Yes, Dev." Katherine freed an arm and held it out. "Get
in here." Looking at her radiant face, he couldn't refuse.
With her frail body between them and her arms tight
around their waists, Devin glared at his brother.

Zander smiled. "Family should always come first, don't
you think? Which brings me to the other reason I'm here."

He paused for a dramatic effect. "I want you to rejoin
Rage."

CHAPTER FIFTEEN

"WHAT DO YOU MEAN, you can't tell me?" Mark's spirits deflated like a three-day-old balloon. He looked at his reflection in the mirrored wardrobe of the guest bedroom, where he'd been checking himself out when Trixie rang.

Since he hadn't brought party clothes, Devin had lent him a hot shirt, black with silver stitching. The material was so soft against his skin it had to be expensive. Tight on Devin, it hung loose on Mark, but he wasn't into fitted shirts anyway, at least not until his body filled out.

"It's…complicated," said Trixie.

"What's complicated about it? If there's more than one woman who qualifies, I'll ask them all. I won't squeal where I got the information from, if that's what you're worried about."

"I think I should make a few of my own inquiries first, okay?"

Was that uncertainty? Mark's fingers tightened on the cell phone. "You know one of them, don't you?"

Her voice was suddenly wary. "I didn't say that…. I gotta go. Let's leave this until Monday."

His mind started to race. Most of the university staff used the library and Trixie was the kind of person who talked to everybody. "Tell me, please. This is important to me."

"I…I can't."

"You *have to*—"

She hung up on him.

Immediately, Mark rang back, and got the message, "This cell phone is either switched off or outside the coverage area. Please try again later." *Shit*. Tossing the phone onto the bed, he put his head in his hands.

There was a knock on the door, then Rachel popped her head in. "Ready to go to this… Mark, what's wrong?"

He was so gutted, he nearly told her. But that would only put a downer on her evening, too. And enough people knew his secret. So he dropped his hands. "Nothing."

She came into the room. "You're pale. Are you sure you're well enough to go? I'd be happy to stay behind and keep you company."

Mark mustered a smile. "No, I want to. I mean how many times do you get to go to a party like this in your life, right?" Rachel was still scanning him anxiously so he made an effort. "You look nice."

She was wearing a halter-necked sundress patterned in swirls of blue, orange and green. Rachel glowed from his compliment. She always acted as if his opinion mattered. It made him feel a little better.

"It's a bit casual," she replied, "but it's all I've got."

Mark had to smile. "Rachel, you always look dressed up."

"To a teenager, maybe." She held out her arm. "Shall we?"

Mark hooked his arm through hers, but his thoughts were already elsewhere. For Trixie to suddenly get this protective, it must be someone she liked. That substantially narrowed the field.

Surely if he thought hard enough, he could work this out.

"Wow, YOUR OLD LADY HAS a lot of friends," the hippie driver said to Devin as the battered island taxi began its descent down the steep, unsealed private road.

From the back, where she sat with Mark, Rachel watched Devin's jaw tighten as he surveyed the emerging spectacle, but he made no reply.

They were catching a cab to the party because he didn't own a vehicle that seated more than two people. It was another reminder that the man was essentially a loner.

Zander's "rental" was a monstrosity of neoclassical architecture that dominated a private beach. At eight-thirty, the sunset tinted the marble exterior a Miami pink, and the giant palms accentuated the tropical glamour.

But what made Rachel smooth the skirt of her sundress were not the few hundred people dotted around the tear-shaped swimming pool, waterfall and lush gardens, but the realization that this event was way bigger than an impromptu Waiheke party.

"I'm seriously underdressed," she said faintly. Her gold strapped sandals had low heels and she hadn't brought jewelry to the island.

Devin didn't turn to look at her. "So am I. Don't worry about it."

The difference was that he made underdressed sexy.

He was wearing slashed jeans and a vermilion shirt open over a black tank. His black belt was studded with silver that picked up the toe cappers on his kick-ass black boots, and the chains around his neck. As usual, his hair was disheveled in the unstudied style that suited his strong, stubbled jaw and wide cheekbones.

He looked exactly what he was, a supremely confident

handsome male who didn't give a damn what anybody thought. And right now that seemed to include her.

Devin had been distracted since Zander's arrival, but after his mother and brother left, his mood had darkened to the point that he'd excused himself and disappeared into his study.

"Maybe he misses the life," Mark had suggested as he and Rachel walked along the sandy beach below the house. "I mean, he only quit because he had to."

She'd thought the undercurrents were more complex than that, but Devin had snapped her head off when she'd asked if something was bothering him. Though he'd immediately apologized, he continued to be remote.

"Oh, hell, pull over," Devin said abruptly, and the cab driver, Tim, slammed on his brakes. They were still three hundred yards from the entrance.

"What's up?" asked Mark.

"Press." Arm on the seat back, Devin turned to Rachel. "It's probably better if we're not photographed together."

"It's okay, I have nothing to hide." Since she was telling Mark the truth tomorrow it wouldn't matter if his parents recognized her in pictures.

"Yeah, but I do." Glancing at Tim, he lowered his voice. "There's a chance I'm going to get newsworthy again soon, so it's better if my private and public worlds are kept separate. I'll walk from here and meet you both inside."

Without waiting for an answer, he handed the driver some notes and got out of the taxi.

"It's like he's ashamed of us," murmured Mark as Devin strode away from them. Camera lights flashed as the press recognized the figure strolling down the driveway.

"That's ridiculous," said Rachel, even though the same thought had struck her.

"I wonder what he meant by newsworthy," her son speculated, ignoring her warning frown. Tim's back was rigid with feigned indifference. "Maybe he's thinking of rejoining the band? And that's why Zander's here—to get him back."

"Man, I hope so." Giving up all pretense of not listening, Tim swung around, his goatee bristling in his excitement. While they waited for Devin to clear the press, he and Mark had an animated discussion on how cool that would be. Rachel listened in growing dismay.

Of course, it made sense. Zander wasn't the type to put his mother's birthday high on the priority list, not after two years of neglect. He obviously had an ulterior motive. And Devin was acting so distant.... She watched his tall figure disappear inside.

He was probably embarrassed to tell her he was leaving, because just this afternoon he'd said he was in love with her. Except he'd only said, "I *think* I'm falling in love with you." There was a big difference.

How lucky then that she hadn't taken him seriously. She stared at her hands, white-knuckled in her lap. "It's not too late to go home," she said to Mark. Both he and Tim looked at her as though she was crazy, so Rachel steeled herself. "Okay then, let's get this over with." Would Zander and Devin make the announcement tonight? *Happy face,* she told herself, *practice your happy face.*

As the cab pulled up to the entrance, one of the photographers peered in at them. "Relax, it's only a couple of locals," he said.

"Bloody cheek," muttered Tim. He made a great show of opening their doors and pulling at his dreads. "What time do you want a pickup, m'lady?" he asked in a fair imitation of an English accent.

Rachel found a real smile. "Eleven would be perfect, thank you, Timothy."

The photographer fell for it. "Over here, please."

Ignoring him, she propelled Mark through an arched gate set in the hedge enclosing the pool and gardens. Among the Nikau palms, chefs supervised roasts of pork and lamb turning on spits. The scents mingled with the night-blooming jasmine and gardenias.

Out of sight of the press, Mark cracked up laughing. "They thought we were important."

Around the pool, young waitresses in tight black skirts and low-cut white blouses glided through the crowd carrying silver platters of tropical cocktails. In keeping with Katherine's era, a fifties-style band in shiny black suits and narrow ties, with pompadour hairstyles, played "All I Have to Do is Dream" over by the pool shed.

"We are important," Rachel affirmed, but as she looked at all the exquisitely dressed guests she was reminded of a recurrent dream she'd had after Steve stood her up for the school ball. She learned later he'd confessed her pregnancy to his parents and all hell had broken loose. But that night she'd still been confident that he would stick by her. In the dream she'd stood naked and alone in the middle of the dance floor, dazed by mirrored balls and strobe lights, while her fellow students pointed and laughed.

Nervously, she touched her bare neck. "I wish I had some jewelry."

"An easy fix." Devin appeared beside her from out of nowhere and took off a couple of his silver chains, twining one around her wrist, the other around her neck. The metal was still warm from his skin.

Rachel started to take them off. "I'd hate to lose them."

He caught her hand to stop her. "Easy come, easy go."

"Is that your philosophy on everything?" She couldn't keep the tartness out of her voice.

But he was distracted, watching Zander, who was holding court with Katherine by the pool. "Sometimes you don't have a choice," he replied. Then he looked down at her and Mark, and his expression softened. "Sorry, guys, this wasn't the weekend I'd planned. Listen, if Zander gives either of you any grief tonight—"

"We'll throw him in the pool," she promised. Privately, Rachel thought Zander wouldn't even notice they were there. She, for one, intended to avoid him. Just as she intended to avoid Devin, at least until she recovered her equilibrium. He still held her hand; she tried to pull free but his grip tightened.

"I'm sorry for ditching you so abruptly earlier. As I said, I wasn't expecting press. Zander swore this was a private party."

Smiling, Rachel broke his hold. "Don't give it another thought." At thirty-four she might be no better at protecting her heart than she was at sixteen, but she'd become an expert at hiding her feelings.

"Zander's signaling us over," said Mark, waving an acknowledgment.

As they started weaving their way through the crowd, Rachel's cell beeped from her clutch bag. "Hang on a second." Pausing, she retrieved it and opened a text from Trixie.

Call me. It's URGENT!!!

Mark caught sight of the message and scowled. "Can I phone her back?"

"Sure." She handed her cell over. He dialed Trixie's number and waited until she picked up. "Oh, so you'll answer when Rachel calls but not me, is that fair?"

Rachel bit back a smile. How was Trixie tormenting him now?

"Does she know this person, too?… Fine, have it your way." Snapping the cover closed, Mark handed the cell back to Rachel. "She says phone her when you've got some privacy."

"You two have a falling-out?" Devin asked Mark.

The teenager shot Rachel a sideways glance. "I'll tell you later. I need to go find a bathroom." He loped out of sight.

"Seems everyone's got secrets tonight," she said lightly.

Accepting two nonalcoholic cocktails from a passing waitress, Devin didn't even try to deny it.

They started making their way through the crush of people, but everyone wanted to talk to Devin, and—if they were female—to touch him. Within five yards he and Rachel were separated. Through the press of bodies, he held out a hand to her but she shook her head.

"Traitor," he murmured, but let her go.

On the sidelines, she sipped her cocktail and watched him greet his admirers. Nearby, two of Zander's entourage were discussing the upcoming tour. "I heard it direct from Zander," said one. "Devin's rejoining Rage." For the first time in her life Rachel wished her drink had alcohol in it.

Across the crowd, Zander's assistant tapped Devin's shoulder and he bent his head to listen. They made a striking couple—Dimity in a silver minidress, impeccably made up with long highlighted hair and even longer tanned legs; Devin in profile, all cheekbones and dark menace. As the blonde leaned forward, she teetered on her stilettos and he steadied her with a hand around her upper arm. Strands of her golden hair brushed his dragon tattoo.

And all the confidence Rachel had spent years rebuilding seeped away until she was sixteen again, awkward, weird and an outsider. She looked down at her 1970s sundress, bought for twenty-five dollars. Vintage was a way of being stylish on the cheap, a way of being individual without competing with other women. Now she simply felt shabby.

And in that moment, she hated Devin for making her forget their differences—the nerd and the cool guy. Hated him for making her feel special when he didn't mean it.

Self-disgust quickly followed. For God's sake, he'd been married and divorced twice. How long would his "love" have lasted, anyway? Five minutes. His entire lifestyle lent itself to easy emotions. And she was a fool for ever thinking otherwise.

What had he said? Easy come, easy go.

"Isn't this fun!" Katherine called, waving for Rachel to join her circle of friends. To her relief, Zander had left his mother's side, the crowd parting before his minders like the Red Sea before Moses. Rachel couldn't like him; aside from his monumental conceit, there was something reptilian in Zander's light eyes, as though he was calculating his next strike.

His mother, however, was charming. As she returned Katherine's hug, Rachel was overwhelmed by a deep homesickness for something she'd never had. With an effort she released the older woman. Dressed as she was in a blushpink chiffon dress with matching pearl earrings, it was obvious tonight where Katherine's sons had got their looks.

"You're radiant," Rachel commented as she handed over the hastily bought present.

"That's because I've drunk too much champagne," Katherine said, laughing. But when she turned to the man by her side, Rachel saw the real reason for her sparkle. "Matthew, this is Devin's sweetheart, Rachel."

Sweetheart. The old-fashioned poignancy of the term struck Rachel like a blow, but she kept the smile on her face. "Not sweetheart," she corrected, shaking Matthew's hand. "Friend."

HEARING THE AMENDMENT as he extricated himself from the crowd and joined them, Devin scowled. His nerves were strung tight since Zander's arrival, and he really needed an ally tonight, but Rachel persisted in keeping him at arm's length. Okay, he'd snapped at her earlier, but he'd apologized and meant it.

Frankly, if anyone needed to cut anybody some slack here, it was the librarian. He'd laid his feelings on the line this afternoon, a difficult thing to do, and she wanted to think about it. Any other woman… He stopped himself. But wasn't that the point? Rachel wasn't any other woman.

Still, sooner or later she needed to meet him halfway, and tonight—especially after what Dimity had just told him—would be a good start. Particularly when Devin was doing his best to protect Rachel and Mark from the media. If he ended up suing Zander, everybody close to them would be embroiled in a media circus.

He'd hedged this afternoon when Zander had asked him to rejoin the band, partly out of shock, mostly because he wouldn't have a showdown in front of their mother. Did Zander honestly think he could placate Devin by waving Rage in front of him? It was a goddamn insult.

Devin looked at the grizzled man with his arm wrapped

possessively around Katherine, and found a target for his anger. "So you must be Matthew Bennett, the guy who's banging my mother?"

He regretted the words as soon as they were out of his mouth. Katherine's face fell and both Rachel and Matthew looked disgusted. Devin wanted to hit something, preferably Zander. As he opened his mouth to apologize, Matthew said quietly, "I think your mother deserves more respect than that."

Devin didn't need to be told how to treat his mother. "Yeah, well, when I want advice from a five-minute fling I'll let you know."

Out of the corner of his eye he saw Rachel flinch, but then Matthew murmured to Katherine, "You haven't told him," and a tingle ran down Devin's spine.

"Told me what?"

"Matthew asked me to marry him today." With apologetic defiance Katherine put her arm around her lover's middle-age spread. "I said yes."

Devin nailed the older man with a hard look. "She hasn't got any money of her own, you know. And everything I've bought for her is in a trust."

Matthew held his gaze. "Not even the boorish behavior of her younger son is enough to put me off. I love your mother."

"How touching. Mom, I'll set you up with a prenup lawyer, first thing Monday."

"Devin, please," Rachel said in a low voice. "This isn't L.A."

All his frustration boiled over. "It's amazing how easy it is for you to care about everyone's feeling but mine."

"You're the one who shuts me out when it's convenient," she snapped.

"We'll talk about this in private." He couldn't discuss his dilemma with Zander in front of his mother.

"Oh, that's right, public and private are kept separate." As Devin tried to work out what that crack meant, Rachel turned her back on him and lifted her glass of orange juice in a toast. "Congratulations to you both. Katherine, I'm sure what Devin is *trying* to say is that he only wants your happiness." With a last glare at him, she stalked off, her dress a swirl of moving color around her legs.

Devin saw his mother looking at him anxiously. "Of course I want you to be happy," he growled. "But I also want to protect you from gold diggers." He shot the man a cursory glance. "No offense, Matthew."

"This works both ways, you know." Matthew's authoritative tone dragged Devin's gaze back to him. "I'm a retired cop and your reputation hardly enhances my good name." With a glint in his eyes, the older man added politely, "No offense, Devin."

He started to like this guy. "That makes for some interesting family dynamics, I grant you." Devin held out his hand. "Maybe we should get acquainted before we jump to conclusions."

The lines on his mother's face deepened as she smiled.

"Sure." Matthew returned the handshake. "I can see why you'd suspect everyone's motives," he conceded. He gestured to Zander's entourage. "It's obvious that hangers-on come with the lifestyle."

"If that's a polite way of saying who the hell are all these people…I don't know. Sorry, Mom."

"I'm enjoying it," she said loyally. "Now go make up with Rachel."

Across the crowd, Zander beckoned. Devin ignored him.

Mom was right. Right now, he had a more important priority. His gaze gravitated to Rachel, who was standing near the hors d'oeuvre table with Mark. Between mouthfuls, the kid was gesticulating with a passion that suggested they were talking about music. At least those two had bonded, so one good thing had come out of this weekend. Devin wished he'd told Rachel about Zander earlier.

He realized abruptly that he suffered when he was out of favor with her; the librarian's opinion had become that important. With every other woman, it had always been easy to walk away. But if Rachel wouldn't—couldn't—love him back, he was in deep trouble.

He was heading over to join them when the background music stopped. The vacuous Dimity clapped her hands. "Zander Freedman would like to say something." Oh, hell, *now* what? Frustrated, Devin turned.

His brother leaped onto the half wall that ran around the courtyard and separated the raised beds of canna lilies and native ferns from the paved courtyard and pool. It was fully dark now and the flaming torches around the garden flickered shadows over his face, making him look every one of his thirty-eight years. "Welcome, everyone. It's great to be hosting Mom's birthday and wonderful to be visiting the country I consider my spiritual home."

A smatter of applause muffled Devin's snort. His brother used that line or something like it in every city and country they ever toured.

You're the rockingest city in the U.S. of A., Pittsburgh!
I've always felt a kinship with the Irish!
Tokyo is my favorite place in the world!

And people bought it. Maybe it was the break in the husky voice, the soulful look in those deep-set eyes, the hand over his heart. Scanning the crowd, Devin saw they were buying it now…. Except Rachel, who stood with her arms folded, frowning slightly. *That's my girl.*

Quietly, Devin resumed weaving through the crowd toward her.

"So, Mom, come up here," Zander called. "Your sons want to sing to you."

Devin stopped dead as the crowd erupted into ecstatic applause.

"And who knows—" Zander winked at the partygoers "—maybe you'll be seeing us performing together more often in future."

I'll kill him.

The Everly Brothers tribute band bowed out, leaving their instruments free. Dimity opened the gate to the driveway and the press started shoving to the front with cameras. Maximum pathos, maximum publicity and— with a sinking heart Devin saw his mother's delight—impossible for him to refuse.

Accepting the inevitable, he made his way to Zander, smiling and waving. "You manipulative son of a bitch," he muttered when he got there.

Zander held out a Washburn electric-acoustic guitar. "It's called marketing, bro." Dammit, Devin should have guessed it was a setup from the instruments, too high-spec for a tribute band. Accepting the guitar, he lovingly imagined bringing it down on his brother's thick skull. Zander's triumph turned to dismay as he read his intent. For a long moment Devin let him sweat, then he put the strap over his shoulder and bowed in Katherine's direction. "Only for you, Mom." As one professional to another he said to Zander, "How do you want to do this?"

His brother's face sagged with relief. "'Love Me Tender' segues into 'Happy Birthday' after the second chorus. I'm thinking the Marilyn Monroe version, but replace the sex with gutsy blues."

Devin nodded. Musically, they'd always been in perfect harmony.

Zander raised his voice. "We'll start with a hit from the decade of your birth, Mom. Something from the King." He nodded his cue; Devin struck the first note. Held it.

Beside Rachel, Mark twitched with barely suppressed excitement. "We're gonna remember this our whole lives."

She didn't respond. Another note joined the first, resonating through the hot night. She closed her eyes. As yet, the melody sounded nothing like "Love Me Tender" except in the mood it evoked—slightly melancholic, heartfelt, deeply emotional. After first meeting Devin, she'd listened to one of Rage's later albums, but was immediately alienated by the hard rock style. Now with this simple solo she understood. Devin didn't play the guitar, he prayed with it.

The tune changed and became familiar. Rachel opened her eyes. Zander began to sing, his deep, powerful voice lifting and falling in a duet with the guitar. Elvis's ballad drew to a close, and seamlessly, Devin changed instruments to a bass, seamlessly transitioned into "Happy Birthday." Together, the brothers sang it like a spiritual, made the old familiar tune both new and extraordinarily moving. Rachel saw her own awe reflected in other people's faces.

Her disappointment over Devin rejoining the band suddenly felt petty and trivial. Who was she to hold him back? She heard the answer in her father's voice. *Nobody.*

The notes faded, the audience stirred. Then the applause

started, rapturous. Wiping her eyes, Katherine stood and embraced her sons. As media and well-wishers swamped them, Devin glanced up, obviously searching for her. Rachel stepped deeper into the shadows. They were done.

CHAPTER SIXTEEN

AT TEN O'CLOCK, when Mark found himself alone with Zander Freedman, he officially upgraded an amazing evening to the best night of his entire life.

It happened by accident. He'd been on his way back from the bathroom when he'd caught the glow of a cigarette, then spotted a shadowy figure alone on a terrace. "Hey, kid," Zander called in his distinctive voice, "Do me a favor and bring me another bottle of Scotch."

Mark didn't need to be asked twice. "Sure." Within a minute, he was back with a bottle. Propped against the glass-and-chrome railing, Zander held out his crystal tumbler and, as he started pouring, Mark registered two things simultaneously. Zander was drunk and the cigarette wasn't tobacco.

"Whoa, careful there, you're spilling it. You know how much this stuff costs?"

Embarrassed, Mark shook his head. At least the half-moon wasn't bright enough to reveal his blush. Somewhere close, the sea hissed against the shoreline.

"Me, neither." Zander's laugh turned into a cough. "Jeez, this local weed is strong." Blowing a smoke ring, he studied Mark through the fragrant cloud. "You're the kid staying at Dev's, aren't you? What's the deal again?"

Mark tried to answer without inhaling. "We're class-mates."

Zander laughed until tears ran down his cheeks. "Yeah," he gasped, "that still cracks me up…. Hold this for a sec, will you?" Handing over the joint, he wiped his eyes on the tail of his black shirt, then took it back. "I thought the novelty would have worn off by now and he'd be back where he belongs."

In his excitement, Mark forgot his shyness. "I *knew* that was why you're here!"

"Right on the money," said Zander. "You want some of this?" He held out the joint. Mark wavered, delighted to be asked and reluctant to offend. Having a cop as a dad gave him a healthy respect for consequences. As he hesitated, Zander peered at him through bleary eyes. "Oh, no, you're a kid. Forget I said that." He took a long drag, held it in his lungs. "So you and Dev are friends, huh?"

"I like to think so," Mark said awkwardly. "I play bass and acoustic, too, and Devin's kinda my mentor."

"Yeah?" Exhaling, Zander looked at him with real interest. "You must be good then. Dev's got a great track record of picking talent. In fact, the guy I replaced him with was once his protégé. I'd hoped it would make my little brother jealous but…" Frowning, he tapped the ash off the end of his joint.

"So…you did ask him back?" Mark ventured timidly.

Zander slugged some Scotch before answering. "Didn't I say that? But on my terms. Devin seems to have forgotten who runs the show. No one has loyalty anymore, kid." He held out his tumbler for a refill. "Exactly how old are you, anyway? You look about twelve."

Mark tried not to look insulted as he refilled Zander's glass. "Seventeen."

"Older than Dev when we started." Zander stared into his drink, silent for a moment. "I used to have to protect him, you know. He's forgotten that."

"No, I haven't." Devin climbed the two steps that separated the paved terrace from the garden. How long had he been there? "Which is why it hurts so much that you've been screwing me over. And you shouldn't be smoking pot in front of a teenager."

"It's fine. I mean, he didn't offer me any," Mark lied. No, that sounded as if Zander was a tightwad. "Not like I'd ever accept." He turned back to Zander. "I'm not trying to sound judgmental or anything," he finished miserably.

The older man laughed. "I like you, kid. You ever need a start in the music business, you come to me. I'll find something for you. Now scram while I talk sense into my little brother."

Mark left, grinning from ear to ear.

God, thought Devin tiredly, *what I'd give for that naïveté again, that faith.* He frowned at his brother. "You're damn lucky Matthew and Mom have left. The guy's an ex-cop."

"I might be reckless, but I'm not stupid." Zander gestured after Mark. "You were like that kid, wet behind the ears…trying to be cool but so not. Jeez, I must've been crazy to let you into the band."

"You were only twenty yourself," said Devin, responding to the ache of nostalgia in his brother's voice. "No more equipped to deal with what happened to us than I was."

"That's where you're wrong." Zander grinned with his old bravado. "I was born to be famous. Yeah. It's all I ever wanted. And I knew how to brand before the cowboys." Flinging back his head, he drained the liquor, then hurled the tumbler into the dark, where they heard it shatter against the rock wall. "Shame your alcoholism screwed everything up for us."

"Drunk, stoned and talking shit as usual." Devin took the joint from Zander's nerveless fingers and ground it out under the heel of his boot. "You might have started by taking care of me, but the reins changed hands a long time ago and you know it. The only way my drinking affected the band was when I couldn't be your buffer anymore, smooth things over with all the people you alienated. That's the real reason you want me back. That and to bribe your way out of a lawsuit."

As usual his brother tuned out what he didn't want to hear. "And to add insult to injury you're turning on me with this legal crap." Patting his breast pocket, Zander produced another joint and a lighter. He lit it and the tip glowed red as he sucked on it angrily. "I made you and I made the band. Without me you'd all be nothing."

Devin leaned against the handrail and folded his arms. "Yeah, so what's happened since we all left, Zander? If you're so pivotal, then why are you having to work so damn hard to sell Rage with new band members? But you made me believe that for a lot of years, the bullshit you spun. Like we'd be laughed out of the studios if they thought a sixteen-year-old had cowritten our songs."

Zander waved a hand. "It was the only way I could force the record label to sit up and take notice. And dammit, you *agreed* I should take sole writing credit to help us get ahead—"

"I was a kid, Zander."

"*And* I've been slipping you royalties on those songs for years."

"But as it turns out," said Devin softly, "not anywhere near my share."

Zander turned away, searching for his glass, obviously forgetting he'd smashed it. "You wanted to be famous, you wanted to go where only I could take you," he said irritably. Giving up on the glass, he took another toke. "Maybe legally you have a case, but morally I deserve the lion's share of royalties. That's why you've never challenged me before."

"I never challenged you before because all I cared about was the next drink. Even sober it took a long time to believe you'd screw me over. Dammit, I trusted you." Anguish threaded his voice. "You were my big brother."

"I'm still your big brother," Zander insisted. "I needed the money, Dev, or I'd never have cut back your payments." He proffered the joint. Devin accepted it to slow Zander down. "This comeback tour is costing me a frickin' fortune."

"Is that why you're considering letting our two biggest hits be used as soundtracks for commercials?"

His brother glanced over sharply. "Dimity told me," said Devin. "'Sweet Stuff' and 'Summer Daze' will flog luxury cars and—wait, let's savor the irony—vodka."

"They're my songs to do what I like with."

"No, Zander, they're *our* songs. And I want my name on them as cowriter so I can stop you destroying all we have left—our legacy. I can't trust you anymore as a custodian."

"And if I refuse?"

Sorry, Mom. "Then I'll sue you and you'll lose the deal, anyway. No one's going to touch songs in dispute. And I'll win, Zander, you know I will. I have original music scores, notes about suggested changes."

"Dev," his brother's voice grew petulant, "if you do that then I can't pay back what I owe you."

Devin looked down at the joint in his hand. He wanted

to stub it out, but that would only prompt Zander to light up another. The habit of looking out for his older brother would probably never die. "I'll let you off the back payments if you commit to visiting Mom once a year. She misses you... I miss you." *I've missed you for ten years or more.*

"Then why the hell are you trying to ruin me?"

"This isn't about you...or me. Some of our songs are anthems—" he remembered what Rachel had called them "—the soundtrack of people's lives. You want to be proud of something, then be proud of that. You can have Rage, you can promote the illusion that our band was all about you, but you're not prostituting our musical legacy. I'll fight for that, Zander. And I'll fight for your sake as much as mine."

Devin thought he saw a flash of comprehension, then his brother shook his head. "Still a frickin' dreamer." He took the joint from Devin. "Come back," he said quietly, and Devin knew he understood all too well.

"The magic's gone, Zand. We're done." He laid a hand on his brother's shoulder. "Move on."

"I can't." Zander looked out to the black horizon, the joint forgotten in his hand. "You're right, in the end it's not about the money. What would my life be if I never heard the roar of a full stadium screaming for me? Never again felt that loved? Some addictions can't be cured."

This was the first evidence of self-awareness Devin had ever seen. Even Peter Pan, it seemed, eventually had to acknowledge a world beyond Neverland. He tightened his grip on his brother's shoulder.

Zander straightened, moved away. "I'll get my lawyers onto it, but it's my idea. Hell, I need the publicity if this tour's ever going to get off the ground."

"And Mom?"

"You weren't the only reason I came home."

"Good."

Zander handed him the joint. "Now if you excuse me, my public awaits."

Devin could see him take on the rock star's mantle as he walked away, the shoulders back, the swagger coming into his stride. The rocker grin, the lovable rogue...the self-destructive ego.

He became aware of moisture on his cheeks; it must have started drizzling. But lifting his face, he saw the sky was still clear, brilliant with stars.

AT ELEVEN, Rachel tracked Mark to the lounge, an ostentatious space characterized by strong angles, vaulted ceilings and tubular-chrome-framed black couches, artfully placed on a pale marble floor that echoed with conversations.

He was sitting on the curved steps leading to the private quarters, eavesdropping on a couple of musicians. To her intense relief, Devin was nowhere in sight. "The cab driver's here," she said. "Ready to leave?"

He stood. "Let me go get Dev."

Rachel laid a hand on his arm. "I'm sure he and Zander have a lot to finalize...and they can't really talk with us around, can they?" As the only person at the party who didn't want to spend time with Devin, she'd found it easy to evade him. And on the couple of occasions he'd run her to ground, she'd avoided a tête-à-tête by staying close to Mark or Katherine and her fiancé.

She might have accepted that Devin was rejoining Rage—the only topic of conversation for most of the partygoers—but Rachel wanted to perfect her happy face before he told her. From the reaction of the photographer on their arrival, that was going to take a lot more practice. And she couldn't bear to give Devin even a hint of how much his impending departure hurt.

"Then I'll just go tell him we're leaving," said Mark.

Rachel's grip tightened on his sleeve. "It's okay, I told Dimity to…" Her voice trailed off; she stepped closer and took another sniff, then recoiled. That smell. Acrid and unmistakable. "You've been smoking marijuana."

"Shhh! Keep your voice down." Mark pulled her up the stairs and into the corridor. "I haven't."

If anything, the smaller space only intensified the odor. The music faded away, the sound of conversation. Rachel's gaze telescoped to Mark's face, taking in each rapid blink, the guilty sideways shift of his eyes. "Who gave it to you?"

Instinctively, he glanced down the corridor toward the back of the house. "Rachel, you're wrong—"

"Never mind." Stalking down the hall, she wasn't surprised to meet Zander coming the other way, a bottle of Scotch in his hand. "If it isn't Ms. Robinson."

He reeked of it. Rachel slammed him against the wall. "Did you give Mark a joint?"

Zander gaped at her in surprise, then flung back his head and laughed. And just like that, seventeen years of repressed maternal instincts were released in a tidal wave of anger. She lifted her fist.

Mark grabbed it. "Rachel, no."

She'd spent the evening feeling sorry for herself when she should have been looking out for her son.

Zander read her expression and sobered. Augmenting Mark's grip on her fist with his own, he held up his free hand to placate her. "I don't offer drugs to children." He gestured outside, beyond the French doors. "Ask Dev. He was with us."

"No," she said automatically. "He wouldn't…" She turned in time to see Devin drop a joint on the stone patio and grind it under his boot. Inarticulate with shock, Rachel put a hand out to the wall to steady herself.

Why wouldn't he? Because falling in love with him had blinded her to his flaws.

Zander shook his head. "Let me guess… You think you're the woman to change him?"

Rachel pushed off the wall and he stepped behind her son. "C'mon, Mark, the grown-ups need to fight." Half staggering, he steered the teenager back toward the party.

Devin was looking at the sky. He glanced her way when Rachel opened the French doors. "This is a nice surprise." He sounded happy again. Not hard to figure out why. The son of a bitch hadn't just pulled the wool over her eyes; he'd trussed her up on a spit and slow-roasted her over a burning fire.

"You smoked dope with Mark." Her voice trembled with fury.

"Whoa, there." He held up a hand. "Zander smoked. Mark and I were bystanders."

She gestured to the stubbed joint at his feet, still releasing a coil of telltale smoke. "So, you were just *holding* it for your brother?"

Devin's mouth twitched. "Actually, yes."

His amusement only added fuel to her anger. "You really think I'm that gullible." Like she didn't already know the answer to that.

His grin faded. "Heartbreaker, you know me better than that."

"Do I?" Or had she let herself be beguiled into seeing what was never there?

"Yes. You *do*." An edge came into his voice. "I was cleaning up after Zander. Mark didn't want any, and even if he had, neither of us would have given it to him." His voice low and persuasive, Devin came closer. So did the smell of weed.

"Even if Mark didn't smoke, how can you act like it's okay when the stuff's illegal? What kind of message is that sending him?"

"If he's going to have a career in the music industry, the sooner he learns how to resist temptation the better. But he does know."

But not from her, not from his mother. And tonight she hadn't protected him. Guilt lacerated her. Teenagers, even sensible ones, made errors of judgment…who understood that better than Rachel? And yet she'd let her feelings for Devin cloud her own judgment. Even when Zander's arrival rang warning bells she hadn't taken Mark home. When she should have been looking out for her son's interests, she'd put romance first.

"This isn't his world. He shouldn't be here," she exclaimed.

"Are we still talking about Mark…or you?"

"Both." All her anguish, all her self-disgust, went into the next words. "You're a bad influence."

His face lost all expression. "Because I don't hide my past like you do? At least I don't keep secrets from people I care about."

"So Zander didn't ask you to rejoin the band?"

"He did, but I'm not going anywhere, Rachel."

She tamped down her relief. "It's no longer important." It was time she got her priorities straight. "After what just happened with Mark, *you're* no longer important."

She saw him take the hit, his shock, the closure. Like a door slamming on an opportunity she'd never had, merely imagined. "So it *was* always about Mark."

She didn't answer. Everything came back to her son. It always had. And she'd made the mistake of forgetting that for a while. Well, no longer.

Moving toward the house, he paused beside her. She'd never seen such cold contempt. "The last ferry back to Auckland leaves at midnight," he said. "Take it."

RACHEL COLLAPSED into a nearby deck chair. Slowly, the noise of the party returned, faint laughter, the underlying bass beat of the music—like the harsh throb of a migraine.

If only she'd trusted her first impression. Instead, she'd let herself be seduced by Devin's charm, disarmed by his honesty. She buried her face in her hands. How could she have been so naive?

She'd been dazzled by his sex appeal and—Rachel squirmed—by his interest in her. And this time she didn't have youth as an excuse. She was pathetic. But she was through being pathetic. She'd tell Mark the truth as soon as they had privacy…tell him and accept the consequences.

If Devin doesn't tell him first.

The thought propelled her to her feet. Oh, God, he was angry enough to. Rachel ran.

Back in the lounge, the music had been cranked up and the lights dimmed for dancing. Rock, loud and discordant, jangled her shattered nerves. Through the shadowy gyrating forms she could see Tim at the door. She'd forgotten all about the taxi driver.

Holding up her fingers, she mouthed, *"Five minutes."*

The cabbie jerked his head in consent. But where was Mark?

Hurrying out to the pool, Rachel scanned the surrounding gardens. Party debris was everywhere, some of it human. Shrieking with laughter, two young women frolicked in the pool, expensive gowns ballooning around their legs.

A hand slid down her bare back. "You look hot when you're mad," said Zander in her ear, his breath sour with whiskey. He fingered the halter bow of her dress. "One tweak and this unties, right?"

Skin crawling, Rachel stepped away. At least Mark was no longer with him. "You don't care who you hurt, do you?"

"Devin can take care of himself. In fact, he's about to do that right now in the spa with a few women. That frees you and me to play."

From the other side of the swimming pool, Stormy watched them, her beautiful face miserable. "And what about your girlfriend?"

"Stormy knows there's plenty to go around." Lazily, Zander ran a thumb down Rachel's cleavage. "So what do you say, you open to sharing the love?"

She shoved him into the pool and headed for the spa.

"COME ON IN, Devin, the water's steaming."

Ignoring the women in the hot tub to his right, Devin stood on the deck overlooking the ocean, letting the wind cool his temper. As soon as the proverbial hit the fan, Rachel had defaulted to what she really believed. That he was irredeemable, an evil influence.

"Yoo-hoo, Devvvin."

What hurt most was that she didn't trust him with

Mark—the kid he'd helped her bond with, the kid he'd kept her secret from—against his better judgment.

She'd exploited his feelings in order to access her son, and later to manipulate him into keeping his mouth shut. Devin felt used, disgusted. And bitter.

"Devin, are you listening? We want to make room for you."

Turning his head, he saw Dimity lounging in the spa with a couple of other women—he recognized Zander's stylist and dietitian—sharing a bottle of Moet.

They were up to their necks in bubbles, inside as well as out. This was the third time his brother's P.A. had hit on Devin tonight. He was about to shut her down once and for all when Rachel spoke behind him.

"Where's Mark?"

Devin pivoted. "I told you to go."

"No more girls," Dimity called petulantly from the spa. "We want Devin to ourselves."

"Not without Mark." Rachel's anxiety gave her away.

Devin leaned back against the railing. "Worried I'll tell him?"

"Tell me what?"

Rachel froze, her expression stricken as she held Devin's gaze. Another painful reminder that she'd never trusted him.

"Dev?" It was natural for Mark to turn to him first. Guilt twisted in Devin's gut. He was supposed to be the boy's mentor, his friend, and he'd put a stupid infatuation before that.

Mark stood by the side of the house, exposed to the northerly wind, his borrowed shirt whipping behind his skinny body like a superhero's cape. His fair hair tangled over his eyes, and he swept it back as he looked past Devin to Rachel.

"What's going on?"

"Nothing," Rachel said hoarsely.

Devin laughed. Behind him, Rachel murmured, "Please."

The three women in the hot tub were whispering among themselves. "*You* can come in, Devin's friend," called the dietitian, a skinny blonde. "But only if you bring Devin with you."

A wet, black bikini top landed with a plop at Mark's feet. He blushed fiery red, visible even under the outdoor lights. It brought Devin to his senses. However much he despised Rachel right now, he couldn't tell Mark here.

"We broke up," he said. "Do me a favor, buddy. Take her back to Auckland."

Color crept back into her pale face. *"Thank you,"* she mouthed. Turning away, she hesitated. "I have to clear one thing up. It wasn't just about…what you thought it was."

He'd thought it was about love. Devin started unbuttoning his shirt. "Yeah, well, like *you* said. No longer important." One benefit of living in the public eye was the ability to pretend you didn't give a damn. "Make room for me, ladies."

He kicked off his boots, then unbuckled his belt. Rachel looked from him to the spa, then back again. She seemed unable to move.

Unzipping his jeans, Devin dropped his pants, to whistles of appreciation from the spa, and stood in black briefs. "So, was there anything else?" he inquired impatiently.

"Yes." Her voice was a whisper. "You don't fool me." Leaving him feeling like an idiot, she turned and walked away. When she reached Mark, he put his arm around her shoulder as he glared back at Devin. *Tough.* The kid would get over it. They disappeared from sight.

A gust of wind made Devin shiver even though it wasn't

cold. Briefly, he closed his eyes, then picked up his clothes and began dressing, his movements tight, economical, verging on vicious.

Heartbreaker. He'd thrown down the challenge and it had come back to haunt him with a vengeance.

"Wait a minute!" Dimity stood up in the spa, her skin as red as an overcooked lobster, her blond hair dripping. "Aren't you joining us?"

He shook his head. "Sorry, girls. Party's over."

CHAPTER SEVENTEEN

MARK SPENT MOST OF THE taxi ride back to Devin's to pick up their bags, then to the wharf, racking his brain for something to say to make things better.

"I'll buy the tickets," he said when they got to the terminal. "You sit down."

"Will you quit worrying? I'm fine." But there was a terrible emptiness behind Rachel's "reassuring" smile. As he waited while she made the purchase, Mark decided he'd lost some respect for Devin. Stripping down for the spa was cruel when he and Rachel had just split up. It was almost like he was trying to punish her.

When she handed Mark his ticket and led the way to the ferry, brightly lit at the end of the wooden dock, Mark overrode her protests and carried her weekend bag. Someone had to look after her.

"This is my fault, isn't it?" he ventured. "The breakup." Rachel stumbled over the ridged gangplank and he caught her by the elbow to steady her.

"What makes you say that?"

"You blame Devin for letting Zander smoke dope in front of me. But what could Dev do, Rachel, wrestle it away from him?"

The wind shook the electric lanterns hanging on the

rail, and light wavered on her set face. "He could have sent you away."

Mark winced. He was not a child. "Well, mostly Devin *trusted* me. I don't think it was a coincidence that he showed up when he did." Over the past five weeks they'd had frank talks about drugs and alcohol. Tonight had only confirmed that being stoned wasn't a good look—even on someone as cool as Zander.

The interior cabin was nearly deserted. Mark recognized a few partygoers. By their shrieks of laughter, they were still partying.

Rachel backed up. "Mind if we sit outside? I know it's windy but I need fresh air."

She did look pale. "Sure." They settled on a sheltered bench at the stern. The ferry chugged away from the dock; in silence they watched Waiheke's smatter of lights recede into the distance. Mark's thoughts turned to Auckland…and Trixie. First thing tomorrow he'd shake the information out of her if he had to. He shifted restlessly on the hard bench.

"Really, our breakup isn't your fault," stressed Rachel, misinterpreting his agitation.

Bracing against the bulkhead to counter the increasing swell as they hit open water, he searched for something to cheer her up. *Zander said he'd give me a job when I want one.* Nope, the guy wasn't exactly top of Rachel's hit parade. Someone at the party had even said she'd shoved him into the pool, but Mark figured that was another rumor, like Devin rejoining the—

He brightened. "Devin's not leaving, you know. You could get back together." But even as he offered the crumb, Mark wondered. There had been something ruthless about their parting, something final.

"It's over." Rachel's flat tone confirmed his suspicions. She mustered another "dead woman walking" smile.

Mark pretended to buy the smile. "You're still young… ish. What, twenty-nine, thirty?" Sheesh, that sounded old. Maybe he shouldn't have mentioned age. But to his intense relief, Rachel smiled—a real one this time.

"Actually, Mark, I'm thirty-five in another month."

He whistled. "Man, you don't look anywhere near that," he said honestly. "I mean, that's old enough to be my mother."

She was still smiling, but her expression seemed to freeze over.

Mark recoiled.

Staring down at her feet, she didn't notice. "Listen," she began awkwardly, "there's something I need to tell you about me."

He sucked in a great lungful of air. "You're my birth mother."

Rachel lifted her gaze to his. "Yes."

Mark felt like he'd been shot. Soon it was going to hurt, but right now the shock protected him. *Rachel*…his mother?

Her cold hand covered his. "I'm sorry I didn't tell you earlier."

He looked down. Even her hands were young. Then what she'd said registered. "Wait a minute…you *knew* I was looking for you?"

"Only for a week."

"A week…" Bewildered, he stared at her then jerked away, tucking his hands under his armpits. "And you didn't tell me?" A week ago he'd gone to her house with… "Does Devin know it's you?"

"Yes." She added quickly, "But the decision not to tell you straightaway was mine. He argued against it."

Trixie had called Rachel tonight, not to ask for advice but to warn her. Everyone had betrayed him. Everyone had taken *her* side.

Rachel was still talking. "You see, I wanted you to get to know me properly before I told you, so that you'd be more open to listening to—"

"Excuses!" Shooting up from the bench, he stumbled on the lurching deck.

"No excuses." Her gaze held his, raw with regret. "I should have told you earlier."

He hated her looking at him like she cared, when she couldn't have—not and kept the secret. The engines slowed to a throb as the ferry edged against the Auckland pier. Mark regained his balance. "Can you even *imagine* what it's like to discover everything you believed about yourself is a lie?" He spat the accusation at her. "Can you?"

"No, and I'm deeply sorry." Her hands twisted together in her lap. "But please know that I had no choice but to give you up."

"Why?" Maybe understanding would somehow help. "Wouldn't your parents let you keep me?"

Momentarily, her gaze dropped. "It's…complicated."

Complicated. Trixie had used that word. "Screw you. I don't want to listen to anything you have to say." Picking up his bag, he stormed back inside, letting the wind slam the door behind him.

Another bang told him Rachel had followed, so he headed for the gangway, toward the people milling on the lower deck, waiting to disembark.

"Mark, please." Rachel clattered down the stairs behind him. "Let me tell you the circumstances." She became aware of the curious stares and dropped her voice. "Come back to my place."

"It doesn't matter." He didn't give a damn who was listening. Let everybody know what she was like. "You were my age when you gave me up. If it happened to me, if I got a girl pregnant, I'd stay in that kid's life no matter what."

"Steady, mate," advised the purser, who was standing near the exit. "Calm down, eh?"

They both ignored him.

"At seventeen, you see your choices as black-and-white, right and wrong," said Rachel. "I did, too. And I thought if you didn't know you were adopted—if I broke all ties—it would be easier for both of us to get on with our lives. I was wrong, Mark."

"You think?"

The gangplank rumbled down; in relief the dozen passengers debarked, heads down in embarrassment. A couple sent back curious glances.

Mark went to follow, but Rachel barred his way. "Your parents tried to talk me out of it—until I made it a condition of the adoption. I'm just sorry that they kept their word, though it shouldn't surprise me. They're good people."

"Better than you," he said, wanting to hurt her. But she only nodded.

"That's why I chose them."

She wasn't even going to fight.

He shoved all the contempt he could into his next words. "I don't want you in my life."

Rachel seemed to shrink. "That's your choice." Even her voice was small as she stepped aside to let him pass.

"Yes," Mark said savagely. "It is." Buoyed by righteous

anger, he marched down the gangway, then turned. "How does it feel being the one rejected for a change?"

IT FELT LIKE HELL.

Except Mark was wrong. Rachel had plenty of practice at being rejected.

All the color leached out of her life. For the first time in her life she was rudderless and bereft of the capable, cheerful identity she'd built block by painful block from the age of seventeen.

Worried that Mark would quit university if she remained on campus, Rachel rang her boss first thing Sunday morning. She told him everything so he'd accept an immediate resignation. He refused to accept it and insisted she take a week's leave to think things over. Rachel didn't have the energy to argue, but knew she'd never go back. It was too hard.

And thinking things over—every scathing, scalding denouncement—was killing her.

Even hating her, Devin hadn't told Mark. How could she ever have doubted him? She'd worried that love blinded her to his faults. Instead she should have worried about how love triggered her own deep-seated insecurities.

The truth was, she'd launched into a blind attack the first excuse she got. Because she'd wanted to shut Devin down before she got hurt. It was ironic that the one time he'd tried to deceive her—stripping for the spa with Dimity—Rachel had seen right through him. He was a good man, struggling to make a new life for himself, and she'd used his imperfect past against him.

Hurt him. And hurt her son.

For the first time in five years, Rachel canceled her

Sunday lunch for students. Bowed by a grief so bone-deep she couldn't cry, she spent the day hunched up in an armchair, or lying in bed staring at the ceiling.

When she'd been a scared teenager living in an Auckland youth hostel, ostracized by her parents and community, the conviction that she'd done the right thing—no matter the personal cost—had saved her. More than that, it had fueled her drive to sit up half the night studying for her library degree while working two dead-end jobs.

With that belief shaken, Rachel felt as if someone had let the air out of her.

The phone rang incessantly with voice messages from Trixie, but she didn't pick up. She had no expectation of hearing from Mark or Devin. Not only had her past lost its meaning, her future had become meaningless, too.

On Sunday night a stormy sou'wester rattled the windows and hammered on the corrugated iron roof of her cottage. Rain stripped the petals off the roses and littered the path with twigs and leaves. The world became the damp, gray chill of her childhood and adolescence, reduced to the clock ticking, light and dark, snatches of restless sleep. Blankness finally settled over her, and even that small inner voice shut up.

When she first heard the banging on the front door at six o'clock Monday night she thought the wind had shaken something loose. It persisted. Despite everything, hope propelled her out of her armchair and into the hall. But when Rachel opened the door it was Trixie standing outside, like a bedraggled black cat. "About bloody time!"

Though her immediate impulse was to shut the door, the maternal part of Rachel wouldn't let her. "How can you go anywhere in this weather without an umbrella? Come in. I'll get you a towel." She headed toward the bathroom.

Squeezing water from her long black hair, Trixie followed. "Why haven't you answered my calls?" Her abrasive tone grated Rachel's nerves. "I've been worried sick about you, particularly after Mark's rant."

She'd forgotten that Trixie knew. In the midst of handing over a towel, Rachel paused. "Is he okay?"

"If foaming at the mouth is okay." Trixie dried her face, her voice muffled through the towel. "He was furious with me for not telling him as soon as I found out you were his mother."

"I'm sorry." The fallout of this just went on and on, and her feeble apologies felt as useful as a Band-Aid on a severed jugular. "You two were good friends."

Emerging from the towel, Trixie said gruffly, "Why didn't *you* tell him as soon as you knew?"

"Because I'm an idiot…. Did Mark mention whether he got my message?" She didn't tell Trixie what it was. If she knew Rachel had resigned her job she'd be here arguing all night. And already Rachel was restless to be alone again.

"He didn't say," said Trixie. "He feels like you really did a number on him." There was accusation in her tone.

Rachel said nothing.

"I still can't get my head around the fact that Mark's your son or that you had a baby when you were seventeen and adopted it out. I mean, you love kids so much, I don't understand how you could have brought yourself to do it."

Again she waited for an explanation; again Rachel remained silent.

"Now if it was me, I'd understand it," Trixie continued blithely, "because I'm the hard-nosed one."

Something inside Rachel snapped. "You're a child playing at dress up. If you ever came up against real hardship you'd fold like a pack of—" She stopped, controlled her breathing. What was the use? Leading the way to the front door, she opened it. "Please go. I don't want to hurt you, too."

But Trixie stood her ground. "I'm sorry, I had no idea…. I speak without engaging my brain sometimes."

"Was Mark at university today?"

"No. Yesterday he talked about going home for a few days to spend time with his par…" Her voice trailed off.

"I'm glad," said Rachel. There was a chill to the wind blowing through the open door. She hugged herself. "At times like this, you need your family."

"What about you? Your family?"

"I'm not important. Mark is."

"Oh, Rach." Trixie stepped forward and wrapped her arms around her.

"I'm okay." Out of courtesy, Rachel waited a few seconds before she tried to free herself. Trixie only tightened her hold.

"He said you and Devin broke up, too."

"I'm okay," she insisted again, but they both knew that was a lie.

Trixie started to cry. "You're giving up, I can tell."

"No, I'm not." Giving up implied you had something *to* give up. And both Mark and Devin had made it clear she had nothing left to fight for.

RACHEL'S MOTHER LIVED in an affluent part of Hamilton, a midsize city bisected by the Waikato River. Her house reminded Mark of his grandparents' home—his *adoptive* grandparents' home—in Cambridge.

At least fifty years old, it was brick and tile, with immaculate paintwork and ornate flowerbeds full of old people's plants—purple hydrangeas; pink and white roses, standard or climbing over freestanding arbors. Even the trees had to be flowering varieties—magnolias and camellias.

Okay, he was procrastinating again. Mark didn't give a damn about the garden. Slowly, he walked up the path to the front door and paused with his finger hovering over the bell. He'd thought telling Rachel to go to hell would be the end of it. But he still had a burning need for answers.

It's complicated, she'd said. What did that mean? Mark wished he'd hung around to find out, except how could he trust anything Rachel said, anyway? Last night—Sunday night, after he'd blasted Trixie—he'd got on the Internet and sourced everything he could about his birth mother. Which wasn't much. Most online references were about Rachel's dad, who'd been some big shot in Hamilton City Council before he died.

Steeling his resolve, Mark pushed the doorbell. A chime rang in the house and set his heart pounding. The idea of approaching Rachel's mother had come to him in the middle of a sleepless night. At seven this morning he'd rung her before he could chicken out. Maureen Robinson had cried when he told her who he was. Yes, she'd tell him everything he wanted to know.

So Mark had caught the afternoon bus to Hamilton, an hour and a half south, with the idea of taking another one the extra forty minutes home to Cambridge after he'd talked to Maureen. At least now he knew his parents weren't the bad guys in this.

The door opened; a plump elderly woman in a mauve housedress stared at him. She lifted her hand to her mouth.

"Hi," he said awkwardly. "I'm Mark."

"Oh, my dear." Dark eyes glistening with tears, she flung her arms around his waist. Tentatively, Mark returned her hug. She was way older then he expected, and her granny perm barely came up to his armpit.

"I wasn't going to do that…embarrass you." She released him, but brushed a hand quickly across his cheek. "Come in, Mark, come in. I have sausage rolls in the oven—I knew you'd be hungry. And a plate of queen cakes…." She bustled ahead of him. Mark had to lengthen his stride to keep up.

"Um, thanks for seeing me. It must be a shock."

She paused and looked over her shoulder. "I prayed for this day…. Now, what would you like to drink? Tea, coffee…juice?" With one hand she opened a cupboard door, revealing cups and glasses; with the other she opened the oven. She reminded Mark of the quails at home, small and pear-shaped. Like her, they flurried.

"Juice, please. You didn't need to go to so much trouble."

Maureen reached for a glass. "You're my grandson." Pulling a tissue from a box on the bench, she dabbed at her eyes. "Ignore me, I'm…" Without finishing the sentence she waved the tissue helplessly.

"Yeah," he said, a lump in his throat.

Mark waited until she'd finished serving the food— enough for a small army—before he spoke again. "I guess I'm here to find out a couple of things, but the main one is how I came to be adopted."

"And Rachel wouldn't tell you." It was a statement, not a question. Maureen poured the juice and set it in front of him.

"She said it was complicated."

Compressing her lips, Maureen pulled out a chair and sat. "No, Mark, it was very simple. We wanted her to keep the baby, but she wouldn't consider it." His grandmother seemed to become aware of who she was talking to, and dropped her gaze in confusion. "I should have softened that—I'm sorry. This is taking awhile to sink in."

Mark managed a smile. "It's okay." *Please know that I had no choice but to give you up.* So Rachel had lied to him. Only now did he realize he'd had hope that this could still turn out all right. His cell rang, a welcome distraction. "Excuse me." Taking it out of his jacket, Mark frowned as he saw the caller ID.

Devin again. Switching it off, he put the phone back in his pocket. "No one important." That betrayal hurt the most. Devin had been his friend, the only one who guessed how much finding his birth mother had meant to him. And he'd chosen Rachel.

Mark looked back at the woman who was his grand-mother. After the enthusiasm of her phone call, he'd expected to feel some kind of connection, warmth. Instead he felt more alone than ever. "You were talking about Rachel."

"She was always so compliant as a child, so good." A fleeting smile lifted the downturned corners of Maureen's mouth. "And then in her teens…well…you hear how kids change overnight, but until it happened to us… We didn't even know she'd been sneaking out at night, so her preg-nancy came as a shock. It hit my husband, Gerard, particu-larly hard. Your grandfather was a man of some standing in the community." Her voice grew stronger. "But we never wavered, not once, in our decision to support Rachel even though the circumstances…"

Her gaze darted to Mark and shied away. She began to fidget with her wedding ring, deeply embedded in one fleshy finger. "But Rachel was determined to give you up

right from the start. She was almost hysterical about it…
I begged her to reconsider, and her father absolutely
forbade the adoption, but she told such lies to the social
worker…such lies."

Maureen's hand crept to the gold crucifix around her
neck. "I still struggle to forgive her for that. You're sweating,
Mark—it's probably too hot in here with the oven." She
bustled to the window above the sink and opened it. Mark
felt the breeze but it did nothing to cool him down.

"Anyway, you're here now. And that's all that matters. Eat
up." Returning to the table, Maureen pushed the towering
plates of sausage rolls and dainty cakes toward him. "I only
wish your grandfather were alive to meet you. He was a wonderful man, Mark. Let me show you some pictures."

She left the room, and Mark stared at the food. A fly
buzzed over the cakes, but they were still too hot to land
on. The thought of eating anything made him nauseous, but
he didn't want to hurt Maureen's feelings, so he hid a few
in his rucksack.

His grandmother came back, hugging half a dozen
photo albums to her ample bosom. "Here we are." Mechanically, he flicked through the ones featuring his grandfather, pretending to be impressed by the faded articles
Maureen had clipped from the paper over the years. His
mind buzzed as fruitlessly as the fly while he tried to
process what he'd heard into something other than rejection by his birth mother. With every word out of Maureen's
mouth he'd felt himself diminish. Until he felt transparent.
It was the strangest sensation.

Rachel had wanted to get rid of him. Except judging by
the holy pictures framed in the hall and the cross around
her mother's neck, he guessed her parents would never

have permitted an abortion. He should consider that lucky, but right now Mark wished he'd never been born, rather than having been so unwanted.

None of the behavior Maureen was describing sounded like the Rachel he knew; but then Mark was still having trouble believing she was his mother. And she'd waited a week to tell him…and lied about having to give him up.

With difficulty, he tuned in to Maureen's prattle. "She didn't even come to her father's funeral, doesn't visit, and all I have are conscience calls…once a week."

Unable to bear any more, Mark stood. "I have to go, catch my bus back."

Maureen closed the albums. "But you'll come again?"

"I'm not sure." *No. Never.* At the door he asked his final question. "Do you know anything about my father?"

"It pains me to tell you this, Mark, but he and his parents washed their hands of responsibility when Gerard refused to discuss an abortion." She crossed herself.

When he'd finally got away Mark walked to the park across the road and stumbled down the path to the river. Had his parents known his history when they'd adopted him? *Let's take* this *baby, he's the most unwanted.* Mom would think like that, and Dad… Tears blinded Mark. Not wanting to be caught crying, he left the path and tramped through the tangle of bracken and undergrowth to the river's edge. One arm around a willow trunk, he looked at the fast-flowing, olive-brown river.

There was a vacuum inside him and his old life wouldn't fill it.

CHAPTER EIGHTEEN

DEVIN WASN'T GOING TO quit school and run back to L.A. with his tail between his legs. Much as he wanted to. His old life was about taking the easy way out; his new one was about finishing things he'd started. Even when they were hard.

He just hadn't expected anything to be this hard.

He'd hit enough terrible lows in his life to know he would survive another, but this was a first for love. A broken heart packed its own wallop, and telling himself the librarian wasn't worth this much suffering didn't seem to make a damn bit of difference.

Fortunately, he had good reason to be away for a few days immediately following his breakup with Rachel. Zander might have agreed to play nice, but he'd renege if left to his own devices. Devin refused to let him out of his sight until they'd made their agreement legal.

That meant accompanying him to Sydney, where his brother had commitments. Devin had expected to be back in New Zealand by Tuesday, but quibbles over the fine print kept him in Australia until Wednesday night. Although he accepted the face-saving reprieve with relief, he knew he couldn't put off the real world forever.

And he was increasingly anxious to make contact with Mark. The kid hadn't returned any of his phone calls—

hardly surprising given Devin's boorish behavior at the spa. Behavior he'd regretted as soon as his anger subsided.

He'd wanted to hurt Rachel, but Devin hated acting like an asshole to any woman in front of Mark. Let alone the woman he'd soon discover was his birth mother. Still, Devin was surprised when he returned to class on Thursday to learn Mark hadn't been at school this week, either.

His ego—always his strength and weakness—didn't allow him to hesitate as he entered the library. But to his immense relief Trixie told him Rachel had taken a leave of absence. Devin quashed his immediate concern for her well-being. Whether she was or wasn't okay didn't matter anymore. He decided it was probably another way to postpone telling Mark the truth. "So where's the kid?"

Trixie's dark eyebrows drew together in a frown. "You mean you haven't heard from him? He's not returning my messages, either, but I figured he was punishing me. He said he was going home for a few days."

She filled him in on Mark's reaction to Rachel's confession and his subsequent diatribe to Trixie about "disloyalty."

So that was why Mark wasn't returning his calls. Devin scowled, a look Trixie interpreted correctly, because she said, "He'll get over it. It's not as if Rachel blamed you or me…he just—"

"Feels like he hasn't got a friend in the world." What a goddamn mess.

"Don't say that. Look, let's call him at home right now." Through directory assistance, Trixie got Mark's parents' number in Cambridge, then phoned and asked for him. Her kohl-darkened eyes widened. "Okay," she said, "well, thanks anyway. Yes, I'd appreciate the number."

Devin started to get a bad feeling. "He's not there?" he said when she hung up.

"No, and they didn't even seem to be expecting him because they told me to call him in Auckland. He canceled their visit tomorrow, too. Said he had to study for a test?"

"He's probably holed up in his apartment to study," he reassured her. *There was no test.* "Is that the phone number?" He rang it and got the answering machine, which gave Mark's cousin's cell phone number. She answered from Dubai and told him she hadn't been home for a week. Devin kept his voice casual as he asked, "What's the street address?"

When he hung up, Trixie said anxiously, "You don't think he'd—"

"No Goth overreactions," Devin interrupted, hiding his own increasing uneasiness. "My classes are finished for the day. I'll call in on the way home."

Her forehead creased in a frown. "I wish I could come, but with Rachel away we're already short-staffed."

"I'll give him your love."

That won him a smile. "Don't you dare. But phone me, won't you?" She scribbled down her number.

As soon as he was out of sight, Devin dropped the laconic stroll and whistled for a cab. Fifteen minutes later he was at the modest apartment block, hammering on Mark's ground floor door and telling himself he was every kind of idiot for worrying. No one answered. A neighbor at the next apartment poked her head out her door, pulling it back like a turtle when she caught sight of Devin.

"Ma'am," he called, "can you help me? I'm looking for Mark White. Have you seen him over the past couple days?"

Her head slowly reappeared and she scanned him from

top to toe with her rheumy eyes. "Are you a drug dealer or an undercover cop?"

The right answer came instinctively. "A friend of his mother's."

"Hmm." She came out, leaning on a cane. "I don't normally see him much but I haven't heard him for a few days...he plays the sound system loud when his cousin's not there."

Shading his eyes against the daylight, Devin peered through a chink in the curtains, and saw a light on in the lounge. "Is there any way of getting in here short of breaking the door down?"

"I have a key. Suzy, his cousin, gets me to water the plants when she's away. Mark has good intentions but he's liable to forget."

Five minutes later, when she turned the key in the lock, he stopped her from reaching for the handle. "Let me go in first."

"You're expecting something bad, son?"

"I hope not." Devin opened the door and stepped inside.

The place smelled shut up. Flies buzzed on the remains of cereal in an empty bowl. The milk had gone sour. Devin started to sweat. *This isn't the same,* he told himself. *Get a grip.*

When he was twenty, he'd lost his best friend, the band's drummer. Devin had found Jeff sprawled across his bed, the TV blaring, the paraphernalia of heroin beside him. He'd been dead for two days.

Forcing himself to walk, Devin moved from room to room until he'd checked through the whole apartment. Empty. His relief was so great he had to sit down. But it was short-lived. Where the hell was Mark?

"YOU DIDN'T PHONE on Sunday." There was accusation in her mother's voice.

She immediately felt guilty, even though there'd been nothing to stop Maureen ringing her. "I'm calling now," she said.

"Four days later."

"Mom, please…" Rachel massaged her temple. Why had she thought she might find comfort here? "This is obviously a bad time. I'll phone again when—"

"He came to see me." There was a strange satisfaction in her mother's voice.

Rachel tried to remember what they'd been talking about last week, but the world had spun on its axis too many times since then. "I'm sorry, I don't recall—"

"Your boy…Mark."

Rachel's grip tightened on the phone. "No."

"He wanted to know why he was adopted."

She went rigid. "Mom, what did you tell him?"

"The truth, of course. That your father and I wanted to keep him, but that you rejected—"

Rachel cut the connection and punched in Mark's cell phone number with trembling fingers. Trixie had told her he wasn't answering calls, but at least she could leave a message. "Mark, it's Rachel. I know you've been to see my mother. There are two sides to every story. Please call me."

She hung up. Briefly, she considered calling his parents' home, but dismissed the idea. Whether he'd told them about her or not, this was a private matter between her and Mark. And Rachel wouldn't force her way into his life without an invitation. Her son had to have some place of refuge.

Desperate to do something, she sat down at the dining

room table and started writing a letter. If she posted it today, he'd get it tomorrow.

She'd only written three lines when the phone rang. Caller ID showed it was her mother. Rachel didn't trust herself to pick up. Even if she could rip through Maureen's fantasy that their life with Gerard Robinson had been normal—and right now she was angry enough to try—it would serve no purpose.

Her mother would never love her, and Rachel would only be stripping an old lady of a defense mechanism that had probably kept her sane.

"He sets high standards, darling, and gets so disappointed when we don't follow them."

"Getting drunk occasionally doesn't make your father an alcoholic. He works hard and needs to vent."

"Oh, I always bruise easily. Goodness, I'm so clumsy."

And when the injuries were too obvious to laugh off: "Darling, I'm not feeling well, I'm staying in bed for a couple of days. You look after your father."

Her father. The town councilor, the church elder, the treasurer of the Rotary Club, the manager of a bank...the great bloke. And in public, he always was.

The answering machine picked up.

"Rachel, I'm disappointed in you, but not surprised," said her mother. "If you'd listened to Gerard and me none of this would be necessary." She hung up with a disapproving click.

Almost immediately, the phone rang again, the library's number. Trixie had promised to ring if she heard from Mark. Rachel snatched up the phone. But the news only ratcheted her tension.

"What's the address?"

"Yeah, that's why I phoned…." As soon as the call ended, Rachel ran to get her car keys. To hell with a hands-off policy.

The front door of her son's apartment was open. Without giving herself time for second thoughts she tapped on it. "Mark?" Stepping inside, Rachel stalled.

Devin was checking through discarded papers on the dining room table. Instinctively, she took a couple of steps toward him.

"Trixie said you were coming." He didn't glance up from what he was doing. "Mark's not here, Rachel. He hasn't been here for a few days."

Pressure tightened like a vise around her lungs, making it difficult to breathe. "Not here…then where?"

"I don't know." He gestured in frustration. "No one does, which is why I'm searching this place for clues."

"He went to see my mother in Hamilton on Monday." She started speaking faster and faster. "She told him that she and Dad didn't want to give him up for adoption. If no one's seen him since then—"

"He came back." Devin picked up the newspaper spread across the dining table in front of him. "This is Tuesday morning's paper. Wednesday's and Thursday's were still on the doormat along with his mail. It looks like some clothes are missing from his closet and there's no sign of his guitar. If he's taken that, he's still okay."

She absorbed the news and tried to think. "Is there anyone else he'd confide in, someone else he'd go to?"

"In Auckland, there was only Trixie and me." His tone held no accusation, no hint of rebuke, though they both knew she was to blame for this. His boots echoed on the linoleum as Devin entered the kitchenette. "I'm hoping he left a note for his cousin somewhere."

The internal vise wound tighter. "Why don't you just tell me it's my fault?"

"Because it won't help find him."

He was right. Rachel got a grip on herself. "Did you check his cousin's bedroom?"

"Only scanned it. Take a closer look while I search in here."

About to head in the direction he indicated, Rachel hesitated. "If I'd listened to you, or at least left you out of it, Mark would have had someone to turn to. I'm…sorry, Devin. For everything. You always had our best interests at heart."

"Apology accepted." Devin's expression was opaque; he'd completely withdrawn from her. Rachel shivered.

She searched Suzy's room but didn't find anything on the dresser or the bedside tables. About to leave, she glimpsed the corner of a white envelope poking out from under one of many pillows and bolsters piled on the double bed.

The envelope was addressed to his parents. A Post-it note attached to it read "Suz, please post this to Mom and Dad. Rent's paid until the 25th. You shouldn't have trouble finding another flatmate. Mark."

She must have made a sound because suddenly Devin was with her. Sitting her on the bed, he took the note from her nerveless fingers and read it. Then without hesitation, he ripped open the envelope and scanned the contents.

Rachel cleared her throat. "What does it say?"

"'Dear Mom and Dad, I guess I should have told you I was looking for my birth mother. Well, I found her.' There are a couple of lines scribbled out hard…he obviously doesn't want anyone deciphering them." Devin held the letter up to the light from the window and she saw that his hand, with its dragon tongue flicking across his knuckles, shook. Maybe it was the same tremor of exhaustion as hers. But Rachel didn't have time to wonder why he hadn't been sleeping. "I can only make out one word." He stopped, a hard question in his eyes as he looked at her. " 'Rejected.' "

"My mother told him I didn't want…" She shook her head, unable to finish. Tears were a luxury she wasn't entitled to.

Something like sympathy flashed in Devin's eyes, then he returned to the letter. " 'I know you're going to be disappointed but I really need some time by myself to figure out…' He's crossed out 'who I am' and replaced it with 'stuff.' " Devin frowned. " 'I will call, I promise, hopefully even before Suz comes back from Dubai and you get this letter. Don't worry, I have a job lined up already. Love, Mark.' His cousin isn't due back for another three days," Devin explained, "so he's not expecting his parents to get this until next week."

Devin frowned as a preposterous idea came to him. He pulled his cell out of his pocket. Zander had left a couple of messages in the night, which he hadn't had a chance to return. Trying not to get his hopes up—surely Mark wasn't that credulous—he rang his brother, turning to the window because he couldn't bear to look at Rachel suffering. Didn't want to be moved by it.

"Thank God," said Zander by way of greeting. "When I arrived home yesterday I found Mark on my doorstep. Apparently I told him I'd give him a job. I would cut him loose but he's like a goddamn puppy that's been kicked too many times."

"Don't! The last thing he needs is more rejection," Devin declared. Behind him, he heard Rachel gasp. "Keep him busy until I get there and don't, whatever you do, tell him I called." Devin snapped his cell shut and turned, trying to ignore the dark shadows under Rachel's eyes. She'd brought this on herself. "He's safe."

Still sitting on the bed, she dropped her head in her hands. Her long dark hair, normally glossy and thick, hung limp. "Thank God…oh, thank God."

Devin couldn't doubt the sincerity of her affection for her son. Grudgingly, he added, "He's with Zander in L.A."

She lifted her face, startled. "Why would he go there?"

Devin filled her in on Zander's throwaway invitation to Mark. "I'm going to get him."

Her throat convulsed as she stood up. "I know you hate me but—"

"Yes," he interrupted. Rachel flinched. Did she really think he could switch her off so easily? Irritated, he finished his sentence. "You can come, too."

But I haven't forgiven you.

RACHEL HADN'T THOUGHT about getting to L.A. beyond packing a bag and grabbing her passport. Devin had said he'd organize the flights, which she'd assumed meant traveling on a commercial jet. So it was a shock when he told her to drive her car past the international departure terminal at Auckland Airport in favor of a smaller terminal where a narrow-bodied Boeing Business Jet was being readied for takeoff, against the backdrop of a blazing West Coast sunset.

"Is that yours?" she said stupidly, pulling into the private parking lot. They'd taken her hatchback because it had a backseat, necessary for Mark. Devin had conceded when she'd made that argument. She hoped he wasn't humoring her.

"Yes, but more often than not it's subleased to other customers. Because of the short notice, we're sharing it today, but I've commandeered the bedroom for you—you need sleep." She stepped into the customs and immigration building, instinctively raising a hand to shade her gritty eyes from the bright lights and well aware she looked terrible.

Self-consciously, Rachel fumbled in her handbag and held out a wad. She'd withdrawn fourteen hundred dollars from her savings account to pay for her flight. "Obviously, it's nowhere near enough but…"

He looked at it curiously, then at her. "You'll use me to get to your son but you're coy about accepting a lift?"

"I didn't use you—" She broke off because the customs official was coming toward them. The flight, including a refueling stop in Hawaii, would be sixteen hours. Plenty of time to set the record straight.

After the formalities, Devin shepherded her aboard the aircraft. Already dazed, she found the luxurious interior only disoriented her more. While Devin went into the cockpit to talk to the captain, an attendant—Kristy—ushered Rachel past the camel-colored leather couches and armchairs, the four-seater dining room table and lavish bathroom to a smaller, private lounge, where she settled her in one of the armchairs. "I'm so sorry you're sharing the flight," she apologized.

Despite her gnawing anxiety for Mark, Rachel smiled. "That's fine," she assured her.

"Let me stow that for you." Kristy took Rachel's overnight bag and placed it in a lacquered maple cupboard. "Anything to eat or drink?"

"No, I'm not—"

"When did you last eat?" asked Devin from the doorway. When Rachel hesitated, he turned to the attendant. "Feed her, please, Kristy." He glanced back at Rachel. "I'm assuming you don't want to join the others?"

She shook her head. Small talk was the last thing she wanted.

"Then I'll check on you later." He disappeared again, obviously unwilling to spend any time with her.

Kristy looked at Rachel, the question evident in her eyes. *What did you do?* Then, recollecting herself, she smiled, indicated the bedroom and en suite, and said she'd be back with a snack. Left alone, Rachel stared out the porthole at the last traces of smeared gold and pink streaks on the horizon.

She didn't see Devin again until halfway through the flight. By that time her thoughts were driving her mad.

He stopped at the door when he saw her. "I thought you'd be in bed."

"Don't stay away on my account."

Devin glanced over his shoulder as a burst of laughter came from the main cabin, then shrugged and stepped in, holding a briefcase. "I have work to do that needs quiet."

Rachel attempted a weak joke. "If you need help with your homework…" She'd meant schoolwork and realized too late that the comment could be read as sexual. It fell into an awful silence.

Grim-faced, Devin sat and opened his briefcase. "It's copyright paperwork on some of my early songs." Briefly, he filled her in on the reason for Zander's visit—to rub salt into the wound, Rachel suspected.

"I knew Zander had invited you to rejoin the band. I

thought you were avoiding telling me because you were embarrassed about…" She stopped, picked up her cold coffee and sipped it, for something to break the sudden tension in the cabin.

"Embarrassed because I'd said I was falling in love with you and didn't mean it? No, my embarrassment came later."

"I should have trusted you." she said.

"Yeah," he said, "you should have. But it wouldn't have solved our basic problem. I was never more than a novelty toy to you, someone to play with while you waited for Mr. Right."

He'd made that accusation before. This time it wounded the part of her she'd vowed never to expose again—her heart.

"You're so wrong," she said, but he'd already stood.

"I'm going back to the other cabin."

"No!" Her anger came out of nowhere, explosively loud in the small space and catching them both by surprise. "I shouldn't have let Mark walk away without an explanation and I'm damned if you will. Sit down."

He folded his arms. "Make me."

She launched herself out of the seat and kissed him, not lightly, not tentatively, but passionately, with everything she felt for him—all the love, all the aching regret. His lips tightened under hers. His hands closed around her upper arms like steel traps as he put her away from him.

Humiliated, she returned to her seat on the couch, but Devin made no move to leave.

"Steve—Mark's father—talked me into smoking a joint the night I got pregnant." Rachel couldn't look at Devin, picking up a cushion and running her palm over the silky fabric. "I was crazy about him at this stage and he'd been teasing me about not drinking. He said it would make me happy. And oh, boy, it did. Happy and irresponsible." She choked on a laugh, looked up. "When I smelled it on Mark…well, it was easier to blame you than admit I'd failed to protect him."

Devin's eyes were grave. "It was more than that, Rachel. You wanted to believe the worst of me."

"No, that's—"

"All the qualities that made me a danger to Mark—the wildness, the bad boy history—made me safe to you. Because I'd never ask you to marry me or have children with me, never make you confront the things you'd have to if I was the right kind of guy. Like why you're so damn scared of anything approaching real intimacy. When I told you I loved you I broke the contract."

"No guy is the right guy," she cried. "I always chose men I couldn't love. You were supposed to be another one. If anyone broke faith, it was you."

"So you love me but you don't want to. Thanks, that makes me feel a whole lot better."

She had to make him understand.

"Just because I did the right thing in giving Mark up for adoption doesn't mean there aren't scars." She hugged herself, but it didn't help. "At seventeen, you think of self-sacrifice as something worthy, something good and enno-bling that will carry you through the loss. You don't know that the scab will still fall off on his birthdays, that you'll still ache every time you hold a baby and smell that sweet, soft baby skin. At seventeen I made the sacrifice and at thirty-four I'm still paying. You're just the latest price."

"Rachel." Devin sat down beside her and reached for her hands; she pulled them away.

"I know what you want. You want all of me and I

can't…love you like that. Giving up my baby changed me…. I can't love anybody that much again, can't risk that kind of loss. It hurt too much. It still hurts." She swallowed, forced herself to meet his gaze. "My only regret is that I hurt *you*."

For the rest of her life she'd remember the compassion in his eyes. "I'm a big boy. I can survive a few rounds in the ring with the Heartbreak Kid."

A laugh escaped her, then a sob. Ignoring her protests, he sat beside her and put his arms around her.

"I can't do this," she whispered against his shoulder, "not even for you."

"It's okay." There was nothing but comfort in his hold. "You don't need to explain. It's going to be all right."

She lifted her face. Devin had never seen such agony. "Is it? Now Mark's making me doubt the only thing I thought I got right."

Tears slid down her pale face, silent sobs shook her body. Rachel put her hands over her mouth, trying to stop.

Devin stroked her hair. "Let it go."

Shaking her head, she stood and stumbled to the adjacent bedroom, shutting the door. He followed her. She lay face down on the bed, her shoulders heaving with the effort of self-control.

He locked the door, then lay down beside her and gathered her into his arms. Rachel pushed him away, trying to curl in on herself and disappear. He pulled her arms free and put them around his waist, pushed down her bent knees and entwined their legs. He wrapped himself around her, trying to cover as much of her as he could with his body. "Let go."

Rachel stopped fighting and burrowed into him, her nails digging into his back as she cried, jagged heartrending sobs that seemed as if they'd been held in check for seventeen years.

At last the weeping abated, her grip on him loosened and her body slowly relaxed against his, until Devin felt as if he held something ethereal, she lay so lightly in his arms. Exhausted, Rachel slept.

Releasing her, he swung his feet off the bed and stood up. Moving stiffly, his muscles still tight from absorbing her tension, he took off her shoes and pulled the covers over her inert form. She slept like the dead. Then he sat on the bed, pushed damp tendrils of hair away from her face and stared at her, his emotions mixed and powerful.

He still had the ability to minimize the damage she'd done to him, to protect himself with emotional distance.

In her sleep, Rachel sighed deeply.

Devin laid his palm against her cheek. Had anyone really loved this woman? It didn't seem so. And yet she'd still had the courage to defy her parents and do what she thought was right by her unborn baby, even at the cost of her relationship with them. She'd been alone in the world from the age of seventeen.

His life had been charmed by comparison, his losses self-indulgent. He'd been a kid in the world, too, and stumbled; but she hadn't. Not his Rachel.

Because she was his, no matter what she said. All his trials had been preparation, strengthening him to become a man capable of loving a woman who so deserved to be loved—and who might always hold something back.

He loved her anyway.

CHAPTER NINETEEN

MARK WAS IN THE sound booth of OneRing Recording Studios, cleaning up after the latest round of coffee takeouts, when Devin strolled in on Friday morning. He started, his grip tightening on a polystyrene cup, and coffee dregs splashed the recording console.

"Watch it, dipstick!" One of the junior techs—bumped up the ranks through Mark's internship—shielded it protectively. "The VPR 60's worth more than your life."

But Mark wasn't listening. He answered his former mentor's casual greeting with a scowl. Untroubled, Devin turned to the studio technician and recording engineer. "Hey, guys, long time no see."

Both men stood to high-five and man-hug him. Even the session musicians tuning up in the isolation booth dumped their instruments to come through.

"Man, you're a sight for sore eyes."

"Good to see you! Back for good, I hope?"

Mark waited for a lull. "What are *you* doing here?"

In all that friendliness and back-thumping, his accusatory tone struck a harshly discordant note. The other guys turned to stare at him.

"Among other things, catching up with old friends," Devin said coolly, and turned back to his buddies. Mark had imagined that when he saw Devin again, his mentor would be full of hangdog apologies, might grovel even. His first wild thought on seeing him was that Devin had come to talk him into going home. Now Mark wasn't so sure.

"So no one sent you to find me?"

Devin glanced over. "Why? Are you lost?"

Mark swallowed hard against a rush of homesickness. He'd been miserable in his week in L.A. Not because Zander mistreated him; in his own careless way the man had been kind, even getting him this job.

"No one sent me," Devin added, then looked at the studio manager. "Okay if I take Mark away for a few minutes, Tom?"

"Rehearsal room four is empty."

"We'll catch up later, guys." Devin left the sound booth, not even checking to see if Mark followed him. Mark dawdled to stress his resentment. Rehearsal room four was a large empty space with white, soundproof walls, a parquet floor and a comfortable couch. Devin sat at the grand piano—the only instrument currently in the room—running his hands lightly over the keys, seemingly unaware that he'd just been taught a lesson.

Bunching his hands in his jean pockets, Mark remained standing in the open door, trying to look aloof instead of sulky.

"Called your parents yet?"

Mark tried not to look guilty. He'd been meaning to call, except he couldn't deal with their questions or inevitable hurt. "I'm getting round to it." He had another day before Suz got home from Dubai and posted his letter.

He braced himself for criticism, but Devin only said, "What do you think of this?" and started playing.

"Sounds old-fashioned," he said impatiently.

"It came out before you were born. Listen to the lyrics."

"It's kinda schmaltzy," said Mark after a few minutes. "All this holding on through the coming years. It makes me think, get another girlfriend and get over it."

"What if the singer was female, sixteen and pregnant, and had just made the decision to adopt. What if it was a love song to her baby? Does that put a different spin on it?"

Devin sang another chorus, and suddenly Mark could feel the anguish in the song. He put his hands over his ears. "Stop."

Devin closed the lid of the piano. "It's Rachel's favorite song."

Mark clenched his hands at the mention of *her* name. "Why did you do it, Dev? Why didn't you tell me as soon as you found out it was her?"

"Because she asked for time to get to know you." His expression softened in the same frustrated, affectionate way Dad's did when he was explaining some crazy female foible of Mom's. "She wanted you to like her first."

Mark snorted.

"It wasn't her best idea," Devin conceded, "but was she wrong to worry that you'd never give her a chance to explain?" With an effort of will, Mark held that penetrating gaze. "When she finally tried, did you listen?"

Mark clung to his righteous anger like a martyr to a hair shirt. "You know what I think? She never wanted me to find out she was my birth mother and that's why she conned you into not telling me."

"No, that's—"

"She's a liar, Dev. She said she gave me up because she had to but—" he paused to clear his throat "—her mother told me they wanted to keep me, and Rachel was the one who said no."

"What if they were both telling the truth?" Devin stood up from the piano. "Mark, you need to hear Rachel's side."

He shook his head. "If it's so damn important that I understand, then where is she? Why isn't *she* here defending herself?"

"I am here," Rachel said behind him.

MARK PALED, and tried to push past her. Heart pounding, Rachel blocked his way.

"Five minutes, then I promise you don't have to see me again."

He hesitated. To her relief he flung himself on the couch, glanced at his watch and folded his arms.

Devin got up to leave.

"Stay," she croaked, "I want you to hear this."

"And I don't want to be alone with her," Mark said savagely.

Rachel wiped her damp palms on her skirt. This was the most important conversation of her life and her mind was a blank.

Still standing by the door, she looked helplessly at Devin, trying to draw strength from his smile of encouragement as he joined Mark on the couch.

"This is a waste of time," said Mark.

"The only time Dad ever hit me was when I told him I was pregnant," she said. Rachel looked at her hands. "It was the only time Mom let him, although when the body blows started she intervened. I think that's why I made contact after he died, but…" She glanced at Mark. "Did she show you the photo albums?"

He nodded.

Rachel went over to sit at the piano stool. "My father was influential in council, in the community, in our church…. I don't think there was a charity he wasn't involved in. He never had any problem knowing exactly the right thing to do, the right way to dress and speak, the right opinions to have." She grimaced. "Of course, he spent his life constantly disappointed in other, more fallible, people."

She wasn't seeing Mark anymore, seeing only the past.

"In our home everything revolved around Dad. He was a secret drinker, always brooding over some slight, real or imagined. It infuriated him when he wasn't given the respect he deserved, and he'd take out his frustrations on my mother. The meal wasn't hot enough, the house not clean enough, she was letting herself go…letting him down."

Discordant notes echoed through the room; inadvertently, she'd leaned on the piano keys. Carefully Rachel closed the lid. "And my mother always agreed that it was her fault, always made excuses for him even when he'd hit her. Even now, when she's finally free of him, he's still a saint in her memory."

She moved restlessly on the stool. "I couldn't raise you on my own, but I couldn't let them raise you, either. For a while I put my hopes in an open adoption, but I couldn't trust Dad to leave you alone. So I canceled it." Her words were coming out all wrong—bald and harsh—but if she gave way to emotion now, she wouldn't finish what she had to say.

Rachel became aware that she was dusting the piano lid, over and over with the sleeve of her silk blouse, and stopped. "All I could give you was a future—parents who would raise you with stability, security and love. I'm sorry, but I can't regret that."

She'd promised five minutes. Rachel started to go.

"Devin said you wanted me to like you first and that's why you delayed telling me," Mark murmured.

Silly, so silly. "I'm sorry," she repeated. He was looking down, kicking the toe of his sneaker against the floor. The lace was untied.

"My real dad wanted you to have an abortion?"

"Yes." Rachel swallowed hard. "But I never considered it, not for a minute." She looked to Devin for more unspoken support.

Mark bent down and tied his shoe. "Still," he said gruffly, "three parents who wanted me isn't so bad."

Rachel smiled.

Her son lifted his face. There were tears in his eyes. "And I do like you," he said.

Her own vision blurred.

CHAPTER TWENTY

IT TAKES AWHILE to believe that the person you started out thinking was all wrong for you is the one you're meant to be with.

But he was a patient man, her friend, Devin Freedman.

"I'm not going to push this," he'd said when they had a private moment on board the flight home. "But I'm not going away, either. I'm backing off until you get used to the idea that I love you. Because I'm damned if I'm doing the 'panic and dump' scenario you put the last two guys through. We're friends until you decide you're ready for more. And by more I mean love, marriage, kids—the whole shebang."

"And if I can't?" Because it wasn't a matter of won't any longer.

He'd simply smiled at her with all his lazy rock star arrogance. How could he be so confident? So sure of what he wanted? "Oh, and one more thing. Start something with me—a flirtation, anything that crosses the friendship boundary—and I'll take it as a yes." He'd leaned closer, so close Rachel felt his body heat, like a faint promise of a long, hot summer. "Because a kiss is not just a kiss, Heartbreaker, it's a commitment."

They all settled back into university life. Rachel met Mark's parents, taking Devin with her and trying not to think about how much she needed him at her back. She fought for and won an increase in her departmental budget. She got to know her son—relishing the slow, natural growth of his affection. She resumed her Sunday lunches and said no to a tattoo—a present from Trixie on her thirty-fifth birthday. And she regained her equilibrium in a very different world.

A world with family in it, even if she hadn't approved one of them yet.

She knew she was testing Devin; after all, the man had two failed marriages and a lot of wildness behind him. But over the next three months she came to trust his feelings. And hers.

And still she made him wait.

KATHERINE FREEDMAN MARRIED Matthew Bennett on a wet, blustery day at the end of June when the winter whitecaps caused more than one guest arriving by the Waiheke ferry to heave with the boat.

Standing beside Mark, watching Devin and Zander walk their mother to her groom's side, Rachel's stomach fluttered nervously. It was a small wedding, only fifty close friends and family, and today she intended to signify her readiness to move from the former into the latter.

Outside, a cold wind shook the bare grapevines in the fields surrounding the mud-brick restaurant. Inside, it was as snug as a hobbit's burrow.

Tall tapers flickered in candelabras on two oak barrels by the arched window where they were to exchange vows. Tea candles lined the long tables, drawing the eye like landing lights on a runway. Overhead, fairy lights spiraled the rough-hewn beams.

A fire crackled in the stone hearth, roaring back at the weather every time a gust came down the chimney.

In a soft apricot suit, Katherine made a beautiful bride. Her sons had dressed to match the wedding party, in conventional dark suits, but to Rachel's relief nothing could civilize Devin's dramatic good looks. His hair would never play nice and the two brothers' diamond cuff links, diamond ear studs and chunky rings threatened to out-bling the bride's. Amid the cops that made up many of the groom's guests, they looked like two elegant thugs waiting for the right moment to pull machine guns out of their guitar cases.

"…to have and to hold," said Katherine, "to love and to cherish…"

Devin captured Rachel's gaze. Normally the fire in his eyes was banked, though it always smoldered under the guise of friendship. Today it blazed.

But then she had dressed provocatively. Lifting her chin, she sent back a sweet, innocuous smile, reminding him who was in charge here. With her doubts settled, there was something fun, something dizzyingly, deliciously female in being the object of unrequited desire. In making Mr. Have-Any-Woman-He-Wanted wait.

His eyes glinted. Suddenly hot, Rachel undid some of the buttons of her 1950s Dior brocade swing coat, tempted to take it off.

The color of raspberries, patterned with gold starbursts, the matching sheath underneath had a deep V in the back, which closed to a large flat bow above the curve of her bottom.

"Sexy as hell," Devin had said when he'd given it to her for her birthday. "But think of the coat like a matador's cape. Only take it off if you want trouble."

Okay, she'd deliberately stoked the fires by wearing

this outfit today. But was she ready for this much Toro Bravo? She wavered.

"I now pronounce you man and wife," intoned the celebrant. The reflected light burnished the smiles of the guests and illuminated the glow of the bridal couple. Matthew kissed his bride with a tenderness that softened Devin's expression. Taking a deep breath, Rachel reached for the last button.

As the applause and conversation restarted, Mark said beside her, "You next. Devin's already asked me to be his best man."

Rachel moved the hand on the button to her hip. "What?"

"When the time comes."

"I think he's getting a little ahead of himself," she said tartly. Maybe she'd make him wait *another* three months.

"I said I'd have to ask you first in case you might, you know—" her son's shrug couldn't quite hide his shyness "—like me to walk you down the aisle or something."

Tears sprang to Rachel's eyes, the offer was so unexpected, so moving.

Mark grinned. "I guess that's a yes?"

Blinking hard, she nodded and hugged him. "I'll keep you posted," she said gruffly. He felt so good, her son, hugging her back.

Devin joined them. "Can I have one of those, Heartbreaker?"

"A hug or a yes?" said Mark. The innocence of his query suggested a conspiracy.

"Both."

Releasing her traitorous son, Rachel glared in mock anger. "You said you'd be patient," she reminded Devin.

"Heartbreaker, you made up your mind weeks ago." His eyes were very green. "Now you're playing me."

"Well, you are fun to play with," she said reasonably, and escaped to congratulate the bridal couple. Dried lavender strewed the flagstones underfoot, its astringent scent mingling with those of the guests. In future she would always associate the old-fashioned fragrance with an anticipatory thrill.

Katherine and Matthew welcomed her with open arms.

"The celebrant's here for another half an hour, Rachel," hinted the bride.

"Why is everyone ganging up on me today?"

"Because I don't want to be the only normal person in this crazy family," said Matthew.

"So what number wife would that make you?" teased Zander, who was already hauling off his tie. He still hadn't entirely forgiven her for the swimming pool incident.

"The last," said Devin as he joined them with Mark.

Rachel frowned. "Excuse me, but I still haven't said yes yet."

"First a cop in the family, now a librarian?" Zander shook his head. "God help my image."

"Musicians are as much geeks as petrol heads and computer nerds," retorted Rachel, "but to repeat, I haven't said yes yet."

Zander turned to his brother. "You do know she'll be teaching you big words like *virtuous* and *respectable.*"

"I was working on those anyway," said Devin. "No, what the librarian's done is extend my emotional vocabulary." The teasing left his voice. "Taught me what love means."

Rachel stared at him. "Oh, you're not playing fair," she whispered.

He picked up her hand. "I know where I belong. With you. Now take off the coat, Rachel."

She dropped his hand, trying not to laugh. "You're incorrigible."

"So put me in my place again, Heartbreaker."

Rachel laid a hand over her heart, palm open, and tapped it gently. Devin's gaze followed the gesture then lifted swiftly, all the teasing gone.

He kissed her, right there among the guests, and it wasn't a chaste public kiss but a toe-curling, carnal one that left her disheveled and breathless. They broke apart amid laughter and cheers.

"Let's get out of here," he said huskily.

They'd started walking before she came to her senses. "We can't, we're at your mother's wedding.'

"That's right," Katherine called across the room. "Mark, go stop the celebrant from leaving." He tore out.

Rachel's heart started to pound. "That's crazy."

"You can't stay on the kids' carousel forever," said Devin. "It's time for the roller coaster."

She could barely breathe for the hammering against her ribs. She wanted to say yes but... Helplessly, she stared at him. "Devin..."

He pulled her aside. "Tell me," he said gently.

"How do you know this is different...from the others?"

"Those relationships started with a bang—literally—followed by rapid disillusionment. With you, the feelings only get stronger."

She remembered their first encounter and smiled. "You thought of me as a fossilized conservative—"

"Who transformed not herself, but me," he said seriously.

Mark returned, panting. "The celebrant's coming back."

Devin held out his hand to her, the dragon's tongue flicking the tip of that one knuckle. Outside, the clouds broke; rays of sunlight shimmered through the sheets of rain, tinting the bleak gray mist with gold, streaming in the window to burnish his smile, his hair, his eyes. "Be my wife," he said, "my one true love."

Rachel shrugged off her coat and handed it to her son, then took Devin's hand. "Yes."

Maybe she would get that birthday tattoo Trixie offered. Perhaps a tiny sword-wielding female knight on her rump. It was a joke that Devin would appreciate.

* * * * *

LA CINDERELLA

BY
AMANDA BERRY

All the characters in this book have no existence outside the imagination of the author, and have no relation whatsoever to anyone bearing the same name or names. They are not even distantly inspired by any individual known or unknown to the author, and all the incidents are pure invention.

First published in Great Britain 2011
by Mills & Boon, an imprint of Harlequin (UK) Limited,
Eton House, 18-24 Paradise Road, Richmond, Surrey TW9 1SR

© Amanda Berry 2010

ISBN: 978 0 263 88897 3

23-0711

Harlequin (UK) policy is to use papers that are natural, renewable and recyclable products and made from wood grown in sustainable forests. The logging and manufacturing processes conform to the legal environmental regulations of the country of origin.

Printed and bound in Spain
by Blackprint CPI, Barcelona

Dear Reader,

This is my first time writing one of these, so bear with me. *LA Cinderella* was a joy to write. In creating my story, I wanted to find a rich and powerful man. Royalty came to mind at first, but I wanted something more. For many years I've heard that Hollywood actors are our royalty in America. They deal with a very glamorous life that can also be hard on relationships because of the constant spotlight.

The setting made for great research. How often can you call watching *E!* research? Looking for restaurants and clubs in LA? Watching the Oscars? Very fun stuff. I've hopefully built a world that seems real and fascinating at the same time.

I have dreamed of being an author since I was a little girl, and I'm so proud that Chase and Natalie's story is my first book into that dream. *LA Cinderella* was fun to write. Chase and Natalie both shined with their love for each other.

I'd love to hear from my readers. Please visit my website at www.amanda-berry.com. Thank you.

Amanda Berry

To my family and friends, who help inspire me to be a better writer, and especially my mom, who gave me my first romance novel.

Chapter One

Natalie Collins tucked a strand of brown hair behind her ear as she shuffled down the hall. How on earth did she manage to get a job at Pandora Productions? Tall, swanky women and beyond-gorgeous men strode down the hall as if on a catwalk. It was hard not to gawk. Her conservative black pantsuit paled in comparison to the rainbow of colors.

The corner of a binder bit into her side. She shifted the two overstuffed binders, trying to balance them. Her glasses slipped down to the tip of her nose again. Of all the rotten luck, to have one of her contacts rip the day before the replacements arrived. Leaning her shoulders back, she tipped her head and tried to wiggle her glasses back in place. She shifted her load again to keep it from falling and ran into a wall.

Her glasses slid to the floor, but she kept hold of the binders. After steadying herself, she glared at the wall. Only the blob in front of her definitely wasn't a wall.

Oh, no, she'd run into someone, probably disrupting their strutting.

A hand gripped her elbow. "Are you all right?" The deep voice caused shivers to course down her back. "Let me take those."

The weight of the binders was lifted from her and she squinted to try to make the man in front of her come into focus. "I…I'm fine. I just lost my glasses."

"How very Velma of you," the voice said, followed by a chuckle.

The voice sounded so familiar, and Natalie's stomach started twisting. What if it was…no, it couldn't be. She heard the thud of her binders on a counter. The man-blob stooped down briefly.

Her heart sank as the glasses brought the face of her rescuer into sharp focus. Chase Booker. Unruly, sun-kissed blond hair fell on a face that angels would envy. Brilliant green eyes sparkled with amusement. A fan girl she was not. A squealing teenager she was not. A hot-blooded woman she unfortunately was.

So much for hoping he wouldn't be as attractive in person. She realized her mouth was agape and he'd put her glasses on her. A little piece inside of her trilled in happiness as his knuckles brushed her cheek.

Hot waves of embarrassment came up quickly, making her face burn. She closed her mouth. "Thank you, Mr. Booker. I'm terribly sorry I ran into you. I hope I didn't hurt you." Oh, somebody stop her from talking. Maybe the wall would open up and swallow her whole.

"No problem. Let me help you carry these."

"No, I've got it. Really." She tried to get there first and bumped up against his side. She knew from his last movie exactly how ripped that side was and the rebellious little piece inside her squealed in delight. She was really going to have to have a talk with herself when she got out of this.

"I insist."

With that face and that body, he could pretty much insist on anything and get it. Her face was probably as red as a beet by now. She dropped her gaze and backed away.

His smile took her breath away. "So where am I taking these?" He held the binders with one arm. His eyes met hers and she had to resist the urge to sigh.

She knew why so many leading ladies went out with him. One look from those emerald eyes and they were goners. She fussed with an imaginary piece of lint to break the contact. "To accounting. My desk is outside Mr. Morrison's."

"You're new to Pandora Productions." It was a statement of fact, so Natalie wasn't sure she was supposed to answer. He led the way down the corridor.

Natalie fought to keep her gaze on his broad shoulders and off his legendary butt. Also very prominent in his last film. She cleared her throat. "Accountant. I'm the new accountant."

He set the books on the desk and turned back to her. Could beauty blind? He held out his hand. "Welcome on board."

She took his hand and a pulse ran through her. Would she ever get her face to stop burning? Probably not with him around. "Thank you, Mr. Booker."

"Call me Chase." He released her hand.

Had he held her hand a little longer than normal?

She gripped her own hands together tightly. Attraction to a magnificent man was perfectly normal. She would definitely get over it after working with him for a while. After all, he was probably spoiled, used to getting what he wanted, overbearing and his eyes were gorgeous. She had to snap out of it. "Thank you…Chase."

He smiled again and she could have sworn she saw a spark of interest in his eyes. Not possible.

"I look forward to working with you…"

"Natalie Collins."

"Natalie." The word rolled off his tongue like a caress. Her knees turned to jelly. It was one thing to drool over him in a movie, but to drool on her boss wasn't professional at all and not a good way to start a business relationship.

She had better get over this quick.

With a cup of steaming black coffee in one hand, Chase Booker stared at the mounds of paper on his desk. Two months of filming on location had taken its toll on the wooden surface. He swallowed some of the hot liquid and glanced at the clock.

In five minutes Martin Morrison, his CFO, and Robert Addler, his partner, were supposed to come in for a meeting. The warmth of the coffee filled him even as the caffeine seeped into his veins. His flight from London had been delayed, so he was dealing with jet lag and fatigue.

The shoot had gone well and even though his production company, Pandora Productions, hadn't produced the action film, he'd loved every minute of it. Especially his married costar. For once he hadn't had to pry off the tentacles of an actress trying to make a name for herself.

After the breakup with Alexis Brandt, he needed something different. It was always the same. Some attractive, no-name actress needed a step up from the D list to the A list. Knowing his track record for giving his girlfriend that extra boost to her career, the actress sets her sights on him. Regardless if he was single or still involved.

He rubbed the bridge of his nose. Maybe it was time for something different. Large brown eyes behind glasses flashed in his mind. The little accountant. Barely over five feet tall. Her brown hair pulled back in a ponytail.

He smiled. In the movies, the librarian takes off her glasses and lets down her hair and she's the most beautiful woman alive. Natalie Collins may not be that type of beauty, but there was something about her. He couldn't put his finger on it.

Maybe the jet lag had gotten to him, but she seemed like the type of woman he wouldn't mind coming home to. Soft eyes not jaded by Hollywood. An innocence the women he went out with only pretended to have. Totally wrong for him, and he was totally wrong for her.

Even if the spark of awareness hadn't been so intense, he still would have found himself captivated by the upturned corner of her pink lips. He'd been down that path before. A path he had no intention of going down again.

A sharp rap on the door brought him out of his brooding thoughts.

"Come in."

Robert came through the door first with his trademark easy smile and loose gait. Chase stood and gripped the hand he offered.

"Good to have you back." Robert's hand tightened on his.

"It's good to be back. I missed the sun."

Robert stepped back and Chase noticed Martin lingering in the doorway.

"Martin. How's our company doing?" Chase gestured for the man to come in.

"How was your flight, sir?" Martin came forward and sat in the chair, shuffling his papers. He never met Chase's eyes. Robert had assured Chase it was just him. When Chase was gone, the CFO didn't act like a mouse in front of a cat. Star envy or some such bull.

"A hassle, but it's over." Chase sank into his chair as Robert sat next to Martin.

"How was filming?" Robert sprawled back in the chair. "Another Oscar award-winning performance?"

"I don't think *Assassin's Target* is Oscar-caliber, but it was great to get back out there. I forgot how much I missed it. The money was nice, unlike *Night Blooming*." Their production couldn't seem to find its way out of the red into the black.

Martin cleared his throat and shuffled through his papers again.

"Do you have the numbers, Martin?" Chase glanced at the stack on the man's lap.

Martin riffled through and pulled out two sheets. His hand shook as he handed one to Robert and passed one across the desk. "These are the preliminary numbers. There are still a few receipts outstanding and a couple of expense reports we are waiting on."

Chase glanced down. The numbers above the line didn't tell him much, but the number in parenthesis at the bottom indicated they'd run over by a hundred thousand dollars instead of making money. He slammed the paper down on his desk, causing Martin to jump.

"How can this be?" He met both men's eyes before looking at the paper again. The numbers hadn't changed. "*Night Blooming* was number one at the box office for several weeks, plus the early release to DVD. The Golden Globe nominations and the Oscar talk. We should be in the black, not the red."

Martin shifted in his chair. "There were costs we hadn't anticipated."

"How could that be?" Chase leaned back in his chair. Every extra dollar counted. The loss would mean one less project they could back this year. "This isn't our first film. Robert, you came up with the budget. You're not green."

"I don't know, Chase," Robert said. "My budgets are pretty tight. The only thing I can think of is to have accounting look into it."

Chase turned back to Martin.

Martin cleared his throat. "Um. I hired a new assistant who will be auditing this budget first thing. I need to start working on the financial reporting for the month."

The little accountant. His pulse jumped. "This is our priority, Martin. We need to get to the bottom of this."

"Natalie!"

Natalie cringed as Martin barreled toward her desk. The CFO liked to yell at her when telling her to do something. He wasn't demeaning or anything, just loud. If anyone was nearby, they always turned to look.

"Yes, Mr. Morrison?" She placed the papers in her work tray and waited for the next project about to be yelled at her.

"Come into my office." He pounded past her desk and into his office.

She grabbed her notebook and pen and followed him.

"Close the door."

She shut the door and sat down across from him, her pen ready. The reams of papers and folders built up on Martin's desk looked as if at any moment they could topple over. He slammed the files down on top of one of his stacks. She jumped. A few papers lifted slightly but didn't dare move from their assigned spots.

He turned as if just noticing her. His brown eyes narrowed and then cleared. "Do you remember when I interviewed you how I told you we need to audit the expenses on productions?"

"Yes, sir." Experience she needed if she wanted to move up in the accounting field. She hadn't wanted to go into audit or tax after college like many of her classmates. She wanted to be like the man in front of her. Well, maybe not exactly like him, but the opportunity to be more than just a staff accountant had been irresistible.

Reaching behind him, he picked up a large folder and handed it across the desk to her. He leaned down, picked up a binder and another folder twice as thick and passed them, as well. The pile on her lap now reached her chin.

"Print out the expenses on *Night Blooming*. These should be all the files, but you may have to pull some more out of the drawers. Go through each expense and make sure you have a corresponding paid invoice and that invoice is for *Night Blooming*. It should have a charge number and be signed by myself or Robert Addler. Any questions?"

"No, Mr. Morrison."

"You've been authorized to work overtime to get this done. I expect you to work at least fifty hours this week and next."

"Of course." It was already Tuesday. She'd only worked seven hours yesterday because Mr. Morrison had sent her home early. She'd have to work over ten hours a day for the remainder of the week to catch up. Not that she had much to go home to. Her roommate, Rachel, who had a life, was always traveling or staying out late.

"Put aside everything else. Mr. Booker wants the numbers as soon as possible."

The sound of his name sent a little shiver through her, but she shook it off.

Martin waved his hand in dismissal, and Natalie hefted the files into her arms. Balancing them precariously, she opened the door and managed to make it to her desk without losing anything. The stack looked imposing as she sat behind it.

Pulling out her keyboard, she typed in the parameters to run the report. She glanced up as Chase's door opened and he stepped out. Her stomach tightened. So much for an easy week.

Chapter Two

Natalie had to go home. The pile of expenses looked as large as when she started, but her stomach growled and her vision was getting blurry. Her computer clock read 8:00. She started to restack her work so she would know where she was in the morning.

Everyone else had already left, including Mr. Morrison. A door opened and footsteps sounded on the tile floor. Her pulse leapt. Who else was here this late?

Startled, she stood to glance down the hallway and saw the broad shoulders of Chase. Her pulse jumped again as she sat back down. She hurried to get her purse from the bottom drawer. Maybe she could beat him out and not have to talk to him. She was so tired she was bound to make a fool of herself.

Sliding the drawer shut, she tried to move away, but her pant leg had caught in it. She cursed silently and bent down to fix it.

"I thought I was the last one here." Chase's voice rippled over her spine like a light caress.

Darn it. "I was just leaving." Her pant leg freed, she looked at Chase and her breath caught. Even fatigued, he was magnificent.

His smile lit his face. "I'll walk you out, then."

Wait…what? "Okay." She could do this. She'd walked to her car with coworkers before. Of course, none of them made her feel weak in the knees and tingly in places she'd rather not mention.

Her hand shaking, she reached to turn off her desk lamp, but it tilted to the side. His hand reached out and steadied it before it fell.

"I got it."

Was there a shade deeper than beet-red? She clung to her purse as if it were a shield as she hurried around the desk. She barely came up to his chin. Not that she wasn't used to being short; it was just that he made her aware of how small she was compared to him.

"So how long have you been working here?" he asked as they started to walk.

"About a month now."

Reaching around her, he flicked off the light for the hallway they'd just left. Her nose filled with his subtle cologne, spicy and rich, tantalizing. She wanted to lean into him and… Whoa.

"Do you like working for us?" He didn't seem to notice her distraction.

"Yes, it's a great opportunity."

They stopped at the door to the outside. Before he could reach across her again, she flicked off the switch and smiled uncertainly.

The only light came from the emergency backup in the

corner. His hand gripped the doorknob, and he stopped. His eyes gazed down into hers, and the air was sucked out of the room.

His mouth opened as if to say something but then shut again. Her heart hammered against her chest. Finally he smiled and turned the knob.

"Sorry, I'm a bit jet-lagged." He held the door open while she passed through. He closed the door and locked it. "I had to get through some files on my desk. If I'd been at home, I'd already be in bed."

An image of him on black satin sheets raced through her mind. She swallowed hard. "Well, I won't keep you. My car's right there. Good night, Mr. Booker." She started to walk away.

"Chase. Good night, Natalie."

She could feel his eyes on her back as she walked. Almost dropping her keys, she finally got the car door unlocked and slipped inside. She glanced back to where he stood in the streetlight.

He appeared puzzled about something, but he smiled and his face cleared. He lifted his hand and waved. She waved back and pulled out of the parking lot.

Ignoring the man in a parked car with a camera strap around his neck, Chase punched in the gate code and pulled through. The garage door opened and he pulled the BMW into its spot next to his Aston Martin. He wasn't surprised to see the paparazzi on his street. They practically lived here with so many big names on the block.

He'd only let the paparazzi get to him once before he realized that his life really was different from everyone else's. Back when he was just a boy in love with a girl.

He walked into the dark kitchen. Its massive size and

the lack of light made it cold and unwelcoming. Maybe sleep would help get his little accountant out of his head. Natalie's large brown eyes sat in his mind like a warm beacon. Most likely due to jet lag.

Distraction was needed. In the morning he'd wake up and figure out where to go this weekend, who to go with and who to leak the information to. With a new movie in the editing room, he needed his name to be on the tip of everyone's tongue.

Going out with him was a first-class ticket to any actress, but hell for a normal girl like Natalie. His high school girlfriend, Becca, had been like Natalie. Not looking for glory or her fifteen minutes in the limelight. Becca couldn't handle the spotlight. The people digging into her past and her family's past to figure out why Chase Booker, son of three-time Academy Award-winning Matt Booker and screen diva Madeline Caine, was interested in her.

In the spotlight before birth, Chase grew up and became used to the attention. Unfortunately Becca hadn't.

He checked the answering machine.

"Hi, Chase. Alexis. I heard you were done filming in London. We should get together this weekend. I'm also available Sunday if you still need a date."

Sunday was the Golden Globes. Alexis, like so many others, struggled to get ahead in a business where publicity was key. He'd liked Alexis and they had a great time together. He'd been a stopping point on her climb to fame, and when she decided it was time to move on, he hadn't wanted to stop her.

She knew how the business worked and hadn't minded the persistence of the cameras. In fact, she'd relished the attention. It had helped her land a starring role, but she wasn't the kind of woman he wanted to come home to.

When they broke up, he found himself wanting more. He wanted a woman who could be with him for who he was and not for the fame he could bring her. He wanted something simple for once in his life. He wanted someone who made him feel alive. And let him be just Chase Booker.

His attraction to Natalie was something new and unexpected. She tantalized his senses and pretended not to be interested. It intrigued him and made him want to explore further, but he had no right to bring her into his life and into the sharp focus of the camera lens.

By Friday, Natalie was ready to pull her hair out. The numbers swirled in front of her eyes even while she slept. Her contacts hadn't arrived, and she was tempted to duct-tape her glasses onto her head to keep them from falling down.

The government could come in and declare her desk a disaster zone. Precarious stacks of papers covered every available surface and spread out along the floor. She'd been over the numbers a hundred times, but still couldn't get to that final number. Something was missing.

"How's it coming along?" Martin shut his door and turned the key in the lock. Even though she was staying late, he left every day at five o'clock on the dot.

"I've got a few more accounts to go over and the expenses that just came in. I also have the actors' expense reports." She moved a paper from one pile to the next.

"Very good. Here's a list of all the actors who worked on *Night Blooming*." The list was three pages, each filled with double columns of names. "Some of our extras had expenses, too."

Natalie stifled a groan as she thought of all the expense reports for the six months of shooting.

"Have a good weekend." Martin shouted behind him as he hurried toward the exit.

"Yeah, right," she said to herself. She set the list aside and plunged back into the pile she'd been working on.

The next time she surfaced, she glanced at the clock. Almost eight. Every night, Chase had insisted on walking her to her car. She'd tried to work later and hoped he'd leave, but he'd wait. She couldn't leave any earlier or she wouldn't get her hours in, and she refused to work on Saturday.

Every night she figured was another opportunity to humiliate herself. It was only a matter of time before he caught her with a goofy grin on her face when she looked at him.

She'd seen him already today. Every time he'd walked past her desk, she'd stopped working and watched. She'd tried not to, but her nose would catch the faint whisper of his cologne, and her head would jerk up in response. And there it would be, his behind clad in denim. He wore jeans the way jeans were meant to be worn.

How many times did the man really need to go past her desk during the day? Seriously. Sure her desk was in the main thoroughfare of the office, but still…

Every night it was awkward walking with him. He always asked how her day went and was amazingly nice. He seemed genuinely interested in her work life. She had hoped to be over her little infatuation, but the guy wasn't demanding and didn't expect star treatment.

He seemed really down to earth for someone who had a star on the Hollywood Walk of Fame and probably an Oscar or Golden Globe for every room of his house. Genuine. She hadn't expected him to walk her to her car or hold the door open for her.

She glanced at the clock again. She could sneak out a

few minutes early, and she wouldn't have to see him again until Monday.

She slid her chair out and reached for her purse. The computer beeped as the screen went black. She winced and glanced down the hall toward his office. Nothing.

After grabbing her purse, she shut off the light and rushed down the hallway. Every few seconds she glanced over her shoulder to make sure he wasn't there. At the door, she heaved a sigh of relief.

With one last look back before opening the door, she was home free.

"Excuse me," a soft, feminine voice said.

Startled, Natalie let out a small scream and almost dropped her keys. Alexis Brandt stood in the now open doorway. From her blond hair to her perfectly manicured fingers, she was everything rich and fabulous. She was also Chase's last girlfriend. Ex-girlfriend, if the tabloids were to be believed. Natalie's roommate Rachel kept her informed of everything going on with her boss and everyone else in Hollywood.

"Is Chase still here?" Her voice was low and husky. Her perfume wafted in waves of floral scent to Natalie.

"I don't—"

"I'm here, Alexis." His voice was directly behind Natalie.

Her heart slammed against her chest. She'd almost made it. Alexis swept through the door, brushed past Natalie and wrapped her arms around Chase.

"Darling." She kissed the air next to his cheeks. "I was so glad you called."

Natalie tried to fade into the wall and slowly slide toward the open door.

"Natalie." His voice was stern as if she'd done something wrong. Sure she'd tried to sneak out before he had a chance to walk her out, but he obviously had his hands full now.

"Yes?" Natalie didn't dare turn around and watch the blonde pressing her over-endowed body into his.

"Wait here for a minute." His words were directed at Natalie and he meant business.

She sighed and gazed longingly at her car a mere half block away in the parking lot.

"Natalie?"

She glanced back. Alexis had moved behind Chase, feigning interest in a picture on the wall. Chase's eyes warned Natalie not to disobey him.

"Yeah, I'll wait." She let the door slide closed and leaned against the wall as Chase led Alexis down the hall to his office.

He was her boss. She shouldn't be acting this way, but every time he came near her, her instincts said *run*. Every time he accidentally brushed against her or held the door open, she couldn't help thinking he was interested in her, which couldn't happen in a million years. But it confused her and she didn't like anything confusing in her life. She stared at the second hand on her watch.

He'd only said to wait a minute. She glanced to make sure he wasn't coming yet. When a minute was up, she was out of here. Thirty seconds. She'd have all weekend to try to get over her crush on him. Twenty seconds. Almost there, come on. Fifteen. Ten.

Chapter Three

Chase smiled as Natalie leaned against the wall staring at her watch. Probably counting down the seconds. His little accountant had tried to leave without him. He justified walking her out every night because she left so late.

But in reality, he just wanted to be close to her. Even if he couldn't think about being anything more than her boss, he couldn't resist the calmness and sweetness she exuded in spite of her nervousness. Not to mention the gentle swaying of her hips, the curve of her calves. And he could feel like just a normal guy walking a girl to her car.

She was so focused on the watch she didn't hear him slip up next to her.

"Ha." She smiled and looked up. The smile disappeared and a look of chagrin crossed her face. "Oh."

"You do know this neighborhood isn't safe at night."

She dropped her eyes and her fingers fiddled with her purse. "I guess."

He leaned across her to push open the door. Awareness singed him where her body brushed against his. The clean scent of her floated in the air with just a touch of sweet, fruity scent, maybe strawberry, from her hair. Her gaze jerked to his. Had she felt the sizzle, too?

Her tongue darted out to wet her lips. His body tightened. He fought against the urge to drag her into his arms and find out if her lips tasted as sweet as she smelled. She was his employee, and he was her boss.

Clearing his throat, he said, "How was your day?"

She took his offer of escape and slipped out the door. "It was fine."

Every night, it was "fine." He wondered if she would ever just tell him about her day. He'd seen her working hard all day long. Strands of hair had escaped her usual ponytail and fell softly around her face. His fingers itched to push it behind her ears or release it all from the ponytail and sink into the rich strands.

He followed her out to her car. Her blue business suit and low heels were a refreshing change from the plunging necklines and stilettos Alexis wore. During the day every time he saw her, his imagination ran rampant wondering what Natalie wore under those clothes. The cut of her suit left a lot to the imagination, and he had a great one.

"Thank you," she said, not turning. Her keys jingled.

"Natalie." He wanted to see her wide brown eyes one more time to get him through his weekend spent with the privileged and the jaded.

The keys fell to the ground as she looked at him over her shoulder. Her eyes widened. He stooped down to pick up the keys, using the distraction to keep himself from kissing her until her eyes melted like chocolate.

He stood and handed her the keys.

"Thanks." Her cheeks and neck were red. How far did the blush go?

He stuffed his hands in his pockets. "Have a good weekend."

"You, too." She stared up at him.

Her lips were barely parted. Mentally, he shook himself. She worked for him and he was mooning over her like a teenager. *Move, you fool*. He backed up a step, giving her room to open her door and slide into her car. He walked back to the building, pausing to watch as she sped off into the night.

When he entered his office, Alexis pounced from the chair. "There's this new part that I'd be perfect for. The Golden Globes are Sunday. If we're seen together there, it could help my chances. We can say we're still friends. We are still friends, aren't we?" She pouted her famous pout.

He sighed, thinking of the woman he'd just left who didn't want anything from him. Not even for him to walk her out to her car.

Alexis continued to chatter about going and being seen, but he couldn't concentrate on her prattle. What would Natalie do if he asked her out? What if like other stars he had a relationship that wasn't broadcast over every available airwave?

Alexis would serve his purpose of getting the paparazzi to stop guessing who he was going after next. He could see if this spark between him and Natalie could be coaxed into a flame, which was a ridiculous thought. Maybe he just needed a break from dating. Alexis would keep the other women at bay without putting the pressure of a relationship on him.

"Are you even listening to me, Chase?"

He brought his attention back to the woman seated across from him. Every hot-blooded male wanted Alexis and would do anything to go out with her, but Chase wanted more than stunning good looks. Innocence and intelligence wrapped up in a small frame lingered in his mind.

"Sure, Alexis. We can go and be seen."

"I have the perfect thing for this weekend."

Natalie rolled her eyes to the ceiling. "I'm not going out. I just finished working an eleven-hour day."

Rachel tended to be the life of the party and tried to drag Natalie with her. A habit that started when they'd roomed together in college and continued when they'd both decided to stay in L.A. after graduation. Rachel would just have to go without her this time.

Rachel came out of the kitchen holding a stack of DVDs and a bowl of popcorn. "Nope, we're staying in. I've got ice cream in the freezer, too."

"Chocolate?"

"Of course. Pick the first movie." Rachel tossed the DVDs on the couch next to Natalie.

Picking up the first one, she groaned. *She didn't.* Natalie spread out the three DVDs. Emerald eyes stared at her from the cover of every DVD. *She did.* Natalie sighed in resignation—so much for getting Chase Booker out of her mind this weekend. She picked up *Into the Hereafter.*

Rachel plopped down next to her. Her blue eyes sparkled with mischief. "I couldn't let you be the only one staring at that hot bod all day." She reached across Natalie and snatched *Riddle Beach.* She turned over the DVD. "This one has nudity. I vote for this one first."

"Fine." Just what she needed—an image of what he

looked like undressed for Monday morning. That wouldn't be at all awkward. *What'd you do over the weekend, Natalie? Oh, stared at your naked body on DVD.*

She grabbed the burgundy throw from the arm of the couch and helped herself to a handful of popcorn. At least there wasn't a chance of this Chase catching her looking at his hot bod.

The opening scene came on the TV. Alexis was the female lead in this movie. Her body flowed across the room with grace and elegance in her forties dress. Her outrageous red lips jumped from the screen.

Natalie's hand formed a fist around her blanket. "Alexis Brandt came by the office tonight." The words spewed from her mouth before she could stop herself.

"Oh, do tell. Dirt before it even hits the stands. How cool is that? Were they, you know, together?" Rachel tucked her legs under her. She couldn't spend an hour without checking the entertainment blogs or news.

Tightness spread through Natalie's chest. Maybe she was coming down with something. She reached over for her drink and took a sip before answering. "I don't know. She did the air kiss, and I left them alone in the office."

"A little office nookie." Rachel's voice quivered with excitement. "Oh, I bet they are having sorry-things-didn't-work-out sex all over the office. I wonder if they'll go to the Globes together."

Natalie gagged on a piece of popcorn. Rachel thumped her hard on the back. Chase having sex in the office—yet another image Natalie didn't want in her brain for Monday morning. Or any morning, for that matter.

On the TV, Chase walked on the screen. Dressed in a long trench coat and derby hat, he sat at a table to watch Alexis's character sing a soulful version of "Fever."

"That's probably not even her voice," Natalie murmured under her breath.

"Is he really that good-looking in person?" Rachel didn't wait for her answer.

Of course, Natalie would have had to admit he looked better in real life. On screen he was larger than life, but in reality, he seemed like a normal guy. A gorgeous normal guy. She could feel the heat flood her cheeks from just thinking about him.

"We have to have lunch this week. I can come to the office to pick you up and try to snag a view of Mr. Sexiest Man Alive for myself."

"I don't think that's such a good idea. I have a lot of work to do next week." Natalie reached for another handful of popcorn.

Rachel was more Chase's type than she was. Her dark hair never had a strand out of place. Rachel also had killer curves. Natalie knew from experience that men wanted Rachel.

Not that Natalie wanted Chase to want her.

"It's just lunch. Nobody would fault you for going to lunch. Besides—" she shoved her hand out toward the TV, "—you can't deny me my one opportunity to meet the man of my dreams."

Natalie snorted. "I thought the man of your dreams was Matt Damon."

"Well, normally, but since Matt isn't available I'll settle for Chase. C'mon, Natalie, you know you can't say no."

A fact her roommate used against her constantly. But one she wasn't willing to fight about right now, or anytime, for that matter. Confrontation made her ill. The camera pulled in tight to Chase's eyes, and she coughed to cover the sigh that tried to escape.

"You know I'll just keep pestering…"

"Fine, we'll do lunch, but I meet you at the door and if he isn't around, we leave. Now, can we just watch the movie?"

Rachel squealed and shook Natalie's arm, knocking popcorn all over the floor. "I get to meet Chase Booker. Oh, this is the scene where he walks across the room naked. Shhh."

Natalie wanted to roll her eyes, but couldn't take them off Chase's body. It had to be touched up in editing or a body double. No one could look that good in real life.

Of course, Monday morning, Natalie found herself staring at Chase as he walked by. The images from the movies played in her head. She tried to detect a difference in the walk to see if they'd used a body double. But his swagger was definitely unique and the perfect butt was again outlined in jeans that should be a sin for him to wear.

"How's the audit going?" Martin's stern voice rang out behind her.

She jumped in her chair. Her face flushed from being caught watching the owner's butt as he strolled down the hallway. Picking up a few papers, she turned. "I've been making progress. I've pulled all the expense reports and started itemizing them in a spreadsheet."

His mouth tightened. "Good. I expect you to continue working late until we get this thing figured out."

"Yes, Mr. Morrison." Though it wasn't really "we" working this out.

He nodded to her and returned to his office. Turning back to her desk, she lost herself in expense reports for all sorts of weird things: haircuts, manicures, massages, personal trainers. Not so weird for a Hollywood production, but really weird to her, especially the amounts for each one.

When she got to a claim for toilet paper, she stopped.

Sliding off her glasses and setting them on the desk, she closed her eyes and rubbed them. The numbers had begun to swim on the page. In her business class, they'd gone over legitimate expenses. Even though this was a movie set, the expenses were ludicrous. Who needed twenty-four dollars' worth of toilet paper for two days at a shoot? Maybe he had diarrhea. She smiled slightly.

"You look like you're in a good mood." Chase's voice curled around her ear and slid down her back, leaving a pleasant shiver in its path.

Resisting the urge to groan, she uncovered her eyes to stare at the blurry blob of Chase Booker.

"Did Velma lose her glasses again?"

She could hear the smile in his voice. Patting the desk in front of her, she gripped her glasses and forced them back onto her face. Maybe she'd have been better off not wearing them. At least when he was a blob, the only thing seducing her was his voice.

"No, I was just…" Her gaze dropped down to the huge amount of paper on her desk.

"Trying to find your way out of the recycling bin?"

Her gaze met his. The smile on her face froze as the unbidden image of him naked on the TV screen flashed in front of her eyes. The heat crept up from her chest until she swore it was going to pop out of the top of her head.

"I like it when you do that." His voice was soft and intimate.

Oh, God. What did he like? That she was visualizing him naked? Was she that obvious?

"There it goes." His eyes sparkled.

"What?" she managed to get her thick tongue to say.

"Your smile."

Seriously, flames should be bursting from her skull any

moment. Her papers—she could look at her papers. Numbers didn't make her heart race, her palms sweaty or her mouth dry. She couldn't take her eyes from his, though.

"Have lunch with me."

"What? Why?"

When he smiled, his eyes lit from within and crinkles formed at their corners. Why was he asking her? Did he do that with all the employees? Was she reading too much into his question? Was his interest in her only as an employee?

"There you are, Natalie. I waited up at the front like you said, but… Oh, hi." Rachel stopped next to Natalie's desk, turned on her hundred-watt smile and tossed her perfect black locks over her shoulder.

Natalie kept her eyes on Chase, trying to read his expression. Once men saw Rachel, Natalie became invisible. Or worse, they pretended to be interested in her to get close to Rachel.

She knew she shouldn't have let Rachel talk her into lunch.

"I'm Rachel McAllister." She stuck out her hand to Chase.

"Chase Booker."

Rachel didn't let go of his hand right away. Natalie's stomach clenched. Even though she knew Chase couldn't be interested in her as more than an employee, she didn't want him to be interested in Rachel.

"You were in our apartment all weekend." Rachel smiled as she released his hand.

Natalie choked back a groan and wished the paper would come alive and eat her whole right this minute.

"'Our apartment'?" Chase raised an eyebrow.

"Natalie and I had a movie fest this weekend." Rachel kept grinning. "We watched all your movies. Since it was newly released we watched *Night Blooming*, even though you weren't in it. The award ceremony was spectacular. I loved your tux. Congrats on the wins." She batted her eyelashes up at him.

Natalie pushed back her chair abruptly and stood. Her boss did not need to know that she'd ogled him all weekend. "We were just heading to lunch. We'd better hurry if you want to get back to work on time."

Rachel turned bright blue eyes to her. "We don't have to leave right now."

Ugh. Natalie didn't like the look on Rachel's face as Rachel turned her smile back to Chase. Frustrated, Natalie blew her bangs out of her face and glanced at Chase. His teasing grin had returned.

"Thank you," he said politely to Rachel before turning back to Natalie. "So, Natalie, which movie was your favorite?" His interest was far too intense. Was it because of Rachel or because he was interested in her?

Resisting the urge to shrink behind Rachel's tall figure, Natalie quickly ran through the titles in her head, trying to remember which one he was completely clothed throughout the entire film. "*Night Blooming*." Ha.

His eyes focused in on her lips and she realized she was smiling. His comment earlier froze the smile on her face. What if he really liked her?

"Don't be silly, Natalie. Of course, she loves *Riddle Beach*. I mean who doesn't." Rachel's eyes practically devoured Chase. "After all, how often does a woman get a feast for her eyes?"

Screw the papers; maybe the floor would swallow her whole. She tugged on Rachel's arm, trying to get her to back off and just go, but Rachel jerked her arm back.

"I figured Natalie's favorite would be *If Only*."

Her eyes snapped up to Chase's face in amazement. To

be honest, it *was* her favorite. She loved the story. The love, the purity, it gave her body tingles just thinking of the kiss at the end. Such perfect buildup, such beautiful emotions. Such an unattainable love.

Her mouth opened, a thousand questions on her tongue tumbling over each other to find their way to the surface. She clamped her mouth shut before they spilled out.

She managed to get out, "We should go."

"Natalie, stop being rude. Of course, Natalie loves that one, too. It never leaves the DVD player. That last scene… Natalie, what's that last line?"

Natalie pressed her lips together. Not that Rachel would notice, as her full attention remained on Chase.

Rachel continued without even blinking an eye. "Oh, what is it? There's that song going on in the background, and she's almost out the door, but she stops when he says it? Natalie, you know what it is."

"'I can't lose you.'"

Natalie's head jerked up at Chase's voice. He wasn't looking at Rachel. He was looking at her. His green eyes touched her so deep. Her breath caught in her throat.

"Yeah, that's it. But there's more," Rachel said.

Chase continued as if Rachel weren't there. "'I'd give up my entire world for one more moment in your arms. One more night by your side. I want it all. All of you. I want you to have it all. All my love, all my heart, all of me.'"

Her purse hit her foot, jerking her out of the moment. It felt like he was really saying it to her, not Elizabeth, the heroine in the movie. Which was ridiculous even to think. Actors acted. He was just acting. She pressed her glasses back up her nose and reached down to pick up her purse.

"Wow, you are good." Rachel's appreciation was too much for Natalie. This whole situation was too much for her.

"Let's go, Rachel. Chase has more important things to do." Again Natalie took hold of Rachel's arm. "'Bye, Chase."

"Okay, okay, I'm coming." Rachel finally took the hint. "It was nice meeting you, Chase."

"Natalie?"

She risked looking at him again. The flames engulfing her face hadn't died down the entire time. "Yes?"

"Think about what I said." He nodded to Rachel and headed down the hallway.

Chapter Four

Think about what he said? How could she think of anything else? Even with Rachel prattling on across the table about how surprised she was that Chase looked that good in real life, she couldn't get those words out of her head.

Maybe he didn't mean to make her obsess about the ending lines that gave her that feel-good feeling when she needed a pick-me-up. Seriously, the man did not need writers making him sound romantic when he could just say "come here" to a woman and she'd be all over him. But if it wasn't that, what else had he said?

Besides, the kind of love found on the movie screen was nowhere near what real life was like. Men like Chase didn't go for women like her unless something more was going on, or it was part of a script.

"Oh, on the blogosphere this morning, Chase and Alexis were seen at Hyde on Friday night and at Spago on

Saturday. Not to mention the Golden Globes. God, I wish I had her body and that dress. Wow." Rachel took a bite of salad. "Mmm. Their reps wouldn't comment on their relationship. You know what that means?"

Maybe it was lunch. That's right. He'd asked her to lunch sometime right before Rachel had appeared. Probably a thing he did with all new employees. It wasn't like she was special in some way.

"Natalie. Natalie!"

"What?" She focused on Rachel's eyes. Rachel's eyebrows were raised and she stared at Natalie like she was from outer space.

"Where are you?"

"What do you mean? I'm right here. With you. Having lunch." Natalie glanced down at her plate, surprised to find it still full.

"No, you weren't. You were in la-la land." Rachel speared a cherry tomato with her fork. "Besides, you didn't answer my question."

Natalie sifted through the last bits of conversation she'd heard. Something about Alexis and Chase? *You know what that means?* "What does it mean?"

"It means that Alexis and Chase are on again. That's the way of the world, you know. They break up, and then after their next big movie, they get back together and finally get married. Maybe have a kid, if it's fashionable at the time. Then have a messy divorce where they swear they'll stay friends for the children."

"So, Alexis and Chase are an item again?" Natalie ignored the knot in her chest.

"Of course. But they won't say anything about it for a month or so."

"Oh." She tamped down the disappointment that rose to

the surface. She knew she'd been dreaming, but… Okay, so she'd hoped a little of his attention had been because of that spark in his eyes. Not that she was any good at reading men, but maybe, just maybe someone like Chase for two seconds thought of someone like her.

She stabbed her fork into a pile of lettuce and shoved the whole thing in her mouth. It tasted bitter.

Uh-oh. Natalie reread the numbers and double-checked the signatures. *Uh-oh.* She picked up the expense report on top of the other stack and lined up the signatures again. Not good.

"I'm heading out."

She snapped the papers together and leaned over her stacks as Martin walked out of his office. Wide-eyed, she tried to keep her face neutral and forced a slight smile.

His eyes narrowed slightly. "Is there anything you need?"

"Of course not. Why would there be anything I need? I'm good. I'm real good." *Stop babbling!* Clamping her lips together, she smiled tightly again.

"Fine." He tucked a newspaper under his arm and narrowed his eyes on her again. "How's the audit going?"

Realizing she was hovering over her work like a pro-tective mother, she stiffly leaned back in her chair. Every night he asked the same thing and she was beginning to understand why. "Fine, I'm almost done with this stack and then I've got those over there to go through, but everything looks fine. Just fine."

"Well, as long as you finish by Monday. Chase and Robert want a full report." He locked his office door. "Have a good night."

He disappeared down the hall. She breathed a sigh of relief. Glancing left and right down the hallway to ensure no one was watching, she picked up the last document she'd been working on.

After working through tons of documents with Martin Morrison's signature and handwriting, she was confident she recognized his writing. Paul Alan, an extra, had similar handwriting and had been paid in cash per Mr. Morrison's instructions.

So had another extra, Jan Robbins. The handwriting is what caught her attention. Both Jan and Paul had eerily similar handwriting, and it bore a strong resemblance to Mr. Morrison's.

She needed to know how cash payments were handled. Glancing over her shoulder at the closed door, she knew she couldn't ask Mr. Morrison even if he were here. If he were guilty of fraud, he'd know she was onto him, and she'd get fired. If she told him what she suspected and she was wrong, she'd still end up fired. Being fired a month into her first job would look really bad on her résumé.

It was after five-thirty on Thursday, which meant the office was practically empty with the exception of her. And possibly Chase. The office staff left early on Thursdays for happy hour.

She hadn't been alone much with Chase this week. Even though she felt relieved, that little part of her couldn't help being disappointed. The past few nights, Robert Addler had walked out with her and Chase, which was perfect for her. Chase couldn't bring up lunch again if they weren't alone. Unless it was purely business. So if he hadn't brought it up, did that mean it was personal?

Robert wasn't here today. She stood and stretched her stiff muscles. Maybe she could just root through the files and figure it out. She stared at the large filing cabinets that stored this year's bills. Four long drawers filled with paperwork sorted by vendor.

Maybe if she knew the rules on picking up cash and how it was given to the extras… She heaved a sigh. Walking around her desk, she stared down the hallway to the only light left on in the office. Her heart thudded against her chest. He would know how the process worked. Besides, she'd have to tell someone sometime. Someone above Mr. Morrison.

Wondering if she was making a huge mistake, she headed to Chase's office. Even with the little trill of anticipation to see him again, she walked slowly down the hall. Not only was she going to accuse the CFO, who had been here a lot longer than herself, of embezzling, but she had to make sure she didn't make a fool out of herself over Chase and her little attraction.

Every time she was near him, her body responded as if she were a cat in heat, and her brain went on vacation. She hadn't figured out how to control it yet.

Natalie paused outside the slightly open door.

His low voice reached her ears, freezing her hand in mid-knock. "Alexis, I don't think so…. No… I know how important this is to you, but I just… Yes… Have you tried Robert?… No, I'm not saying… If you would just… Sure, we'll talk tomorrow."

The phone click, as it was returned to the cradle, barely penetrated the fog in her brain. What did it mean? Were they back together? She rolled back on her heels and tried to slip back before he noticed her.

One step. She stopped at a rustling in the office, followed by footsteps. She squeezed her eyes shut. Oh, yeah, like that really hid her. She opened her eyes. A blue shirt filled her view. Oops.

Tentatively she raised her eyes to his bemused expression. As always, heat flushed through her and her heart slammed against her chest.

"Eavesdropping?"

"No, of course not. I was coming to ask you a question. Just a question. I didn't mean to overhear…. Not that I heard anything… I mean…" Oh, God, someone stop her.

His grin seemed to increase the further she dug herself into the ground. Seriously, someone needed to make an emergency escape hatch one could fall into after one embarrassed oneself sufficiently.

"It's okay, Natalie. Come on in." He stepped back into his office.

He gestured to the leather guest chair before sitting behind the desk. She slid into the chair, and her eyes darted around the room. She crossed her legs and clasped her hands in her lap.

She'd never been in here before. The tiled floor from the hallway flowed into the nice-size office, not huge but bigger than Mr. Morrison's. Beige paint and framed movie posters covered the walls.

Finally her eyes rested on the man behind the desk. Somehow he seemed closer than when he'd walked her to her car. Maybe it was his uninterrupted attention on her. A low thrum of energy sizzled through her body, and she involuntarily shivered.

"What was your question?"

Question? Oh, yeah, question. She'd had one. Things seemed to flit out of her brain when he was around. What had she been doing?

"Yes, umm…"

His mouth turned into a soft smile. "Take your time."

"Well…" She chewed on her bottom lip. Mr. Morrison.

"When extras are paid in cash where does the cash come from?"

The smile faded from Chase's face, and he came to attention behind his desk. "We don't typically pay extras in cash."

Her hands tightened. "These are for expenses. You know, expense reports turned in and instead of a check they request cash?"

"Where are these expense reports?" Suspicion lurked in Chase's eyes.

She recrossed her legs and swallowed. "On my desk. I just noticed it today. Isn't that the way it's typically done?"

Chase stood and ran a hand through his hair. "Get the reports and meet me in the conference room. We need to figure this out."

"We?" she squeaked out.

He walked around the desk and gripped her elbow, helping her out of the chair and steering her toward the door. "Yes, we. Now, go get the documents, and I'll order us some Chinese."

"But I should go home soon." The conference room wasn't very big, so he'd be close, which made that little piece in her trill again. But if she were alone with him, she was sure to make a fool of herself. His hand on her elbow burned through the silk of her blouse. Why had she taken off her jacket? She'd definitely make a fool out of herself if left alone with this man for any length of time. But she did want to get to the bottom of this.

"Hot date?" Chase's voice sounded slightly gruff.

A fresh wave of heat swallowed her face. "No, but—"

His green eyes settled on hers. "I won't take no for an answer."

Chapter Five

By the time they were settled into the conference room, only two chairs weren't covered in papers. However, the chairs were right next to each other. If Natalie moved that stack…

Before she could move anything, Chase spoke up.

"Sit down and we'll discuss what you've found while we eat." His tone was all business. Maybe she'd read too much into their earlier conversations.

She could be businesslike, too. Relieved, she breathed deep and slid into the chair. When he sat down his denim-clad leg brushed against her cotton skirt. She sucked in a breath, but covered it by opening one of the takeout bags. She crossed her legs away from his.

"I wasn't sure what to get, so I got a couple of different things. We can share," he said.

She picked up the containers and opened them. The

rich sauce filled the air with the aroma of ginger and garlic. Settling on beef with broccoli, she found one of the rice boxes.

"What have you found so far?" Chase said. His leg brushed against hers again. Her body tensed. She wondered if he did it on purpose. His warmth radiated to her side. The woodsy smell of his cologne wafted over her.

"The…uh." She cleared her throat. "Um, well, I was going through the expense reports and I noticed the hand-writing was similar on a few of them and…" Should she tell him that she suspected Mr. Morrison wrote them? She closed her mouth. She didn't want to accuse an innocent man. She only knew that the numbers told her that someone might be taking money.

"And?" he prodded. His gaze bore into hers, but it suddenly softened.

What had they been talking about? Was there a woman alive who could resist him? He didn't even have to put forth any effort to be irresistible. That kiss—her eyes dropped to his lips. That kiss at the end of *If Only*. She could feel her lips separate. The red-hot wave flowed over her face. She dipped her head as her food suddenly was way too interesting. After all, there was white, brown and green.

Way better to look at that than the slight scruff along Chase's chin. She was definitely going to make a fool out of herself.

When she dropped her gaze to her food, Chase leaned back in his chair. Trying to draw out this timid woman was like digging for diamonds. It took forever, but he just knew something special was hiding in there.

He'd already begun to suspect his chief financial officer

wasn't on the up-and-up. Every time Chase approached him, Martin shook and started prattling on about this and that.

Chase also suspected the reason Martin had hired Natalie was because of her timidity and lack of experience. What Martin hadn't figured on was the intelligence lingering in the depths of her gorgeous brown eyes.

Setting down the box of noodles, Chase studied the woman next to him. She drew him with her quiet strength and a warmth he'd never experienced before. She wasn't what Hollywood considered beautiful—few people were—but the delicate tilt of her chin, the gentle upsweep at the tip of her nose, her wide, innocent brown eyes and her lips, all drew his eyes and he found himself captivated by her.

He loved watching her lips curve into a smile, tighten when she was upset or part slightly on a breath. Real, that's what she was. He shifted in his chair. She jerked her head up again. Every nerve in his body longed for more contact than his knee against hers.

Women like her should stay as far away as possible from men like him. Even as he lost himself in her eyes, he could see her pushing him away. She might trust him in the beginning, but when some reporter speculated he was cheating, or when he was gone for months on a shoot, he'd lose her. Distance rarely made the heart grow fonder.

Her gaze fluttered down again, breaking the connection. He couldn't resist trying to have her. Just for a little while, not forever. Just enough to get her out of his system.

"Show me the expense reports you found." He cleared his throat.

Her shoulders relaxed beneath her cream blouse. He made her nervous, but he figured everyone did. She reminded him of a small bird ready to take flight at the least provocation, except when she was talking work.

She put aside the barely touched food and pulled forward some papers. She handed him the first two reports.

Her gaze never left his face while he looked over the reports. It was intense, but not sexual in nature. It was the stare of someone waiting for a connection to be made.

The handwriting was similar on both reports, just enough difference to prevent someone from questioning them if they went through on the same day. He noticed the signature authorizing cash payments. *Martin Morrison*.

"Let's separate all the ones authorized for cash payment first." When she started to pull more papers her way, he stopped her. "After we eat."

She nodded and went back to playing with the box of food. Her tongue swept over her lower lip. How soft would her lips be? He took a deep breath; it was going to be a long night.

After they ate, Natalie stood and cleared the table. Her slight body moved efficiently. She didn't overemphasize any moves, like some actresses. Her blouse was loose on her frame, but her skirt tightened at the waist, and the cut was tight to the legs. As she bent over the table, he couldn't help appreciating her backside.

It was going to be a *very* long night.

She straightened, and he noticed her ever-present blush. Would she ever not blush around him? Did he really want her to stop?

"I'll be right back," she said, as she walked out the door with the bags.

Chase took in the amount of paper. They had hours of work ahead of them. Natalie slipped back in and returned to her seat.

"If you want, you can go through that one while I go through this one," she said. Her eyes didn't meet his, and he could tell that she was struggling. She wasn't used to giving orders.

"Sounds good." Pulling the stack closer, he looked for the same signature on the front page. As the smell of brown sauce and egg rolls dissipated, the scent of strawberries and other sweet smells started to permeate his nose.

He glanced over at Natalie's bent head when he was about halfway through. Precariously balanced, her glasses had slid down to the tip of her nose. His fingers itched to push them back and brush the gentle curve of her cheek. Her finger pushed the lenses back into place.

He brought the paper in front of him back into focus. As the pile of cash payments grew, Chase's temper rose along with it.

Martin Morrison had come highly recommended. Chase couldn't imagine the slight man committing fraud against the company, but as the evidence kept mounting up, he couldn't deny it. The handwriting on all of them resembled Martin's. But without seeing them together, Chase would have never seen the similarities. Martin was in charge of accounting and therefore the checks.

He doubted Robert would have noticed the handwriting, but how had Robert missed so many expenses paid out to extras? He paused on the expense report for Dana Bradley. It was a cash payment of almost a thousand dollars, but all the expenses were below the fifty-dollar receipt limit they'd established to keep the files smaller.

Robert's signature was on it, just like the others. Too much like the others. Chase grabbed the last one and put the sheets together. They were exactly the same signature, no variations.

Not only was Martin stealing from the company, but he was forging Robert's signature, too. This explained why

Night Blooming had lost so much money, and it made Chase skeptical of the other productions that hadn't been losses, but hadn't been as profitable as he'd expected.

Apparently, Martin had gotten greedy.

"Can I see one of your expense reports?" Maybe hers would have Robert's real signature and not forgeries.

Natalie pushed her glasses back up her nose as she handed him the one she was looking at. He compared Robert's signatures, and again they were exactly the same.

"Mr. Morrison gave me a list of extras when he gave me the files."

"Do you have that in here?"

She retrieved a larger document than he'd expected. When Robert and Chase had originally discussed the crowd scenes, they'd decided to use computer rendering for the people. But when other costs increased they decided it would be more economical and more realistic to use extras.

Extras who weren't supposed to turn in expense reports. "Are all these extra expense reports?"

Her gaze analyzed each pile for a moment. "All except those three."

"Okay, let's focus on the extras only. Keep a running total."

"Okay." She actually seemed excited by the idea of adding what had to be hundreds of numbers. Her eyes brightened, and she flipped on the adding machine.

Only a slight bit of pink tinged her usually red cheeks. That quiet feeling spread through his chest looking at her. The intelligence sparkling in her eyes drew him. If his life were a little simpler, he'd think nothing of coaxing this woman into his arms.

He shook his head and went back to work. The light tapping of keys followed by the ticking of the numbers printing lulled him as he kept adding to her pile.

"I think that's it." He leaned back. The piles had shifted from one side of the room to the other. Her rhythmic typing continued. Her finger trailed down the page. She typed in the number, then lifted the sheet and added it to the other pile.

"That's the last one." She pressed the equal sign and then pulled the tape out of the machine.

"What's the damage?" He leaned forward.

She studied the number and then handed him the paper.

"Five hundred thousand dollars? This can't be right."

She looked back at the piles. "I can add it up again to double-check." She pulled the stack she'd just added back over.

Without this amount, *Night Blooming* would have been around the initial projections. They would need to have everything together if they were going to accuse Martin.

His gaze went back to Natalie. Watching her work was better than hanging out at clubs by a long run, but when she started to trail her finger down the page, he covered her hand with his. Startled eyes met his. A faint tinge of blue had appeared under her eyes. Most of her brown hair floated around her face, framing it.

"You can rerun the numbers tomorrow," he said, gently. When her gaze flitted to his hand on hers, he reluctantly pulled it away. Standing, he reached his hand down to her.

She glanced up at him before sliding her hand into his. His body came alive, but he resisted every temptation to pull her into his arms. The gentle curve of her mouth was almost too much. As soon as she stood in front of him, he released her hand.

"Let's get these back to your desk." Grabbing a pile, he headed out the door, away from her sweet scent. He thought he caught the sound of a sigh as he left the room.

Chapter Six

Grabbing a stack, Natalie followed, too confused and tired to argue. Not that she would have. She passed Chase in the hall on the way to her desk. Her hand still tingled as if he still touched her. She rubbed it on her skirt when she was in the conference room.

She bent and picked up more reports. When she stood, her glasses slid down her nose. Tipping her head back, she tried to wiggle them back.

"Here, let me help."

Before she could protest, he gripped the sides of her glasses and adjusted them on the bridge of her nose. Her breath caught in her throat. She held the papers as a make-shift shield to keep her treacherous emotions at bay. He was just helping her. That was all.

As if he couldn't resist, his fingers trailed down the sides of her face. Her pulse jumped, and desire pooled in her core. Papers on the floor behind her blocked her automatic urge to retreat. Surely, he hadn't meant anything by it. Certainly he hadn't meant to make her feel desire.

He dropped his hands and took the load from her without a word. She released it, thinking he'd take it and she'd grab the next. Her breath passed out over her lips.

He set the papers on the table and turned back to her. Her mouth opened, but nothing came out. She'd seen the look on his face dozens of times. Her heart threatened to pound its way out of her chest.

That was the look he'd given the heroine right before he kissed her. A look that had invaded her dreams where she played the part of Elizabeth in *If Only*. This was where the music would crescendo.

But this wasn't a movie. Chase wasn't playing a character, and neither was she. He stepped closer until a mere breath separated them. Obviously giving her the chance to stop him.

She should stop him. She wasn't what he wanted. She couldn't be what he needed. She didn't want to be famous. But with that look in his eyes and those eyes on her, she didn't think she could bear to stop him.

The back of his hand caressed her cheek. Her head leaned into the warmth as his hand left a trail of fire in its wake. His gaze held hers captivated, as his hand slipped to the back of her neck.

One last chance to say something. Her pulse raced through her veins. She licked her lips. One last chance to stop this. One chance, one taste, that's all she needed.

He closed the distance until a breath separated their mouths. Her hands came up and grabbed the front of his shirt. His mouth touched hers, a whisper of a kiss.

Her eyes fluttered shut, and she jerked on his shirt. His lips pressed against hers, gently touching, tasting. They were soft and full. Her heart was pounding so hard she was certain he could hear it.

Her mind swam in a sensual fog. Chase Booker was kissing her. Natalie Collins. His tongue met hers and her knees buckled. It wasn't just *the* Chase Booker kissing her, but this man. The one who opened doors for her, walked her to the car, made her feel pretty even with her glasses on.

But he shouldn't be kissing her. He was her boss. His mouth slid to her cheek and sent a searing bolt between her thighs. She pulled in air, desperately trying to surface. She needed space. She needed to think. Pulling back, she rested her forehead against his.

His jagged breathing matched hers. His thumb rubbed the side of her neck, sending an echoing ache through her. Lifting his head, he smoothed her hair back from her face.

She opened her eyes. His were filled with desire, need and frustration. Her body responded to his, wanting to invite him in.

"I should walk you to your car." His tone was cool. His hands dropped, and he turned.

Ice water splashed through her, cooling her overheated body. He hadn't meant to kiss her. Was he trying something for a new role? Had she just been convenient? Or something different?

Jerkily, she picked up a stack of papers and walked around him.

"I'll do that," he said.

She couldn't look at him or speak. She just continued down the hall to her desk. Her eyes burned with tears, but as long as she didn't talk or stop, she could hold them back.

As she set down the papers, she felt him behind her. His hands rested on her shoulders. She could feel the walls crumbling all around her. There wasn't a hole big enough to sink into.

"I'm sorry. I didn't mean to…" he started.

Her body started to shake.

"No, I did mean to, I just—"

"Stop, please. Just stop." The first teardrop crashed down on the desk. She felt so stupid for actually thinking a man like him would want her. She couldn't turn around. She couldn't see the look on his face. Jerking from his grasp, she went around the desk and grabbed her purse.

Without looking at him, she hurried down the hall. Tears blurred her vision but didn't fall. He was behind her, but he let her go.

She didn't stop until she was behind the wheel of her car. She'd been stupid to think someone like him would want someone like her. He'd stopped at the building door and stood there watching her.

She could still feel his lips against hers. Desire clung to her. She'd kissed Chase Booker. It was like going to the sun. She should have known that she'd get burned.

Chase purposely arrived late the following morning. He'd had a long talk with Robert about Martin after Natalie had fled last night. They decided to keep things normal for now, so Martin wouldn't suspect that they knew anything.

He hoped Natalie had time to get settled before having to see him. He'd acted impulsively last night and moved too fast, but he'd needed to know how she tasted.

It'd been more explosive than he'd imagined. He hadn't wanted it to end. It shouldn't have happened in the first place, but he definitely wanted it to happen again.

When he entered Pandora Productions, the receptionist

turned to smile at him like she always did, but froze and pretended to pick up a call instead.

Damn it. He'd hoped his foul mood wouldn't show, but he had no desire to act right now. No desire to force niceties. He only cared how one person was doing today.

When he walked past her desk, she wasn't there. He stopped in the hallway. Had she stayed home? Had he pushed her too far?

"Don't forget to get through the audit today. I have to leave early, but I expect it on my desk first thing Monday morning." Martin's voice carried into the hallway.

"Yes, Mr. Morrison," came Natalie's timid voice. "It shouldn't be a problem."

Chase continued down the hall before she came out. She was here. He'd almost expected her to take a sick day or something, but he was glad she hadn't. Maybe he hadn't screwed things up for the company and for himself. They needed her to help with this audit. Who was he kidding, he needed her.

As he entered his office, he saw an envelope in the center of his desk.

Chapter Seven

"What the hell is this?"

Natalie had been prepared for Chase's reaction, but she'd thought he'd be relieved. She hadn't expected anger. She straightened the crumpled letter of resignation he'd tossed on her desk.

"I… It's obvious, isn't it?" She kept her eyes on the paper.

"No, it's not." He paused and his tone softened. "Damn it."

Her eyes jerked up to his. Anger and frustration poured off him. His usual smiling face seemed tired this morning.

"I don't have time for this right now. You will have lunch with me today to discuss this letter." He acted like *letter* was a four-letter word. Without waiting for her answer, he disappeared down the hall.

Natalie glanced down the other way to see if anyone had witnessed his blowup. No one was around. Relief flowed through her. Well, she knew it would be awkward to see Chase this morning. Whatever she'd expected, it hadn't been anger. He hadn't gotten that upset when she'd told him about the fraud.

She folded up the letter, which gave two weeks' notice, and stuffed it in her purse. She'd just have to give it back to him at lunch. It would be much easier to talk to him in a crowded restaurant than in his office alone or, worse, at her desk where everyone at work could see, and the memory of last night's kiss lingered in the air.

Tugging a pile of documents closer, she sighed and began adding up the numbers again. She tried to lose herself in her numbers, but her mind kept jumping from the fraud to the kiss. She hadn't known what to say to Mr. Morrison. *Yeah, Mr. Morrison, we found a bunch of expenses that just shouldn't be there. Don't worry, though. I'm fairly certain you were the one that put them through.*

Every squeak of Mr. Morrison's chair made her heart skip a beat. Already keyed up by the fact Chase had demanded she have lunch with him, she kept expecting Chase to pop in front of her any moment. Then, what if Mr. Morrison figured out what she'd discovered by sneaking up behind her and seeing what she was working on?

When her desk phone rang, a small scream escaped her throat. Maybe she should have just stayed home. Picking up the phone and glancing around to make sure no one had heard her scream, she said, "This is Natalie. How may I help you?"

"Hi, Natalie. This is Jared Anderson from *Element Magazine*. I hear you're new at Pandora and was wondering if we could meet for lunch sometime."

A reporter? Calling her? "Um, I don't think that's a good idea."

The man's voice remained cajoling. "Look, we could have

a mutually beneficial relationship. But I don't want to discuss it over the phone. They can't be paying you that much."

"I'm sorry, but I don't think so." A flash of movement in front of her desk captured her attention. She looked up into Chase's eyes. Her lips parted. The spark of desire flared to life. Her whole being shook with the force of his gaze.

Jared's voice continued in her ear. "We're always looking for someone to help us find the good stories. We're not asking you to rat out your boss or anything. Just a bit of an inside scoop on how Chase runs things down there."

"I can't. Really. I don't know anything about…" Her gaze dropped from Chase's quizzical expression. What if he thought she'd called the magazine? "…that and don't really want to talk to anyone at your…" She glanced up at Chase. "…business."

"Why don't you write down my number? Just in case you change your mind—"

"I won't. Thank you for calling." She set the phone back on the cradle. The papers in front of her could be straighter and were a lot easier to look at than Chase at the moment.

"Let's go, Natalie."

Her heart leapt in her throat. She nodded slightly, still not making eye contact. Picking up her purse, she moved to follow him out of the office. She kept her head down, not wanting to meet anyone's gaze. Her pulse jumped as she brushed against him when he held open the door for her.

Her resolve to hand in her resignation increased. She couldn't be expected to work with this man and not want him. Maybe every other woman in the office wanted him and just coped daily with it, but she wasn't like those women. Maybe he'd kissed every one of them, too. Hell, he could have slept with all of them.

Her chest crushed in on her heart. Though she wasn't a

part of the gossip mill at Pandora Productions, she was certain someone would have mentioned that particular trait of Chase's. Or Rachel would have told her, since that kind of behavior wouldn't have escaped the attention of people like Jared Anderson. Why would a reporter call her?

Chase's hand lightly brushed the small of her back, guiding her to his car. Her breath caught, and she stumbled a little. He gripped her elbow to steady her.

He stopped them. After a moment, she looked up at his chin.

"Are you okay?"

No. "I'm fine." She pressed her glasses back up her nose and examined the concrete beneath her feet.

When he didn't continue to the car after a few moments, she dared a peek up at him. The wind tousled his blond hair, giving him that just-rolled-out-of-bed look. Her hair whipped loose from its clip and slapped her across the face.

"Do you ever say how you really feel?" His hand smoothed her loose hair behind her ear. His touch sent tingles coursing through her body. He glanced over her shoulder and frowned.

She followed his gaze and saw Mr. Morrison standing next to the door, cigarette in hand. He lifted his hand and waved. Chase's lips tightened, but he didn't say anything, just steered her toward the car again.

Chase remained silent while they were shown to a private corner booth. They'd come in the back entrance and hadn't drawn any attention.

Sliding into the seat, Natalie knocked over an empty glass. Chase caught it before it rolled to the floor. Her skin flushed pink as he slid in after her.

The table was small, but she tucked herself as far away

from him as possible. He didn't know whether to be frustrated or to laugh. What he really wanted to do was pull her back into his arms and keep her there for several hours. But he knew they'd both be better off if they repaired their working relationship and forgot about the tantalizing prospect of that kiss. At least until this mess with Martin was over.

She picked at the napkin and stared at the menu.

The sweet, clean smell of her lingered in his nose. His fingertips itched to turn her face up to his. He cleared his throat. Her gaze leapt up to his, her eyes wide and wary.

"Do you know what you want?" He smiled, trying to reassure her and calm her down.

Her eyes widened further, and she leaned away from him. She looked like she was ready to bolt.

"To eat, Natalie. What do you want to eat?" He picked up his menu. "I typically get shrimp scampi, but everything here is really good."

"I'm sure it is." Her eyes darted back to the menu. How could he make her relax?

The waiter stopped by and filled their glasses. They both ordered, and he left, leaving them quite alone in the secluded booth.

She started to fiddle with her fork. He laid his hand over hers, stilling her fidgeting. Her eyes were warm pools of chocolate as they met his, but her body tensed.

"I'm not going to pounce on you."

Panic and disappointment warred on her face before her shoulders dropped slightly. "I know," she said, as if she knew he'd never do something like that.

He wanted to shake her. His whole body ached to pull her into his arms again and prove to her that even though he said he wouldn't, he wanted to.

"Natalie." He waited for her eyes to meet his again.

"You are a very attractive woman. No, don't deny it. I find you incredibly attractive, but—"

"There's always a but," she said under her breath.

He blew out a breath and took a drink of water. He'd never have this much difficulty on a set. Everything was scripted already. He knew exactly how the other person was going to react. Natalie eluded him. He couldn't figure out her character, couldn't put her into a category.

"As I was saying, you work for my company. I shouldn't have taken advantage of you last night." He should say he'd never do it again, but something stilled his tongue.

The moment their lips had met he'd felt something he'd never experienced before. Desire and passion had been full-force in the front, but something had lingered in the back of his mind keeping him awake all night pondering the feeling. He'd felt protective and possessive. Feelings he had no right to have, but she'd felt right in his arms. He couldn't say he wouldn't be tempted again.

"I could have stopped you." Her voice was barely above a whisper.

The hesitation in her voice increased his pulse rate. He had to change the topic. "Have you had a chance to go through the papers again?"

Her body relaxed, and her hands stilled. "Yes, and I came up with the same number. As soon as Mr. Morrison leaves for the evening, I plan to go through the bank statements and figure out if he used a check to get the cash or if he made a withdrawal."

The confidence she exuded when talking about her job always amazed him. The pink receded from her cheeks, and her eyes were animated. This is the way she should always be. This is the way she should be with him.

His body tightened, but he shoved the desire back. For now, she couldn't be a part of his life except through work.

He remembered the look on Martin's face in the parking lot. He wasn't sure if the man suspected anything was going on between them, but he wouldn't put it past Martin to say something to the press.

"We'll have to take things carefully, if the files continue to point to Martin." Chase turned his thoughts back to business, a much safer subject. "He has his fingers in everything at Pandora. Robert and I talked this morning. We'll need a list of every bank account he has access to."

"I was just hired to help out. He hasn't given me a lot of things to do or shown me much."

The waiter reappeared and set down their lunches.

"The biggest thing is what he will leak to the press when he leaves. There's no telling what he'll make up or what he suspects." He hoped that was enough to warn her. He didn't want her to start with the two weeks' notice again. Martin probably wouldn't try to bring Natalie into it, anyway.

He needed to make sure Martin wouldn't insinuate anything. That look on the man's face when he'd seen them in the parking lot had worried Chase. Surely, Martin wouldn't think anything was happening between Natalie and Chase. Maybe he should stay away from her desk during the day.

They ate in silence. When the waiter removed the plates, Chase turned to Natalie.

"We'll need someone to help with the transition until we get a new CFO if Martin is implicated. Can I trust you to stay with us until then?"

She hesitated for a moment, and he held his breath waiting for her reply. "Of course."

"Natalie, will you give me—Pandora Productions—another chance? I think you have a brilliant mind and would be a great asset to our company."

The red crept up her cheeks. She nodded slightly and lifted her eyes to his. "I'll try."

Chapter Eight

Natalie sat on the edge of her seat, waiting for the clock to turn five. Mr. Morrison had left at the same time every day for the past month she'd worked here, but tonight he was supposed to leave early. With her luck, he'd probably stick around.

Chase had been avoiding her desk all afternoon. After the first hour of waiting for him to pass by her desk, she'd started to relax. She ignored the twinges of disappointment as time continued to pass.

It would be better for both of them if they kept their relationship purely work-related. She could forget how his lips had caressed hers and how the warmth had flooded through her from the touch of his hands.

The door slammed behind her, and she almost fell off her chair. Mr. Morrison locked the door and turned his shifty eyes to her. "I expect the report first thing Monday morning. Just because Mr. Booker took you for a long lunch doesn't mean you can neglect your work."

Her cheeks were on fire. "Of course not, Mr. Morrison. I've got the numbers tied into the expense reports and just need to categorize two more reports before I'm finished." She hoped he was convinced by her lie, because she could hear the tremor in her voice and could feel the tightness of her smile.

"Good. I'll see you Monday morning." He hefted his briefcase in his hand and was out the door before she could say anything else.

Now she just had to wait for the rest of the office to clear out. Which shouldn't take long. Over half the staff hadn't come back after lunch and half of those remaining had taken off early. They had places to go and be seen.

Her phone rang. She stared at it for a moment. The caller ID came up as Unavailable. She really didn't want to talk to Jared Anderson again, but he wasn't the only one who had her phone number.

Tentatively, she picked the phone up from the cradle. "This is Natalie. How may I help you?"

"Nat," Rachel's voice yelled above the background noise. "Brian finally asked me out."

"Good for you."

Rachel had been trying to get Brian from work to ask her out for months now.

"Don't wait up, sweetie. I don't think I'll be home tonight."

"Be careful."

"Hey, sorry about the mess in the kitchen, I was experimenting last night with cupcakes. Turns out I can't cook, so I picked some up at the store this morning. Would you mind cleaning it up? Just in case Brian and I end up back at our place?"

Natalie had seen the mess when she'd come home last night but had been too exhausted physically and emotionally to do anything about it. "Sure. Be safe."

"Thanks, sweetie. See ya." The line went dead.

She set down the phone and stood. Time to wander through and see who was left in the building. The hallway runway was quiet as she headed down to fill her water bottle.

She held her breath as she passed by Chase's closed door and breathed a sigh of relief when nothing happened.

After filling her bottle, feeling confident that no one was left in the building besides Chase and her, she stopped at his door and knocked tentatively.

"Yeah?" She heard from within. She cracked the door open.

"Chase, Mr. Morrison has left for the day." As she pushed the door open, a pair of feminine legs came into view. Someone was sitting in the guest chair. "Oh, I'm sorry."

Alexis Brandt was back for her Friday-night pickup.

"It's all right, Natalie." Clearly distracted, Chase looked up from some papers on his desk. He held out a set of keys. "Let me know if you need anything."

She nodded to Chase, took the keys and pulled the door closed. Her chest had tightened, and she could barely breathe. She walked on wooden legs back to Mr. Morrison's door. Her hands shook as she inserted the keys to find the right one.

She had no reason to feel jealous. She didn't have any claim to Chase—just because he'd kissed her last night didn't mean anything. Hadn't he said that? The keys made a heavy thud when they slipped from her hands.

Squatting, she picked them up and shoved her glasses back up her nose. She was being ridiculous. Guys like Chase went for girls like Alexis. Just because he'd kissed her didn't mean he felt anything for her. He kissed women as a career. Maybe he'd just been practicing.

She found the right key and pushed into the office. Get what she needed and get out. The sooner she was done, the sooner she could be away from Chase for a whole weekend. A weekend to strengthen her resolve to stay away from him.

Papers covered Mr. Morrison's desk. Boxes of files covered the floor in front of five gray filing cabinets. This was going to take hours. Natalie shoved the keys into her jacket pocket.

Picking a drawer, she started methodically rummaging through the files. She was so absorbed in the files she tuned out the noises from down the hall. She didn't care what those two were doing, anyway. It wasn't any of her business.

After an hour she stretched, trying to loosen her muscles before heading out to her desk.

There had to be a better way. She keyed in her password but didn't have access to the reports she wanted.

Chase would have the access she needed. Her face grew warm. She didn't want to interrupt whatever was happening with Alexis.

But this would go a lot faster if she could look at the information in the computer first. If they were waiting for her to finish, this would get them out the door faster, too.

Smiling, she stood and headed down the hall. She stopped when she noticed his office door was open. He wasn't behind his desk. Had he left? Usually he stayed until she was finished, but it wasn't unfathomable that he'd left because he had better things to do than wait for her.

"Did you need something?" His voice came from behind her.

She spun on her heel. "I thought you'd left."

"I was just walking Alexis to her car. Didn't you hear us pass by the office?" He smiled, and his gaze roamed over her.

"I was working." Her words came out breathy. She cleared her throat and tried to tame the desire surging through her as his eyes settled on her lips.

Breaking eye contact, he walked around her into his office. "Have you found anything?"

Natalie took in a deep breath. She could do this. She could ignore this attraction and focus on work. She followed him into his office. "Do you have complete access to the computer system?"

"I should. What do we need to look up?" He opened his laptop, logged in and looked up at her, expectantly.

She stepped around the desk to stand behind him. Trying to ignore the smell of him, she leaned down to focus on the screen. She pointed to the icon of the reporting system. "Click there."

He followed her instructions until the report she was looking for came up.

"Can you print that out?"

"Sure. Is there anything else?" He leaned back, and his shoulder brushed her hip. She nearly leapt out of her skin. She'd been so focused on the computer. She hadn't realized she'd gotten so close to him.

"Um." She stepped back.

His chair swiveled toward her. "Natalie, it's okay." His eyes sparkled like emeralds. "People touch all the time in business. It doesn't mean anything."

Unfortunately, no one told her body that. Every touch catapulted her rational thoughts out the window, leaving her a pool of desire. Just because he didn't feel it, didn't mean she could stop.

"Of course." Warmth surged to her cheeks as she

realized she'd pressed herself against the wall as far from him as possible. Forcing herself to relax, she stepped forward again.

"Is there anything else I can do for you?" His voice had a husky quality to it, but she ignored the corresponding push from her insides.

"Bank account statements. Do you know where they would be in Mr. Morrison's office?"

He stood and she resisted the impulse to step back, but she couldn't control the wince at the expected contact. When he didn't brush against her, she raised her gaze to his face.

"I'll show you."

She couldn't breathe, let alone move. What was he going to show her? Heat poured off his body, infusing her with a drowsy feeling. Her body wanted to sway into his to see if the heat would explode into flames.

"Natalie?"

"Hmm."

"Martin's office?"

"Oh, yeah. Sorry." She turned and caught herself before she stumbled. He didn't touch her, but she could feel him directly behind her, ready to help if needed. Straightening, she walked down the hall before him, silently chastising herself.

"Here, I'll show you the drawer," Chase said.

What was she doing here with this man? He was supposed to be condescending and overbearing. He'd been raised to be a Hollywood star, a highly publicized birth followed by a childhood in the limelight. Speculations about what features he'd get from each of his beyond-gorgeous parents had been rampant.

Critically acclaimed performances had shot him beyond the shadows of his famous parents. He'd taken on risky performances and made them his own. Now he was kneeling in front of a filing cabinet, rooting through bank statements.

And all she could think about was how soft his lips had been, how he'd tasted like a hint of mint and how his body had melded against hers. Why had she let his warm eyes and smooth words convince her she could work with him? She would die a little every time someone like Alexis strutted down the hallway to his office.

She was halfway in love with this man, and if she stayed much longer, she could find herself hopelessly in love with him. Someone like him could never love someone like her. A burning sensation formed at the back of her eyes.

"Found it." Looking at the papers in the folder he was holding, he stood and walked toward her. "All the bank statements are in here. This should have the information you need."

When he met her eyes, he froze. A moment of panic flashed over his face and flowed into resignation.

"I'll come back in tomorrow to finish up." She managed to speak without a single hitch. Even though her heart ached and she could barely breathe. She dug the keys out of her pocket and held them out to him.

"Nata—"

"Please. Don't. I can't." She turned and ran out the door.

Chapter Nine

The rain started as soon as Natalie pulled out of the parking lot. Chase stood in the doorway and watched her drive away.

He'd let her go for the good of the company. He'd done the right thing.

He set the folder with the bank statements back on her desk and closed and locked Martin's door. Her usually neat desk looked like a tornado had hit it. Every night before she left she straightened the piles. Tonight she couldn't get away fast enough and had almost left her purse behind.

Maybe he should ask Robert to come in tomorrow to help her out. His chest felt hollow. While he'd promised to back off, he couldn't resist seeing her. He just wanted to be around her, smell her sweetness, touch her soft skin. Feel like he'd finally found something real.

She could never fit into his world. She'd crumble under

the pressure. He'd lose her before he ever had her, so he went back to his office and turned off the computer and lights. On his way past her desk, he noticed something sparkling under her desk.

A cell phone lay on the floor under her desk where her purse usually was. He picked it up and flipped it open. The display showed a field of flowers and her name.

He slid it into his pocket, knowing it was the wrong thing to do, but the crushing weight on his chest lifted as he opened Martin's office again. This time to get Natalie's address.

The ice cream box was almost empty by the time the movie was at the halfway point. Elizabeth was telling Chase's character, Tom, how they were meant to be together, but Tom was blowing her off, even though he loved her. Usually Natalie didn't require a tissue box and way too much Chunky Monkey ice cream to get through her favorite film. But with every close-up of Chase's face, she helped herself to a huge bite of ice cream.

It didn't help that she'd become way too familiar with his face. Seeing the expressions he'd given her on the television made her pulse pound and her heart ache.

She'd cleaned the kitchen with a vengeance first thing when she got home. Then she'd changed into her comfiest pair of jammies and popped on *If Only*. She hadn't bothered with dinner, figuring she'd get enough calories from the ice cream.

Now tucked under her blanket, she began questioning her sanity for picking the movie she'd always loved in the past. It only served to remind her of Chase's larger-than-life world. That, coupled with the magazine Rachel had left open to pictures of Chase and Alexis last weekend. Natalie wondered what else she could do to sink the dagger further into her heart.

She tried to find comfort by reminding herself she wouldn't be able to handle watching him kiss other women onscreen if he were hers. She sighed. If he were hers… The words burned in her heart. A wish that could never come true, no matter how many stars she wished upon.

Besides, she wasn't ready for a man in her life. She'd been down that road in college, and it had always ended up with her hurt and crying on Rachel's shoulder. She needed to focus on her career and worry about guys later.

Chase flashed back on the screen.

She'd have to see him in the morning. She had to finish the work before Monday. He'd said he'd be there as early as she wanted. If she could get some sleep, she might be able to deal with him in the morning.

She didn't move from the couch. She was wide awake, and though the movie made her sink further into misery, it was noise. She didn't want to fantasize about emerald eyes that burned with desire and blond hair that would be silky to the touch. She didn't want to run out to the store and find the cologne he used and wear it. She probably couldn't afford it anyway.

She shut her eyes as his image came back on the screen.

"How do you know?" his character said to Elizabeth. "How can anyone know?" His voice trickled down her spine.

She opened her eyes to see him lift his hand and caress Elizabeth's face. She imagined Chase's hand against her cheek. He didn't kiss Elizabeth in this scene. The only kiss was the one at the end of the movie. Natalie couldn't skip to the end. What made that kiss was the journey, the tangle of emotions that preceded it and made it the most beautiful kiss she'd ever seen.

A knock at the door startled her out of the movie. She hit Pause on the remote. Who would be knocking on the door at eleven on a Friday night? She grabbed the aluminum bat they kept near the door and opened the peephole.

The night was dark and rainy. Chase stood in front of her door, dripping wet. The bat slipped from her grip, and she yanked the door open.

"What are you doing here?"

His hair was plastered to his head. Rivers of rain flowed down his face and over his grin. "Can I drip on your floor?"

She nodded, still stunned by his appearance on her doorstep, and stepped back to let him in. She closed the door and locked it automatically. Leaning against the door, she stared at him.

He smiled down at her. "I don't suppose I could use a towel?"

"Uh, yeah. Just a moment." She walked around him into the bathroom. Her brain couldn't wrap around the fact that Chase was in her home. It was almost as if she'd conjured him from the movie. She grabbed two towels and headed out to the hallway again. He'd removed his shoes and put them on the mat near the door.

She held the towels out at arm's length for him.

"Pink. Nice."

After he took them, she wrapped her arms around her middle, suddenly vulnerable in her own home. This wasn't the office or a public restaurant, and she was in pajamas. She wondered if her overactive imagination had brought him here somehow.

He rubbed the towel over his head, leaving his hair sticking up. Feeling her fingers tingle, she wanted to run her hands over his hair and smooth it back down.

"Was there something you needed?" she bit out, having a hard time forgetting her fantasies of him, now that the reality of him stood before her. Her body throbbed with un-fulfilled desire.

He shouldered off his jacket and hung it on the doorknob. His shirt wasn't quite as wet so it didn't cling to the muscles hiding underneath, but she'd already seen that part of the movie and knew how sleek and rippled his body was under that dark shirt.

After he dried off, he reached into a coat pocket and pulled out her cell phone. "I found this in the office."

"You didn't have to bring this to me. I could have gotten it tomorrow." Wishing she'd brought the ice cream to the door with her, she reached out her hand for the phone.

When Chase lifted his gaze to hers, she inhaled. A thousand curses on the writer of *If Only*. A thousand curses on the director, who'd decided on those scenes. She'd seen that look before. The reason she watched *If Only* a million times was because of that look. But Chase was more than his performance, he was real and thoughtful and that scared her more than the desire racing through her.

"I should go." He pressed the phone in her hand. His touch coursed through her, and he didn't lift his hand from hers.

She couldn't think as desire swelled within her. Nothing she'd experienced before compared to what Chase was making her feel. Her heart fluttered against the cage of her chest.

He closed the distance between them slightly. "I should go." His voice low and his eyes hooded.

She nodded slightly, not trusting her voice, not really meaning it. She didn't want him to go. His presence filled her vision. Her body shook with the need to be touched, but he was still holding back.

His hand slid off hers, leaving the phone in her palm. A heartbeat separated them. Much as she wanted to, Natalie couldn't drop her gaze from his. Never would she imagine Chase Booker looking at her this way. Never could she imagine Chase Booker being in her apartment. She could imagine losing her heart to him.

Not because of the fabulous roles he played, but because of who he was. She didn't see Tom from *If Only* in front of her. She saw the man who said he liked her smile. The man who picked up her glasses. The man who looked at her as if she were the only woman in the world.

She saw Chase. Her hand shook as she set the phone on the counter next to her. Risking everything for that look, she lifted her hand slowly. Her shaking fingertips traced the rough scruff along his chin.

His eyes sparked with her touch, but he didn't close the last bit of distance between them. Her fingers wandered up into his slightly damp hair. She rubbed the strands between her fingers. So soft.

"Natalie."

She pulled her gaze from his hair and met his eyes. She didn't care why he was here, just that he was here. With her. Seeing her. Making her feel beautiful.

His eyes shut, and he leaned into her hand for a moment. When he opened them, they were filled with regret. Covering her hand with his, he smiled softly. "I should go. We…we're not from the same world."

The little piece of hope that had flared to life went out. Not from the same world. He was Mr. Popularity and she was the nerd. That may not be what he meant, but that's how it felt.

She slid her hand out from under his. His hand clung to hers until it was freed. He flexed his fingers as he dropped his hand to his side. He wasn't unaffected by her, but she wasn't enough to tempt him to stay.

His fingers lifted her chin until she met his eyes again. "I…" He dropped his hand. "I've got to go."

Turning, he shrugged on his coat and stepped into his shoes. She leaned against the wall for support. She had nothing to add. She couldn't have spoken if she wanted to.

He didn't look at her as he struggled with the locks and the doorknob. Stepping forward, she brushed his hands aside, undid the locks and pulled the door open. The scent of rain, fresh and clean, filled the small space.

He stepped out. "I'll see you in the morning."

"Yeah," she rasped as she eased the door shut. Before it closed fully, it stopped.

Natalie stepped back from the door as it slowly opened.

Chase stood in the doorway, hands braced on the door frame. Rain coursed over him. His head hung down. His fingers curved into the wood as if some invisible wall separated them.

"Natalie, tell me to leave and I will." Haunted green eyes rose to meet her eyes. "I don't want to leave, but if you tell me to, I will."

Her heart struggled against her chest. "I…" She dropped her gaze to the puddle forming at his feet. What would it mean if she let Chase in again? Would they make love and then just forget about each other? Would it be enough?

"Natalie?"

She lifted her gaze to his. Could she resist this opportunity? Did she want to? God yes, she wanted him. She clamped her lips together to stop her doubts from emerging and held out her hand.

He dropped his head again before pushing off the door frame and into the apartment. "To hell with right and wrong." His foot kicked the door shut as his hand closed over hers.

He yanked her into his arms, and his mouth crashed

down on hers. Her jammies were soaked within seconds but she didn't care. A flood of desire pooled in her core, and her body tingled where his warmth radiated through his clothes.

The intensity of his kiss thrilled her down to her toes. He lifted her against him. His arousal pressed into her stomach as an answering pulse surged between her thighs. A sensuous fog of lust clouded her mind as his mouth trailed away to her neck. Her feet met the floor again and he released her. She whimpered.

He smiled as he kicked off his shoes and dropped his jacket on the floor. He closed the distance between their bodies and tipped up her face to his. His mouth stopped above hers, and his eyes delved into hers. "I couldn't leave you now. I need you, Natalie. You. Only you."

His mouth pressed against hers. Her hands sank into his wet locks and held him there. She wanted this moment more than she wanted to breathe. He gathered her in his arms and worked her backward down the hall.

His head lifted and his forehead rested against hers as they both gulped down air. His heart raced against hers. "Which way do we go?"

She opened her eyes to his deep green ones. His hand brushed over the back of her neck, and her eyelids slid shut. His chest rubbed against her breasts. Her lips parted. Had he asked something?

Her eyelids lifted. His eyes smiled down at her.

"Don't you have a roommate?" His voice was husky and deep. It sent shivers down her spine.

"Rachel?"

"Much as I love the camera, I don't want to put on a show tonight. I want you all to myself." His fingertip traced the curve of her ear.

"Oh." His words penetrated the fog invading her mind. "She's out tonight." The smell of rain and his woodsy scent overwhelmed her nose. It coursed down her body to settle in her belly.

"Where's your room, Natalie?" His teeth nipped the tender skin of her jaw, and her pulse leapt. The desire reflected in his gaze finally broke through the fog.

She turned within his arms. His hand lifted her hair from her neck, and his mouth caressed the back of her neck. If his arm hadn't been around her, she would have melted into a puddle at his feet.

"Room?" His warm breath fanned the nape of her neck.

Right, room. She led him into the living room. He'd mercifully lifted his head from his torment of her neck, giving her some space to think. His arm remained around her waist. The backs of his fingers skimmed down the side of her breast.

She stopped in her tracks. Her breath caught in her throat at the whisper of a touch, and she leaned back into the warmth of his chest. A drop of water splattered on her forehead.

His finger brushed away the drop. "I could use another towel."

This was really happening. Chase was in her living room, touching and kissing her. Not just in her mind or on the screen. Screen? Her gaze darted to the TV still paused on Chase's face.

The red-hot lava of embarrassment filled her cheeks even as pools of liquid fire gathered between her thighs and his mouth worked down the side of her neck again. Maybe he wouldn't notice.

"Not the best still frame, but definitely a good scene." His breath was hot against her neck as he spoke.

So much for hoping he wouldn't notice. Normally, she'd

wish for the floor to swallow her whole, but she didn't want to be out of Chase's arms for one second. "I think that's one of your best smiles."

His mouth curved into a smile as he dropped a kiss on her lips.

"I stand corrected," Natalie said as she struggled to control her breathing. "That is your best smile."

He leaned down until his lips were next to her ear. "You ain't seen nothing yet."

His hand trailed from her waist to cup her breast. Her nipples hardened, and she fought to control her breathing. His body was hard against her back. She completely forgot the TV as urgency filled her. Her body pulsed.

His thumb stroked her nipple through her damp pajama top. His other hand relinquished her hip and worked on the buttons of her top. Her hands found his hips, something solid to cling to as desire pulled her farther down. When the top few buttons were undone, his hand slipped inside. His flesh brushed against her nipple. Warmth pooled between her legs.

"Natalie." Her name was a growl upon his lips.

Her shirt fell open when he finished with the buttons. His hands brushed the shirt down her arms and it slid to the floor. His mouth caressed the sensitive area between her neck and her shoulder.

His hands stroked back up her arms. She was beyond lost. Any doubts she may have felt went up in smoke. She turned in his arms.

Looking down into liquid pools of chocolate, Chase shuddered at the trust and longing revealed there. Gently he removed her glasses and set them on the table next to him. Unable to resist the parting of her lips, he lowered his mouth to hers, taking his time to savor the sweet taste of her.

He lifted his head and yanked his shirt over his head.

Pulling her tight against his chest, he rejoiced in the feeling of her flesh sliding against his, but it wasn't enough.

His hands smoothed over her back down to the waist-band of her pajamas. They were hardly the sexy lingerie he'd had the pleasure to see and remove, but somehow the tiny kitten print on cotton suited Natalie.

She rested her head against his hammering heart. Her hands wrapped around his back. Her fingers were tentative on the top of his jeans, but her touch left a trail of fire. Damn it, he wanted to get her to a bed. He wanted to be everything she desired, but she didn't seem to care where they were, which enflamed his desire for her more.

His hands slipped below her waistband, curving over her bottom and pulling her tight against his arousal. Her fingernails scraped his lower back, and a shiver rippled down his spine.

Her fingers found their way below his waistband. Unable to deny himself any longer, he held her shoulders to push her away. She gazed up at him as he lifted her to meet his mouth. Her legs wrapped around his waist.

The center of her rubbed intimately against his arousal as his mouth caressed hers. His tongue touched her lips and she opened them, greeting his tongue with hers.

Natalie felt as if she were falling as his shoulders bunched under her fingers. As he lowered her to the floor, his smooth skin warmed under her touch. The carpeting brushed her back, and he settled on top of her.

His mouth never left hers as his hands returned to her waist. Pushing her bottoms off, he broke contact briefly before returning to her lips. Maybe he was worried that she'd change her mind, but she couldn't stop this. Her hands brushed over his back to convince herself he was here and not just a dream from sugar overload.

She reached for the buttons on his jeans. His chest brushed her tender nipples as he pushed off his pants. He reached into his pocket to pull out a condom before flinging his pants away.

His flesh warm against hers. Her body ready and aching to know the feel of his. His hands lifted her hips. As his mouth ravished hers, his erection pressed against her opening.

This was real. She was awake, and it was really happening. Chase was with her.

Instinctively, her hips rocked against him, longing to draw him in. He lifted his mouth from hers and held still.

"Open your eyes, Natalie." His voice was on the edge of control and the complete loss of control.

Her eyes met his and he buried himself in her. Her lips parted at the sensations pulsing within her. Again he waited until her eyes met his before he began to move within her.

His eyes held hers as the pressure within her boiled to the breaking point. The intimacy of watching his eyes filled with want and restraint pushed her over the edge. Her eyelids fluttered as she peaked, free-falling into the abyss. But she kept her eyes open and locked with his.

When she began to relax, he moved within her again. Sparking her sensitive flesh into a renewed fever, she gripped his shoulders and they surged together. His forehead rested against hers as his body tensed and released.

She relished the weight of him against her as he relaxed over her. Her mind was a jumbled mess, but she knew it wouldn't last. She'd just slept with Chase Booker, become another notch on his bedpost. Had the most intense orgasm of her life.

She closed her eyes.

Her arms and legs were wrapped around his sweat-slick body. He covered every inch of her. She didn't want to move, but she could barely breathe. Holy crap, she'd had sex with Chase Booker.

Chase lifted his weight on his forearms and looked down into Natalie's eyes. His heart swelled in his chest at the shy smile she gave him. "So which one was your bedroom?"

Her head rolled to the side, and she pointed to one of the doors. "That one, I think." She squinted "It's a bit blurry at the moment."

He sat up and reached over onto the table where he'd set her glasses. He stretched out beside her and lowered her glasses to her face. The blush that usually disappeared into her blouse's neckline spread over the tops of her breasts.

Unable to resist, he trailed his finger where the blush faded into pale skin. Her skin reddened even further. Her hand reached up to the blanket on the couch, but he caught her wrist.

"Don't. I like looking at you."

Her hand curled into a fist, but she made no move to cover herself. Even though she was short, her body was well proportioned. Her breasts were small and unaltered. They were perfect. He traced his fingertip over the tip. The nipple puckered under his touch.

"Shouldn't we go to the bedroom? Or turn off a light?" Maybe he'd be willing to let her light a candle instead of having lamps on. He seemed mesmerized as his fingers trailed lower. Over her slightly rounded belly, his finger left a line of fire in its wake. The fire shot straight to her core, building her arousal again.

They'd had sex in her living room. On the floor. She closed her eyes as embarrassment warred with desire. She wanted him to stop so they could cover up somehow, but she didn't want him to stop what he was doing.

His hand flattened on her stomach, and she inhaled deeply of his cologne, the rain, him. Her belly quivered as his hand dipped lower until his fingertips slipped between her thighs.

Her breath hissed out between her teeth. His lips touched hers as his fingers gently moved over and in her. His tongue traced her lower lip as his finger circled her sex. Her fingers sank into the carpet as her body arched into his palm. Her side pressed into his warm, hard muscles.

When he removed his hand, she whimpered with need. The condom package rustled. He covered her with his body and entered her smoothly. Her body buzzed with pent-up frustration, and her desire soared as she crested the edge again. His climax followed close behind hers, and he collapsed against her.

She had the overwhelming urge to laugh. Her body had always been wound so tight, and now she felt as if the spring had finally broken. Her limbs were like water. She'd never been so satisfied in her life.

When he raised his head and peered into her eyes, her breath caught. Her heart flipped, and she knew she was in trouble.

Chapter Ten

Light peeked through the slightly parted curtain to torment Natalie. She squeezed her eyes shut and rolled straight into a solid, warm object. A very naked solid, warm object whose very naked arm was wrapped around her very naked body.

Cracking open her eyes, she stared at the slightly blurry image of Chase. His chest rose and fell gently. Her hand rested on his well-formed abs underneath her lavender sheets.

Her body ached pleasantly, and she smiled as she recalled gathering up the clothes strewn across the apartment and managing to make it to the bed for round three. Her comforter was half off the bed and pillows were scattered throughout the room.

She rested her cheek against his chest and listened to the rhythmic pace of his heart. She wished the sun would go away and leave her forever in the night with Chase.

Morning meant responsibility. Morning meant work. Morning meant regret.

As she snuggled against him, she wondered if he'd regret last night. She couldn't. Chase had wanted her. It still seemed unfathomable, but he wanted her.

His chest shifted under her, and his fingers lightly brushed down her hair. "Good morning." His voice was satisfied and low. His lips touched her forehead.

"Morning." Should she add more? What were the expectations when someone woke in the arms of the Sexiest Man Alive? But that's not who she'd been with last night. She'd been with Chase, just Chase. The suave heartthrob from the screen had disappeared, leaving behind the man who made her feel beautiful. Who cared enough to give her a choice. Who was flesh and blood, not just a character on a show.

His arm tightened around her waist. "Relax. Everything will be fine." His heartbeat increased under her ear, and she felt his growing arousal next to her thigh.

"We should get to work," she whispered. Her sore body flooded with heat.

His hand slipped down to cup one of her breasts. "You're right. We should." His other hand reached over to the nightstand for a condom.

She gasped as he shifted her on top of him. His full arousal rested against the junction of her legs. "Chase." His name came out on a breath as she lowered her hips to meet his.

They came together slowly. Bodies sliding against each other. His hands controlled the pace of her hips. Her core rippled with each slow withdrawal and excruciating slow return. Her mind melted with the fire of her arousal until she lived for the next caress, the next brush, the next penetration.

As she found climax, she arched and cried out. He sat up with her, drawing her body against his, and continued to raise and lower her hips until his climax took him. They fell back to the bed. Her thighs trembled as she lay on top of him.

She couldn't remember a time she'd been so thoroughly sated. Her breathing returned to normal, and her heart slowed its frantic beat. It was time to get back to the real world, where he was larger than life, and she was happy being a flower on the wall.

Natalie sat on the floor of Mr. Morrison's office surrounded by files. She stared out the window as her mind wandered back to the care and tenderness Chase had shown when they'd shared the shower. She'd been beet-red the entire time, but she'd enjoyed every moment.

They'd managed to get out of the apartment before Rachel came in, which had Natalie counting her blessings. Meeting Chase in the office was one thing, but finding he'd spent the night with Natalie would definitely blow Rachel's mind.

Now, he sat down the hall in his office, while she picked through files. When she could get her mind to focus on them. Every time she heard a sound she'd jump. She didn't think Mr. Morrison worked on the weekends, but she knew her luck couldn't hold out. Then there was Chase. She just didn't know what to expect or how to react to him today.

She'd been a permanent shade of pink this morning. He didn't seem to want to let her out of his sight, though he did allow her some privacy in the bathroom. She'd also convinced him to let her drive her car instead of riding with him.

The kiss he'd given her before they left the apartment had ricocheted through her sore body. He didn't just kiss with his mouth. He kissed with his whole body, drawing her so close.

She'd sagged against her car waiting for him to get in

his, before shaking herself. Time to get on with it. Maybe she was just a fascination. Something different from what he usually went after. He'd cast her aside when a shiny new something passed by.

She returned her attention to the file in her lap. Whatever it was between them, it couldn't last. Maybe she should end it now before she got too hurt. She rubbed the ache that began in her chest at the thought. Yeah, it was definitely too late to avoid pain, but she did enjoy the pleasure.

Chase stood in the doorway of Martin's office and took in his little accountant surrounded by mounds of paper, an expression of intensity on her face. A soft smile teased the corner of her lips. He'd put that there.

He wanted to see where this thing between them could go, but the moment the press got ahold of it they'd latch on and shake it until it broke. He could protect her from that, if they were careful. Maybe this hadn't been his best idea—the press was already sniffing around because of the breakup, and he needed the publicity for his upcoming film.

His thoughts flew out the window when she turned her face up to him and that crimson flush covered her cheeks. For a moment, he allowed himself to sink into her wide eyes and feel the wholesomeness of her. Her lips parted in a silent invitation he wasn't sure she was aware of.

He cleared his throat. "How's it going?"

Her eyes wandered over the folders. "I don't think I'm going to be able to get through this today. I need more time."

He longed to smooth his fingers over the creases in her forehead. "I think we can put Martin off for a few days, while you continue to investigate. You give him a report that doesn't mention the expenses. Everything matched up, right? Receipts and expenses are all accounted for?"

"Yes, there are forms for everything, but when will I be able to work on it with him being here during the day?" Frustration poured off her.

He leaned against the doorway. "We'll stay late and go through it together. I always thought Martin was a good man and want to make absolutely sure before I accuse him of anything."

Her gaze flitted up to his. Her eyes spoke volumes as worry, fear and desire whipped through them. What did she fear? Him? "Together," she said, resigned.

"Let's clean up this mess and get out of here. We could pick up some takeout and go back to my place?" Suddenly, he was nervous, like a boy asking a girl out for the first time. After last night that was a ridiculous thought, but it was there, a tingle of anticipation and fear of rejection.

If he ended it now, they wouldn't have to worry about the press. No one would ever find out, and Natalie would stay happy in her simple life. And he'd go back to dating the same women he'd always dated. But what if this was the only shot he had at something real?

She started stacking the files without looking up at him. "Do you think we should?" Her hands trembled as she set the papers down. "I mean, don't you have plans with Alexis? It is Saturday night."

He knelt beside her and used his finger under her chin to turn her face to his. A sadness lingered in her eyes. "The only person I want to be with tonight is right here." He traced her lower lip with his thumb. "Please say yes."

The warring factions continued for a moment within her eyes. Her face flushed, and her shy smile appeared, easing the tightness in his chest. "Yes."

Chase's house was bigger than Natalie had imagined. He lived in Hollywood Hills with the A-list celebrities. The houses lining the streets weren't simple homes, but complexes with long, gated drives.

She followed in her car up the drive and around to the back of the house. Two garage doors opened along the huge building. She pulled her Honda Fit in next to an expensive-looking silver car.

The garage door closed behind her. She stepped out into a huge room with a high ceiling and painted concrete floors. A couple of the cars had shrouds over them, but she could tell by the shape that they were sport cars.

She'd been happy when she'd qualified for the loan on her Fit, which she would pay off in five years. She highly doubted there were loans on the six cars in this garage. Each one was probably at least five times the new price of hers.

Chase strode to her side. "Do you like cars?"

"Um, well, they get me from here to there, but not really." She was lucky to have the old beater that got her through college. She hadn't needed a car before that, since her mother had homeschooled her.

His fingers laced into hers. "C'mon. Let me show you my house."

She tried to ignore the fizzle of awareness that coursed through her at his touch. His grip was strong and gentle as he pulled her through the door connecting the house to the garage.

The kitchen was enormous. Cream-colored tile swept across the floor. Dark wood cabinets and sparkling stainless steel appliances filled one end of the kitchen, while the other end had floor-to-ceiling windows and a simple kitchen table with chairs.

Chase set the bags of food down on the table and tugged her into his arms. Kissing him was like kissing an electrical socket. Her whole body sparked to life, aware of every inch of him pressed against every inch of her. His hand loosened the knot in her hair before cradling her head.

When he came up for air, she could barely stand. Her knees turned to jelly, and her core pulsed with need.

"Welcome to my home." He smiled down at her and kissed the tip of her nose.

"Is that always part of the welcome?" She held on to his arms to brace herself.

"For you, it should be." His smile was warm as he set her aside. "Now, if you'll stop groping me—"

"I'm not the one grop—"

He brushed his lips over hers. "We can eat. Then I can show you around." With his hand on her lower back, he guided her to one of the chairs surrounding the cherrywood table. He moved around the kitchen efficiently.

"Do you cook?" Natalie asked.

When he returned, he set the table with china, silverware and wine glasses. "I get by. My housekeeper keeps the kitchen stocked with essentials. I like to cook and don't always order out if that's what you're asking." He winked before heading to the fridge.

"It's just…I suppose I thought…"

He uncorked a bottle of white wine.

"You thought that I wouldn't want to?" he offered. As he sat, his thigh brushed hers, sending little ripples of desire racing through her. His eyes danced.

"Maybe." She couldn't think much of anything when he was near.

After he poured the wine, he pulled out a couple of containers. "I hope you like La Bouche Paisible." His hand brushed hers as she took the glass.

"I've never eaten there before." She didn't think her paycheck would cover the dinner. Not to mention she'd need something better to wear than her current wardrobe could provide to get in the door. She shoved her glasses up her nose, wishing her contacts would magically appear.

"Well, you are in for an experience."

She was already having an experience that was beyond belief. And she was more than willing to follow this golden brick road until she found her way back home.

After he dished out the contents of the containers, there was still one left.

"What's that?"

He smiled mysteriously. "Dessert."

Her plate overflowed with food. A filet steak with brown gravy, new potatoes with herbs, grilled asparagus and the scent—her stomach rumbled from the delicious smells emanating from her plate.

"Where'd you grow up?" he asked before taking a bite of steak.

"What makes you think I'm not from here?" she asked, trying to sound serious.

His eyebrow lifted, causing her to laugh.

"I'm from the Midwest. Illinois. We moved out to California my senior year when dad got a transfer. I've been here ever since."

"Do you see your family much?"

"No, my older sister stayed in Illinois when we moved, and Dad got transferred again while I was in college. We see each other at holidays, of course." Natalie bit into the steak and her mouth exploded with flavor. "Oh, wow."

He smiled, pleased with himself. "Yeah."

After she swallowed the small piece of heaven, she turned to him. "What about you?"

"For the most part, my birth and subsequent childhood are public record."

"Assume I don't know anything, because I wasn't around when you were born." She wanted to know how he felt about growing up with his family, not what the press reported.

"Well, I spent a lot of my time on movie sets or in foreign countries. I had a tutor and a nanny. My parents tried to keep me out of the tabloids, but when I started auditioning all bets were off."

"How old were you?" she asked gently.

"I was eight." He set down his fork and picked up his wineglass. Staring at the contents, he continued, "I was ten when I had my first crush. She was an actress, too. We made it into all the teeny-bop magazines."

"I never read any of those."

His gaze pivoted to her and gave her an assessing look. "I don't suppose you would have. When it ended, I talked to my parents about going to a real high school. After all, I'd played a high schooler on TV, how hard could real life be?"

"I never went to high school. Mom homeschooled me, but I bet you were the coolest kid in school." She pushed her plate away and picked up her wineglass.

His hand covered hers on the table. "Not really. Sure, I had all the toys boys like and the best clothes, but I'd never really socialized with kids my own age before." He picked up her hand and turned it over. His finger traced the lines on her palm. "I found a group and dated a little, but they either resented me for who I was or wanted something from me."

Something troubled him, but she didn't press. The more she learned about him the more real he seemed. The harder it would be to let him go.

He pushed back from the table. "Come on. I want to show you my home. I'll bring dessert."

He grabbed a couple of spoons and the container before taking her hand and leading her across the kitchen.

The rest of his house was as amazing and intimidating as the kitchen. From the crystal chandeliers in the dining room to the antiques in the living room. From the extra-large-screen TV in the media room to the red-lined pool table in the recreation room. The splendor and richness made her head spin.

"How long have you lived here?" She knew the man was a multimillionaire. She knew he wore expensive clothes, even if they were casual, but it hadn't really hit her. Now it slapped her across the face. Her apartment could fit into his media room.

"This was my parents' home. I inherited it." He seemed to choke up on the statement before it passed. "Besides, it's small compared to the one I own in Italy."

Her head still reeling, he opened a door and pulled her into a darkened room. She slammed into his back as he halted and flipped a switch. Soft lights lit the interior of the room.

She stepped around Chase and her mouth dropped open. Before her, tropical trees and flowers filled the room in bold colors, reds, yellows, greens and blues. The scent of the flowers and the leafy smell of the trees perfumed the air. A glass roof and walls enclosed the garden.

A stone path wound its way along the floor through the trees and disappeared into the foliage. She could hear the chirps of birds somewhere in the room.

"My favorite room." Chase's hand rested at her lower back.

"I can see why." She gaped up at the large, colorful flowers as he led her farther into the room. The back was blocked off and filled with tropical birds of all colors. She stopped as a large toucan swept down to the ground where a bowl of fruit rested near a small pond. It was unbelievable. Almost like stepping through a doorway onto a tropical island.

"Here we are." He led her into a small gazebo open to the sights and sounds of the room, but secluded from the door to the rest of the house.

"You could forget where you are in here." She settled on the pillows covering the floor, still trying to absorb all the colors and scents.

"That's the point. I can't always make time to escape to a tropical location, but I can usually slip into this room. I'm pretty good at pretending." He lowered himself down beside her and stretched out on his side. "Dessert?"

Tearing her gaze from a beautiful orange flower, she found herself captivated by his eyes, and her breathing hitched.

She knew why she'd agreed to come here to his house.

She wasn't strong enough to walk away from Chase. She didn't want to walk away from the attraction between them. When it was over, she was fairly certain it would be him doing the walking.

But that didn't mean she couldn't enjoy the ride. "What did you have in mind?"

His grin was positively wicked. He popped the lid off the last container. "Dark chocolate mousse."

He handed her a spoon and dug his into the creamy mousse. He lifted the spoon to her mouth and waited.

Her gaze never left his as she leaned forward and took the spoon and chocolate into her mouth. The sweetness and the slight bitterness of the chocolate combined to form ecstasy in her mouth. She closed her eyes and savored the taste rolling around on her tongue.

Before she could open her eyes, soft lips pressed against hers. His mouth tasted like the wine they'd been drinking flavored with the chocolate of the mousse. She didn't resist when his body shifted, pushing her back into the pillows.

His hands lifted her glasses from her face before his mouth returned to the gentle assault on her senses. She'd never experienced anything quite like Chase before. Every opportunity he could touch her, he did. Every chance to kiss her, he took.

As his lips caressed her neck, she wondered if this wasn't a good idea. "Maybe... maybe we should stop." Her fingers dug into his shoulders as he sucked her earlobe into his mouth.

"Mmm-hmm. You're right. We haven't finished dessert yet." His mouth returned to hers. His tongue slid along her bottom lip. His hands caressed the sides of her body, pulling her firmly up into his body. Her flesh warmed beneath his, responding to his fire.

"Chase?" she murmured against his lips. He raised his head and she forgot what she was going to say at the gentle smile on his lips and the desire in his eyes. That was a look she'd never seen in his movies. Any protests she may have had died on her tongue. She hadn't really meant them anyway.

"Would you like more dessert?" His finger lightly brushed over her nipple.

A shudder coursed through her. Resistance was futile. "Yes, please."

Chapter Eleven

Sitting cross-legged on Chase's king-size bed wearing only his T-shirt, Natalie picked up one of the chocolate-covered strawberries from the tray. She couldn't wipe the ridiculously pleased smile off her face and didn't really want to.

Sunday afternoon had never been her favorite day or time. Usually it was reserved for doing laundry or running errands. But after spending the last few hours in Chase's arms, it was definitely moving to the top of her list. Unfortunately, Monday morning would follow closely on its heels.

She glanced at the open bedroom door. Chase had discovered her weakness for sweets and had promised her the best hot chocolate ever. He'd kissed her soundly before insisting she stay in bed and conserve her energy.

She'd never felt so pampered or so thoroughly loved before. Her muscles and body ached, but it was a pleasant ache. It couldn't possibly last, though. Tomorrow was Monday, after all.

While this fantasy had been fabulous and she never wanted it to end, Monday changed everything. Back to the real world. Back to being an accountant beneath notice and an actor on the cover of *People*.

"Whoa, what happened to that smile?" Chase in only a pair of boxer briefs stood in the doorway, balancing a tray. "There it is." He set the tray on the massive nightstand and joined her on the bed. "I'm sorry to inform you that I'm out of chocolate, but I found some protein instead."

He produced a plate with a turkey sandwich cut into squares. "Eat. You need your energy."

She smiled and pushed her glasses back up her nose. "Thanks." Taking a sandwich, she smiled at him.

He lay down beside her on the bed and rubbed the hem of her shirt between two fingers. The back of his fingers brushed her skin, fanning the ever-present flame.

He helped himself to a sandwich square and a chocolate-covered strawberry. She couldn't keep her mind from their shared bath last night or the morning spent in this bed.

She picked off a corner of the sandwich and chewed it thoughtfully. "What are we going to do about tomorrow?"

He dragged his finger lazily up her leg. "What about tomorrow?" He kissed her thigh and looked up at her with his lazy grin.

Her heart leapt, and her body responded with a pulsing need. She needed to focus. "Work. Chase, stop that. We need to talk about work."

He picked up her plate and set it on the table. He handed her a bottle of water and sat up on the bed with her. "What about work?" This time his eyes were serious as he watched her drink.

She almost spilled from the intensity of his gaze. She capped the water before it ended up all over the bed.

"Well?" He took the bottle from her and set it aside.

"Well, what do we do about this?"

He scooted behind her and pulled her back to his front. She leaned her head back against him. He wrapped one arm around her shoulder and the other around her stomach, pulling her tight against him.

His voice was quiet and soft when he asked, "What do you want?" His arms tightened around her.

She turned her head so that her cheek rested on his bare chest. His heartbeat echoed in her ears. He made her feel warm and safe and beautiful.

She sighed. She wanted to stay like this forever, but that wasn't likely to happen. A whole world waited outside those doors. "I...I don't know."

"Stay with me."

"I can't do that. What about the media?"

His cheek rested against the top of her head. "What if I weren't famous and a line of paparazzi didn't hang on my every move?" His voice had an edge to it.

"I—I don't know. I—I—" She'd almost slipped and said "love." "I like you, Chase. I like spending time with you, but this can't possibly work."

"What if we didn't go public? What if we kept this to ourselves?" It sounded reasonable, but how many other girls had thought the same thing and ended up as tabloid fodder.

"Has that ever worked? It seems like those relationships always get caught. I can't be that girl. I don't want that kind of attention."

Desperation filled her. She didn't want to stop seeing Chase, but what choice did she have? She wasn't made of the stuff needed to be a Hollywood star's girlfriend. She would be compared to all his ex-girlfriends. There was no way she could measure up against the likes of Alexis Brandt. Eventually Chase would realize the mistake he'd made by being with Natalie.

His arms squeezed her. He shifted them until she lay under him. In the move, the soft T-shirt had bunched up at her waist. He lowered his mouth to hers. Afraid this could be over, she met his lips with all the desire she felt. Her hands grabbed his head to hold it there.

His hands skimmed down her sides to her panties, and her body arched up into his erection. This could be the last time. She didn't want this to ever end.

He shifted slightly while he retrieved a condom from the nightstand, but his mouth never left hers. His teeth nipped at her lips. He slid into her as his mouth continued to devastate hers. She sighed against his lips, and her body shuddered with longing.

She'd wanted to feel this all her life. The connection, the intimacy. It swelled up within her. How could she ever let this go? But she had to—she wasn't cut out for his lifestyle.

He lifted his head and gazed down into her eyes. She needed his mouth back on hers. She needed him to move within her and take them over the edge. He was an addiction, and she just needed one more hit.

His eyes searched hers. "Don't leave."

Her core pulsed around him. "But—"

"No *buts*. We don't have to go public. I want you." The muscles in his arms shook as he held himself above her.

He moved within her slowly, maintaining eye contact. She could feel him touching her soul as he slowly drove her insane. She didn't ever want this to end.

"Natalie?"

She met his heated gaze and felt the pressure building within her.

"Stay."

Her resolve to end it now before it would hurt too much crumbled at the look in his eyes. It was going to hurt when it ended, but she couldn't bear to let go. She'd take all she could get. Her body shook with her decision. "I'll stay, Chase."

His mouth covered hers, and he thrust within her again. Her body convulsed around him as she returned his kiss. Joy filled her heart. His body arched into hers once more before he collapsed against her. Her fingers tangled in his hair as they both drifted back to themselves. Where was the harm in trying?

By Monday morning the weekend rain had passed, leaving everything greener and brighter. Natalie had gone home Sunday, and Rachel hadn't even missed her. Rachel had asked what she'd done last night, and Natalie had mentioned going out to a movie or shopping or something.

Her heart had been full, and her body had been relaxed. She'd slept wonderfully last night, with only thoughts of Chase racing through her brain.

Natalie had come in early this morning to get the report finished for Mr. Morrison. Her heart jumped every time the exterior door opened, knowing that Chase would be here soon.

When Mr. Morrison showed up at nine, Natalie had handed him the report with trembling hands, sure he would sense she knew. Mr. Morrison took it and didn't spare her another glance as he made his way back to his office.

The morning dragged on, but still no Chase. Natalie lost herself in her work. When Mr. Morrison went out for lunch, she pulled out the copies of the bank statements and listed the cash withdrawals. She made sure they were put away before he returned.

She took a quick break to run and get something to eat at her desk. By then she figured Chase wasn't coming in. She didn't want to arouse anyone's suspicions by asking the receptionist about him. Her nervous energy drained off as she spent the afternoon engrossed in an audit of another film that Mr. Morrison wanted her to do.

"Good night, Natalie. That was a fine report you put together."

She broke away from the list of numbers she was adding to look up at Mr. Morrison blankly.

"Chase and Robert have it on their desks now. Don't worry about working late this week." Mr. Morrison locked his door and left before Natalie could think of anything to say.

Her head was spinning. Was Chase here? Why hadn't she noticed him go by? Why hadn't he said anything? She picked up her water bottle and headed down to the kitchen. She at least could check to see if his light was on.

It wasn't like they'd actually made any plans for today. Maybe he'd had time to think about it and really didn't want to be with her anymore. Maybe it'd just been a line to make her feel better. Her stomach dropped. Well, it wasn't like it was going to last.

She slowed her pace as she reached the end of the hall near his office. His door was shut, but light peeked out from under the door. Was that the sun or his desk light?

She sighed and went into the kitchen. Why did she care? They were just going to have an affair. It's not like they'd decided to date. She had been the one to try to cut things off. The water ran over the top of her bottle.

Maybe he'd decided that she was right. Her heart twisted but she ignored it. Maybe this was for the best. Not sparing his door another glance, she headed back to her desk. Putting it out of her mind, she filed what she was working on and pulled out the documents for *Night Blooming*. Chase wouldn't hide from her. Obviously, he had to do stuff away from the office sometimes.

She shoved her glasses up on her nose. She'd checked the shipping documents online for her contacts. They were supposed to be delivered today. Maybe she would call it an early night. After all, hadn't Chase said they should work on it together?

She heard the door close as the last person left. Well, she thought, the last one, except for her and potentially Chase, if he really was in his office. She sighed. She had it bad.

Her computer fan shut down, leaving the office in silence. She glanced down the hallway. She could knock to see if he was there and tell him she was leaving for the night. If he wasn't there, no one would know. If he was there…well, she could cross that bridge when it happened.

As she moved to stand, her desk phone rang. It was almost six o'clock. Who would be calling her at work?

"This is Natalie."

"Hi, Natalie. Jared Anderson. Before you hang up, let me apologize for the way I came off the other day. I'm just trying to show people the real Chase Booker."

She almost hung up the phone, but his last sentence stuck with her. "The real Chase Booker?"

"You know, the man behind the legend. The real Chase Booker, not the public persona."

Actually she was very familiar with the real Chase Booker, or at least the Chase Booker he'd shown her. How could she really trust that was the real Chase? He was a great actor. Award winning. What made her think he wasn't acting with her?

"Hello? Are you still there?" Jared's voice cut across the phone line.

She cleared her thoughts. "I'm sorry. I really can't help you."

"That's fine. I'm going to send you an e-mail with my contact info in case you change your mind. Good night, Natalie."

She hung up the phone. Maybe he was right. Maybe no one knew the real Chase. Her mind wandered back to this weekend. Her pulse kicked up a notch and she released a breath. If that hadn't been real, she didn't know what was.

Or maybe she just didn't want to know if it was faked. Maybe she wanted to cling to those feelings for a little while longer.

Chapter Twelve

Chase set down the phone. All day it had been one disaster after another. He'd avoided going anywhere near Natalie today for fear he wouldn't be able to resist pulling her into his arms.

His life had always been filled with beautiful women willing to give him anything. Whenever he was available, another woman would slide effortlessly into the role of girlfriend. Natalie's reluctance to be a part of his public life was something he'd never dealt with before. Even his high school girlfriend had loved the extra attention at first.

Everything about Natalie felt different, and he was afraid of letting her slip through his fingers. For once in his life, he wasn't sure what to do.

He'd hoped to catch her before she left for the day, but at five a director had called him to work out some issues with their next production. An hour later, he'd worked through the details, but feared Natalie had already left the office.

Pushing back from his desk, he strode to his door and yanked it open. Natalie stood there looking achingly uncertain. Her pale face bloomed red as she met his eyes.

Quickly glancing down the hall and seeing no one, he grabbed her hand and pulled her into his office. He slammed the door and slipped his arms around her, gathering her close. He lowered his head and found her lips with his. The stress of the day fell away as her arms clung to his neck, and her lips responded to his.

It'd only been a day since he'd seen her, but it felt like forever as his hands skimmed her backside. Her hands sank into his hair holding him close, but not close enough for him. He reached behind her and clicked the door lock into place before lifting her. Still rediscovering her sweet mouth, he set her on the edge of his desk. Her fingers worked on the buttons of his shirt while his worked on hers.

His hands skimmed over the satin of her chemise. The softness eased the ache within him slightly. He took a breath and smiled down at her.

"Hi." He pushed her shirt down her arms and kissed her collar bone.

"Hi."

He looked up in time to catch her smile, the one she only gave to him. Her cheeks and neck were flushed, but he knew it was due to arousal rather than embarrassment.

He smoothed his hands up her thighs, raising her skirt as he went. "I missed you last night."

She scooted forward on the desk until her body was pressed against his. "I missed you, too." Her voice trembled. "Maybe we shouldn't do this here." But she made no move to push him away.

He pressed his mouth to hers and ran his hand up her inner thighs. "Do you have someplace better in mind?"

Her sharp inhale was followed by a tightened grip on his arm. Her eyes unfocused as his hand reached the juncture of her thighs. Her lips parted.

Unable to resist, he captured her mouth as his hand slipped beneath her underwear to the warm, wet flesh beneath. He caught her gasp in his mouth.

His cell phone vibrated on the table. He ignored it, knowing it would go to voice mail, and nothing was more important than Natalie at this moment.

He pulled away from her to slide her underwear down her legs and slid off her sandals. Her hands sought his chest, his shoulders, his back. Every touch branded him as hers.

He made quick work of his jeans and a condom before drawing her into his arms. He tried to ease into her, but she linked her legs around his back and pulled him into her fully.

The air escaped his lungs at the feeling of her surrounding him, her legs around his waist, her hands on his shoulders, her breasts crushed against his chest. He withdrew and sank into her again. His lips sought hers as they came together at a frantic pace.

Had it only been a day since he'd been with her? Her sex clamped down on him as her body pulsated around him. He strained as he felt his own climax approaching, surrounding him, pulling him down with her. He held her to him as if she would slip away if he let go.

He could feel her heart thundering along with his. Her panting echoed in his ear. Slowly, his pulse returned to normal and he eased away from her, holding her to keep her from falling.

When she looked up at him, he smiled. "Hi."

"You definitely know how to greet a girl." Her smile was

shy and tentative, even after the weekend they'd shared and what they'd just done on his desk.

"It was probably about time to break in the desk." He brushed his lips across hers as he bent. He pulled up his pants and then picked up her discarded clothing. He held them out to her. Before she could take them, he snatched them out of her reach. "Come back to my place tonight."

A worried look crossed her face. "Do you think that's smart? What about the paparazzi?" She reached out for her underwear and shirt.

He held it out of her reach. There had to be a way. "I'll follow you home, and you can ride there in my car." He smiled, problem solved.

"Then how do I get home? Can we discuss this with my underwear on?"

He waggled his eyebrows at her. "I think some of our best discussions have been when you aren't wearing underwear."

She laughed. "Usually there's not a lot of talking at that point."

He waggled his eyebrows again. "I know." He kissed her soft smile. "Come home with me."

She snatched her clothes from him. "Fine, but we better not get caught."

"That's part of the fun."

It may be fun, but it definitely wasn't comfortable. Sure the backseat of Chase's car was plush, but Natalie had been right to worry. As they pulled up to the gate, she stared out the tinted back windows at three cars parked along the street with cameras in the windows waiting for the money shot. Butterflies flew haphazardly in her stomach.

Fortunately, no one had followed Chase and her or they would have been caught. Chase had assured her the only reason paparazzi were on his street was the multiple homes that belonged to celebrities.

But Natalie knew at least one reporter who wanted to find out what was going on with Chase. Though they were in the clear tonight, it couldn't possibly last.

She just couldn't imagine not being with Chase every opportunity she had. As they pulled through the gates, her cell phone rang. Rachel.

"Hello?"

"Natalie, are you going to be late tonight?"

She glanced at Chase's eyes in the rearview mirror. "Yeah, I probably won't get in until you're asleep." From the look in Chase's eyes, she probably wouldn't be home until right before Rachel woke up. Her body tightened in anticipation at the promise in his eyes.

"Could you pick up my dry cleaning when you pick up yours tomorrow?"

"Yeah, sure, anything else?"

"Nope that's it. Did you hear that Alexis isn't with your boss anymore? She was seen this weekend, but Chase was nowhere to be found. Do you think he's found someone else?"

Chase pulled into the garage and turned in his seat to look back at her. His eyes sent shivers down her spine.

"I don't know."

"Oh, well, keep me up on the dirt. Talk to you later."

Natalie clicked the End button.

"We did it." Chase opened his door and stepped out. He opened her door. "Not one photo snapped."

She took his offered hand, and he spun her in a circle into his arms. She laughed. She refused to think about tomorrow or next week. This sexy man wanted her now.

But if he wasn't being seen with Alexis… "How long before the press starts to wonder if you're with someone?"

His face turned thoughtful. "They're always speculating. It will probably get intense around the Oscars as they wonder who I'm bringing or who I'm not bringing."

A month until the Oscars. Surely, they'd be out of each other's system in a few weeks.

He led her into the house. A buzzing sound went off in the kitchen. Natalie started and looked around, positive that someone had found them out.

"It's just the gate buzzer." Chase dropped a kiss on her mouth, before moving over to a panel on the wall. He pressed a button. "Hello?"

"Chase, I thought we were going to talk this weekend." Alexis's sultry voice blared through the intercom.

"Alexis, now isn't a good time. Can we talk later?"

Natalie sank into a kitchen chair. Was he trying to juggle two women? Why was she one of them?

"Well, maybe if you'd answered your cell phone when I'd called, I wouldn't have driven all this way."

"Sorry to make you drive, but tonight isn't a good time to talk." Chase sent Natalie an apologetic look.

She smiled tightly. She didn't have the face or body that Alexis had, but Chase didn't seem to care about that. After this weekend and the office… Her face flushed thinking about it. She clasped her hands tightly on the table.

"Oh, I'm sure these nice photographers standing listening to our conversation would love to know why you aren't inviting me up to the house. Wouldn't you, guys?"

Natalie could hear the smile in Alexis's voice.

"Fine, Alexis. Let me buzz you in." Chase released the button and dropped into the chair next to Natalie. His hands covered hers.

"Do you want me to go?" Natalie whispered.

"No, I don't, but I don't want her to see you here."

Her lips tightened, and she tried to ignore the ache in her chest. She started to pull her hands out from under his.

His hands tightened. "Natalie." His voice was soothing. "It's not like that. She would love to cause a scandal where she was the woman wronged, but that's not what this is about. She's trying to get ahead and using me as a stepping stone. She and I were never real. Do you understand that?"

Not looking up, she nodded.

"The only woman I want to be with is you. Why don't you go upstairs and get tucked into bed? I'll be up in a few moments after I get rid of Alexis, and I can show you what we have is real." His finger brushed back a stray hair and then tipped up her chin. "I'll even bring ice cream."

He seemed sincere, but the man acted for a living. She couldn't lie worth a damn, but his career was to pretend and make people believe him. Something in his eyes drew her and reassured her. Maybe she just wanted to be reassured, and he was spewing crap, but she wanted him to be speaking from his heart, even if they were doomed.

"Natalie?"

She focused on his eyes again. Her heart clenched, but she wasn't ready to face the truth. She didn't want him to be using her.

"Please."

She nodded. He brushed his lips over hers. She stood and strode across the kitchen. Without looking back she walked through the dining room and out into the entrance hall where the stairs were.

Even though her eyes were on the marble tile beneath her feet, she caught a movement out of the corner of her eye. She stopped and looked through the glass door with horror. On the other side stood Alexis, her hand raised to press the doorbell.

They stared at each other through the door. Oh, no.

Chapter Thirteen

Chase had hung back in the kitchen for a few minutes before heading to the door. Alexis had probably stopped and made sure the photographers got a few key shots of her driving through his gate. Maybe even a few on his front porch.

As he entered the foyer, his heart stopped. Natalie and Alexis stared at each other through the glass door. Chase cursed his stupid luck as he brushed past Natalie and jerked open the door.

"Come in, Alexis." He shut the door behind her and led her farther into the room, away from telephoto range, which fortunately Natalie was out of. "Ladies, I believe we need to have a discussion. Let's go to the media room."

Alexis strutted through the door leading to the media room. Chase took Natalie's hand. Her face registered shock and panic.

"I'll fix this."

Her eyes were wide. "How?"

He had no idea how, but he couldn't tell her that. She looked like her dog just died. "I'll fix this."

Taking Natalie's hand, he led her into the Media room and sat her in a chair before closing the door.

"Alexis, I believe you remember Natalie from the office." Chase stood beside Natalie's chair while Alexis leaned against the bar with a satisfied grin.

"From the office? Oh, yes, the little girl who does the books. Chase, this is worse than Jude's nanny fiasco."

He could see the wheels turning in Alexis's head. "This is nothing like that, Alexis. You and I aren't dating."

"Yes, but you're still screwing the hired help."

Natalie jerked in her chair as if Alexis had slapped her. Why hadn't he asked Natalie to go upstairs and not subject her to Alexis? He rested his hand on her shoulder, and she winced under his hand. He squeezed her, hoping to reassure her. This night was going from bad to worse. "Look, Alexis, we're adults here. You and I aren't a couple anymore."

Alexis's eyes narrowed and her famous lips tightened. "You're right, we're not, but they don't know that." She flung her arm out in an arc. "What *they* will see is that the Sexiest Man Alive prefers his bookkeeper over me. Do you know what that will do to my image?"

"What do you want me to do, Alexis? Put my life on hold so you can try to make an even bigger name for yourself?"

Her body curled down into a seat. "No, but I think we can find a mutually agreeable solution."

"I'm listening." He didn't need Alexis to start attacking Natalie again, and the quickest way to get Alexis out of here was to figure out what she wanted.

Natalie tensed under his hand again. If he hadn't driven her here, she probably would have already bolted, which would have been impossible to clean up after the entrance Alexis made.

Alexis flashed her smile. "We've already been seen at the Golden Globes."

He waited for her to go on. He'd forgotten how melodramatic she was. Everything had been an act with her. He wondered if she even knew herself anymore.

"There's been Oscar talk...." Her eyes gleamed with her self-importance. "If you go, I want to be on your arm."

Natalie shifted in the chair. It wasn't a lot to ask. It wasn't as if Natalie wanted to go. Or did she? There's nothing he'd like better than to have her by his side on award night, but that would bring her under the spotlight. She barely wanted to be seen at the best of times. He knew it from the way she'd try to shrink behind things or pull into herself when they spoke.

If their relationship ever hit the stands, it would simultaneously hit a wall. She'd be gone, out of his life forever. He had no doubt about it. His chest ached. It wasn't like this could last.

"Fine. On one condition. My relationship with Natalie stays out of the tabloids. If there is even a hint of her name or face on a page, no Oscar night."

"That's not fair." Alexis stood and stomped her foot to emphasize her point. "What if you guys get sloppy or someone else finds out?"

Chase leaned back against the wall. "That's the risk you'll have to deal with. Take it or leave it." He was confident Alexis would do anything to keep the tabloids from finding out about Natalie just to go to the Oscars. That would at least give Chase a month of not having to worry that Natalie would turn tail and run. One month would have to be enough.

Alexis's mouth curled into a smile. "All right, but you have to go out with me a few times during the month, too." Her red-painted nails curved around her arms like claws.

Make a deal with the devil and you're bound to get burned. Isn't that what his grandpa had always said? If it allowed him to keep Natalie, he'd do almost anything.

"Sure, whatever."

Alexis smiled dangerously. "Seal it with a kiss?"

"Not if my life depended on it." He heard the breath rush out of Natalie. How long had she been holding it?

"Well, then it was a pleasure meeting you again... Natalie, was it? I'll see you this Friday and Saturday, Chase." She drifted across the room.

"Friday only."

She stopped. "Friday night and Saturday dinner. You'll be home early enough to do whatever or whomever you like."

"Fine."

She smiled like the cat that'd caught the canary and swallowed it whole. "It's a pleasure doing business with you, Chase."

Alexis swept from the room. Chase sighed. The arrangement would keep their relationship hidden for a while longer. Natalie could stay.

"Can you take me home?" she whispered. Her voice shook as if she were about to cry.

He dropped to his knee in front of her. Brushing her hair back from her face, he looked up into her large brown eyes. "You don't have to go home, Natalie. Besides, if we leave now, the photogs will definitely follow." Please stay with me, his heart pleaded, even though he knew this couldn't last.

She grimaced.

"Stay, Natalie."

"Why?"

He sensed there was more to that question. Something huge lurked beneath that question, and he wished she'd let it out. Trust him enough to deal with whatever doubts she may be having. He chose to ignore the lurking monster and answer her question as posed, even knowing that lurking monsters usually pounced on you when you least expected it.

"Because I want you to stay. Because I want to hold you tonight. I want to feel you in my arms when I wake."

"Why? Why me?" She refused to meet his eyes. "Why not her?"

He wanted to shake her and pull her into his arms and never let her go. "Because she's not you."

Her face was flush with color. "I'm not like Alexis. I don't want what she wants."

"Natalie, please. We can figure out where this will go tomorrow. Be with me tonight." He wrapped his arms around her waist and laid his head on her chest. "Just tonight."

She wrapped her arms around his head, and he sighed. She was his for at least tonight.

Friday morning came too quickly for Natalie. The week had flown by.

Night Blooming had been nominated for seven Oscars. The whole office was ecstatic. Chase and Robert had taken the production team out to lunch to celebrate the news.

Every night after everyone left, Chase and she had worked on figuring out how much Mr. Morrison had taken. The evidence kept piling up. And after crunching numbers, Chase would take her to his house, and they'd spend the night in each other's arms.

They'd talked about his tutors and her mother. How their classrooms of one had been lonely at times. He'd shared his secret desire to go to college. She'd told him about rooming with Rachel in college, and how different it had been from anything she'd ever experienced.

She wasn't getting as much sleep as she needed, but she was deliciously tired. During the day, the strutting down the hallway couldn't intimidate her anymore. Her contacts had come in on Monday, and she no longer had to wear her old glasses.

She smiled remembering Chase's reaction. He'd actually missed the darn things and made her promise to bring them with her to his place.

"Are you ready?" Chase was there in front of her.

Her smile grew until she remembered what they were about to do. Martin Morrison was about to get his walking papers. Well, not exactly. There would be a police escort waiting to book him for fraud.

Her smile slipped. She turned her head to look at the door behind her. Chase had insisted she be a part of this, even though she had tried to argue with him. She still wasn't good at saying no.

"Okay." She stood and followed Chase down the hall, trying not to focus on his butt in those fabulous jeans. He stopped abruptly, and she crashed into his back. Steadying herself, she stepped back.

He glanced over his shoulder and smiled the smile that melted her heart every time. She couldn't even blush anymore around him. Except when she thought about what he did to her, his gentle exploration, the slow burn that ignited whenever he was near. She sighed.

"Are we ready?" Robert's voice interrupted her daydreams.

"Yeah, we have all the evidence. We just need to call in Martin. Natalie, you can wait in my office." His voice was all business, but she couldn't seem to lift her gaze from watching his lips move.

His words penetrated her brain, and she nodded and stepped around him into the office. She took one of the chairs along the back and crossed her legs. By the time the men filed in, she'd squeezed her hands so tight her knuckles were turning white.

She didn't want to be in here. Confrontations were not her thing, but Chase had insisted. She tried to fade into the corner as the men took their seats.

"As you know, Martin, we've been looking into the production expenses."

Mr. Morrison glanced over at her in the corner, but didn't so much as raise an eyebrow. He focused his attention on Chase. "Yes, Chase. We finished up the audit on Monday, and I provided you with our report. All the expenses tied in. The numbers were correct."

"Not exactly, Martin." Chase leaned back in his chair. "We found some things that didn't seem right."

Robert chimed in. "Like expense reports from extras."

"We typically allow actors certain expenses while on set." Martin's voice changed pitch slightly. His head swiveled from Chase to Robert. "I see nothing wrong with a few expenses."

"Martin, we know about the cash payments. We also know that the extras didn't turn in any expense reports." Chase was calm and matter-of-fact. He didn't project the anger or betrayal that Natalie knew he felt. He was cold and direct.

"I don't know what you are suggesting, Chase, but I haven't done anything wrong." He swiveled in his chair and pierced Natalie with his gaze. "What did you find that you didn't bring to me?"

Natalie cowered in her corner. Her palms sweated and her stomach churned.

"Natalie did her job." Chase drew Martin's attention back to him.

She breathed in and out slowly.

Robert stood and walked around the desk behind Chase. "The police are here to take you into custody, Martin. I'm sorry it's come to this."

"Not as sorry as you'll be." Martin stood and straightened his jacket. "Not as sorry as you will be." He glared at Natalie as he walked out the door.

Natalie couldn't slow the beating of her heart and knew it was only a matter of minutes before her breakfast made a repeat performance. She lunged out of the chair and out the door. Shoving into the bathroom, she made it to the stall before the heaving began.

"Natalie?" Chase's voice was directly behind her. His hand soothed her, running down her back.

Mortification filled her as her stomach turned over again. His hand continued slow soothing circles as tears streamed down her face. His hand left her, and a moment later, he draped a wet towel over the back of her neck.

Her stomach finally stopped convulsing. She slid from her knees to lean against the stall wall. Her eyes closed as exhaustion overwhelmed her.

Something wet touched her face, and she jerked her eyes opened. Chase gently wiped her face with a towel. He brushed away a tear with his thumb.

"We need to get you home." His hand smoothed back her hair. He leaned over her as if he were going to pick her up.

She wanted to rely on him, to give in and let him take care of her, but she knew what was on the other side of the bathroom door. Martin's very public exit from the company had drawn a number of press vans. Chase couldn't carry her out of even the bathroom without making a scene. She wasn't prepared to deal with that.

She placed her clammy hand on his warm arm. "No, Chase."

"What?" He seemed genuinely confused.

"You can't. The press."

"Damn it." He slammed his hand against the metal stall. "What does it matter? Maybe I'm just a really good employer."

"That's not the way it works, Chase, and you know it." She pressed her shaking hand against his cheek.

"So now I can't even take care of you." His jaw was tight. He'd push it if she let him.

She wanted to let him and that scared her. Instead she lifted her head. "I'm fine, Chase. It's just nerves. By the way, you know you're in the lady's room, right?"

His eyes narrowed, and he didn't smile like she'd hoped. He stood and helped her to her feet. "Go home, Natalie. Get some sleep."

He tossed the towel in the trash and left the room. She stumbled over to the sink and turned on the faucet. So much for another week or two. She splashed water over her face and swished some in her mouth to get rid of the taste.

Her makeup was nonexistent. Her face was pale. She had work to do, but the boss had told her to go home. With the hours they'd put in she'd already worked a forty-hour week anyway. She could face the fallout on Monday morning, especially if anyone had witnessed Chase following her into the bathroom.

Besides, Chase was upset with her and she didn't want to face the anger in his eyes.

Did he want to get caught together? She didn't think he

did, but she was the one who'd put the restriction on their relationship. He hadn't protested, so she figured he didn't care. She'd thought he understood.

She pushed away from the sink and dried her face. The real problem was for one moment she hadn't cared that the press surrounded the place. She'd just wanted Chase to continue looking at her like that. Concerned and caring. She'd wanted him to carry her out and take care of her.

Instead she'd go home to her empty apartment. Maybe she'd pop on a movie. She wasn't going to see Chase any other way tonight.

It was Alexis's turn. Her stomach clenched again, but there was nothing left. She definitely had to leave before Alexis came to retrieve her prize.

Chapter Fourteen

Chase's head lolled back on the cab seat. He snapped it upright again. "Here, turn here." He handed the man a hundred-dollar bill as he pulled to the curb. "Keep the change."

His eyes weren't working quite right, but he could still put one foot in front of the other. It had been Alexis's idea to leave his car at her place for the night while they went clubbing. He was really too old to go clubbing. The stairs wavered before him as he climbed them.

He raised his hand and pressed the button. The chimes rang inside the apartment and he pressed it again. One more time. Why was he pressing this button again? Oh, well, press it again.

"I have a bat and I've called nine-one-one." The sweet sound of Natalie's voice reached his ears.

"Rapunzel, Rapunzel, let down your fair hair."

The door snapped open and the light blinded him. "Chase?"

"Ah, my fair Rosalynn, let me slay a dragon for you, my fair maiden." His grin felt like it would split his face.

He stumbled into the apartment and heard the door shut and the locks snick into place.

"What are you doing here, Chase?" Natalie was suddenly directly in front of him.

"Why, I'm here for you. To slay whatever needs to be slayed. To lay whatever needs to be laid."

Her nose wrinkled, and she raised her eyebrow. "How did you get here, Chase? Please tell me you didn't drive."

"Of course not. I'm the spokesman for drunk driving. I mean, against drunk driving."

Her image wavered before him, and he reached out to steady her. Maybe those shots hadn't been the smartest move.

"Chase, you can't stay here."

"Why not? A bed is a bed. Your bed is serviceable if I recall. Of course, the floor is good, too. We could always try the wall." He moved in close to her.

Her cheeks turned bright red, and she stepped back right into said wall.

His body flared to life as he noticed her kitten pajamas and a smudge of chocolate on the corner of her mouth. "Do you know I find kitten pajamas very sexy?" He tugged on the hem of her shirt.

"Chase, you should go home. Let me call you a cab." She tried to slide along the wall, but he put his hands on either side of her head. "Chase?"

"What, Natalie? Are you afraid someone will find out? Are you afraid someone will snap a shot of us kissing inside your apartment?" He leaned into her until his mouth brushed against hers when he spoke. "Or are you afraid you'd like being watched?"

"Chase—"

His mouth covered hers, cutting off any protests she might have. He'd had an Altoid in the cab. She tasted like chocolate, smooth and creamy. The mint and chocolate blended perfectly. Her tongue was cold as it brushed against his. Ice cream. He smiled.

He lifted his head. "Did you want me to leave?"

"No." Her voice was light and airy. "But maybe we should go to your place. Rachel will be home soon. And if we leave now maybe the shutterbugs will still be outside the clubs."

Though Chase hadn't always been friendly with the paparazzi, they were a part of his life. A part he had had to learn to live with and they weren't going away anytime soon. It didn't matter tonight. All he wanted was Natalie.

He brushed back a strand of brown hair and tucked it behind her ear. "Why don't you drive us back?"

Her eyes fluttered as she leaned into his hand. She turned her head and kissed his open palm.

"How soon did you say your roommate would be home?" He rubbed his thumb across her lips.

"Too soon."

He replaced his thumb with his lips. She opened beneath him. Her hands gripped his shirt and pulled him closer. He gathered her into his arms and backed her down the hallway.

He dragged in a breath. "Haven't we been here before?" he said as he pushed through the living room door.

Her smile took his breath away. "I'm sure I have no idea what you mean."

As he traced the sensual curve of her lower lip with his fingertip, he glanced over her shoulder and saw the credits rolling on *If Only*. "At least this time you got to finish."

Her eyes sparkled up at him. "I always finish with you." Wherever this playful woman had come from, he hoped she'd stick around for a while. His beautiful accountant seemed to be blooming all around him.

She took his hand and pulled him toward her bedroom. He went willingly. Even though he'd had a few shots, the effects were starting to fade, leaving behind that easy, relaxed feeling.

He sank on the edge of the bed and held his arms out to her. She stepped between his knees, and he wrapped his arms around her.

"I'm sorry," she whispered as her hands stroked over his hair. Her heartbeat was strong beneath the cushion of her breasts.

"For what?" He never wanted to let her go, but knew it was coming. The pressure of a public relationship would kill this tender thing they had. His arms squeezed her tighter.

"For being so damned paranoid." Her hand brushed the side of his face.

He closed his eyes and absorbed what she was making him feel. His heart filled his chest and he knew he wouldn't be able to let her go. He lifted his head and took her face between his hands. "All I want is you, Natalie."

Their lips met. He surrendered himself to whatever would happen in the future as he pulled her down to the bed with him.

"What was that?" Natalie put her hand against Chase's glistening shoulder. "Chase?"

His head lifted from her breasts, and he looked at her with passion-laden eyes. His body brushed against hers, tantalizing all the fine nerve endings as he moved up to take possession of her mouth again. The sound receded in her mind as he slid into her, filling her.

The sound of the door slamming shocked Natalie. "Chase?"

He moved within her. "Hmmm." His movements were slow and lazy. She got lost in the movements as her passion swirled higher and higher with each stroke.

"Natalie, why are all the lights on?" Rachel's voice pierced through the wood of her door.

"Uh-oh."

Rachel knew no boundaries. She could open the door and find them. Chase's naked body completely covered hers. Not that Rachel hadn't seen Chase's butt before. Almost every woman in America and across the globe had seen Chase's butt. Her body tensed at the combined approach of her orgasm and the footsteps outside the door.

"Chase?" she whispered. She groaned against his lips. He seemed determined to drive her out of her mind, and he was doing a great job of it, too. His lips moved over hers, capturing whatever she might have said. Her body exploded all around him.

He swallowed all the sounds she made. His body tensed over her, and he let go.

"Are you even here, Natalie?" Rachel's voice was on the other side of the door.

Natalie started pushing on Chase. He had to get off her before Rachel opened the door. He cuddled against her body and a little snore escaped his mouth.

"I'm not dressed, Rachel." That much was true. "Sorry, I…" *I just had incredible sex with Chase Booker and can't tell anyone.* "I spilled ice cream all over myself."

The arms around her tightened. Chase rolled until she was on top of his chest. Oh, yeah, this was a much better view for Rachel. She lifted her head to glare down at him and found his laughing green eyes open.

The urge to shove him off the bed almost over-whelmed her. She tried to scoot off his chest, but his arms held her still.

She turned her head to watch the doorknob. Her ear was next to his mouth and she about jumped when his quiet voice whispered, "I'd lick the ice cream off for you."

"Oh, okay." Rachel's voice drifted away from the door. She must be walking away. "I'm going to head to bed. We have to talk in the morning. I can't wait to tell you what I found out about Chase."

"I bet you could tell her a thing or two." He sucked her earlobe into his mouth, sending shivers of pleasure rippling through her.

The door to the other bedroom closed, and Natalie relaxed against Chase's chest. Sure, she could tell Rachel that Chase was an unselfish lover. He snored. He was ticklish on his sides. His lips were as soft as velvet. He slept wrapped around her as if he never wanted to let her go. And she was hopelessly in love with him.

She rested her head against the steady beat of his heart. One of his hands stroked down her back while the other rested in her hair. She'd been wrong. She should have stopped earlier. She should have never gone to his house. She should have turned him away at her door. She should have stopped that first kiss.

She was too far gone now. When she thought of ending it, her lungs seized up, and she fought for air. She shivered as she thought of the long, lonely nights ahead of her. Lonely nights made worse because she knew what it was like to not be alone. To be made love to so thoroughly that no one would ever be able to replace him.

Her eyes burned, and she took short, quick breaths to stop the flood that threatened. He rolled them to the side and lifted her chin. Seeing the concern in his eyes broke her. The tears slipped out even as she fought to hold them back.

"What's wrong, Natalie?" His thumb brushed aside the tears, smearing them on her cheeks.

"Nothing." *Everything.* She tried to smile and blinked back the tears. Maybe it was worth the risk. Maybe he was worth the exposure. And maybe she could have a pony, too.

He tightened his arms around her, pulling her against his chest. "Let's go home," he whispered against her hair.

Not his house. Home. The place she belonged.

Chapter Fifteen

Natalie sipped the hot tea Chase had made her. Wearing only his T-shirt, she sat on his kitchen counter while he cooked eggs for her on his industrial range.

The world seemed bright and cheery this morning like nothing could touch them. He worked on the stove like a pro, cooking an omelet without a spatula, showing off by sliding it around the pan before flipping it in the air and catching it.

"You wouldn't do that if you had to clean up the mess." She set the mug down and used her hands to brace herself while she leaned back.

He glanced up at her. "I don't make messes that I don't clean up." His free hand roamed tantalizingly up her thigh toward the hem of the T-shirt.

She playfully swatted at his hand. "None of that. I need some food before another round."

"Thankfully, food is done." He eased the omelet onto a plate and turned off the stove. He grabbed her waist and lifted her down to the floor.

"My hero." She grabbed her plate and went to the kitchen table.

Chase joined her with a wicked smile on his face. "Eat up."

The man might be an Academy Award-winning actor, but he could cook one mean omelet. Of course, it helped that he had all the finest ingredients and fresh vegetables to pick from.

The shrill ring of the phone broke the amicable silence. Chase got up and left the room to pick it up.

A few seconds later "Glamorous" by Fergie sounded from the depths of her purse. Setting down her fork, she dug out her phone. A picture of Rachel showed on the screen.

She hit the Talk button. "You changed my ringtone."

"Not now. Where are you?" Rachel's voice was impatient.

Natalie leaned against the wall and looked down the hall to where Chase stood talking on the phone. She could feel the silly smile on her face and didn't care. "Having breakfast."

"Where?"

"Why?"

"Natalie, do you know what's going on?" Rachel seemed upset by something.

"No, what's happened? Are you okay?" She straightened from the wall. Chase's eyes widened as his gaze met hers.

"That CFO Chase fired talked to some reporter and said that Chase was having an affair with someone at work."

Natalie's heart stopped. She almost dropped the phone. "Do they know who?" Her voice sounded distant to her own ears.

"They say whoever it is he's been seeing her and Alexis.

Do you want to tell me something, Natalie?" Rachel was her best friend. Natalie could hear the hurt in Rachel's voice.

"Where do they say Chase is?"

Chase had set down the phone and was striding across the room toward her.

"They think he's at Alexis's. At least, that's what one report says. But another report says an eyewitness saw him get into a cab and leave Alexis. They haven't been able to talk to the cabby yet."

Natalie broke out in a cold sweat. Thousands of cameras could be lined up all over the street just waiting for her to step out of his house. The delicious omelet sat like a lump in her stomach. Chase stopped in front of her.

"I've got to go." She shut the phone on Rachel's voice.

"They know," she said. The illusion shattered around her. It was over. "I've got to go."

Chase grabbed her shoulders before she could walk around him. "Why?"

What did he mean why? Didn't he know? "They know, Chase. Martin leaked it to the press. They are probably out on the street, just waiting for me to walk out. Oh, God, they are going to take pictures of me."

"Natalie?" His fingers tightened on her shoulders.

"What, Chase?" She glanced at the windows. Photographers might be lurking in the bushes, behind the trees. "Maybe they aren't here yet. Maybe I can still get out."

"I talked to Alexis."

Her gaze shot to his. The look in his eyes didn't alleviate her panic. This was worse than she thought.

"She's leaked to the paparazzi that I spent the night at her house. They're waiting over there to talk to me. She's putting them off, but she has to go out sometime today."

Relief flowed over her in a gush. "Then I can leave. I

can get out before they realize you are here. No one's going to think anything of my little Honda leaving. They'll just think I'm the paid help."

"You aren't the hired help." His voice was forceful. "Don't go."

"I can get dressed—what?" She refocused on him.

His face was drawn tight as if he was fighting with something. "Don't go."

"But if I don't, they'll find out." Where was he going with this?

"So what? Let them find out." A hardness filled his eyes.

She stared up at him. Her mouth parted to ask why, but no sound came out.

He closed his eyes and dropped his hands from her shoulders. "You're right. Go get dressed. I'll clean up down here."

He turned his back on her and walked to the kitchen table. She didn't want this to end, but the situation had spiraled out of her control. She wanted to go to him and wrap her arms around his waist and say everything would be okay, but he'd already closed himself off from her.

She drew in a breath. She had to go. There was nothing more to it. Their affair had been fun to Chase while it was hidden, but he'd realize she wasn't what he wanted in the bright glare of the spotlight. The carefree days were over. She had to let Chase go.

Chase slammed the refrigerator door. He wanted to throw plates across the room. He wanted to tear something apart. Instead he leaned his forehead against the stainless steel door.

She was leaving. Damn it. He couldn't stop her. She never wanted to be part of his world. His shrinking violet preferred the dark to the glare of the spotlight.

He'd known that from the start. They'd both known this

would happen. This time would have come eventually; he'd just thought when it happened she'd want to stay, or he'd be ready to let her go.

He shoved away from the fridge and stormed through the house. He took the stairs two at a time until he reached the bedroom.

She sat on the bed looking forlorn. "I found my sock." She held it up. "But I can't find my other shoe." Her lower lip trembled.

Scanning the room, his gaze fell upon the missing shoe. He scooped it up and knelt on the floor at her feet. She wouldn't meet his eyes.

He snatched the sock out of her loose fingers. Lifting her foot, he pulled her sock over it and then slipped on her shoe. He stood, tugging her up with him.

She studied his chest. He tipped her face up so he could look into her brown eyes one last time. Tears swam over her eyes.

One more taste. His lips found hers. Her arms wrapped around his neck, holding him close. Desperation tainted the kiss.

She yanked her head away and dropped her arms. "Good-bye, Chase." She hurried out the door.

A pain stabbed through his chest. What if…

He caught up to her at the bottom of the stairs. "Wait."

She stopped and dropped her chin to her chest. "Don't make this any harder than it already is."

"How much harder can it get?" He could hear the tremor in his voice, but ignored it. All that mattered was that Natalie didn't give up on him.

"Please, Chase. Let me go." She moved in the direction of the kitchen, but he blocked her. She swung around toward the front door.

He grabbed her arm. "I love you." The words slipped from his soul.

She stiffened as if he'd hit her, but she didn't meet his eyes. The words lay like a gauntlet thrown down between them. He hadn't meant to say them. He wasn't even sure what those words meant, but it felt right with Natalie.

Her words were whispered to the door. "You pretend to be in love for a living." Her arm shook under his touch. "How do you know what's real?"

Her words cut him to the quick. He drew her away from the door and turned her. He tilted her face up. Tears streamed down from huge eyes. Her eyes were devoid of hope. It ripped through him.

"You're real. What I feel is real." How could he convince her? What more could he give her?

She closed her eyes and shook her head. "Pretend. Make believe." She jerked her arm from him and swiped at her cheeks. "Someone to play house with. Someone to pretend to have a normal life. You'll never have a normal life. You're Chase Booker, movie star, producer—"

"I'm a man, dammit." Chase could feel the years slip away, and he was that teenage boy trying to explain to his girlfriend to ignore the cameras. They didn't matter. Only the two of them did.

Natalie tried to walk past him to go to the garage again, but he blocked her way. He pulled her into his arms and kissed her. She jerked away with tears in her eyes, pressing her fingers to her lips.

"We can't, Chase. We can't be in love. We don't live in the same world." She spun and yanked open the front door.

"Fine." He wouldn't crucify himself anymore. If she wanted to leave, she'd leave. If his love wasn't enough to keep her, she could go.

Her shoulders slumped and she nodded. She glanced back over her shoulder at him, but he maintained a look of indifference. He'd begged enough.

As she looked forward again, a flash went off.

Chapter Sixteen

"Back to our catch of the day," the television blared. "It would appear Alexis Brandt has been replaced by a younger woman. Photographers got these pictures of the young woman leaving Chase's house earlier today. The woman hasn't been identified yet. Friday, allegations of an office romance had been released by Pandora Productions' ex-CFO, Martin Morrison."

The TV showed Natalie's Honda Fit racing out of Chase's driveway. What it didn't show was that she'd managed to get away before anyone was able to hop into their cars. She'd driven around a little before returning home, just in case.

Why had she gone out the front door? Because she couldn't stand to walk around Chase and through his house to escape. Because if she'd walked through his house, he might have changed her mind, and she would have stayed.

"We don't have to watch." Rachel plopped down on the couch next to her and handed her a bucket of Cherry Garcia ice cream and a spoon. Rachel swiped at the used tissues that littered the couch and the floor.

"I know." Her insides were hollow. It didn't matter. None of it mattered. Chase had told her he loved her, and she'd thrown it back in his face. Because she thought it was for the best.

"Do you want to talk about it?" Rachel straightened the blanket over Natalie's legs.

"No." The tears overflowed her eyes again. It hadn't been for the best, because the paparazzi were going to figure out who she was. She couldn't avoid work. She'd promised Chase she would carry the workload until they could hire a CFO.

"Wanna watch a movie?"

"No." Her favorite movie that saw her through the bad times would never be the same again. She couldn't watch Chase on the screen and not remember those same eyes staring into hers, that body pressed against hers, those words.... Those simple words that meant everything to her, but weren't enough.

Natalie and Rachel decided if she wore her glasses maybe the swarms of paparazzi wouldn't be able to recognize her. She'd pulled her hair back in a ponytail. It had been down when she'd left Saturday morning and had obscured part of her face.

Natalie could barely breathe let alone walk and talk. A sense of numbness surrounded her. She borrowed Rachel's car to get to work.

When she pulled up to Pandora Productions, it was worse than she'd imagined. A crew from *E!* stood outside recording an intro piece. The parking lot was filled with photographers leaning against their cars waiting.

She hoped they wouldn't realize she was the woman they were waiting for. She parked the car and steadied herself. Pushing her glasses up her nose, she walked toward the door.

"Chase Booker and Robert Addler brought allegations of fraud against their CFO on Friday morning."

She breezed past the camera crew and made it through the door. The receptionist glanced up at her and went back to the computer screen.

Shrugging her purse back over her shoulder, Natalie shuffled down the hallway to her desk. She flipped on the computer and glanced around. No one felt the urge to strut this morning, which suited Natalie just fine. She didn't need to be reminded she wasn't tall, thin and gorgeous on top of everything else.

Her water bottle was empty, but there was no way she was going to pass by Chase's office to get more water. What if he was in there? She had to pretend he didn't matter.

She opened her e-mail, and the computer downloaded two messages. Both were from Jared Anderson. Sighing, she clicked on the first one. It was his contact information, along with a note of how they'd talked on the phone.

She closed it and opened the second one, which had been sent this morning. *If you need to talk, you know where to find me. S*he deleted the e-mail. It was inevitable that people would put two and two together and figure out she was the one Chase had been seeing.

But she wasn't going to help them along. She pulled a stack of invoices over and started to enter them into the computer. She needed to keep herself busy.

* * *

Walking into Pandora had been a nightmare of saying "No comment" and "I have nothing to say." His sunglasses helped to hide the rings under his eyes from his sleepless night.

He'd already told his publicity director to give no comments. Alexis had agreed to keep Natalie's name a secret as long as she could say that she dumped him and the office worker was a rebound. He hadn't cared. Business as usual.

The receptionist glanced up and gave him a wan smile before returning to her work. He walked up to her and waited for her to hang up the phone.

"Hold all my calls. If anyone asks, Robert and I will have a press release this afternoon about Martin's departure." He'd been so wrapped up in Natalie that he hadn't even thought about firing Martin, which had served to increase the number of reporters outside.

"Yes, sir." She dropped her eyes back to the computer screen and answered the line.

He straightened his shoulders. Natalie would be here already. He had to keep her secret for as long as possible. The hallway was mostly empty as he walked toward his office.

He glanced nonchalantly toward Natalie's desk. Her head was bent over some papers and her glasses dangled on the tip of her nose. He almost stumbled, but ripped his gaze from her and continued forward.

Taking a deep breath, he unlocked his office. Ten minutes after he settled behind his desk to read a script, Robert came in.

"We need to talk."

Chase set down the script. He hadn't been able to read it anyway. The image of Natalie half-naked on his desk kept interrupting his train of thought. "What's on your mind?"

"Are the rumors true?" Robert slumped into the chair.

"Which ones?" Chase looked up at the ceiling. He should have stayed home, but every room smelled of her. Her smile followed him. Her words haunted his steps.

"Well, let's see. How about the ones that include a certain accountant?" Robert had been his friend for years. Part of the reason they became friends was his no-nonsense attitude.

But Chase didn't want to talk about Natalie. He tightened his lips and leaned back.

Robert shifted. "Okay, how about damage control? You know, the other employees are talking about how she slept with you to get the CFO position."

"That's ridiculous."

Robert held out his hands. "I'm only saying what they're saying. You need to figure out how to handle this and quick. There are leaks in this company that would make a sieve jealous. The press is going to find out about Natalie, and it's going to blow up in both of your faces unless you do something about it now."

Chase dropped his head into his hands. "I know, but what am I supposed to do?"

"Don't tell me you love her? I thought you were just getting over Alexis." Robert held up his hands again.

Chase stopped glaring at Robert, but he still wasn't happy. It would be a while before he was happy again. "We'll deal with it when we deal with Martin."

"We should also consider changing who she reports to."

Chase slammed his hand down on the desk.

Robert stood up. "She'll start reporting to me. We'll start interviewing for the CFO position tomorrow. I already told Anne to call recruiters."

"We're not together anymore. She can still report to

me." Chase rubbed his hands over his face, feeling his hard-earned control slipping.

"It doesn't matter if you are still together or not. We have to maintain appearances. And maybe if she isn't reporting to you, she might actually stay with the company. If you hadn't noticed, she has a good mind and a knack for numbers."

"I noticed."

"Good, then we'll move forward with my plan." Robert moved to the door and looked back. "Man, you must have it bad." He slipped out. Chase's pen hit the closed door.

The whole morning he stayed in his office trying to get through the script. Every few minutes someone else would knock on his door. By noon he was a mess of tension.

He'd finally managed to put aside the disaster his life had become and get into the script when a tentative knock on the door brought him out of it.

"What?" Chase bellowed at the door.

The door opened a crack. "Um, if now isn't a good time, I could come back later." Natalie stood in the doorway, looking like she'd prefer to run down the hall than come in and talk with him.

"Why are you here?" he snapped. Chase's heart beat unsteadily in his chest. The smell of strawberries wafted between them, making him want to grind his teeth together.

A tinge of pink covered her cheeks and neck. She slid her glasses back up her nose. "Robert asked me to meet him here." She glanced toward Robert's office. Her uncertainty and discomfort made him feel a little better, but it also annoyed him.

He'd covered her blushes with his kisses. Brought smiles and sighs to those lips. Slipped his hands around her waist and held her body against him.

"Maybe I should wait in the hallway...." Her voice brought his attention back to her face.

"Don't be ridiculous. Have a seat. I'm sure Robert will be here in a minute."

Natalie considered turning tail and running for the door. Chase's intense gaze turned her knees to water, while it caused her battered heart to leap up in her throat. She glanced once more toward Robert's office and then at her watch. He'd said noon. It was five past.

She couldn't make any more excuses. Her legs were stiff as she walked into Chase's office and perched on the edge of the chair. Her cheeks were on fire, even more so when his gaze dipped down to her breasts. Having not gotten the memo, her body responded instantly.

She pressed her knees together and straightened her skirt. Her hands turned white from clutching them together, and her stomach started to churn, just like the last time she'd been in here.

"Relax, Natalie. I'm not going to pounce on you."

Her gaze jerked to his eyes. She remembered him saying that to her before. She couldn't place when, but it raised the ghost of Saturday morning. The things she'd said. Her gaze dropped to her lap.

The urge to run out the door raced through her, but she stayed. Chase didn't say anything else, but she could feel his eyes on her. The silence relentlessly continued. Maybe she could come back later? Or he could call her when Robert came in. She raised her head to suggest it, but stopped before saying anything.

Pain. For a moment, his eyes seemed like an open wound. A wound she'd caused. But then it was gone like she'd imagined it. Maybe she had. He couldn't possibly love her. It just didn't make sense. As soon as the next actress crossed his path, he'd be fine. He probably wouldn't even remember her name. A pain stabbed through her heart at the thought.

"Sorry, I got caught up on a phone call." Robert swept into the office and closed the door. "Wow, you could cut the tension with a knife in here."

Chase broke their eye contact to glare at Robert. "What is this about, Robert?"

Robert smiled. "Well, I figured if we were going to ruin this woman's life she should be prepared."

"What?" Natalie's hand began to shake.

Robert gave her a sympathetic smile and reached over as if to take one of her hands. A growl from the other side of the desk stopped him.

"We have to make this go away, and the only way to make something go away in Hollywood is to be up-front and honest so there is nothing to find. Then wait for some huge, new scandal for them to sink their teeth into."

Natalie's heart tightened, and her gaze flitted to Chase's stern face. His lips were pressed into a thin line.

"Natalie," Robert began, "we have to put all the facts out there. Chase has already said your relationship is over, which will make the press only wonder why it ever happened and probably make them back off. Especially if they think it was just another boss-banging-the-worker story."

Natalie winced at the harsh words. Chase had told Robert they were over? She'd known when she left Saturday there'd be no turning back, but it didn't stop the shooting pain through her heart or the upheaval in her stomach.

"You'll be reporting to me from now on and the new CFO when hired. I suggest that both of you—" Robert's fatherly stare went between them "—stay away from each other. The less you are seen together the more seriously our statement today will be taken."

"That won't be a problem. I'm going to help Reggie in Ontario later this week. He's been having issues with some of the scenes." Chase brushed his hand through his hair.

Her fingers itched to smooth it back down. Something she'd never do again. He was leaving? For how long?

"That's a good idea. With you gone, the focus should go with you. What about the luncheon next week? Our nominations?"

Chase stood and walked to look out the window. "I'll be back for it."

Natalie could feel the tears rising, and her stomach rolled, as well. She cleared her throat. "If that's…if that's all, I'll go to lunch."

Robert gave her a sympathetic look and nodded. "Sure, Natalie. Why don't you go home for the rest of the day? I think after the news conference this afternoon things are going to get crazy here."

"Thank you." She rose and walked to the door. She glanced back at Chase's profile. "Have a good trip."

"Are you sure?" Rachel eyed her as if she'd gone out of her mind.

Maybe she had. Maybe she'd lost it the moment she'd run into Chase that first day. If not her mind, she'd definitely lost her heart.

Natalie set her pizza down on her plate. More comfort food that just wasn't comforting. She shoved the plate across the coffee table and pulled her blanket tighter around her shoulders.

"I've got to know what they are saying. I need to be

prepared for tomorrow." Natalie's eyes were dry, too dry. The kind of dryness that only happened after all the tears were gone.

Still watching her, Rachel clicked the remote for the TV and turned her laptop on. The bright light from the TV hurt Natalie's eyes, but she didn't care. Chase had caught a flight out in the afternoon, that much she knew.

"In a surprising turn of events, Pandora Productions in the news again shortly after their nomination for Best Picture for their production *Night Blooming*. The company has brought charges of fraud against their former CFO, Martin Morrison."

A picture of Mr. Morrison being escorted from the building appeared on the screen behind Ryan Seacrest.

"Shortly after his arrest, Morrison leaked to the press that Chase Booker, co-owner of Pandora, had been having an affair with one of his staff."

A shot of her escape from Chase's house Saturday came up on the screen. She curled tighter into the corner of the couch. Clips of Alexis and Chase started to show on the screen.

"Alexis Brandt stated today that she and Chase never really got back together, and she was as shocked as everyone else by this turn of events. This afternoon, Chase Booker and Robert Addler spoke with *E!*"

The screen cut to the news conference. Chase stood behind Robert as he spoke to the crowd. "We have turned all our evidence on Martin Morrison over to our lawyer and the police. We were sad to see Martin go as we had always considered him an asset before all this came to light."

Robert glanced back at Chase before returning to the microphones. "We are currently looking for a replacement CFO. We will not be promoting anyone within the company.

In addition, we have shifted the accounting department to be more fully under my direction. This will enable Chase to spend more time in the field and to star in more films."

He shifted behind the podium. "Martin also claimed an ongoing affair between Chase and one of our staff. Chase was trying to protect the woman from the misguided attention of the paparazzi. Regardless, the affair is over, and the woman would prefer to remain anonymous. I would hope that the press would respect her and Chase's privacy in this matter. Thank you."

The TV cut back to the studio. "We were also told that Chase would be going to Ontario to help work on Pandora Productions' filming. Meanwhile, Britney Spears—"

Rachel hit Mute on the remote. "Okay, here's what the entertainment news is saying. Some say you were a rebound and the real reason he's going to Ontario is to see Madeline Stark, who recently dumped Andre Pratt."

"Do you think that's why he went?" The tears began to burn at the back of her throat again. Had she really just been a rebound?

"I don't know, sweetie." Rachel rubbed her hand on Natalie's leg in a comforting way.

Natalie fought down the tears. "What are they saying about me?"

"Let's see." Rachel's eyes roamed the page as her hand moved the mouse. "Here's something. They suspect you are the woman in the picture, but no one will confirm it. A source, one of your stupid coworkers, claims that you and Chase worked late for the past two weeks and seemed very chummy in the office."

Natalie picked at the threads coming out at the end of the blanket. She needed to know more. She needed to know why Chase had picked her. She needed to know why he'd been with her. "What else does it say?" she choked out around the held-back tears.

"Natalie, I don't think you want to know." Rachel shut the lid on the laptop. "It's just the normal catty stuff."

"The stuff you enjoy?"

Rachel brushed a stray piece of Natalie's hair behind her ear. "Only when it's about someone ridiculous, which you aren't. Are you sure you don't want to talk about it? I swear I won't leak it to the press." She smiled softly.

"I know you won't." Natalie tried to return her friend's smile but wasn't sure if it came across. "I just…I want to understand, is all."

"Understand what?"

"Why me?" A tear slipped over the edge. The rest of the tears, seeing the escapee, pressed forward.

Rachel handed her a tissue. "Why not you, Natalie? You're bright, intelligent, loving, pretty. You take care of anyone you care about. What's not to love about you, Natalie?"

The tissues kept coming as Natalie's vision blurred behind the tears. "He said he loved me." She sniffled. "He said he loved me, and I said he didn't."

Chapter Seventeen

The week that followed was the hardest of Natalie's life. From the guy digging around in her trash to the car that followed her to work, at first she wondered if she was just paranoid. When a camera flashed as she left the grocery store, she knew she wasn't.

It was so subtle she barely noticed it at first. Rachel kept showing Natalie pictures of her when she hadn't even known anyone was around. The receptionist held all calls to Natalie's phone.

Robert had been especially nice to her and had even had a meeting with the staff informing them that the new CFO would start in two weeks. Natalie buried herself in the piles of paper. Eventually the strutting down the hall picked up again, and people didn't stop talking when she came into the room.

Her heart ached every time she passed Chase's empty

office. It had to be easier than actually seeing him every day. Rachel stopped informing Natalie of Chase's comings and goings when she continued to break down into tears and run from the room.

Natalie sighed with relief as the hour turned to four. One more hour and then she'd have the whole weekend to lock herself away with tubs of ice cream and her favorite mov—

Pushing aside the folder on her desk, she realized she couldn't watch her favorite movie. The constant ache in her chest throbbed. Maybe she'd rent some horror flicks instead, or a good chick flick.

Her phone rang, and she didn't think twice about picking it up. "This is Natalie."

"Natalie, Jared Anderson. Before you hang up, give me a minute of your time."

She held the phone to her ear instead of slamming it down. "I'm listening."

"Good. Why don't we meet somewhere? You could get your side of the relationship on record. It could launch your career. At least get you on a reality show."

Her mind blanked. "Is that all you people think about? Do you really think I like having my name in headlines or my face in your papers? Well, I don't. I don't want to be any part of this industry. I'm an accountant, for Pete's sake. Not someone waiting for her big break. I'll thank you to never call me again."

She slammed the phone down and felt better than she had all week.

"Nice job." The voice stilled her heart.

She couldn't look up. She wasn't ready. She couldn't see him. She couldn't resist. Her gaze trailed up the jean-clad hips to his black T-shirt, the planes of his body as familiar as her own.

Her heart pounded within her chest. His lips were curved into a wary smile and his eyes... Why did they have to be so green? "Chase." His name slipped out of her mouth on a sigh.

"I heard what you said."

Had she been talking? His eyes appeared tired, and there was a strain around his lips.

"Sorry?" Her brain had flown out the window when she'd heard his voice again.

"The reporter? I couldn't have said it better myself." He pointed toward the phone and her gaze followed, completely dumbfounded.

Heat rushed into her cheeks as his words sunk in. "Oh."

"I've got to..." He gestured down the hall with his thumb.

"I hope you had a good trip."

He nodded and disappeared down the hall. She dropped her head down to the desk. So much for being intelligent. What was he doing back? What had he been doing? Did he hook up with that actress up there?

She lifted her head and grabbed her cell phone. If any one person knew all the goings-on in Hollywood, it would be Rachel.

Chase closed the door behind him and leaned his forehead against it. It had to be the best performance of his life. Pretending he wasn't falling apart without Natalie. If he could convince her, he could convince everyone else.

Her eyes had been wide and tired. Good. He hoped she wasn't getting any sleep, because he wasn't. When he would finally drift off, he'd reach out to pull her close, and she wasn't there.

He dropped his briefcase inside the door and collapsed

into his chair. His head in his hands, he ignored the knocking on his door.

The door opened. "Why did you come in at all?"

"Leave me alone, Robert."

The door shut. "The director called to say you left earlier than expected." Robert was trying to lead Chase, but Chase didn't feel like discussing the real reason he'd left early. He'd been drawn back like a moth to a flame.

He wanted to see her before the weekend. When he'd walked in and seen her behind the mountain of paper, his heart had lifted. Then he'd heard her on the phone with the reporter, and he remembered.

She didn't want to be in the public eye. She had no intention of ever being in the public eye. There was no future for them. But he'd managed to stand there and act as if his chest weren't ready to explode.

"So you aren't going to say anything?" Robert sank into the chair. "Are you going to ask about the new CFO?"

Chase leaned back in his chair and narrowed his eyes on Robert. "You sent me the résumé. We did the interview via conference call. Is there something I missed? You called every day."

"No, Chase, you called every day. You avoided talking about Natalie every time, as well. You look like hell, man."

"I just got off a plane—"

"And you rushed over here to—what? Sit in your office and rest your weary head? Give me a break. I saw you stop at Natalie's desk—"

"I just was checking up—"

"You stood there like a man presented with water after crossing the desert. Why not talk to her? Her eyes are red and puffy every morning. You both are hurting, so why not end the games and just get together already."

Chase stared at his partner with astonishment. "She doesn't want any part of the fame or this industry."

"We're not talking about the industry. We're talking about you, Chase."

"The industry and me are the same. It's always been a part of who I am. A part I can't escape, and I don't want to escape it. I may hate being followed sometimes, but it's part of my life and she doesn't want any of that."

"Have you asked her?"

Chase could feel the rage rising within him. "Why would she? That part of my life is never going away. Even if I had never gone into acting, I would still be the son of Matt Booker and Madeline Caine. If she doesn't want that life, we can't be together."

Natalie was having difficulty breathing. When someone moved down the hall, she'd hold her breath and not release it until she knew it wasn't Chase. This had to be the longest hour of her life.

Since it was Friday a lot of the staff took off early. People were constantly going past her desk. Rachel had at least eased her fears that Chase hadn't already moved on. Not that she cared, but it had made her feel better to know he hadn't dived right back into the dating pool. Of course, that could also mean that he really did love her, which made her feel even worse.

Life shouldn't be so hard. He'd gone out of his way to keep their relationship discreet, which was what she wanted. Wasn't it? Someone started down the hall.

Hold it, hold it. Just another model. Release. This was ridiculous. She glanced at the clock. Close enough. She bent and got her purse, and when she came back up she screamed. Not a bloodcurdling scream, but that oh-my-

God-you-scared-the-last-year-off-my-life scream. Chase stood in front of her desk.

Her hand covered her racing heart, and she took several deep breaths.

"I didn't mean to startle you." His smooth voice awakened the desire that was always on simmer just for him.

Her face flushed as hot flashes of him making love to her burst within her mind. "Not a problem," she said hurriedly. She clutched her purse to her like a shield as she stood up. "I was just leaving." Did he know she was picturing him naked?

"Natalie."

She stopped and stared at the ground. Please don't come near. She could survive hearing his voice, but she'd explode into tears if he touched her. Or worse, she'd throw herself into his arms and plead with him to forgive her.

Her eyes squeezed shut when she felt him move behind her. She wasn't this strong. She could bolt. She could run for the door and pray she didn't trip.

"Can I…"

Can he what? She lifted her face and stared straight ahead at the door. "I really should be going."

"Can I walk you to your car?"

She spun and almost fell back. She hadn't realized he was directly behind her. He reached out to steady her by her elbow, but she jerked out of his reach and banged her elbow against the wall.

"Are you okay?" He reached out to steady her.

She pressed herself against the wall avoiding his hands and held her elbow as her funny bone throbbed. "I'm fine."

"From that face you're making, I highly doubt that." He dropped his hands.

Her body relaxed. His eyes were resigned when she finally lifted her gaze to meet them.

"We can't be friends, can we?" His shoulders dropped.

"I…" She wanted to tell him they could. She didn't want to let him out of her life, but she couldn't be with him and not watch his lips and remember. She shook her head and said softly, "I don't think so."

He nodded. "Can I walk you out?"

The door was a long way away, but outside a few stubborn photographers lingered, waiting for just the right photo op. "I don't think so, Chase."

His smile was a shadow of the one he used to give her. "You are probably right. Have a good weekend." His hand lifted as if to brush her cheek.

Her breath caught, and she couldn't move. He dropped his hand and spun on his heel, leaving her in the hall with a throbbing elbow and a broken heart.

"I know you're in there." Rachel yelled through the door.

"No, I'm not," Natalie told her pillow. She hugged the pillow closer, knocking a dozen tissues off the edge of the bed. It still smelled like him. It was only a throw pillow, but it smelled like him.

"I don't have to go out of town. I can tell the company I have personal business to attend to." Her voice was muffled by the door.

"You need to go. I'll be fine."

"I got more ice cream." There wasn't enough chocolate ice cream in the world to make the pain go away, but Rachel didn't need to know that. "I'll have my cell phone on. If you need me, call. I don't care when or why. I'll answer. I also picked up some of those frozen meals that are low-fat. You know, to counteract the ice cream."

"Thank you." She lifted her face from the pillow. "Go. I'll be fine."

"Okay, I'll see you Wednesday. Try to get out of bed sometime between now and then."

Natalie waited until the door closed and she heard the snick of the locks. She pried herself off the bed and wandered into the living room. Grabbing the remote, she cued up *If Only* and wandered into the kitchen to grab a fresh carton of ice cream.

There was a note on the fridge. *Try to eat something besides ice cream. R.* "Well, chocolate sauce isn't ice cream."

She piled her blanket, the pillow that smelled like Chase and her ice cream onto the couch with her as the beginning credits rolled.

She found herself caught up by the story. The pressure on her chest lifted as the love affair between Tom and Elizabeth played upon the screen. Every touch, every gesture placed so perfectly to create this growing love that echoed within her chest. She rode the wave of their love, so thoroughly enraptured that when the final scene came the ice cream had been set aside, and she hugged the pillow to her chest.

Tom stood on the stage watching Elizabeth walk out of his life for good. He looked down at his hands and flexed his fingers as if realizing she was slipping through them.

"I can't lose you." Tom called out to her.

"It doesn't matter," Elizabeth responded, her hand on the doorknob. "If you can't accept me for who I am, there is nothing left of us."

Tom jumped down from the stage. He opened his arms wide. "I'd give up my entire world for one more moment in your arms. One more night by your side. I want it all. All of you. I want you to have it all. All my love, all my heart, all of me."

Elizabeth turned with tears filling her eyes. His stride

ate up the distance between them and he drew her into his arms. Their mouths met and the camera held until the end credits rolled.

That man playing Tom wasn't Chase. Those smiles and looks she'd thought were so similar to the movie weren't. They were smiles Chase only gave to her. The kisses, the touches, the looks, they'd all been real. He hadn't been onstage. He'd been with her. And when he'd told her he loved her and wanted her to stay, she'd thrown it in his face.

Her hand on her lips, Natalie whispered, "What have I done?" She shrugged out of the blanket and raced to her room.

Chapter Eighteen

A half hour later, Natalie's car stopped in front of the intercom outside Chase's gate. Her heart still thundered in her chest from her mad dash through her apartment, jerking on clothes over her jammies and tying her hair back.

Her hands shook as she coached herself. *You can do this*. She glanced down the street at the man sitting in a car with a camera around his neck. If this didn't work, she would be shooting herself in the foot.

The headlines would read Accountant Couldn't Take a Hint. But what was the point of being in love, if you didn't at least try?

She pushed the button and squeezed her eyes shut. An eternity passed while she waited, her heart in her hands. Maybe he wasn't in. Or worse, what if he already had someone there?

Fearing the worst, she put the car into Reverse.

"Hello?" The muffled sound of birds came across the intercom with Chase's voice.

"Chase?" Oh, crap, why hadn't she practiced what she was going to say? Everything she'd thought of on the drive over slipped out of her mind and left her fumbling for the words. Mercifully the gate opened, and she didn't have to make a fool of herself to the box on a stick.

The photographer shifted up in his seat and put the camera to his eye. She couldn't tell if he was taking a photo or not. She didn't care. The car pulled through the gates.

A garage door was open, and she drove the car into it. The garage door closed behind her with finality. She couldn't go back on her decision now, but she didn't get out of the car. Her pulse beat so loudly that she couldn't find the train of her thoughts.

What if he wouldn't forgive her? What if he didn't want her anymore? What if he'd never loved her? What if he laughed in her face? Her eyes burned as tears worked their way to the surface. No, he'd loved her, even if he didn't now. He'd loved her.

The thought gave her strength. She stepped from the car, expecting to find Chase in the garage. She glanced around and didn't see him. She ran clammy hands over the back of her jeans.

Maybe he was in the kitchen. She forced her feet to propel her forward. The kitchen was empty, except for the memories. They clung to her as she moved forward. She could picture him making her an omelet.

She peered into the dining room and spun through the media room, where they'd spent an evening watching movies and laughing as he'd shared stories from the set. Her curiosity built as she made her way toward the greenhouse. Why not meet her out in the garage? Why force her to find him in his favorite room?

She pushed through the doors and swallowed the thick, fragrant air. The whispered rustling of wings and the discord of birdsongs filled the room. The hot moisture clung to her, and she discarded her sweatshirt, leaving it behind on the path. It didn't matter, nothing mattered, but Chase.

Yanking out the tie in her hair, she let it slip from her fingers to the stone below. The atmosphere of the room pulled at her. The fact that after everything he wanted her in here had to count for something. His favorite room.

She rounded the bend and stared up at the colorful birds perched on branches as if waiting for her. As one they lifted off, flooding her view with rich colors.

Leaving the birds behind, she moved down the path to the gazebo. She could see his shadow in there. Her heart pounded in her chest, and her stomach clenched. She reached up to straighten her glasses only to realize she wasn't wearing them.

She stopped at the door to the gazebo. He stood inside leaning against a pillar. His face was in shadow. Her hand went out to the door frame to steady herself. What if he hated her?

"Why are you here?"

She couldn't take her eyes off his. This was it. She either wimped out or tried for the gold. She cleared her throat. "I'm scared."

"Of what?"

"Of you. Of me. Of the cameras. Of what I feel."

He straightened from the pillar. "Why are you scared of me?"

"Because I can't tell when you are acting." She held up her hand to stop him from speaking. "My past experiences with guys haven't been great. You know I was home-schooled before I went to college?"

He nodded but didn't interrupt.

"Well, my first boyfriend, Bill, seemed to care about me until after we had sex. The door didn't even hit him on the way out. The guys who pretended to like me to get close to Rachel were even worse. I trusted them, and they lied to me." She still couldn't see his face to read it. "Your performances are award-winning. Theirs weren't."

His body relaxed back against the pillar.

"I never felt for any of them what I feel when I'm with you. I want it to be real." She stepped into the gazebo, dropping her hands to her side. "What I feel is real. I love the way I feel when I'm with you. I love that you take care of me. I love you." Her heart pounded in her chest.

He didn't move toward her.

"How do I know you aren't acting? How can I know what we have is real?"

"You can't know, but you need to trust me. We can't go further with this, if you don't trust me," he said.

"I want to trust you. I want to be with you. I didn't mean what I said that day. I didn't mean any of it." The words could barely make it past the lump in her throat. What if…

"I did." His voice was steady as he stepped forward. Within touching distance, he stopped. His eyes searched hers. She could only hope he would find what he was looking for within them.

"I…" She cleared her throat. Tears sprang to her eyes. "Chase? I love…I love you. Please forgive me."

He didn't move. She stood there open, vulnerable, more naked than she'd ever been in all her life.

"My life hasn't changed." He held back still.

A tear slipped down her cheek. "I know."

His hand lifted as if to brush the tear away, but stopped. "They'll take your picture and follow you around, waiting for something spectacular to happen."

She caught his raised hand between hers and brought it to her lips. "If I'm with you, it will be spectacular." She pressed his hand against her cheek and closed her eyes, enjoying the spiral of warmth that radiated through her body at his touch.

"Natalie?"

She opened her eyes. He still stood there stiffly. Releasing his hand, she reached up and pulled his face down to hers. Her lips pressed against his, and for a moment he didn't move. Had she been mistaken?

His arms curled around her and dragged her into his body as his mouth claimed hers. A wave of pleasure swept over her, drowning her in sensations of his hard length pressed against her.

The pain of the past week disappeared as her heart filled her chest. She pushed forward to back them into the gazebo. He pulled her back with him until he sat on the bench.

Standing between his legs, she stared down in wonder at the love in his eyes. This amazing man loved her. The feelings inside her were so overwhelming, so pure.

"I love you, Chase." She brushed the hair away from his face and kissed his forehead. "I love you so much."

He captured her face with his hands and brought his lips to hers, but he didn't kiss her. Her eyes opened and stared into green as pure and deep as the leaves of the forest surrounding them. "I love you."

A spear of heat hit her core. He brushed his lips over hers, a gentle back and forth motion. So slowly it was driving her insane. She straddled his lap, placing her knees on the cushioned bench beside his hips. His erection pressed against the juncture of her thighs.

The rich smell of him assaulted her nose, filling her with need, but he kept up his relentless brushing never deepening the kiss and not allowing her to. She rubbed her breasts against the hardness of his chest.

Her brain suffered meltdown as the heat between them intensified, but he did no more than brush his mouth over hers. A low rumble started in the back of her throat as the pressure continued to build within. Her clothes were too tight, and there were way too many layers between their bodies.

She stepped back from the bench. His eyes were glazed as he watched her, but he didn't pull her back to him. Kicking off her sandals, she jerked off her pajama top and shimmied out of her jeans and underwear.

His eyes took in her body, but she was beyond being embarrassed. Her body was on fire, and she needed him. She stalked toward him. She yanked his shirt out of his pants and up. He held his arms up for her to get the shirt off, but didn't help or say anything.

When her breast brushed against his cheek, his mouth closed over her hardened nipple. She froze as the pulling reached down to her center. Her core pulsed in time with his gentle suction. She caught her bottom lip between her teeth to keep from exploding.

She ripped the shirt the rest of the way off and flung it to the side. Her naked flesh slid against his, warm and moist. He smiled up at her with passion-laden eyes, but he made no move to take over. She wrapped her arms around his chest and pulled him up to stand with her.

Her body pressed into his as she popped open his jean button. Her knuckles brushed against his stomach causing shivers of anticipation to course through her.

She lowered his jeans and his boxer briefs and pushed

him back on the bench. She knelt at his feet and pulled the jeans and underwear off the rest of the way.

Crawling her way back up onto his lap, she straddled his hips again. This time nothing blocked her flesh from his and she groaned deep in her throat as the velvet softness of his erection pressed against her stomach.

It'd been too long. A week of longing to be with him. A week of feeling horrible for the things she'd said to him.

Her mouth lowered and captured his. His hands remained at his sides. She would go insane if he didn't touch her soon. Her body was fevered and pulsated with desire.

She slid along him. Her tongue parted his lips and sought his. Her core pulsed with its emptiness as he parried with his tongue.

He leaned over and grabbed a condom from his discarded pants. She guided him to her throbbing center.

Gripping his shoulders, she lowered herself fully on him. Her lips parted and a sigh of relief passed out of them. His mouth captured hers and his hands found her hips.

He didn't move her, just held her. She slid up excruciatingly slowly enjoying the friction of his flesh on hers before lowering herself again. She repeated the process and Chase groaned.

His mouth moved with the desperation she felt and his hands took over her rhythm, sending her soaring higher until all that existed was the pulsating within her. His flesh against hers. His mouth on hers.

Her body clenched around him and her mouth opened in a silent scream. His fingers convulsed on her hips as their bodies continued to strain together. Her fingernails dug into his shoulders as her body rocked into another orgasm.

She could feel his answering pulse within her. He held

her body still as he found his own release. Wrapped around him, she opened her eyes and looked down into his.

"I love you." Her voice trembled and was weak, but very, very satisfied.

He brushed her hair away from her face and kissed her softly. "I have never loved anyone the way I do you."

Chase still couldn't believe Natalie was here, asleep in his bed. He trailed a lazy finger down her back, from her shoulder to her waist where the sheet rested.

He'd been in misery the entire time he was in Ontario, but he couldn't have stayed here. Being close to her was torture. Knowing she was only a car drive away had almost crushed him since she'd made it clear she wasn't willing to be in the spotlight.

She didn't know what she was getting into. She hadn't begun to be pursued by the paparazzi. As an ex-lover she'd been interesting, but to be his girlfriend meant a whole new level of scrutiny. Her nose crinkled in her sleep. He gently brushed her hair off her face.

Would they be able to see what he saw when he was with her? Beautiful, intelligent eyes. A smile that made his heart swell every time she gave him one. When she looked at him, he knew he could do anything, be anyone.

When he'd been gone, he'd lost the peace that seemed to settle over him when she was near. What had changed? Did he really want to question why she was here? Wasn't it enough that she was? That was it, wasn't it? How long could she handle the pressure? How long before she left him for good? How long would love be enough to hold her to him? Would he ever be sure she was here to stay?

He couldn't know, but he didn't want to go back to the

way things were before. He didn't want the superficial Hollywood romances. He wanted Natalie.

His fingers tangled in her shoulder-length hair. He leaned down and kissed the pale skin of her shoulder. When he lifted his head, he caught the slight smile on her lips before it disappeared again.

His hand trailed down her spine while he kept careful watch on her face. The little minx was pretending to sleep. His hand didn't stop at the sheet, but continued under and over the curve of her buttocks.

When his hand slipped between her thighs and cupped her, a moan escaped her lips. Gently he stroked her as his other hand wrapped under her to lift her rear up. She rocked against his hand.

The flush of arousal coated her but she kept her eyes closed. Would anyone know the secret beauty who shared his bed? This wonderful creature who dominated his thoughts. Her lips parted.

He grabbed a condom off the nightstand and shifted on the bed until he was behind her raised hips. He replaced his hand with his erection and pulled her up against his body.

"Good morning, sleepy," he whispered huskily in her ear.

Her arm draped up over his shoulder to clutch his neck as he rocked gently against her. "Morning."

His arm crossed her chest, holding her to him as his other hand found the moist center of her. His fingers slid over her as he continued to rock inside her.

She shattered all around him. Her body shook as she came hard. Her sex clamped down on him. He lost control as his body shuddered in hers.

He lowered them to the bed still inside her, cradling her against his body.

"Definitely a good morning." Her voice was soft as she

stretched against him. She gently turned into him to face him. Her eyes reflected his satisfaction.

"Let's go out to breakfast." If this was going to work in the real world, she had to get used to going and being seen. That part of his life wouldn't change.

She stiffened slightly. What if she wasn't ready? Would she ever be ready?

Her body stretched against his again. Her wide, gorgeous eyes smiled up at him. "Where did you have in mind?"

Chapter Nineteen

How could Natalie say no when all the joy had been wiped from his face? Even though she'd wanted to run to the bedroom door and lock it and throw away the key, she knew that at some point they'd have to go out in public. Obviously Chase thought the sooner the better, though Natalie would have preferred to save it for a rainy day.

They sat on the patio of the Polo Lounge at the Beverly Hills Hotel. It was as if Chase was testing her. Thankfully she'd been able to shower and had the sense of mind to run home and change, but she still felt underdressed in jeans, sandals and a light top.

Everyone else was in jeans and T-shirts, but her labels paled in comparison to theirs. Chase sat across from her soaking in the sun. His smile was almost blinding this morning.

She'd managed to hold back the jaw-dropping at some

of the famous people she saw sitting around her. They didn't seem to pay attention to anyone around them and completely ignored the photographers across the street.

While Chase would have a nice tanned look to him in any photos that were taken, she would look like she'd spent days in the sun. Her cheeks burned with the feeling of being watched.

Chase leaned across the table and placed his hand over hers. She jerked.

"Relax, Natalie. It's breakfast. No one's going to run up and kidnap you or anything." Chase was obviously joking.

She let out a nervous laugh, but then she glanced around the streets. "Does that happen?"

His hand brushed her cheek, and her focus centered on him and the warmth that engulfed her when he was near. "Just relax and eat. We're just two people having breakfast."

"Yeah, but normally when I have breakfast it doesn't appear in the *Enquirer*. Normally no one notices me at all."

"I notice you." His smile made her insides churn in a good way. "Now eat something, and I'll take you for a walk to some shops."

She gulped as she looked down at the giant croissant on her plate. While Chase had tried to get her to eat a big breakfast, she'd insisted on bread. Bread was less likely to come back up, in her experience.

She picked off small pieces and ate. Chase smiled and shook his head at her before tucking into his quiche. A motion caused her to look up. A group of giggling twenty-somethings was heading toward their table.

"Oh, my God, are you Chase Booker?" a petite blonde from the front of the group squealed.

"Can I get your autograph?" A brown-haired girl shoved a pad and pen toward Chase.

He took it and smiled at them. "Who do I make it out to?" He glanced at Natalie briefly.

Was this another test? One of the girls in the back nudged another girl with her elbow and whispered something behind her hand while looking at Natalie. The other girl giggled.

They obviously didn't think she belonged with him. Their laughter and whispered words cut through Natalie. Would it always be like this with Chase? Ignored or ridiculed? Being ignored was fine, but ridiculed behind her back… Her stomach dropped.

Natalie quickly changed her focus back to Chase. He loved her. She loved him. Wasn't that what mattered most? He'd written the autograph and handed back the pad.

"Can I get your picture?" The blonde held up a camera.

"Sure, but then I really must get back to breakfast before it gets cold." He flashed her a smile Natalie had seen a million times in the newspaper.

The girls giggled a thank-you and wandered away. Chase turned back to her. "What's got you smiling?"

Her smile broadened. "Your smile. They think that smile is brilliant, but they've never seen the smile you give me."

His hand reached across to take hers. A flash went off in her peripheral vision, but she ignored it. If she wanted Chase, that had to be part of her life, too.

When they finished up breakfast, Chase took her hand and led her down Rodeo Drive.

Natalie stared in the windows, but when Chase tried to lead her into Gucci, her feet ground to a halt. His surprised eyes met hers.

"Don't you want to go in?"

"Yeah, but I can't afford anything in there, and I'd feel like Julia Roberts in *Pretty Woman*. Girls like me don't go in shops like that. We stand outside the windows like street urchins and stare at the pretty things." Her gaze shifted to the gorgeous dress in the window. Something she had absolutely no need for.

"What if I wanted to buy something for you?" His hands were on her upper arms, and she longed to be in the privacy of his house or her apartment. Though she relished his touch, she fought the urge to back up and duck her head.

"You don't need to buy me anything."

"What if I wanted you to go to the Oscars with me? Would you let me buy you something then?" His eyes swept over her body like a physical caress.

When he looked at her like that, she'd give him anything he asked. The street and store disappeared, and it was just the two of them. Her mind cleared. Had he just asked what she thought he'd asked? "What?"

"I asked if you'd like to accompany me to the Oscars. There's no one else I'd rather take with me." His fingers brushed the hair from her face and tucked it behind her ear. "Say yes."

His smile would convince a nun to give up her vows for him. Natalie wasn't strong enough to resist.

"I couldn't afford a dress." She tried to drop her gaze, but his held hers, enraptured.

"I'll take care of it. I know just the person to ask to help."

"When Chase told me he was sending me a project, I'd hoped it would be more than this." The woman pursed her lips as she gestured toward Natalie. "I need a smoke."

Natalie smiled weakly.

The woman sashayed out of the room, leaving Natalie sitting in her office. Natalie pulled out her phone and quickly texted Rachel. *Pls reply. Need dress for Oscars. Crazy Lady went out for smoke. N*

She hit the send button and waited. Her phone beeped in her hand. *So jealous. Insist Vera Wang or Oscar de la Renta*. She dropped her phone back in her purse.

She wouldn't mind switching places with Rachel right now or even to have Rachel with her. The woman, Charity Christian, was anything but charitable. Her dark hair was yanked back so tight it pulled the edges of her eyes out farther than seemed possible. Charity had taken four smoke breaks in the past half hour. Every time the woman looked over at Natalie, she insisted on a cigarette.

Natalie wasn't Alexis Brandt—beautiful, but the ice cream hadn't yet taken its toll on her figure. She didn't have anything to push up, but what she had was all hers.

Charity drifted back in on a gust of cigarette smoke. "I've called around, and I think we might be able to find something. Your eyes are quite nice."

Natalie's lips remained tightly pressed together as she tried not to breathe in the smoke cloud that hovered in the room.

"I know Vera could probably do something or maybe Donna Karan. Stand up again." Charity had picked up a long, pointed stick like people used in presentations.

Unable to disobey the fierce-tongued woman, Natalie stood. Charity's critical eye roamed over every inch of Natalie's body.

"Definitely not red. Especially if you continue to blush like a schoolgirl." Her stick poked at Natalie's lower back. "You have a nice waistline, and you need to remember to smile."

"Umm, is this going to take much longer? I'm supposed to go back to work." Natalie's gaze tried to follow the woman as Charity critically assessed all her faults.

Chase had been thoroughly enamored with her body for the past two nights. Charity's disapproval had nothing on

Chase's rich eyes undressing her as she walked across the room. She was doing this for Chase. Somehow she'd manage to put aside her feelings of inadequacy for a while. The dress, the cameras, the Oscars. How on earth does a girl like her get invited to the Oscars?

She kept expecting to wake up or else find herself walking down the red carpet with nothing on. She'd always been thankful to wake up from naked-in-public dreams. But this wasn't a dream; she'd be wearing a dress, shoes and jewelry that would equal her entire year's wages, probably closer to ten years' wages. And she'd be with Chase. A little twitter raced through her.

She definitely had a Cinderella vibe going, except her fairy godmother, Charity, could definitely use some work, along with a breath mint.

Charity muttered under her breath as she whipped out a measuring tape from her pocket and tightened it around Natalie's chest, waist and then hips. She returned to the opposite side of her drafting desk and waved her hand dismissively. "You may go. I'll call you tomorrow and let you know when your fitting will be."

Natalie retrieved her purse. "Thank you." She slipped out of the room and drew in a deep breath of fresh air. She could be everything Chase wanted her to be. Elegant, unabashed, fearless. The butterflies in her stomach kicked up into full flurry. Even if she'd prefer to watch quietly at home, she'd do this for Chase.

Natalie pulled her Honda into Pandora Productions' parking lot and almost pulled right back out. A group of men with cameras lounged across the street, but when her car stopped, they perked up.

The mirror on the visor left a lot to be desired, but her

hair hadn't completely escaped her ponytail, and her subtle makeup was not all gone. Her emotions were so jumbled this morning.

She couldn't wait to see Chase, but she didn't want to face the cameras or the other employees who by now knew she'd been at Chase's all weekend. Chase had offered to go with her this morning to the stylist and then drive her into work, but she couldn't let him take her everywhere forever. At some point, she'd have to stand on her own.

A knock on her window threw her heart into palpitations. Her hand blocked her heart's escape through her rib cage. As she turned her pulse increased pleasantly. Chase smiled at her and her mouth curved into a responding smile. He loved her.

She unlocked her door, and he opened it for her.

"Good morning, Natalie." Chase held out his hand to help her from the car.

Her face burned as she recalled exactly how good her morning had already been, and the night before and yesterday afternoon. She slipped her hand in his and a sense of completeness surged through her.

He drew her out of the car, but didn't back up, leaving only an inch between them. Natalie's gaze shot to the cameras that were currently going off. Life would be so much simpler if the cameras weren't at every corner ready to go. She stepped back from him.

"It's okay." Chase's smile was reassuring. "We'll go straight in and not talk to anyone." His fingers linked with hers, and together they walked across the parking lot. "How was Charity's this morning?"

Words flew through Natalie's mind: awful, discouraging, ego wrecking. "Fine. She's going to call me about a fitting tomorrow. When is the luncheon today?"

Chase stopped right outside the door. "Anytime you say 'fine,' it doesn't really mean fine. You mean something bothered you, but you don't want to discuss it."

When she looked at the ground, his finger lifted her chin, and she reluctantly met his eyes.

"It's okay." The words were beginning to sound like he was trying to steady a skittish horse.

"You are beautiful." He brushed a strand of hair behind her ear. "Charity can be really harsh, but she does a damn fine job dressing people. I have no doubts she'll find you the perfect dress, and that you'll look absolutely stunning in it."

His head dipped down to hers, and she quickly turned her head to the side so that his lips brushed her cheek.

"We should really go inside," she said. Her pulse thundered through her veins, and she resisted the urge to turn and taste his minty breath, to forget about the cameras and lose herself in his warmth and taste.

His deep voice in her ear sent little shivers of desire coursing down to pool between her legs. "I'll let that one go. This time."

She avoided his eyes as he lifted his head and opened the door for her. Slipping into the relative safety of the office, she hurried past the receptionist, whose eyes were about to pop out of her head. She managed to make it to her desk without melting into a puddle on the floor. Chase was hot on her heels. Her breath caught at the hot look he gave her.

"I'll see you tonight." Both a promise and a threat lingered in his eyes.

She sank down into her chair as he continued down the hallway. How was she going to concentrate with such a tantalizing offer hanging over her head?

One of the statuesque beauties from the administrative department strutted by and gave her a belittling look. Natalie quickly buried her face into a stack of work.

The hours quickly passed as she concentrated on work and not on the jealous or curious looks of the amazingly large number of people who had to pass her desk during the day. Chase sent her a smoldering glance as he left for his luncheon with Robert.

"So, trying to get ahead by dating the boss?" The catty voice caused Natalie to stiffen in her chair and tear her gaze away from her computer screen.

The woman could have been a runway model, from her choice in clothing to her makeup to her outrageous look-at-me hairstyle. Her three-inch heels had her towering over Natalie's desk as she looked down her nose.

"I'm sorry." Natalie couldn't have heard the woman properly. This woman had never spoken to Natalie before. She probably thought Natalie was beneath her.

The smile that twisted the woman's face was anything but friendly. "We all try to get ahead by any means possible. But no one has been able to capture Chase Booker's attention. He only dates actresses, not…" She didn't continue but let her gaze slide over Natalie.

If only Natalie were more like Rachel, she'd have a snappy comeback ready and be able to put this wannabe in her place. Instead she wished the warmth would lessen in her cheeks. At least her mouth wasn't opening and closing like a guppy's.

"So how'd you capture the elusive man? Did you get naked in front of him? Did you go down—"

"Excuse me. I'm trying to work here." She glanced down the hall to make sure no one else was hearing this woman. What was this woman's problem?

"Why bother? You have Chase—isn't that what every woman wants?" The woman's eyes shot daggers through Natalie before she pivoted gracefully and strutted away.

Natalie stared after her for a few moments before she stood stiffly and walked down to the bathroom. Is that what everyone thought of her? That she was just trying to get ahead by going to the boss's bed?

She shut herself in the stall and tried to calm her rushing nerves. At least here she was out of sight of all those people. She suddenly felt like the outsider again. A frumpy, short woman among the jungle of beautiful people. Before she'd been beneath their notice, but now she was with Chase. She hadn't considered the reactions from her co-workers when she'd driven to Chase's house. How was she going to cope with this?

The bathroom door opened, and women's voices wafted through the opening. She quickly stood on the toilet without really thinking about it. *What am I doing?*

Just as she was about to step down, the door clicked closed, and the voices became distinct.

"Can you believe the nerve of her?" the woman who'd stopped at her desk said. "I mean, to strut in here with Chase Booker on her heels like some sort of lapdog."

"I know, right?"

Natalie didn't recognize the second woman's voice.

"I heard he's using her to get back at Alexis Brandt for breaking up with him." The first woman's voice got close to the stall door and stopped.

Natalie held her breath and kept completely still. Her gaze was riveted to the doorknob. She'd locked it, but would it hold?

She heard the rustle of fabric, and the woman's heels clicked back toward the sink.

"I think he's doing it as a publicity stunt. Something to slap Hollywood in the face."

Was that all she was to Chase? He loved her. But had it all been make-believe?

"Totally. He can use her, and Hollywood will keep trying to figure out why. That's probably the real reason. Besides she'll sink back into oblivion when he's done with her."

Natalie's heartbeat echoed so loud she wondered why the women didn't hear it.

Her heart tightened painfully as the door closed behind them. Was he trying to prove something to someone by toting her around everywhere? By dressing her up and taking her to the Oscars? Was that some kind of slap in the face of the Hollywood engine?

She stepped down off the toilet. She had to get out of here. She needed to go home. She needed to get away from these people. She waited another few minutes in the bathroom before venturing out into the hallway.

Rushing to her desk, she grabbed her purse and switched off the computer screen. Hoping to avoid the women from the bathroom and everyone else who obviously thought she wasn't worthy of Chase's attentions, she hurried out the front door without meeting anyone's eyes.

Once in the safety of her car, she glanced around. Her eyes stopped on the men with their cameras. How did actors do it? How could they prevent the cameras from catching them when their hearts were on their sleeves and tears were in their eyes?

Chapter Twenty

The luncheon took up more time than Chase remembered. Between the photos and everyone stopping to ask about his latest project or film and, in turn, telling him about their latest project or film, Chase couldn't wait to be near Natalie and not have to worry about the rest of the world.

After saying good-bye to Robert, he dialed Natalie's cell phone on his way to his car, but the call went to voice mail. He called her office number but got voice mail there, too. Tipping the valet, he slipped into his car before dialing the office.

"Pandora Productions," the receptionist said.

"This is Chase. Is Natalie still there?"

"Um, no." There was hesitation in the woman's voice. "She left a few minutes ago."

At the slightly guilty tone of the receptionist, Chase's heart dropped. What had happened while he was gone? Natalie never left work early unless someone told her to. Had he pushed too hard? Was she going to leave him like Becca did?

He hung up the phone without saying another word. He'd have to wait until he saw her to make any conclusions. She seemed so sure that she was ready to be a part of his public life, but he couldn't help wondering when it would become too much. When would she leave him again? He wasn't ready to let her walk out of his life, but what choice would he have?

Maybe this was a mistake. He never should have started something with someone who wasn't part of the industry. It seemed only a matter of time before Natalie left him for good. He couldn't offer her the life she wanted. Quiet. Unassuming. But he also couldn't stand the thought of losing her again.

Would she go to his place or would she go to her apartment?

He decided to head back to his place. He'd asked her to meet him after work and, if she still wanted him, she would be there. If she wasn't there, he'd have to deal with that when it happened.

He'd given her the gate code as well as an extra garage-door opener. All he could do was hope that she had used them.

Remote controls were evil. Chase had sworn to her that the remote he had for his media center was user-friendly. Apparently not if that user was Natalie. She'd found the DVD for *If Only* and, after another fifteen minutes, figured out where to put it in.

She had the remote in her lap and stared at the blank touch screen. It was one of those high-end ones that controlled everything from lighting levels to the popcorn machine.

Well, probably not the popcorn machine. She'd just be

happy if she could figure out how to turn on the damn remote. She'd tried touching the screen, and nothing had happened. She'd turned it over and all around to see if there was a switch somewhere. She found a few places to plug in cords.

She sighed. All she wanted to do was lose herself in her movie and be here when Chase came home. In his house, she was surrounded by a wall that kept out the outside world. She could pretend that this calm space in his life was all there was. That the cameras, catty women and unwanted attention didn't exist in this house.

Her emotions were completely wrung out, and the damn frustrating remote wasn't helping to hold back the tears burning behind her eyes.

Whatever the reason Chase wanted her didn't matter. It didn't matter that those women thought she didn't deserve him. He wanted her. He'd made it clear so many times that she was the one he wanted. He'd proved it to her with his words, with his lips, with his hands.... She shook off the desire that spread from the center of her at her unruly thoughts.

Remote. Chase had shown it to her. He'd picked it up and pointed it at the TV, and it had worked. For him. But for her, it obviously wanted a blood sacrifice or something.

She set it down on the chair next to her. There had to be a way to make it all work without the remote. The large screen stared back at her, but no buttons were in sight. The shelves of black boxes with a dozen lights and buttons looked like something from a sci-fi movie. Overall it was intimidating.

"Evil remote." She glared down at it.

"I don't find it at all evil."

She swiveled around to meet Chase's smiling eyes. Her

heart filled, her pulse kicked up a notch and the worries from the day seemed to fall away in his eyes.

"In fact I find it a lot easier than dealing with the twelve that came with the components."

"It probably is, once it's turned on."

Chase sat down next to her and leaned across her to grab the remote. His cologne touched her nose. His arm brushed against her breasts, and a shimmer of awareness rushed through her.

"Now, let's see here." He glanced up at her and then down at the remote. Taking his thumb, he placed it in the center of the screen. The main menu came up instantly.

"But I did that." She reached out, and he handed it to her. She squinted down at the menu and touched Play DVD. Glancing up at the TV, she saw nothing happen.

"Here," Chase said and held out his hand. She held out the remote but he grabbed her hand instead. "Your fingers are probably too cold."

He brought her fingers in front of her mouth and blew hot air across them. "We just need to warm them up." With both of his hands, he massaged her hand.

Her ability to breathe was lost as he made slow circles on her palm with his thumbs. His gaze remained on her hand as he brought each fingertip to his lips and kissed the pad. He cupped her hand and blew against it.

"Now try it." He lifted his gaze to hers.

Her brain had ceased to function, except to send shivers of desire throughout her body. Gently he took her finger and pressed it against Play DVD. The screen came to life.

"There. See, all better." He drew her back against his side and set the remote down. His arms gathered her close, and she relaxed into him. Whatever his reasons for wanting her here, she was here in his arms. He said to trust him, and she did. And even if he was faking it, he was a very convincing actor, because she truly felt loved and cherished and desired.

She settled into him and rested her head against his chest. The steady, rhythmic rise and fall of his chest, and the movie lulled her. His fingers skittered up and down her bare arm.

With the familiar movie in the background, Natalie relaxed. This is what she wanted. Just him and her. No outside world trying to get in.

"Why did you leave work early?"

"It wasn't that early."

He shifted beside her until he tipped her face up to meet his gaze. "You don't normally leave early."

"I…" What could she say to Chase? *I was confused, frightened? I don't know if I can be your girlfriend.*

"You can talk to me." Chase drew his thumb across her lips.

"It was just something someone said." She dropped her gaze to his chin.

"Do I need to fire someone?"

She jerked her gaze up to his at the seriousness of his voice. "No. No one needs to be fired. They just…I just…I don't understand."

"What don't you understand?" He gently brushed her hair behind her ear.

Her heart hammered against her chest and her lungs squeezed. "Why me? Out of everyone, everywhere. Why me?"

His gaze softened, and his hands cupped her cheeks. "Why not you, Natalie?"

She closed her eyes. "Because I'm nothing fantastic. I'm not fabulous. I'm just convenient."

His lips brushed gently against hers, and he drew her

into his arms. Her head rested against his beating heart. "You're right. There are hundreds of women out there that want me. Who wouldn't think a thing about dating a man with a hundred cameras in their face on a daily basis.

"Women who wouldn't mind me being out of the country for weeks at a time and spending my time with beautiful women."

"This isn't making me feel better," Natalie mumbled next to his chest. His hand stroked up and down her back while his spicy scent filled her nose.

"I've never met someone who makes me feel the way you do. You're beautiful and kind. You make me feel like I could walk on water for you if you wanted me to." He set her back from him and tipped her chin up with his finger.

She couldn't help the tears that swam in front of her vision, making him hard to see. She'd never thought she'd be able to find anyone like Chase, and his words were overwhelming.

"I love it when you smile at me. When you blush because of something I said. When you lean over your desk, poring over numbers as if nothing else exists in the universe. When I wake up and your face is the first thing I see."

His thumb brushed over the tear that spilled down her cheek. "No one has ever made me feel the way I feel for you. I love you, Natalie."

The music from the forgotten movie crescendoed in the background as his lips met hers. Her heart filled her chest and she wrapped her arms around his neck. Maybe fairy tales did come true.

Rachel arrived home in time to accompany Natalie to Charity Christian's studio to try on Oscar dresses. Chase had offered to go with her, but she wanted him to be surprised. And she wasn't ready to face Charity by herself.

"Do you think she'll have anything in my size?" Rachel said wistfully as she picked up a pair of gorgeous sandals encrusted with sparkling gems.

"Those are worth ten thousand dollars a shoe," Charity's disapproving voice preceded her through the door. Her smoke cloud followed in her wake.

Rachel made an *oh* face and set them carefully back down with covetous eyes.

"Now, I was able to get a few designers to send some things on such late notice." Every word out of Charity's mouth always made Natalie feel like a naughty little girl.

A small woman pushed in a rack of dresses before shuffling back out. Natalie wished she could get away from Charity as well, but the urge to see the dresses was greater than her fear. She stood and wandered over to the dresses.

Rachel stood beside her and thumbed through the materials. The colors were all fantastic, light creams, blacks, rich shades of gold and brown, deep blues and dark green. Natalie ran her hands over the silk of the dark green gown. Any woman would look stunning in these gowns.

She hadn't dressed up for Chase before. Her heart swelled thinking of him. There had been no prom for her. No best friend going shopping to find the perfect dress. No tux and limo. Now she'd be able to dress in designer gowns and ridiculously expensive shoes and jewelry. And be beautiful, if only for Chase.

"Get undressed, so we can start before I need another cigarette." Charity's voice penetrated the daydream Natalie had been having about Chase in a tux spinning her in circles around a dance floor.

"Right. Where's the changing room?" Natalie looked around but there wasn't a curtain in the room.

"You're in it. Now let's get on with it. You don't have

anything either of us hasn't seen before." Charity puckered her lips and gave Natalie a once-over before turning to the rack. "We'll start with this one."

"I think she should try the Oscar de la Renta," Rachel offered. They bantered back and forth while Natalie tried to tone down the blood flowing through her ears. She was barely comfortable being naked in front of Chase, but she wasn't certain she could stand in a room in only her bra and underwear in front of Rachel and the dragon lady.

He may love her flaws, but she didn't need to see the looks from Rachel and Charity. Those looks that questioned why Chase had picked her over any number of women.

For Chase. That's why she was doing all this, for Chase. He was worth every minute of torture because he always matched those minutes with hours of passion that far outweighed the torture. That, and she'd get to wear a gorgeous dress and maybe for once feel like she belonged on the arm of the Sexiest Man Alive.

While the women were distracted with the dresses, she quietly disrobed down to her plain cotton underwear and bra. She'd made sure to wear undergarments that wouldn't leave a line, but she wasn't about to take Rachel's suggestion to go with a thong.

Charity turned and what might have been a smile crossed her lips. "I swear, those clothes should be burned. They do nothing for your figure."

Natalie's face burned. She guessed that was the best compliment she'd ever get from Charity.

"Lift up your arms."

Natalie unwrapped her arms from her waist and held them up while Rachel and Charity lowered a cream dress over her head. The fabric slid against her flesh like a second skin. It was absolutely stunning, but the back dipped down so low, she couldn't help imagining walking down the red carpet with plumber crack.

"This isn't it." Charity stood back with a critical eye.

"Definitely not." Rachel moved to Natalie's side and helped tug the dress off.

They went through the dresses one by one. There were problems with each one. Natalie wasn't comfortable with the cut of some. Rachel wouldn't let her wear anything with a big bow or flower. She swore it was a huge risk. The fashion police loved it or hated it. Charity just wasn't happy, but Natalie wasn't sure the woman was ever happy.

As they worked their way through the rack, Natalie became less aware of the fact that she was standing half-naked most of the time. Even the dresses that didn't work made her feel beautiful, special.

The green silk dress flowed over her head and settled softly on her shoulders. Thin straps held up the empire waist gown. An intricate lace-and-diamond ribbon wrapped around below her breasts. The layered skirt draped from the ribbon and fell softly to the ground. A fairy princess never looked this good.

Rachel stood behind her looking into the mirror. "Vera Wang certainly knows how to drape a woman."

"It definitely has potential." Charity's critical eye followed the lines of the dress and pinched a few places. "With the right hair and makeup, this could work. I'll pin for the adjustments, and then you'll come back next week to make sure everything fits. We'll also have the hairstylist here so we can try out everything before the big day."

Rachel smiled a big grin at Natalie in the mirror. "It looks like Cinderella gets to go to the ball."

Chapter Twenty-One

"No, Chase, it's fine. Pick me up from Charity's studio."
Holding the cell phone to her ear, Natalie bent her head to
the side as the makeup artist worked on her eyes. "I'll see
you when you get here."

She snapped the cell phone shut and watched the transformation in the mirror. Braids of her brown hair had been
gathered into a diamond clip at the back of her head. The
makeup artist performed a miracle involving tweezers and
dark eyeliner. It wasn't overdone, but it was more than Natalie
had every worn. A mask to hide behind on the red carpet.

Charity paced in the background. Her hand curved as if
holding an imaginary cigarette. She puffed out each breath.
The woman looked as nervous as Natalie felt.

"You remember how to walk?"

"Yes." Natalie had practiced for the past two days
walking and posing in the high-heeled shoes Charity had

picked. Her feet and ankles were wrapped in diamonds. Diamonds dripped from her earlobes and a larger diamond fell gently to lie between her breasts over the silk dress. Armed guards seemed like a good idea. Her body's net worth at the moment far surpassed her retirement goals.

"And the pose? You remember that? Never put both your hands on your hips at the same time. Don't face directly into the camera. Don't forget to cock your hip." Charity's words shot out of her mouth, not allowing Natalie time to speak.

"Finished," the makeup artist said, and stepped back as Charity shoved her way in front of the chair. Her critical eyes swept over Natalie's face.

"None of that," Charity snapped.

Natalie attempted to control the blush that had tried to surface. Her hands trembled as she reached up to adjust the necklace after the paper was removed from her neck.

"Beautiful." Charity's face crumpled into that kind of smile. "Stand up so we can make sure there aren't wrinkles on the back."

Natalie straightened, and for a moment was disoriented as she gained a few inches from her heels. Her heart fluttered in time with the butterflies in her stomach.

Charity circled around the back of her and picked at the fabric. She hurried over to a pile of purses and scarves and came back with a small beaded handbag. The lipstick she dropped in it filled the bag.

"This is all you need."

Natalie nodded and stared at the transformation in the mirror. Someone else stared back at her. The dress made her appear taller and was the richest fabric she'd ever touched. Tall and elegant just wasn't her, but if it made Chase happy…

She sighed. Who was she kidding? These past weeks had been the most trying of her life and the most wonderful. Seeing her picture in the magazines Rachel read was disconcerting. Next to Chase, she looked like a small, insignificant girl. But she was with him.

Being in his spotlight was the only way to be in his life. She wasn't sure how much more of the spotlight she could handle. The woman staring back at her in the mirror looked like she could take on this world, but inside Natalie couldn't help wondering if this was who she was. If maybe life would be better without the constant scrutiny.

When one magazine had done a spread of Chase's past lovers, she couldn't help noticing that she was shorter, less blond, less leggy and less everything compared to them. Chase loved her and showed her every night. Her body tightened. But would she be enough? When would he tire of his dalliance with an accountant from the Midwest?

"Chase should be here to pick me up in a few minutes." Natalie felt the need to reassure Charity and maybe even herself that this was real.

"You'll do fine if you remember everything I told you. Just remember the way you present yourself reflects on Chase and on me." Her eyes softened slightly before hardening again. It passed so quickly Natalie wasn't sure it had actually happened. "I need a smoke."

Charity breezed out of the room. Natalie almost sat down but then thought of her dress. How was she supposed to not sit all evening? Would she have to stand in the limo Chase was bringing?

Every move had been rehearsed. Chase had gone over how the red carpet would be. How he would do interviews down the line while she stood back with a handler or was shown to her seat. One misstep would be played for a decade on *E!* in some red-carpet oops show. She wasn't afraid of a wardrobe malfunction in this dress, but she could easily fall off these heels.

A movement in the mirror caught her eye. Her breath stuck in her throat as Chase stepped into the room. He was positively stunning in his tux. From the devilish glint in his eye to his slightly tousled blond hair, Chase looked every inch a movie star.

His appreciative gaze drifted slowly over her, taking in everything from her hair to her painted toes peeking out from under her hem. Her body flushed where his eyes touched.

He stood utterly still as his gaze returned to hers. "I've never seen anything more beautiful."

She fought the urge to duck her head and stare at the floor. Chase strode across the room and took her hand. "I'd kiss you but I don't want to smudge your lipstick." He brought her hand to his lips, and little shivers rippled through her.

"You don't look half-bad yourself." Her heart spilled out, making her face pull into a wide grin.

"Shall we?" He led her out the door and past Charity inhaling a cigarette. The limo driver held open the door, and Chase helped her into the back.

After they settled and were on their way to the Kodak Theatre, Natalie's nerves started to fizzle. She was about to walk down the red carpet with Chase in front of thousands of people with cameras everywhere. Live TV. Her chest tightened, and she struggled to draw in a deep breath. Her hands felt soggy as Chase wove his fingers through hers.

"Are you nervous?" His voice startled her in the darkness of the limo.

"Aren't you?" She managed to control the shaking that was starting in her hands.

"I used to be, but I never really had stage fright. One of my teachers told me that old adage, think of the audience naked."

"Oh, God, now I'm going to see everyone naked. I think I'm going to be sick." Natalie struggled with the controls on the door, frantic to get some air.

Chase leaned across and gently moved her hand to the right button and helped her depress it. She gulped in the cool air that floated in. His hand rubbed her back.

"It will be okay, Natalie. I won't let you out of my sight. We'll get through this together." His tone was reassuring and helped to calm her down a little. "Besides, it's not like you'll be the first one to vomit on the red carpet."

Natalie turned to glare at him.

He held his hands up. "It was a joke, love. Only a joke. You'll do fine."

The limo drew to a halt, and Natalie saw the lights through the tinted window. It was now or never. How the heck had she gotten here? Cameras were prepared to take pictures of Chase and, because she was with him, Natalie.

"I love you." His whispered words and the gentle caress of his lips on her ear sent shivers down her spine.

She turned on the seat to face him and rested her forehead against his. "I love you." She couldn't imagine a day without him in her life. This was just another test, another trial by fire that proved she loved him.

This was his life and if she wanted to be part of his life, she had to be part of this, too. She tried to absorb his confidence. He wouldn't have brought her if he didn't think she could handle it, right?

Her heart slammed against the cage of her ribs as the door opened, and lights flashed in her eyes. A thousand voices rushed into the limo. Her ears ached from the volume, and her hands tried to move toward her ears, but Chase's hold on her hand reminded her where she was.

He brushed his lips across her knuckles and preceded her out the door. Standing for a moment, as cameras created a strobe-light effect in the interior of the car, he turned and offered her a hand.

She stared at it. Could she just sit back and ignore his hand? She wouldn't have to go in front of everyone and make herself available to their ridicule. The butterflies in her stomach threatened to make an escape attempt as she continued to stare at his hand.

Chase leaned in the door. His smile was the one she'd grown to love, the one meant only for her. "Come on, Natalie. What's the worst that could happen?"

She could probably name a hundred things that could happen, each one worse than the next. The one that came to mind was stepping on her hem with her pointed shoes and falling while tearing off the dress. Not only would she be facedown on the red carpet, but also only in her underwear. The heat rose to her face as she met his eyes. "I could trip?"

He clasped both of her hands and tugged gently. "If you fall, I promise to catch you."

She allowed him to help her to her feet outside of the limo. She tried her hardest to ignore the flashing and focused on his smiling face. He was worth it. She tamped down the butterflies as he wrapped one of her hands in the crook of his elbow and gently led her away from the safety of the limo.

The red carpet loomed before her. It glowed bright from the many lights. Colorful gowns swished and dark suits blended to create a beautiful picture. Crowds of people milled along the outskirts and pressed in on the flimsy barriers holding them back. The color left Natalie's face as they passed people she'd only seen on a movie screen. Her fingers clenched into Chase's flesh. What was she doing here?

"Smile, Natalie." His warm breath tickled her ear. "Relax, it's going to be all right."

She forced a smile as they passed a crowd of people chanting the actors' names as they passed. Chase stopped and signed a couple of autographs before moving to the line for reporters.

His hand covered hers on his sleeve, and she looked up. "It will be over soon."

She tried to smile at him, but a fake grin was frozen on her face as the butterflies threatened to burst through her stomach like a scene from a horror movie. His smile softened, and his hand brushed a stray hair from her cheek. His touch energized her. The look in his eyes brought the butterflies under control.

She relaxed her sore cheeks. His hand still over hers, he led her forward again. She barely noticed when Chase nodded at a man who Natalie could only assume was one of the handlers she'd been told about. The one who would rescue her from the reporters and take her to her seat.

When the man returned the nod and turned away, Natalie's butterflies revolted again. She tried to get Chase's attention, but he was pulling her forward to the microphones and cameras. Her instinct to grind her heels was overridden by the paralyzing fear that coursed through her. Besides, if she tried to run, she probably would end up in her underwear as part of the carpet.

She could see Chase's mouth move as he talked to the reporter, but the warning bells ringing in her head blocked out his voice. He'd said she could go with the handlers.

He'd said she didn't have to talk to the reporters. He'd said a lot of things. Did his promises mean nothing to him?

Her heart ached as he looked down at her expectantly. What did he really expect from her? She'd never desired this kind of attention. She wanted to be with Chase. He made her feel things she'd never felt before, but this mass panic in her body was not one of the things she loved.

A flicker of concern went through his eyes, and he turned and told the reporter who designed her dress and mentioned Charity. An eternity went by as she stared helplessly at the red light on the camera. Chase gently tugged her arm to lead her to another line.

She knew the pictures tomorrow would show her with a panicked look on her face. Chase would be humiliated. She already was humiliated. Why had she agreed to this? This wasn't her. If he really wanted her for who she was, couldn't he see that?

Instead of getting in the line for the next reporter, Chase led her to a relatively quiet area out of the spotlight. Her shoes sparkled in the lights. Something she didn't think she'd ever be able to do.

He blocked out the red carpet with his broad shoulders and drew her into his arms. The fuzzy, warm feelings of love chased the specters of fear back into their corner. She leaned into him, drawing from his strength.

Why couldn't it just be the two of them? Why did the whole country have to be involved in their love affair? He pushed her back slightly. He wanted her to look up, but she was afraid. She couldn't keep up this act. She wasn't built for this kind of situation. She had no delusions of what she looked like. She was ordinary, which was fine for everyday life, but someone like Chase needed one of those women, the ones who were extraordinary.

"Natalie?"

Unable to resist his soft, deep voice, she shifted her gaze up.

"I have to do the interviews. I want you to stay with me. Do you want to stay with me, or do you want to go to your chair?"

She nibbled on her lip. Was this a test? Would she fail if she went to her chair? Would he be disappointed if she went to her seat? Could she stand to go back to the cameras?

"This is a part of who I am." Chase's eyes were intense as they gazed down into hers. "It's not going to go away. I don't want to do it alone. I want to share this with you. I want to share all of me with you."

She drew in a deep breath. "I want to be with you, Chase. I just…" She dropped her gaze back to the floor.

He lifted her chin with a finger and dropped a brief kiss against her lips. "Then share this with me, Natalie. Come and be a part of it. Don't hide in the corner. Trust me. I won't let you down. I promise."

Her eyes glittered with unshed tears. No one had ever loved her like Chase did. She wasn't willing to let that go without giving it a chance. She forced herself to nod. Her reward was a glowing smile from Chase.

His lips brushed over hers. His gaze traced her lips, checking to see if he'd smudged her makeup before he led her back to the line. She'd finally realized what the worst thing that could happen was.

She could lose Chase.

Chase felt like it was the first time he'd taken the stage. His heart hammered in his chest. Adrenaline rushed through his veins. Natalie stood stiffly beside him, but the look of panic was gone.

He'd seen it in her eyes, known she was weighing her options. Knew he was pushing her, but if he didn't now, what would happen when he was on set and someone showed her a picture of him with his costar? He didn't want to go to his movies and the award shows alone. He wanted to experience it with Natalie.

He automatically answered the reporter's questions, gave his dazzling smile and continued on, all the time aware of his little accountant at his side. Her smile wasn't quite as bad as it had been, but it was definitely forced.

Maybe if he'd reminded her of how much he loved her. Maybe if he'd told her that whatever happened he'd still love her. Maybe if he'd told her how beautiful she was. Maybe she would have relaxed enough.

This was something she could get used to. When they got home tonight, they could share some ice cream and watch the award show and laugh at how nervous she'd been over nothing.

"And what about you, Natalie? How are you enjoying the evening?" The woman reporter put the microphone close to Natalie's lips.

Chase held his breath and squeezed her hand with his. It was like he was the one on the spot, not her.

"It's all very lovely." Natalie's voice was slightly higher pitched than normal, but at least she'd managed to talk. Her cheeks had a slight flush to them. Chase smiled down at her as she answered the "who are you wearing" question.

Her hand released a little from gouging into his arm, and he led her to the next interview. He leaned down and whispered in her ear, "That was great, love."

She flushed, but didn't look up at him as they confronted the next reporter.

"And now I'm here with Chase Booker and his girlfriend, Natalie Collins," Rick Jones said to the camera. He turned and stuck out his microphone. "Chase, your movie *Night Blooming* has been nominated for seven awards. How do you feel about your chances tonight?"

"I think all the nominees are wonderful across the board. We're up against some tight competition. It should be an interesting night." Chase kept Natalie tight against him.

Rick asked Natalie who she was wearing, and Chase watched Natalie relax slightly and answer. As she spoke, he couldn't help but realize how lucky he was to find her.

He led her away, noticing how her body shook next to his. He'd pushed her enough for the evening. The interviews were over for now. They stopped for a picture before heading into the theater.

The usher escorted them to their seats. Chase took Natalie's hand in his and brought it to his lips.

"You did wonderfully, Natalie."

She blushed softly and smiled. "It wasn't as awful as I thought it would be."

"No falling or puking. I think that's a pass."

Her gaze roamed the crowd. Her expressions captivated him as she recognized actors she'd seen in movies or TV. Chase had already med most of them, either through his parents or during his own career.

"Chase," Robert said as he and Alexis sat beside them. "Natalie, you look stunning tonight." Alexis had chosen a daring gown. Obviously she was aiming for a best-dressed nod. Even worst dressed would help get her the attention she craved.

"Good evening, Chase." Alexis pouted her full lips his way. "I'm so glad you decided not to bring me. Robert is such a fine escort." She ran her hand over Robert's arm.

Robert gave Chase a helpless look. Robert typically avoided bringing anyone to shows. He was a confirmed bachelor and rarely dated. Women tried all the time to get him, but he remained cool and aloof.

Natalie's face tilted his way. Chase knew he was hopelessly lost when it came to Natalie. He'd been trying to break her all week. Clubs, dinner and finally the Oscars. Maybe he was wrong to push her, but he wanted all or nothing. He'd rather lose her now than years down the road when it would be harder to let go.

He followed her gaze to see Shannen Matthews, his costar from *If Only*, standing beside his chair. Chase rose from his seat.

"Chase, how are you?" Shannen leaned forward and kissed the air beside his cheeks.

"Good, good, and you?"

"Missing London. I swear L.A. gets hotter every year." Shannen's blond hair brushed his sleeve as she turned her head and waved at someone.

"It has been a warm year. Natalie is a huge fan of *If Only*." Chase glanced over his shoulder at Natalie, but she wasn't looking at him.

She nodded in Natalie's direction. "I must find Bill. We'll catch up at the after party." She kissed the air again and sauntered farther down the aisle.

Chase sat down as the lights began to dim. Natalie's hands were clasped on her lap. He reached over and plucked one of them. He folded his fingers in with hers and listened to the opening act.

"Have you worked with Shannen Matthews after *If Only*?" The tentative whisper tickled his ear.

"Yeah, we're supposed to do something in the future. Some sort of period romance," he whispered without taking his eyes off the stage, where they were announcing Actor in a Supporting Role nominees.

"Oh."

He glanced over at her, but her eyes remained riveted on the stage. What had that been all about?

The ceremony continued. Natalie clapped and watched along with the rest of the crowd, but something was off. Something in the way she smiled alerted him that something was wrong. Her fingers restlessly pinched at her satin dress. Her cheeks were stained pink and her lips were drawn tight. Had he done the right thing by bringing her? Was it too soon?

Becca had been a teenager when she left him. Natalie was a grown woman. Her shyness was one of the things he'd fallen in love with. Her reluctance to be brought into the spotlight charmed him. She made him happy, and she was trying so hard.

She'd taken everything he'd thrown at her this week. He'd stopped worrying that today would be the day she'd leave him. He'd begun to hope that they could make this last. That he could make a life with Natalie even though she wasn't an actress.

Maybe he could make it up to her by skipping the after parties and just going home. They could cuddle up with some chocolate ice cream, and he could show her once more how much he loved her.

Chapter Twenty-Two

Natalie laced her fingers together. Chase loved her. Would that be enough? They hadn't talked long term, but she couldn't begin to imagine a life without him in it. But to have to brave this scrutiny every year…every month…every day….

Her normal, boring life would change. Not that it hadn't already. After all, she sat next to Chase Booker at the Oscars. Never in a million years would she have imagined being here. She would have never considered it a possibility or wanted it.

The goals she'd set for herself had nothing to do with fame. A good career, a solid man, a few children, retirement. Nowhere in her future had she wished for cameras intruding on all the moments in her life. Strangers wouldn't have wanted to know what she was doing. But as long as she was with Chase, her life would be open season for reporters and so would her children's lives.

Her eyes drifted to Alexis's beautiful profile. Chase had dated Alexis. The woman personified sex, from her lush curves to her to-die-for lips. When Chase went to his next movie set, a woman as gorgeous as Alexis would be waiting for him.

They'd kiss passionately because Chase always got the woman in the movies. How would Natalie's kisses measure up? How would he feel coming back to L.A.? To her? Natalie Collins, petite brown-haired wallflower. How would they ever have a private life? Chase's life was public. Had always been public, would always be public.

His smile was radiant as he watched the next presenter. He did look like Prince Charming. Unfortunately, she didn't qualify as Cinderella.

He reclaimed her hand. Her traitorous body tingled in reaction to his touch. His eyes met hers. How long before he realized he'd made a mistake? How long before he wound up in someone else's bed because she wasn't cut out for this kind of life?

"Are you all right?" Chase ran his fingertip down the side of her face, leaving a trail of bittersweet desire behind.

She tried to steady her wayward thoughts. All relationships were built on trust, and she trusted Chase. Even though she preferred a quiet life, she loved him.

"Natalie?"

The crescendoing music kept time with her pulse as an Oscar winner left the stage.

She smiled at Chase and touched his cheek. "I'm fine."

His eyes narrowed, but the next presenters began their speech for Best Picture. Chase and Robert's faces appeared up on the big screen as *Night Blooming* was announced.

"And the Oscar goes to Chase Booker and Robert Addler for *Night Blooming*." Applause sounded all around them.

Chase's face cleared of all the concern in a heartbeat as he flashed his winning smile at the camera. He leaned close to her. "We'll talk when I get back."

He moved to the aisle and strode toward the stage with Robert. The music had stopped, and Chase and Robert were getting ready to deliver their speech.

"We'd like to thank the Academy." Chase's voice filled the auditorium. "There are so many people who were part of this film and helped to make it happen."

He continued congratulating the whole cast and everyone involved in production, and she'd never felt more proud in her life. Her heart filled with love and warmth for Chase.

At the end of his speech, he turned to face her and gave her that smile that was hers. When he smiled at her like that, she was willing to give up everything, just to be with him. She cheered with the rest of the crowd as he was ushered backstage. Everything would be okay.

Alexis leaned over the empty seat. "They'll be a few minutes backstage. We can head out if you'd like." Her smile was predatory, but Natalie assumed it was always that way.

"Sure, but I'd like to find the restrooms first."

An usher happened to overhear her and escorted her to the bathroom.

The doorman opened the door, and Natalie swept into the relative emptiness of the foyer. Natalie froze at the landscape beyond the doors of the theater. Though it was night, the exterior of the Kodak burned as bright as if it were noon. The rich and famous posed and paraded outside.

Alexis hadn't waited for her out here either. Breathing deeply, Natalie moved toward the doors. It couldn't be any worse than before. Except then she'd had Chase with her. Being next to Chase made her feel more beautiful, made her feel like she belonged.

She stepped out onto the red carpet and stopped to scan the crowd for Chase. Her gaze flowed over the other actors and zeroed in on Chase.

Her smile froze as she saw Alexis curving into his side as the camera flashed. Suddenly everything clicked into place.

Alexis wanted fame and attention. She didn't need coaxing to get into the spotlight. Someone like Alexis would be there for him and look beautiful doing it. She didn't mind the attention. She didn't want a quiet life. She didn't want simplicity. She'd fit in Chase's life, where Natalie was a square peg trying to shove into a round hole.

Tonight she felt gorgeous with the dress, jewelry, makeup and shoes, but tomorrow she'd go back to being just Natalie. How long would just Natalie be enough?

No, that was stupid. Chase loved her. Natalie trusted him. He'd said he didn't want anyone but her, and she believed him. For now, she was who he wanted to be with, but what about a month from now? Six months? A year?

Alexis turned and pressed her lips to Chase's cheek for the next photo.

Natalie spun as her heart plummeted. This wasn't who she was. She wasn't strong enough to watch her man pretend to be in love with someone else. She wasn't strong enough to walk toward him and claim him from Alexis. But somehow she'd find the strength to walk away.

She jerked open the doors and went back into the theater. There had to be a back exit. She picked up her skirt and hurried across the tile floor.

The door slammed open behind her.

"Natalie?"

Oh, hell, all he had to say was her name, and she wanted to stop and let him convince her she was wrong. That she deserved to be with him. That she could take the pressure of being his girlfriend.

His hand closed over her shoulder. She squeezed her eyes shut at the warmth in his touch and the feelings that swirled around inside her.

"Natalie, are you all right?" Chase didn't spin her around or move in front of her, and for that she was grateful.

She couldn't say what she needed to say if she lost herself in his green eyes. Opening her eyes, she stared at the red exit sign that would lead her back home.

"Who are we kidding, Chase?" Natalie's eyes filled with unshed tears. She kept her voice steady. "You don't need me. You need someone like Alexis. We don't make sense."

"I don't want Alexis. I want you." He slowly turned her until she faced him.

She kept her eyes on his tie knot. "For how long?" she whispered.

His fingers tensed on her shoulder. The pain was slight compared to the hurt curled up in her chest.

"Natalie…"

What was going on in his head? Was he going to thank her for calling it quits because he hadn't wanted to hurt her? An unchecked tear slipped down her cheek. She drew in a deep breath and waited for his reply.

"This is who I am. It won't go away. The Alexises will always be there. The cameras will always be there. The speculation will always be there." His fingers fell from her shoulder, leaving her cold. "I thought you trusted me."

Another tear escaped down her cheek. She had moments before the floodgates opened. "I can—" Her eyes connected with the paparazzi outside the window. A small crowd had gathered. Nothing was private, nothing was sacred. Life with Chase was life in a fishbowl. If she walked away now, her life would go back to what it had been before, quiet, unassuming, boring, safe.

He could go back to his fabulous women who wouldn't feel like hurling on the red carpet. Who wouldn't need so much reassurance to get through one evening.

His finger caught one of her tears.

She took another deep breath and stepped back. Her heart shuddered. "I wish I could, but I can't, Chase." Her voice trembled and the words barely left her lips. "I just can't." The tears welled unbearably. Before he could say anything, she spun on her heels and raced toward the beckoning exit sign.

She almost wished she'd fall, but when she reached the door, she turned for one last look. He stood where she'd left him. She couldn't let him hurt her. She had to be the one to leave. The door slid shut behind her.

Chase let her go. What else could he do? He couldn't force her to stay. He couldn't change who he was, who he had become. The box in his pocket weighed heavily on his mind.

He'd wanted to share forever with her, but it looked like their fifteen minutes were up.

A hand clapped over his shoulder. "Tough break." Robert moved to stand beside him. "We've got pictures to take."

Chase watched the door she'd vanished behind. Every second it stayed closed, the hollowness in his chest grew. He'd known better. He'd known it would end this way.

Knowing didn't ease the tightness. "I'm going to take that role."

Robert nodded. "The last-minute replacement."

It had sat on his desk for the past two days as he debated whether their relationship was strong enough for him to leave for a few months. Apparently, it hadn't been strong enough.

"Yeah, I'll fly out Monday morning." Chase turned back toward the theater doors. He'd do what he did best, lose himself in a part.

"Do what you need to do, my friend."

"What are you going to do?" Rachel tucked her feet up on the couch.

"I can't quit my job. I haven't even been there two months. We can't afford not to have my paycheck." Natalie swept through the room with a pile of pillows and sheets. She'd remade the bed, but his scent still stubbornly clung to a few things. A trip through the washer should solve that problem.

It was well past midnight, but she didn't think she'd ever be able to sleep again. Rachel had waited up for her when she used the phone in the limo to call and blubbered in Rachel's ear. The tears were gone now. Just an emptiness remained, and no amount of crying or ice cream was going to fill that hole.

"He probably won't be at work tomorrow. All the after parties last well into the morning." Rachel clicked on *E!* and hit mute.

Natalie headed for the DVD player and hit the eject key. "You're right. It's not like he's around that much. I'm sure he'll start work on something soon, and I don't have to work late anymore since the new CFO starts Monday. I'll just sit at my desk and do my work."

She lifted *If Only* out of the player and pushed it back into its case. She'd walked away from Chase Booker, and even though her heart was broken, she felt like she could do anything. She opened the freezer.

Rachel glanced over her shoulder. "Are you sure you want to do that?"

"Yes, I'm sure." Natalie put the DVD case with Chase's face in the freezer and took out a carton of chocolate ice cream. Even though she'd gone back to her boring life, not everything could stay the same. She dropped the ice cream in the trash and rubbed her hands on the back of her sweats. "I'll get by."

"You'll do fine. Even if you see him, I'm sure everything will be okay."

For a week, Natalie's heart jumped every time someone walked past her desk. No one really talked to her, which was par for the course. Robert had called her into his office to make sure she wasn't quitting and restated that they both thought she was good to have on their team and would hate to lose her.

She'd reassured him that she wasn't going anywhere. After all, where could she go? She had two months of experience, right out of college. She sighed and tabbed back over to the spreadsheet. Chase was in London for the next month or so, which should give her plenty of time to get over their short affair.

Why did it feel like more than just a month had passed? Why did her bed feel empty? And her heart ached for what? A month? She shook her head. There was no room for such thoughts anymore. She'd get over Chase Booker and act as if nothing happened.

Her phone had been turned off to external calls, which had been a blessing. Everyone wanted to know what happened to the flash affair between Chase Booker and his lowly accountant. She brought her lunch and only left with Robert walking her to her car.

An e-mail pinged in the background. Natalie automatically flipped over to the e-mail. It was from Jared Anderson. Her mouse hovered over the delete key, but curiosity got the better of her.

If you need to talk to someone, off the record, give me a call. I've been following Chase for years and have some information that might help.

Might help what? Make him not famous? Make her not shy? Make her trust in him beyond the tabloids? The dull ache stayed in her chest, constantly reminding her that she'd lost the only man she'd loved. Not because of who he was, but because of *who* he was.

The reporter couldn't tell her anything that would change her mind. This was the life she'd chosen. She hit the delete key.

Chase guided Amanda Rogers into the dining room.

"It really has been a pleasure working on this film with you, Chase." Her finely manicured nails pawed at his suit jacket.

"It's a great movie. I was glad the lead dropped out." He smiled down at her. After years of acting, he would have thought he'd learned to hide his true feelings, but he could feel the cracks on the edge of his smile. Hopefully no one else could tell.

He held out her chair and took the one beside her. The rest of the cast and crew were already seated around the table at the old castle where they were filming. The period piece wasn't exactly helping him get over his relationship with Natalie.

He played a hero trying to save the heroine from the

clutches of an evil sorcerer. Every time he stared down into Amanda's beautifully overdrawn face, he saw Natalie's pert nose, wide brown eyes and constant blush.

"Do you think you'll stay in London after the filming ends?" Amanda had been dropping hints all week about starting an affair or a flirtation or anything.

He was confident Natalie was probably hearing that he and his costar were involved in a tawdry love affair. When in reality, he lay in bed at night staring up at the ceiling knowing Natalie was awake and wondering what she was doing. Robert had told him that Natalie had decided to stay on at Pandora Productions.

"I'm not sure what my next move will be." Chase waited for the wine to be poured. "We still have a few months of filming." A few months for him to get over Natalie. Then he could get back to dating women who were used to fame.

"To getting to know each other better." Amanda's red lips curved into an inviting smile. She held up her glass of white wine.

He wished Natalie were here as he tapped his glass against Amanda's. He would have loved to show her England and Europe. They could have escaped up to Scotland for a weekend. Maybe he should take what Amanda was offering. Maybe then he could get Natalie out of his head.

"Chase?"

He lifted his eyes to Amanda's bright blue ones.

"You aren't over her, are you?" Her usually plastic face was soft and knowing. "It's okay, you know. If you want to talk about it?"

Chase glanced around the table. Everyone was involved in their own conversations, enjoying the wine and the food.

"Look, Chase, we need to stick together here. You can't go all moony-eyed on me every time someone mentions her."

"I don't go all—" He turned to catch Amanda's teasing smile.

"I'm not above stealing a man from another woman, but not when he's desperately in love with her. So why don't you tell me about it?" She stabbed a piece of carrot and chewed on it with her attention completely on him.

"She's not one of us." Chase took a swallow of wine.

"You mean she's an alien or something." Amanda's eyebrow rose.

"No, she's not used to being in the spotlight."

"Oh." Amanda chewed another piece of carrot before responding. "So, she's like me before I became an actress."

"I highly doubt that. You probably loved attention. She'd prefer to stay in the background." Chase smiled softly, remembering Natalie's shyness.

"True. I was made for Hollywood. But so what? Why should she adore the spotlight? What's wrong with having someone in the background cheering you on? Instead of having to manage two careers?"

"Because it's part of my life, it's part of who I am. If she can't be in the light with me, when else am I going to see her?" Chase's fork clattered on the plate.

"My God, Chase. What a snob you are." Her eyes twinkled in the candlelight. "You'd give up a chance at happiness because she didn't want to be in front of the silver screen. Do you know how many actors and actresses would kill to find a relationship where they knew the person was after them and not using them to get a leg up in the business?"

Chase stared down at his plate. Her words echoed through his head.

She placed a hand on his arm. "Love doesn't come around

all that often in this business. If you've got it, why the hell would you let it go?" Her words rang through the hall.

The din of conversation stopped. Chase looked around the table to all the eyes turned on him. Could it really be that simple? Would it all be right if he went back and asked her to be with him any way she wanted? Just as long as she was in his life?

"Well?" Amanda's voice drew his attention back to her. "What are you waiting for?"

"Yeah, Chase. Go get her," came from the end of the table.

Chase pushed back his chair. "I'll see you all in a few days."

Natalie pushed up her glasses as she tried to concentrate on the binder in front of her. Her contact had torn that morning, and she'd had to put on her glasses at work. Things had gone pretty much back to normal.

The tall, model-like employees continued to use the hallway as their personal runway except it didn't bother her like it had before. She just kept working.

When she was working, she could keep her mind off Chase. Wondering who he was with? If he missed her? Rachel had assured her that Chase and Alexis weren't back together, which made her heartache worse.

Even if she wanted to live in his fishbowl world with him, she'd burned that bridge. There would be someone for her, but no one would be like Chase. He definitely had been worth the scrutiny, but it had been too much.

She tried to focus on the papers in front of her. What she wouldn't give to get away? Unfortunately, she hadn't been at Pandora long enough to ask for vacation so she could recapture her focus.

A shiver of awareness went through her. Startled, she

looked up, but no one was in the hallway. Her nose tickled with the scent of Chase's cologne. Her heart jumped in her chest, hoping for more than just his scent. She tamped down on her wayward heart.

Someone must be wearing his favorite cologne. Chase was somewhere in England shooting a film with some actress who had likely taken Natalie's place in his bed. Her stomach pinched at the thought. She knew the tabloids weren't always right, but it didn't hurt any less.

She needed one of the other binders from down the hall to figure out this last reconciliation.

She hurried to the file room, still marveling at the way the office cleared out after four on a Friday afternoon. If she could get these last few numbers into her spreadsheet, she could e-mail it to the CFO and leave for the day. Not that she had anywhere important to go.

She shoved her glasses back up her nose and scanned the sides of the binders. Of course, it was the top shelf. She grabbed a stool and pulled it over. Stepping up, she closed her hand over the binder.

"Do you need a hand?" Chase's voice sent tidal waves of joy pulsing through her body. The heat from his body scorched her back.

Natalie couldn't move. Her arm was still slightly above her head, even with the stool. Her mind blanked, and her heart skipped. "Uh, no. I've got it."

He leaned into her back, and his hand closed over hers on the binder. She closed her eyes against the assault to her senses. The instinct to lean back into him almost overrode her common sense.

Her heart pounded in her ears even as it clutched in her chest.

"Natalie?" His soft words lifted the hair around her ear.

Every nerve in her body strained with the need to turn and fling herself into his arms. She couldn't, though. She couldn't be what he needed.

"Forgive me." His words reverberated through her being. His hand closed over hers and brought her knuckles over her shoulder to his lips.

A gasp of air escaped her at the sensation of his lips on her flesh. Unable to fight her impulses, she spun. She had to see him. Her eyes drank in the sight of him. With the stool they were face to face. A slight darkness underscored his eyes. His hair was a bit more tousled than usual, but he was just as gorgeous as he'd ever been.

His words sunk in. "Forgive you?"

His hand brought hers back to his lips, and he kissed each of her knuckles. "I never should have pushed so hard. There's only one woman I want to be with, and I don't need to share her with the press."

His hand caressed the side of her face and trailed down to her neck. "You ground me. Keep me real. I love you. I can't promise life with me will be easy, but I want you to share it, with or without the cameras. Can you trust in my love for you?"

"What are you saying, Chase?" Her aching heart eased and began to fill her chest with hope.

"What I should have said at the Oscars. However you are willing to share my life—even if you want to stay in the background—I want you there. In my life, in my bed, in my future." He pushed up her glasses. "Will you marry me, Natalie?"

A thousand things rushed through her mind. A thousand what-ifs were stomped down by her heart. She couldn't imagine living without Chase. Her heart had ached every day they were apart. He was worth giving up her private life.

Her hands cradled his cheeks. "I trust you, Chase. I want to be a part of your life. I love you." She kissed him.

He drew her into his arms and captured her lips with his. The weight on her heart lifted. Anything was possible with this man by her side.

Epilogue

Natalie stood silently staring at the reflection in the mirror. The dress was simple, but elegant. Her hair was pulled up with ringlets left loose to float around her face. Her makeup was subtle. She'd never felt more gorgeous.

"No, Charity. It's fine." Rachel's gaze met hers in the mirror, and Rachel rolled her eyes. She continued to talk into the phone, "No, it's not wrinkled. Woman, it's called a vacation. I've got everything on this end. Go relax somewhere." Rachel snapped the phone shut.

"Okay, where were we?" Rachel picked up a slip of paper. "I think we got everything on Charity's checklist."

"I'm surprised she sent you a checklist." Natalie turned and smiled at Rachel.

"I'm not." Rachel set the list down. "But you're gorgeous, Natalie. Every man out there is going to wish he was the one standing there."

A short rap on the door sounded before it was cracked open. "It's time."

Rachel grabbed the bouquets and studied Natalie's face intently. "I'm so happy for you."

Rachel pulled Natalie into a brief hug before handing her a bouquet.

For a moment, Natalie's butterflies took flight in her stomach. After this, Chase and she were headed to Hawaii for a week, where they could be alone. The butterflies settled and she followed Rachel out the door.

Her father took her hand as she entered the church, which normally sat a few hundred. The pews were full, and people were standing along the sides.

As they stepped forward after Rachel, Natalie's eyes connected with Chase's. His smile took her breath away, and even though the paparazzi were outside the church waiting, she couldn't be nervous.

Her future waited for her at the end of the aisle. A future that included the man she loved and trusted to keep her heart safe.

When her father passed her hands to Chase's, Chase leaned down next to her ear and whispered, "I'd give up my entire world for one more moment in your arms. One more night by your side. I want it all. All of you. I want you to have it all. All my love, all my heart, all of me."

Her eyes misted over, and she leaned into him. "I want you for who you are. I trust you with my heart. I love you, Chase Booker, whether the spotlight is on or off."

His finger brushed aside the tear on her cheek. He brought her hand to his lips and pressed a kiss to her knuckles. "Forever."

"Forever." She turned with him to step up the stairs to the awaiting minister. Ready to spend every day in the fishbowl as long as Chase was by her side.

* * * * *

Cherish

NOT-SO-PERFECT PRINCESS *by Melissa McClone*

Princess Julianna's attraction to rebel prince Alejandro is instant—but
her intended is his brother! Can she remain dutiful, or is it time to
follow her heart?

THE HEART OF A HERO *by Barbara Wallace*

All Zoe wants is time to heal her post-divorce wounds in peace.
Until her new neighbour, ex-army captain Jake Meyers, helps her open
her heart.

RESCUED BY THE BROODING TYCOON *by Lucy Gordon*

Harriet is content with her life. She doesn't need the upstart tycoon
whose life she saved ruining it all! Yet can Darius make her see that she
might need rescuing too?

FIXED UP WITH MR RIGHT? *by Marie Ferrarella*

After lawyer Kate's prince turned into a frog, she didn't want a new
relationship—especially not with a client. Then sexy Jackson strode into
her life...

WANTED: ONE MUMMY *by Cathy Gillen Thacker*

Take-charge CEO Jack loves his little girl with all his heart—but he
doesn't believe in happy endings. Could wedding planner Caroline
change his mind?

Cherish

On sale from 5th August 2011
Don't miss out!

Available at WHSmith, Tesco, ASDA, Eason
and all good bookshops

www.millsandboon.co.uk

THE DEPUTY'S LOST AND FOUND *by Stella Bagwell*

Brady couldn't hide his fascination with the amnesiac woman he'd
discovered. He wanted to claim Lass as his own—but what if she was
already spoken for?

HER SECOND CHANCE COP *by Jeanie London*

Widow Riley's made herself a promise: no more romantic entanglements
with police officers. So what is she going to do when seriously gorgeous
cop Scott offers her his help?

AUSTRALIA'S MAVERICK MILLIONAIRE
by Margaret Way

Clio's the one woman who always saw the bravery beneath Josh's
bravado. Now he's ready to prove to her that he's worthy of her love
and trust.

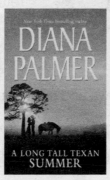
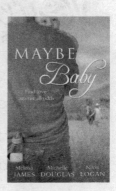

2 FREE BOOKS
AND A SURPRISE GIFT

We would like to take this opportunity to thank you for reading this Mills & Boon® book by offering you the chance to take TWO more specially selected books from the Cherish™ series absolutely FREE! We're also making this offer to introduce you to the benefits of the Mills & Boon® Book Club™—

- **FREE home delivery**
- **FREE gifts and competitions**
- **FREE monthly Newsletter**
- **Exclusive Mills & Boon Book Club offers**
- **Books available before they're in the shops**

Accepting these FREE books and gift places you under no obligation to buy, you may cancel at any time, even after receiving your free books. Simply complete your details below and return the entire page to the address below. You don't even need a stamp!

YES Please send me 2 free Cherish books and a surprise gift. I understand that unless you hear from me, I will receive 5 superb new stories every month, including two 2-in-1 books priced at £5.30 each, and a single book priced at £3.30, postage and packing free. I am under no obligation to purchase any books and may cancel my subscription at any time. The free books and gift will be mine to keep in any case.

Ms/Mrs/Miss/Mr ＿＿＿＿＿＿ Initials ＿＿＿＿＿＿

＿＿＿＿＿＿＿＿＿＿＿＿＿＿＿＿＿＿＿＿

Surname ＿＿＿＿＿＿＿＿＿＿＿＿＿

Address ＿＿＿＿＿＿＿＿＿＿＿＿＿

＿＿＿＿＿＿＿＿＿＿＿＿＿＿＿＿＿＿＿＿

＿＿＿＿＿＿＿＿＿＿＿ Postcode ＿＿＿＿

E-mail ＿＿＿＿＿＿＿＿＿＿＿＿＿＿＿＿

Send this whole page to: Mills & Boon Book Club, Free Book Offer, FREEPOST NAT 10298, Richmond, TW9 1BR.